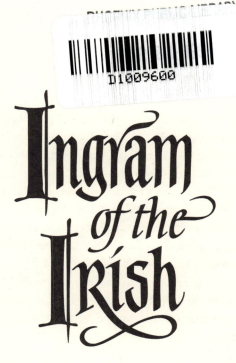

Ingram *of the* Irish

Angela Elwell Hunt

Tyndale House Publishers, Inc.
Wheaton, Illinois

Library of Congress Cataloging-in-Publication Data

Hunt, Angela Elwell, date
  Ingram of the Irish / Angela Elwell Hunt.
    p.   cm. — (The Theyn chronicles ; bk. 3)
    ISBN 0-8423-1623
    1. Knights and knighthood—Ireland—Fiction. I. Title.
II. Series: Hunt, Angela Elwell, date Theyn chronicles ; bk. 3
PS3558.U46747I54 1994   94-8020
813'.54—dc20

Printed in the United States of America

99 98 97 96 95 94
10 9   8   7   6   5   4   3   2   1

We are the same that our fathers have been,
We see the same sights that our fathers have seen,
We drink the same stream, we feel the same sun,
And run the same course that our fathers have run.
—from "Songs of Israel" by William Knox

Your feet will bring you to where your heart is.
—Irish Proverb

Table of Contents

FATHER COLUM
1151

I took you from the ends of the earth,
from its farthest corners I called you. . . .
So do not fear, for I am with you;
do not be dismayed, for I am your God.

ISAIAH 41:9-10

ONE

"I hated God, you see, but never more than on the day I heard her screams."

Colum's throat tightened as it always did when he thought of that day, and he lifted his eyes from the dark wooden floor and reluctantly met the steady gaze of Lady Wynne, his hostess. "Go on," she urged, nodding her regal head in the dim light of the castle chamber. "We would hear everything, Father."

"I was not called 'Father' then, nor did I deserve to be," he answered, folding his hands in his lap as he transferred his eyes to the crackling fireplace at his side. "I was an oblate, you see, given to the church as a babe by poor parents who couldn't afford another mouth to feed. They gained rewards in heaven, and I lost me mother and father. As a child in the monastery, I knew nothing but study and deprivation, but as a young man of twenty, I saw life as it existed for other men." Against his will, his voice trembled. "And I wanted that life for meself."

"How can that be?" Lord Galbert interrupted, frowning. "Men of God are separated from the world, spared the sight of things they cannot possess—"

"English monasteries are very different from those of the Irish, if you take me meaning." Colum shifted slightly in his chair. "The Irish monasteries are—" he spread his hands delicately— "more *relaxed*, shall we say? My task, for instance, was to teach Latin to the sons of farmers, and daily

3

I journeyed from the monastery at Clonmacnoise to a small hut near the farmers' homes. I became well acquainted with the boys, their parents, and their families. After a while, I stayed at the hut for days at a time, able at times to forget that I was a monk."

"And the girl?" the lady persisted. "Where did you meet her?"

"She was not a farmer's daughter," Colum answered, his voice softening. "The day I met her, I was wandering through the forest, cursing my fate and wanting to be anything other than what I was. I heard her piteous cry, ran to her, and saw a sight that chilled me blood—a cloaked youth holding a wee girl on the ground. I froze, not knowing what to do. I knew nothing about women, you see, and even less about a man's proper behavior with a maid. But I knew what I saw violated every law of man and God. When the youth brought the back of his hand across the girl's face, I sprang out, roaring in me anger. The fiend fled away, startled beyond reason, certainly, for he carried a dagger, and I did not. He could have killed me easily."

"You acted valiantly," Galbert commented, his hand instinctively moving to the hilt of his sword.

"I acted impulsively," Colum answered. "And that day marked the beginning of me troubles."

"You were right to aid her," Lady Wynne said, smoothing the embroidery in her lap. "Any God-fearing soul would have done exactly what you did."

"Sure, well, a truly holy man would have given aid, as I did, but his motive would have been different, don't you see? As I beheld the poor girl, I wasn't thinking of saving her soul. I thought instead that I'd been cheated. I'd never have a woman like her at me side."

"The result was the same, was it not?" the lady asked, her dark eyes grave with concern. "The girl was saved?"

"No, my lady, she was not." Colum turned his eyes toward the fire. "She lay beaten, bleeding, and bruised on the forest floor. 'Twas a terrible sight. Her clothing had been torn, so I took me own cloak, covered her, and lifted her into me arms. That's when I made me mistake."

He cleared his throat awkwardly. It was an old story and painful to retell, but necessary if he was to set things right at last.

"I should have taken her straightaway to the monastery infirmary."

"But you—" The lady urged him forward in his tale.

"I took her to the hut I used for teaching, then washed and covered her wounds. I knew I could give me lessons outside the hut and no one would bother her."

He lowered his voice; shadows of nearly forgotten memories rose up before him and danced in the firelight as he gathered the threads of his story. "She was lovely and fragile and the only woman I had ever really known. I told meself she needed time to rest and heal, for the wee colleen's arm was broken. I made her comfortable, clothed her, and determined to stay with her, not caring what penance I'd have to perform when I returned to the monastery. I knew I would not be much missed in the cloister; sure, the abbot was probably glad to be rid of me."

A log shifted in the cavernous fireplace, scattering sparks across the floor, and the three were silent until the last spark darkened into ash.

"In time her arm mended, and within a month I fancied myself in love with her. Ah, faith, don't you know that our love itself was a tragedy, for just as I had been given to God by me parents, so she also had been dedicated to God. She was fifteen when I found her and had been a bride of Christ for two years."

"A nun?" Galbert's dark eyes gleamed with sharp curiosity. "The young scoundrel in the forest dared to attack a *nun?*"

"Aye." Colum nodded. "And she knew the fiend's name, though she would never divulge it to me. I know only that he was of the *aes dana*—"

"What?" The lady put out a jeweled hand to interrupt him.

"The nobility," Colum explained. "The youth was an Irish nobleman's son, a rascal who caught a glimpse of her at the chapel, forcibly stole her from the holy place, and chased her through the forest like an animal."

Colum clenched his hands; he couldn't help it. A most unholy anger always stirred within him when he thought about the young man in the woods. He forced himself to relax, spreading his hands over his knees, and threw a quick, insincere smile to his hostess. "I have yet to learn forgiveness, my lady; I am not a perfect man of God. Ah, no, it wasn't enough for the monster to wound the wee colleen's body. By the time her broken arm healed and she prepared to return to the nunnery, we were sure she carried a child."

"Yours?" Galbert suggested, his question echoing in the room.

Colum shook his head. "I did not touch her," he said, pressing his hands upon his knees with increasing force. "Not ever. God is my witness; the child was not of my doing."

The lady's hand went quickly to her throat, and the lord raised a skeptical eyebrow.

Colum nodded at their unspoken thoughts. "Sure, and you're thinking that because she carried the fruit of the youth's loins, she must have found pleasure in his attentions. Well, naturally, others would have thought the same thing—"

"But surely she did find pleasure—how can babies come without love?" the lady whispered, horrified.

"I assure you there was no affection between me angel and the devil who attacked her," Colum replied, his voice dry. "But no one would believe her, and how could a bride of Christ appear at her nunnery with child? I cast all thoughts of my abbot aside and begged her to remain with me. She did, throughout the rest of the year and into the winter."

"Did no one come for you?" Galbert asked.

Colum nodded. "When me brothers appeared occasionally, asking about me absence, I told them I'd chosen the life of a hermit in order to better reflect upon God. After a while, they left me alone. My conscience hardened with each lie, even as my love for her grew more resolute."

His voice thickened as he continued, and he noted the change with faint surprise. "Truth to tell, I *was* meditating, but upon love, not God. In her company I found what I had been seeking my entire life. I had been but a shell of a man, listening always for God but never hearing him, dressed in a monk's robes but without a monk's heart or calling. But with her in me humble hut, I found completeness."

He leaned back in his chair, the truth of his words striking him anew, and his next words came in a breath of wonder: "I had never seen such evidence of God in the cloister, but, don't you know, I saw the Creator's almighty hand in the woman he brought to me. As I loved her, I understood how God could love man, and as I sought to make her trust me, I realized what drove God to design a plan to unite himself with his creation. Of course, I didn't realize all this right away. I was madly besotted with her and had little thought for anything else. But in her I found meself. And because I found her, years later I was able to find God."

He paused to collect his thoughts and curb the emotions he had thought long dead. Lady Wynne stirred impatiently in her chair; Galbert rose to put a new log on the fire.

When Galbert had settled back into his seat, Colum leaned forward and resumed his tale. "The travail of birth began in the wintry harshness of January. I knew nothing about childbirth and would have brought a doctor, but she would not allow me to leave her side." He drew a ragged breath, struggling with the memory. "The babe would not come. After three days of pain, she had no more strength, and we both knew it. She implored me to cut the baby from her."

Lady Wynne gasped and turned her head, but he could not stop; his words flowed like a river from behind a broken dam. "I did as she asked, for I could refuse her nothing. I cut her belly and pulled the infant out by his legs. I cared not whether the bloody babe lived or died, but through her pain, she smiled and reached for him. With her last breath, she bade me promise that he should be given to God in exchange for her life. Then, with the babe in her arms, she smiled and left me forever."

Colum gave Lord Galbert a pained grimace. "Again, my lord, I felt cheated. I wanted to cradle her. I wanted her last words to be of our love, but her only thoughts were of . . . him."

Lady Wynne held up her hand as if she would speak, but Colum cut her off with a sharp glance. "Can you imagine, my lady, what I felt in that hour? The only love I had ever known lay dead in me hut, her newborn flesh squirmed in me arms, and me monk's robes were forever stained with her life's blood and me own rebellion to the holy church. I did not know what to think or do, but I scribbled a hasty note to explain the body, wrapped the child, stole a horse, and donned the garments of a simple farmer. Despite me promise, I would be accursed before I would surrender meself or the child to the God who had taken her from me. So as Jonah fled from God, I crossed the Irish Sea for England."

"And so you came to Southwick," Lord Galbert said, guessing where the story would lead.

Colum nodded. "We had journeyed as far as Southwick when I realized that I could not keep the baby with me. Milk from cows and goats was not sufficient; the child was perishing with hunger, and, truth be told, I felt no real fondness for the babe. He had killed the woman I loved."

"So you left him at my house." Lady Wynne's voice was tender with gratitude.

"Aye. Twenty-six years ago I left the babe in this place, and I returned today to see him a man grown. Sure, and don't you know, I expected to find him a stable boy, not a handsome and worthy knight."

"He brings honor to this household," Lord Galbert said, sitting upright in his chair. "Of all the knights at Southwick Castle, Sir Ingram serves me and Lady Wynne most loyally."

"He has been like a son to us, second only to our own son, Vinson, in our loving regard," Lady Wynne said. "You can be assured, Father Colum, that you did well to leave him here. Surely God's hand guided your decision."

Colum met the lady's eager gaze and shook his head. "No, my lady, for God knows I acted in rebellion and haste. In the last twenty-six years God has kept me by his mercy and brought me to see his face. Last year I swore upon holy relics that I would return what I took from God's service and once again don the holy robes of the priesthood."

He gentled his voice, watching as the lady's smile trembled. "What I took, dear lady, was the boy. By God's grace, I'll be returning him now."

"No." Lady Wynne's smile faded as she spoke, and something very fragile shone in her eyes. She put a hand out toward her husband. "Galbert, how do we know for certain that our Ingram is the child he left in this place? Perhaps the child he left was found by one of the villeins, and mayhap Ingram came from another unfortunate—"

"I can identify the babe without question," the monk replied. "When I cut the mother's belly, my dagger sliced the infant's left leg. The man who grew from that child undoubtedly bears a scar."

"What knight does not boast a hundred scars?" Lady Wynne asked, her hands fluttering in her lap like a pair of startled doves.

"Don't be denying the truth now, my lady," Colum answered. He wished he could spare her this pain. "What knight will possess a scar exactly as I have described unless he is the babe I brought here?"

The lady slanted her eyes toward her husband.

9

"Galbert, your word is law in this matter. Surely Ingram's place is with us."

Galbert's shrewd eyes shone with an odd mingling of wariness and regret. "What you speak may be of God," he said, his voice subdued. "Our son, Vinson, is due to return soon from his service at another castle, and perhaps it will be easier for him if the valiant and courageous Ingram is gone from this place."

The lord tilted his head slightly as if to urge his wife to see things from another perspective. "Ingram is a colossal star, and Vinson a small one. For our son's sake, dear Wynne, perhaps we should urge Ingram to follow this holy monk."

Lady Wynne bit her lip, and her eyes watered as they darted from her husband to their guest. "We can but ask his wishes," she said finally in an aching, husky voice. "If he wishes to go, he may, but if he wishes to remain, my lord and husband, hold him fast to your side as the sworn knight he is."

Lord Galbert placed his hand over his wife's. "It shall be as Ingram wishes."

Father Colum fingered the rough wool of his robe as he stood alone the next morning in the spacious hall of Southwick Castle. Lord Galbert had agreed to let Ingram join him for a private meeting, and Colum was sure the knight knew nothing of the purpose for his visit to Southwick.

How much of the story should the knight be told? If the entire truth were repeated, the knight might refuse to leave Southwick, for why should a successful knight surrender his hard-won glory for a secondhand calling from God? If the knight was told of the violent act of his conception, he might seek revenge. If he was told of his mother's death, he might sorrow to the point of uselessness.

And sorrow, Colum thought as he watched a tall, handsome knight enter the hall and stride toward him, would not sit well on such a magnificent man. At twenty-six, Ingram of Southwick was slim but powerfully built, with clean blue eyes and golden hair that would undoubtedly shine red in the sun. Even without his armor, in a simple sleeveless sur-coat and long blue embroidered tunic, Ingram appeared to be the ideal Norman knight.

"Father Colum?" Ingram asked, bowing slightly in respect. His confident smile lit his entire face. "Lord Galbert said you had need of me. I am at your service."

"Aye, my son, I wished to see you, but the service shall be mine." Colum gestured toward a table that had been set for the dinner to come at midday. "Sit, please. I have a gift for you."

"For me?" Pleasant curiosity shone in the knight's eyes as he politely waited for Colum to take his seat on a bench at the table.

"Aye," Colum answered, struggling to bend his aging bones onto the narrow bench designed for younger and nimbler men. "Something you have never had, though you may have wanted it very badly. Before I bestow it, though, I would ask a question of you, my son. What would you be knowing of yourself?"

Ingram gracefully slid his tall form between the bench and table. "I know that I am the chief champion of Southwick Castle and the most skilled knight in these lands." He gave the priest an impenitent grin. "I suppose you'll tell me now that I lack humility."

"'Tis not my task to judge a man's pride, sir knight. How long have you been a knight of Southwick Castle?"

"I was dubbed ten years ago by Lord Galbert himself."

"Before that, you were a squire?"

"Yes, here in this castle. I served two years."

"Before that, a page?"

"Yes, here also."

"Before that?"

The last trace of the boyish smile vanished, and his reply

was clipped. "Before that, I was a child. Here. With Lady Wynne."

"Your mother? Surely you know something of her?"

"Lady Wynne has been all the mother I needed."

"Your father?"

"I have no father."

"Don't you—"

"I don't wish for one."

Colum pressed his thin lips together and lightly joined his fingertips. The knight was pleasant enough unless pressed but obviously sensitive about his origins—or, more precisely, his lack of them.

"What I have to offer you, sir knight, is a birthday."

Ingram scowled. "Of what use is a birthday?"

"Och, you eejit, 'tis not just any birthday. 'Tis *your* birthday. January sixth, in the year of our Lord eleven hundred twenty and five, to be exact. You were born in Ireland on that day and promised, upon your birth, to God."

Ingram had stiffened when called an idiot, but he drew in a quick breath of utter astonishment at the monk's final declaration. Colum nodded in pleasure at the profound effect of his words. "I can help you discover more," he whispered, leaning across the table toward the knight, "but 'twill require a sacrifice. You must leave this castle you call home, the lord and lady you serve, and journey with me to the land of your mother and father. You must trust me, ask no questions, and do all that I require you to do."

Disbelief furrowed the knight's handsome face, but Colum did not pause. "I know that upon your left knee you bear a white scar, inflicted at your birth," he said, carefully gauging the reaction of his words upon the doubting knight. "I know how it came to be inflicted and may tell you, sir, if all goes well."

"How can your words be true?" Ingram whispered, his blue eyes shining remarkably like those of the girl in Colum's memory. "I have such a scar. How do you know of this?"

"Later." Colum waved his hand impatiently. "I must have your word. Will you come with me, sir knight? Will you leave this place today, after dinner? Surely that is time enough to take your leave of your lord and lady."

"I-I do not know," Ingram gasped, running his hands through his golden hair. "How can you know these things?"

"I know them well enough; 'tis not for you to doubt me."

The knight's eyes narrowed suspiciously. "I have not lived so long, Father, without learning the skills of ambush and other devious devices. How do I know that you will not lead me into a trap and demand my ransom from the Lord of Southwick?"

Colum raised a finger in salute and smiled. "A worthy question. But know this, sir knight. I am a man of God, and I am commanded by no man on earth but the archbishops and the pope. At no time will I disarm you; your sword may remain by your side. Me quest, I can assure you, is no trap."

"What if Lord Galbert and Lady Wynne will not allow me to go? I am sworn to serve them."

"They'll not stand in your way. I've spoken to them already; they are willing to free you from your vows of fealty if you wish to leave."

"But, my fellow knights! I lead them; we are friends and comrades—"

"You may find more than comrades in Ireland, sir knight. Have you never troubled your head with thoughts of kinsfolk? What price would you pay to know someone whose blood has sprung from the same font as your own? What would you give to stand on land in which your fore-fathers lie buried?"

Ingram closed his eyes as wonder, fear, and curiosity rippled across his face. "Ireland! By heaven, I know nothing of the place! To know my father—" His hand slammed down upon the table in a rush of enthusiasm. "To know my father, my mother—"

"There is no time to be delaying," Colum interrupted.

13

"We shall dine, then depart. It is a fearsome journey and best undertaken while it is day, if you take me meaning."

"Of course," Ingram replied automatically. The monk stood and folded his arms into the sleeves of his dark robe.

"After dinner, then," Colum said, smiling at the knight's confusion.

'Twas better this way, he thought, as he walked from the hall. The less time Ingram had to ponder the unusual situation, the more likely Colum would be to ensnare a willing sacrifice for the monastery.

TWO

There had not been much time to make special preparations for Ingram's last dinner, and Lady Wynne chewed absently on her thumbnail, a nervous habit that had plagued her since childhood. Fresh rushes had been spread on the floor, the tables set with the best cloths, steel knives, silver spoons, and salt dishes. At each place waited a sturdy trencher, a slice of day-old bread that would be topped with the cook's best sauces, meats, and porridges.

She forced herself to lower her thumb and appear calm. Ingram was just a knight, after all, and though she loved him best after her husband and son, still he had no claim to her, nor she to him. He had not been born on the Southwick manor; he had no lands, no inheritance, no titles that could ever benefit or repay Wynne and Galbert for his noble upbringing. Still, he was Ingram, her blond, beautiful boy, and she had loved him far longer than she had loved her own son.

One of the villein women approached, curtsying low, and Wynne rubbed her hand over the garment the woman offered for inspection. "It is fine; it will do," Wynne said, casting an expert eye over the new surcoat, beautifully and elaborately embroidered with the lion of England on one shoulder and the hawk of Southwick on another. "Green and gold—how fitting. Green for his eternal youth; gold for his godly virtue. This will be a most suitable gift for Ingram."

The toothless old woman smiled and bowed again,

leaving the garment with Wynne, and the distinguished lady sighed as she folded it into a compact bundle. Ghosts of the past seemed to haunt the great hall as she looked around: Ingram's adolescent shadow playing leapfrog with the toddling Vinson; Ingram kneeling in gleaming white as all the knights and lords of southern England watched his ceremonious dubbing; Ingram's graceful form dancing with the first and last love of his life.

How tender he had been in love and how vulnerable! She saw love begin as infatuation for Adele, the steward's pretty wife, and did all she could to redirect Ingram's affections. Yet, despite her efforts, the young knight's heart had been broken. Consequently, when Adele and her husband fled Southwick, Wynne did not know how to comfort the disconsolate knight. He had wandered around the castle for weeks, distracted to the point of despair, until Wynne took him aside and told him that love was a commitment to be shared, not an emotion to be mourned.

"What you are feeling is not love but the effects of spring," she said, scolding him. "Fire and water combine in the spring, heating men's blood, and you must not let yourself fall prey to nature's elements. I have a purgative potion, Ingram, that will cleanse your body of these feelings. And since you take pride in subjecting yourself to the trials of knighthood, perhaps you should toughen your heart as you've toughened your body. Seek the God you claim to serve and ask him to clear your mind of all that hinders your devotion to him."

With a single-mindedness characteristic of the young knight, he did as she bade him, and often thereafter she would come upon Ingram kneeling in prayer. By the following fall he seemed to have been restored to his jovial, pleasant self. Once again he accomplished his knightly duties with ardor. Once again his eyes danced with humor and gentle mischief. But though the maids in the castle followed him with discreet glances, Wynne did not think he had loved any maiden since Adele.

He was proud, her Ingram, and would not be defeated twice by any man and certainly not by a woman. In his training for knighthood, he had borne blows and trials without complaint, then risen to vanquish his opponents until he alone stood as the champion of Southwick. The flower and pride of Southwick for years, he had no equal, not even the lord's own son. . . .

Galbert was right. With Vinson returning as heir, perhaps it would be better for Ingram to move on. But to what? Wynne shuddered as she remembered the dark story the monk had told the previous night. No mother waited in Ireland for Ingram; no father would claim him. No matter what illusions Ingram had about his origins, none could be as terrible as the truth.

Ingram must never know how he was conceived, Wynne decided. Though he would undoubtedly choose to go with the monk—for Ingram loved an adventure and challenge—he could not journey to Ireland knowing the dreadful story of his birth. The truth would destroy his pride and confidence, the two qualities most necessary for his success as a knight.

She made a mental note to speak to Father Colum privately, and then she nodded to the trumpeter who waited on the small balcony near the window. He raised his horn and blew the signal that would bring every servant and knight of the castle to what would surely be Ingram's final dinner at Southwick.

After dinner Sir Ingram of Southwick placed a protective hand on the knot of glossy black hair at the nape of Lady Wynne's neck and tried to restrain the unmanly tears that sprang to his eyes. His mistress cried freely, silvery trails of tears shining on her sculpted face, and she caught his hand and pressed it to her lips. He did not trust his voice to respond in words, so he nodded and hugged his new surcoat closer to his chest in appreciation.

Wynne let him go with a trembling smile. Ingram turned to Lord Galbert and knelt at the elder man's feet. "Sir Ingram of Southwick, I discharge you from your vows of fealty," Galbert pronounced as a hush fell over the assembled household. He reached for Ingram's hands, joined them, and placed his own hands over the knight's. The same gesture which had bound Ingram to Galbert years before now symbolized his release.

"They say a lord possesses true wealth only in how many friends he has," Galbert continued, his voice gruff with emotion. "Today, my friend, I am a poorer man than yesterday, for I am sending away a treasure."

"You are not poorer, my lord, for even though God may lead me to journey far from this place, I will be your friend and servant always," Ingram answered, rising to his feet. From his superior height, he smiled down at his master and gently pulled his hands from Galbert's grasp. "I can never repay you for all you have given me. My only wish is to bring you honor in all that I undertake."

"Go with God, then, as we have taught you, and carry his light into dark Ireland," Galbert answered, moving stiffly backward.

"And you, Father Colum, I pray you will remember your promise," Lady Wynne said, nodding slightly to the monk.

The monk bowed to the lady in reply, and Ingram idly wondered what promise this might be. Probably only a sentimental and foolish plea to take care of him, he decided, resolutely turning from the only home he had ever known. Lady Wynne worried too much.

THREE

They traveled on two fine horses provided by the generosity of Lord Galbert. Ingram's handsome Arabian stallion—a Christmas gift from Lord Galbert years earlier, the knight confided—was long-legged and high-spirited. When Colum tried to approach the animal, the stallion reared, and a front hoof missed Colum's head by inches.

"Stick to the gelding, Father," the knight said, laughing. "I'm the only knight in the entire region who can ride this horse."

Colum found his brown gelding more to his liking. Plain and sturdy, the animal traveled like a good monk, bearing the discomforts of the rough road without complaint or protest.

As they trotted through the fading autumn shrubbery of the English forest, Colum studied the back of the knight who rode before him. Tall and straight in the saddle, Ingram handled the skittish stallion with gentle nudges and confident clicks of his tongue. True to his promise, he had asked no questions and said little on the journey but rode with a practiced and wary eye on the countryside around them. It did not seem to matter that he had been freed from his bonds of fealty and knightly service, for he was still a knight from head to heel, a regal warrior with a sword at his waist, a shield by his side, and an iron helmet for a crown.

The new surcoat given by Lady Wynne complemented Ingram's good looks, and the silvery mesh of his chain mail hauberk gleamed through the richly embroidered fabric. "There are kings in Éireann who would kill for such a garment," Colum called up to the knight, urging his horse forward.

"Oh?" Ingram answered, reining in his eager mount until the horses walked side by side. "What's Éireann?"

"Ireland. You are going to have to learn a bit of Gaelic to get along. Haven't you thought of it?" Colum paused to catch his breath. The constant up-and-down motion of the trotting horse had exhausted him. "But I would think the tongue would be in your blood, being that Éireann is the land of your birth."

"I speak French, English, and Latin," Ingram replied, his tone dry. "Why don't the Irish join the rest of the world?"

"Because the Emerald Isle is not a part of the world as you know it," Colum answered, struggling to speak smoothly. "Faith, can't we keep the horses at this pace? Me aged rump is tired of constant jostling."

Ingram gave the monk a faintly indulgent smile as Colum wiped a trail of perspiration from his nose. 'Twas a blessing that monks were sworn to poverty and were more often on foot than in a saddle. Such travel was too jarring for men accustomed to meditation and prayer.

"You haven't said much, Father," Ingram said, glancing sideways at the monk. "How long am I to wonder about what you can tell me of my birth? That scar, for instance. How did I come by it?"

"Do you have faith, me son?"

"Aye, in some things. But not in all men."

"In God?"

The knight stared out toward the horizon and paused before answering. "I believe in God, yes. He is good, and he is powerful. And as a knight, I am sworn to serve him."

"You speak with reluctance, I think."

"I speak as one who has never seen God's hand."

"How can you say that? You are strong and successful. You have had everything a knight could desire—"

"Have I?" The muscles in the knight's face tightened. "Have I known parents? Have I known love?"

"I have not known parents," the monk answered, swatting at a fly that buzzed persistently around the gelding's head. "I was an oblate, given to the church as an infant and raised by the monks. I spent my childhood sitting on a tree trunk while listening to lessons. If my posture bent even a little, I felt the strike of a switch. I spoke only with permission. In my ignorance, I believed all I heard—that I was like an angel, superior to the adult monks, for children were soft wax, completely ignorant of the world, wholly innocent."

"I, too, led a disciplined childhood," Ingram answered, his eyes still on the distant sky. "But I wouldn't call it innocent."

"Innocence is a temporary condition," Colum replied, shifting uncomfortably in the saddle. "Before I could profess me vows, I was assigned to teach farmers' boys, and for the first time in me life, I walked freely to and from the monastery. I saw the world for meself, and me innocence, well . . ." He cleared his throat and gestured uselessly. "It left."

"And have you found it again?"

"Innocence can never be regained," Colum replied, "but sin can be forgiven. Restitution can be made, and that is my purpose here today, sir knight."

"Restitution?" Ingram's eyes left the horizon and turned to the monk. "Pray explain yourself, Father. You speak as if you have wronged someone."

"Aye. I have sinned against God himself."

"And what has that sin to do with me?" The knight spoke slowly, then pulled back on the reins until the stallion stopped. As the silence of the forest engulfed them, Ingram gave Colum a sidelong look. "Are you my father?"

"You agreed to ask no questions," Colum answered, nudging his horse with his boot. "But that one I shall answer. No, me son, I am not your father. Now, we have a long ride to Bristol, and I've heard it shall take us at least thirteen hours if we urge the horses to do their best. Though I'm not sure how long I'll be living if I have to keep me rump in a saddle. Still, less talk and more riding will do us good, I think."

He gave the gelding a swift kick in the ribs, and the startled animal lunged ahead before the knight could protest.

They rode five hours without speaking again. When the short-lived September sun began to dip toward the western horizon and the chill of evening stung through their cloaks, Ingram urged his horse into a canter and pressed forward in search of a hospice. He breathed a sigh of relief when he spotted a small building in a clearing outside the city walls of Winchester. "We should stop here," he called over his shoulder to the monk behind him. "The roads aren't safe after dark, not even for a knight and a holy man. Though I am certain of my valor should we come across a band of thieves, I wouldn't want to be responsible for yours, Father."

"'Tis a sin to tease an old man; haven't I said so?" Father Colum answered, panting. "And I'm brave enough, mind you. Getting on this horse was an exercise in courage for me."

Ingram chuckled softly as he rode up to the hospice and dismounted. A tonsured priest opened the door and bowed slightly to Ingram; he bowed more deeply when Father Colum approached and slowly eased himself from his saddle.

The monk of the hospice led the weary Father Colum inside, and Ingram took charge of the horses, leading them to a stream behind the drab building. As the horses drank deeply, Ingram realized that few days had brought as many changes in his life as had this one. When he had awakened that morning, he never dreamed that nightfall would find him miles away from the only home he had ever known, in the company of a mysterious, guilt-ridden monk who spoke in riddles and kept secrets. How did the monk know his birthday? What else did he know? And how much of his knowledge was truth?

Ingram had a nagging suspicion that the monk had invented the story solely to have the company of an armed knight for protection on what was certainly a dangerous journey. How better for a solitary priest to ward off highway robbers than to ride with a knight in armor?

But if the story was an invention, how did the monk know of the thin, white scar on Ingram's left leg? How had he convinced Lord Galbert and Lady Wynne to release their most valuable knight from his vows of fealty?

Anything less than truth would dishonor God and the priesthood, Ingram decided. If the old man was truly a monk, he had no choice but to trust him. In any event, the secrets the monk *could* possess were so tantalizing that Ingram could not have remained at Southwick. In his entire twenty-six years, Ingram had never dared to imagine that he might find his parents and take his place in a noble family of his own. If the price for finding home and family was to act as a glorified bodyguard for a decrepit monk, so be it.

Ingram was sure God knew the hidden desires of his heart—he had prayed often for some sense of belonging. Perhaps the Lord had brought this holy servant to lead Ingram home. Ingram only hoped Father Colum would reveal his secrets before dying of old age.

They breakfasted on a thick pottage of vegetables and beef, and the monk at the hospice sent them off with a generous loaf of brown bread and a blessing.

Ingram hesitated before lifting his spurred boot to the stallion's stirrup. His companion moved stiffly, shuffling his sandaled feet as though he were in pain. "Are you well, Father?" Ingram called. "Or should we remain here for a day so you can regain your strength?"

"Do you think you'll be needing to rest on me account?" the monk answered, his white hands grasping the gelding's reins. "By all that St. Patrick held dear, I'll not hold us back. Just give me time to catch me breath, sir knight, and we'll be off to Bristol. Mayhap we can even catch sight of that fair city before the day's end."

"Not at our pace," Ingram said, smothering a grin as Father Colum heaved his lanky form across the saddle. For a moment the monk lay across his mount like a sack of potatoes, then groaned as he stiffly righted himself. Ingram vaulted easily into the saddle on the tall stallion. "I think we should walk the horses today, Father. You'll thank me tomorrow."

The monk's eyes narrowed as if he would shake his head; then he reconsidered and gave Ingram a tentative smile. "Perhaps you are right, me boy," he answered. "It could be a good day for us to have a wee talk and become acquainted, don't you think?"

"My thoughts exactly," Ingram answered, pulling his horse's head toward the road. "Walk your horse abreast with mine, Father, and we'll talk of Ireland."

"No fairer subject," the monk answered, slapping his reins. "'Tis not a bad thing to be Irish, you know. You should be glad God smiled on you and allowed you to be born there."

Apparently the night's rest had loosened the monk's tongue, for he chatted freely of bogs and drumlins and peat as their horses walked along the road to Bristol. Peaceful rays of light from the early morning sun streamed across the misty fields outside the village. The air snapped with the promise of winter, but as the sun grew warm, a few lingering birds called to each other through the stillness of the early morning.

Father Colum exulted in his Irishness. "The Irish are a truly remarkable race, you know," he called over the steady *clip-clop* of the horses' hooves. "More advanced in literature and writing than any other country or kingdom, I can tell you. Haven't I been traveling for the last twenty-six years? I've been in places you could only dream about, me lad, and

I've seen barbarism and hate and cruelty. But in Ireland I experienced beauty and poetry and fine writings you could only dream of."

"If Ireland has no faults, why did you leave?" Ingram asked.

"Ah, and that's a good question," the priest answered, raising a finger. "Truth to tell, she has faults, and so do I. I left because I ran from God, me friend, not from the auld sod. I've been running for most of your life. Not until last year did God finally reclaim my wandering soul, just as I'm reclaiming yours."

"Mine?" Ingram shot a quizzical look at the monk, who only grinned in response. "I suppose God went to your lord and lady and demanded your release."

"In a way, he did. I was living in a small community in France—not fitting in very well, mind you—and I met a priest there, a Benedictine called Putnem. A godly man he was, always full of good works and gentleness. Well, after I met him, he took a fever. Putnem was not sure how long he'd be living, so he called his brother monks together and begged them to pray for his sick body and soul. I, too, went down to pray, thinking that maybe God would set aside a wee bit of time to hear me prayers. Even if I was a runaway, still I always knew I belonged to God."

The old man paused in his story, and Ingram turned to glance at him. The monk's lower lip jutted forward as he stopped to consider something, but when he caught Ingram's eye, his homely face rearranged itself into a grin. "As I was saying, Putnem had us all praying, then he died. We watched over his dead body throughout the night, and at dawn, the brother monks headed to bed after saying the long office of the dead. Not being a monk, you'll not understand, but these men were *tired.*"

"I understand tired," Ingram answered, mildly offended. What did Colum think knights did all day?

Father Colum shrugged. "Ah, sure you do. Well, naturally, not having a bed in the monastery to go to, I stayed behind in the chapel with the dead body. There were three others with me—Putnem's abbot, a deacon, and a doorkeeper. The abbot prayed the Lord to vouchsafe once again to show the virtue of his supreme majesty and commanded in the name of our Lord Jesus Christ that Putnem would once again speak with his brethren."

Ingram felt a sudden chill despite the warmth of the sun.

Father Colum lowered his voice to a whisper. "The abbot prayed, and the dead man opened his eyes," he said. "The abbot staggered backward in surprise, but he managed to ask if Putnem willed that we ask the Lord to grant his presence still with us on earth."

"And Putnem answered?"

"Aye." Father Colum's dark eyes gleamed. "He answered. But don't you know, having tried it, he preferred death? He says, 'By the Lord I beseech thee that I be no longer held here, deprived of that perpetual peace in which I did find myself.' Then Putnem looked straightaway at me."

Ingram shivered again.

"Putnem turned his glassy eyes upon me and said, 'Colum of Ireland, our Lord has a word for you: Return to the land of your birth and do there what God would have you to do.'" The old man's voice trembled as he repeated the words.

Ingram took a deep breath to quiet the unfamiliar pounding of his heart and forced a light note into his voice. "Was this the tale you told Lord Galbert and Lady Wynne? I understand now how you convinced them to release me from Southwick, for they are God-fearing folk—"

Father Colum shook his head. "No, sir knight. No one save you, me, and those in that chapel know this tale. It isn't a tale easily repeated, if you take my meaning."

"What happened after the dead man spoke to you?"

"I wanted to die on the spot, so great was me terror, but the abbot prayed again, asking this time that the Lord would take Putnem's humble soul. When the prayer was done, the body of Putnem stilled. The abbot charged me straightaway to obey the word of the Lord. I took my vows that day, donned holy robes once again, and resolved to return to the monastery from which I fled."

"You fled—"

"Twenty-six years ago I fled from Ireland with you, sir knight. I took you because you had been promised to God, as I had; I was confused, angry, and resentful. You were just a babe in arms, but I left you outside the walls of Southwick Castle, charging a villein girl to entrust you to the lady of the manor. There Lady Wynne received you, and you grew—"

"I know that part of the story, Father." Ingram felt himself growing impatient. "What of my mother and father? From what monastery did you take me? What woman left me there? What is my family name? Have I brothers or sisters?"

The monk shook his head. "Ah, sure, why do you want to know about things that are best revealed in God's time? Surely your lord and lady gave you answers of your parents before this. Be content with those for yet a while."

"I found no answers!" Ingram swallowed a surge of angry laughter. "I never had answers, only evasions! I supposed Lady Wynne was my mother, for she reared me in the sanctuary of her chamber, but when she gave birth to Vinson, I was sent to the garrison to live with the knights. I learned on that day that I had no mother or father, that I was never to assume Southwick's noble blood flowed in my veins! I never knew who or what I was!"

"Surely there were other young boys at Southwick Castle in your position."

"No, the others had *fathers!* They were the sons of knights, sons of free men, or sons of villeins who worked the estate." Ingram turned to the monk and reined in his horse. The monk's gelding halted immediately; the air stilled in the silence. "I'm begging you, Father, tell me what you know of my parents," Ingram said, his eyes watering in the bright sunlight. "For years I have prayed in secret that God would reveal my heritage to me. I must know what sort of man I am."

The older man's eyes shone with an odd mingling of pity and tenderness. "God knows what sort of man you are, sir knight," the monk replied, his dark eyes squinting up at Ingram. "And I cannot tell you more than what I have already said. You must trust God, my friend."

Unspent emotion knotted in Ingram's stomach, and the flush of shame burned his cheeks. He had said too much. A knight never invited pity, never asked for compassion. Little boys were routinely left at castles while their fathers marched or rode off to the Crusades or a king's battle and were never seen again. The boys grew into squires and studied the chivalric arts so they could fight the battles of kings and nobles. It was the way of life for a knight's son, and Ingram had always supposed that it was the life to which he had been born.

And yet never had it been more difficult to follow the monk's counsel and trust God than now . . . now, when he was so close to the answers he had never dared hope to learn.

Ingram sighed. God would have to grant him an extra measure of patience to keep him from shaking those answers from the old monk.

A small knot of villeins appeared on the crest of a hill in front of them, and Ingram let his eyes flit over them carelessly until he realized that *he* could have sprung from such lowly folk. Was it possible that he was not the son of a noble or knight but of a villein, a *peasant*?

He stiffened his spine and pressed his lips together. Regardless of what the monk had said, he knew he was Ingram, knight of Southwick Castle, defender of the crown and the cause of Christ. He could ride a horse, lance an enemy, and wield a sword like no other man in the south of England. He had committed his life to God.

Wasn't knowing those things enough?

FOUR

The September sun grew hot, glaring upon the monk's tonsured head until he thought he could actually feel his leathery scalp shriveling. The swanlike clouds that had sheltered him all morning had flown to lands southward, and the forest trees had long disappeared and yielded to pasturelands that gave no shade. According to the last group of travelers they had passed, they were nearing Wiltshire; there they could find a meal and water if they were hungry.

If they were hungry? Colum was starving. The huge meal at Southwick the day before had filled his stomach completely for the first time in months, and now his belly demanded to be refilled. Ingram, however, mentioned nothing of hunger or thirst but kept his eyes fixed on the road ahead, lost in his thoughts.

Colum shook his head in pity. He would have told the knight more of the reason for their journey, but yesterday Lady Wynne had demanded that Colum swear to keep silent about the boy's distressing birth. The lady had insisted that Ingram not know the situation of his conception and the secret of his parentage, and Colum did not see how it would be possible to tell part of the truth without telling the entire story.

Why did it matter so much, anyway? His own childhood had been so filled with reading and writing and oral history that he had found no time for idle speculation about his mother and father. And the monastery did not allow for

sentimental softness—no tenderness, no affection, no touch-
ing, no embraces. *Pray daily, fast daily, study daily, work
daily*—that was the sum and substance of their lives, and so
they had prayed often, eaten sparely, studied the Scriptures,
and worked the fields.

But you left it all when she came, an unbidden voice
chimed from the depths of his memory. *How easily you set
aside the things of God for one of his creations.*

Colum allowed his heavy eyelids to fall as his body
relaxed into the steady, rhythmic gait of the horse's plodding walk. The memory of his love rippled through his
mind like wind on water, and he smiled despite his resolve
to quit thinking of her. It was impossible not to think of her,
when her flesh and blood rode before him, looked out with
her eyes, and moved with her grace!

Slowly he submerged himself into memory, blocking out
the unseasonable warmth of the day and the endless road
before him, and allowed himself to recall an afternoon in the
beehive hut they had shared.

*"Welcome home," she said again, her sweet voice not
dimmed by time. "Faith, it's good to see you, Colum. Sit down
for a wee talk while I find us something to eat."*

*He grabbed her wrists, pulling her away from the low door-
way. "Ah, sure, and why do you want to be cooking for me?" he
asked, his heart about to break merely at the sight of her. He
could feel the warmth of her nearness, and the sensation made
his heart pound and his voice tremble. "You're in no condition
to be scrounging around in the garden. Let me gather up what
I can, but first, listen to me story about the pack of amadons
and eejits I taught today."*

*She laughed, and Colum reveled in the sweetness of her
laughter, amazed by the simple fact that she was wonderful
and she was with him. The burgeoning of her belly bothered
him not a bit, nor did the shining brooch on her cloak that
meant she was undoubtedly from a wealthy family and not at
all of his class. For this brief respite of time and in this place, she
was his, and he was hers. Their world was separate from the*

worlds of men and monks, their love more sacred and pure than that which other mortals shared.

"*Ah, Colum,*" she said, her smile unlike anything he'd ever seen before, "*I'll be wanting to hear all your tales, but first we must eat. I'm perishing with hunger—*"

"Perishing," he said aloud, reaching out for her.

"What?" The knight's voice startled Colum; the memory vanished.

"Nothing." Colum shrugged off the hazy afterglow of his daydream and peered at the road ahead. They rode through deep forest. A wall of tall oaks stood as sentries beside the road, and their shade brought a chill contrast to the warmth of the autumn sun. The knight leaned back in his saddle and stopped his horse; the stallion snorted and pawed the ground nervously.

"Why have we stopped?"

Ingram squinted forward and peered at the dark road ahead. The treetops stirred with the whisper of a warning breeze, and Colum saw the knight's hand tighten upon the hilt of his sword.

"Is there danger ahead?" Colum whispered, feeling goose bumps rise on his legs and arms. "What do you see?"

"It's what I don't see that concerns me," Ingram answered. "For no reason, a flock of birds flew out of the trees up ahead beyond the crest of the next hill. And listen— a magpie who serenaded me with her song has suddenly grown silent."

Colum scanned the forest ahead and gripped the pommel of his saddle. The orange and gold leaves of the oaks twisted in the chill breeze, and sunspots filtered down on the shrubs beneath the trees' canopy. All was quiet. Was the knight trying to frighten him?

"God will go with us through this valley as he did through the fields," Colum said finally, urging his horse forward. "God knows I've promised him my remaining years, and he'll want to get the best of them. There's nothing to bother us, sir knight, so let us proceed."

31

"Halt, Father." The words were an authoritative command, and Colum felt surprise that his first instinct was to obey. But the man beside him was the babe he had brought into the world, and by all rights, *he* should be protecting *Ingram*.

"If there be thieves in the woods, they'll not be attacking us," Colum said, trying not to appear anxious as he snapped his reins and urged his horse forward. "Only an eejit or a blackguard would attack a man of God. And sure, sir knight, upon that fine horse, you are such an imposing picture that no man in his right mind—"

A sudden *swoosh* from an elm tree caught him off guard, and a sharp pinch at his left side sent darts of sensation up his arm. Glancing down, he noticed with some surprise that an arrow lay buried to its feathers in his upper arm. "I'm speared," he called in disbelief, a curious, tingling shock registering in his consciousness. "Like a duck, sir knight, and what would you be thinking of that?"

The pain hit suddenly, a white-hot flame that licked up his arm and shoulder to his brain, and the world went black as Colum slipped from his horse.

Despite his wariness, the sight of the pierced monk singed Ingram's nerves like the quick, hot touch of the devil. Dropping the stallion's reins, he pulled his sword forth with one hand and reached for his lance with the other, determined to face the unseen enemy who dared to attack from an unseen vantage point. "Come out and reveal yourself," Ingram called as the stallion pranced nervously beneath him. "Or would you die a coward's death?"

A clump of bushes shuddered. Ingram aimed his lance and spurred the stallion into a gallop, ducking as another arrow flew from behind the bush and missed Ingram's head by inches. Ingram kept his lance aimed at the bush, and at the last possible moment, a man rose from the greenery and ran. But he was too late. Ingram's lance found its target, and the hapless archer lay still on the ground.

The sound of movement behind him drove Ingram to withdraw the lance and whirl his horse around. Two other men advanced from the far side of the road, their swords drawn. "How dare you attack a holy man on the king's road!" Ingram roared, raising his lance again. "You shall die today like the vermin you are!"

"The only vermin in these woods are Norman!" the first man snarled. "Come down and die, Norman dog! Feel the heat of a Saxon blade in your belly!"

"'Twas a Norman who killed my father; 'twas a Norman who took our lands and enslaved my family," the other man called, drawing his lips in a tight smile as he pulled a dagger from his belt. "You wear the armor of a Norman knight, and so you deserve to die."

"God would not have me kill you without reason," Ingram answered, breathing deeply to steady his nerves. The hand holding his lance shook; the stallion trembled beneath him. "But I will defend my companion and my life."

"Have at it then, Norman dog!" the first man called.

"You speak like the fool you are," Ingram said, steeling his nerves for another assault. "For I am not Norman, nor shall I ever be."

The first man roared and came forward, swinging a sword above his head. Ingram spurred his horse and aimed his lance, but at the point of impact the wily Saxon peasant batted the charging lance away with a stout forearm, upsetting Ingram's balance. He fell from the horse, released his lance, and scrambled quickly to his feet, his sword in his hands.

Though he was well armed and his hauberk protected him from glancing blows, still Ingram found himself muttering a prayer, for he faced two attackers, and the mesh of the hauberk would not stop a direct piercing hit. He had fought enough to know that men armed with the potent fury of righteous anger made dangerous, desperate opponents.

The second peasant sprinted toward the spirited stallion, leaving Ingram with the larger man. The opponent faced Ingram squarely, sheer determination helping him keep pace with Ingram's skilled swordsmanship. They traded blow for blow; then their swords locked overhead, and the two combatants came face-to-face.

"'Tis time to die," the peasant said, his foul breath blowing over Ingram's face.

"So be it," Ingram answered, defensively angling his blade across his body. The peasant pulled his sword away, gripped it with both hands, retreated back two steps, then advanced with a terrible yell, his sword flashing overhead.

Ingram let him come. When the man reached him, he parried the blow, ducked, and turned, bringing his sword cleanly across the man's throbbing jugular.

❖ ❖ ❖

"It's dark . . . so dark. I'll be wanting to confess meself before I die," Colum muttered, his eyelids fluttering. "Can you find me a priest, young Ingram?"

"You're not going to die." Ingram tried to keep the impatience from his voice. "You've received a wound, Father, but I've stopped the bleeding with a tight bandage. It's dark because the sun is about to set."

The monk made an effort to sit up and shook his head. "Sure, so that's why me arm is throbbing." He regarded the bandage curiously, then looked up at Ingram and smiled. "A beauty, for sure. 'Tis me first wound, you know."

Ingram turned his back to the monk and continued his grisly task. The three Saxon robbers lay under the pile of rocks he was gathering, their eyes open and seeing nothing.

"What's that you're doing?"

"Burying the three men who attacked us. If you want to pray for souls today, pray for these poor fools."

The priest's face fell. "Three men died here today? On our account?"

"On account of their own foolishness, Father. My

lance took one, my sword another, and my horse the third—a swift kick to the head." He couldn't keep a bitter smile from his lips. "Peasants should never attack knights, yet still they do."

"Their pride drives them. They are a defeated race."

"Their greed drives them, Father. They hoped to find gold and take our horses."

"'Silver and gold have I none, but such as I have give I thee,'" Colum quoted absently, and the verse struck a chord somewhere in Ingram's memory.

He laid a large stone on the top of the burial mound and brushed his hands together. The monk had risen to his unsteady feet and stood swaying by the side of the road.

"Young knight, I would give you something."

Ingram pressed his hands to his back and stretched. "Another birthday? I don't quite know what to think of the one you've already given me."

"Why would I be giving you another birthday? No, faith, this is quite different." The monk fumbled under the cowl of his cloak and pulled out a brooch that glinted in the fading afternoon sun as he held it out to the knight. "This Irish brooch is me one earthly possession, and it's only right you should have it."

Ingram smiled in gentle amusement. "You don't owe me anything, Father. I've only done my duty as a knight."

"And by doing this, I'm doing my duty for you, don't you see? If something happens to separate us—God forbid—on this journey of ours, methinks this brooch will lead you home."

Ingram rubbed the stubble on his chin and carefully regarded the brooch in the monk's hand. It was much like those the lords of England wore to fasten their cloaks, but this brooch made of bronze boasted a spectacular design of interlaced golden filigree. The head of an animal—what was it, a dragon?—gazed steadily at him from the crescent edge of the brooch, and double rubies gleamed in their settings, as the animal's eyes.

"Is this a bit of Irish witchcraft?" Ingram asked, lifting an eyebrow. "How can a brooch lead a man home?"

"'Tis not bewitched. But 'tis valuable, and you should keep it with you always," the monk urged. "'Tis studded with precious stones, though, so it may be wise to wear it discreetly, surrounded by robbers as we are."

The brooch was handsome and certainly valuable. Ingram had never been offered such a treasure. He took the brooch reluctantly, then held it high as he examined it. To his surprise, the back of the brooch, seen only by the wearer before putting it on, bore even more distinctive artwork than the front. Animals and birds were engraved into the metal, coiling restlessly around two silver panels engraved with unusual curlicues.

Fascinated despite his best intentions, Ingram found himself nodding his appreciation to the monk, who wore a look of grim satisfaction. "I accept," he said, fastening the brooch to his surcoat. "I give you thanks, though I do not see the reason for such a gift."

The monk gingerly patted the rough bandage on his wounded arm. "Trust me, and trust in God, sir knight. 'Tis nothing more than a man should do."

ERIK LOMBAY
1151

*See, it is I who created the blacksmith who fans the coals
into flame and forges a weapon fit for its work. . . .
No weapon forged against you will prevail. . . .
This is the heritage of the servants of the Lord.*

ISAIAH 54:16-17

FIVE

For two days more they traveled, and Ingram found the journey from Wiltshire to the port at Bristol uneventful except for Father Colum's constant bragging about his wound. "Truth to tell, I've never had a wound," he repeated for the tenth time as they neared the city gates of Bristol. "As a monk, as a man, as a scribe in my journeying throughout the world, no one has ever struck me."

"Wear your scar as a badge of honor, then," Ingram replied, his eyes scanning the watchtower behind the city wall for signs of life, friendly or hostile. The city gates had already been closed, for the sun had nearly set. A guard in the tower straightened as they approached.

Ingram signaled for the monk to keep silent and reined in his horse. "We be a holy father and a knight of Southwick," he called to the guard.

"What is your business here?" the guard answered, his voice surly. "We've had troubles with robbers in the past fortnight, and the good citizens of Bristol know to obey the curfew and be inside before dusk."

"We, too, have met with robbers," Ingram replied, jerking his hand toward the bloody bandage on the priest's arm.

The guard's eyes narrowed for a moment as he studied the monk's wound, then he nodded. "Enter then," he called, and the timbered gate on the tall city wall opened slowly as Ingram and Father Colum rode through.

They ate supper at an inn, where the monk regaled the

other guests with a greatly embellished tale of Ingram's bravery in confronting the three Saxon thieves. "Ah, 'tis a tale of continuous trouble," one man said, nodding sympathetically to the monk. "We Saxons have been under Norman leadership for well over eighty years now, and yet some refuse to acknowledge what is obvious to the rest of us. God wanted England to be ruled in decency and order; hence the Normans came to judge us."

"Have you been ruled in decency since, eh?" another man asked, his lower lip protruding. "My Norman master demands all I have. He would wring water from a stone if it were possible."

"'Tis no more than a Saxon king would demand," the first man countered.

Father Colum waved his hand to declare a truce. "God knows, my friends, we cannot judge the Saxons too harshly. I myself have traveled long and far, and I've seen that a man will fight to guard his land and family. Consider my friend the knight here. . . ."

Ingram froze, his spoon halfway to his mouth. He had no desire to be used as an example, but the monk continued. "I had heard of the knight's skill and gallantry, me friends, and had no wish to see it at such close hand, but see it I did. He is a wonder with a sword and merciful to those who deserve mercy. Unfortunately—" the monk paused to cross himself— "these particular Saxons wanted no part of mercy."

Every eye in the gathering turned toward Ingram in profound respect. Feeling their scrutiny, he wanted to drop out of sight, especially when a fetching maiden knelt almost reverently at his feet. But the laws of chivalry demanded that he maintain his composure and continue in his duty.

And his duty, as he had come to see it, lay in guarding the loquacious monk. He had intended to consider the journey an adventure, but the excitement and wonder that had borne him away from Southwick Castle had dissolved into cautious resolve. What if the monk's story was not true? The question plagued him.

And so, to maintain his equanimity and guard his feelings, he told himself that he was merely a knight sent to escort a prattling monk on his journey home. If the monk's fantastic tale about Ingram's birth were true, it would be proved easily enough. And if it were false, Ingram would simply return to Southwick and the role he had played since birth.

But the thought of parents, a home, brothers, and sisters was tantalizing. Perhaps God was answering his prayer through Father Colum. Was it possible that a record of his birth existed? That a woman in Ireland lived and breathed and wondered what had become of the son born of her womb? That a father wished silently that his son, the fruit of his manhood, had not gone to God?

Did they know that he had been spirited away by a rebellious monk? Did they care?

"Aye, they'll not see our like again, will they, sir knight?" Father Colum's bragging tone brought Ingram back to reality. "Sure, don't I know that it was a tragedy that three men died the other day on our account? But they shouldn't have tangled with me fine son here, Sir Ingram."

"Your son?" The question came from the maiden. Though she spoke to the monk, her eyes remained steadily on Ingram. Her mouth curved in a supple smile. "Surely you err, Father, for what monk boasts of sons?"

"Some of the Irish monks do," Colum answered, raising an unsteady hand. "They have wives, you see. 'Tis better for them to marry than live in sin, if you take me meaning."

The man was drunk! Ingram closed his eyes and drew a slow and patient breath. He had never willingly tolerated drunkenness in his knights, but how did one reprove a tipsy priest?

The girl seemed to find nothing unusual in the monk's condition. Still fixing her eyes on Ingram's face, she laid a long and slender hand on the monk's shoulder. "So this

knight is your son? But he has none of your features, Father.
His height, his golden hair, his eyes are nothing like yours."

"His father?" Colum asked, pointing drunkenly in
Ingram's direction. "Holy Mary, no. I wish I was, you see,
for I loved his mother, but Ingram, me boy—" the monk
clasped his hand on the knight's knee and looked into
Ingram's steady gaze— "truth to tell, I'm not your father."

"So you've said." Ingram straightened himself. The
monk was not his father, but he had known and loved his
mother! Lady Wynne had always said that drunks and small
children do not lie, and Ingram had no reason to doubt her
wisdom.

"My mother," Ingram said, reaching casually for the
cowl of the monk's robe. He made an effort to smile pleasantly as he gathered the fabric and pulled the monk toward
him. "Who was my mother? Where did you know her,
Father?"

Colum closed his eyes for a minute and smiled stupidly.
"Me arm feels much better, sir knight," he said, his sour
breath streaming across Ingram's face. "And faith, I think
I'd better be off to bed now."

He tried to stand, but the slight pressure of Ingram's
unrelenting hand upon his robe was enough to pull him
down. Still smiling, the monk collapsed in a drunken pile at
Ingram's feet.

While Colum slept off the effects of the previous evening's
ale, Ingram left the city and traveled down to the port, glad
for the chance to be alone. The autumn sun illuminated the
forest in a kind and golden light, and as he rode along the
wooded road that led to the port, Ingram reviewed the tasks
at hand. He first had to book passage for himself and the
monk across the Irish Sea. But more importantly, he had to
find a way to entice Colum to reveal his mother's name.

The monk had loved her! Ingram savored this new fact,
turning it over and over in his mind. How could a monk

love a woman? Had he met her at a monastery? Often nobles and their wives stopped during their travels at the hostelries of great monasteries; other women traveled to monasteries on behalf of their noble husbands to bequeath gifts to the church.

As he rode, Ingram mused on several possibilities. Perhaps his noble mother had visited a monastery while pregnant, and the monk had loved her on sight. If that was how Colum met his mother, the reason for his secrecy was obvious. The woman had been married, probably to a powerful man, and Colum, a young monk, had fallen in love and had to keep his feelings hidden.

Ingram felt a strange excitement. The pieces fit: Colum had loved the woman, heard that she intended to surrender her child as an oblation, and stolen the child away. Love was the motivation, and as a knight knowledgeable about the rituals and demands of courtly love, Ingram could understand the monk's love completely. Love demanded secrecy and sacrifice, especially when that love was forbidden.

Burning with suppressed energy, he spurred the stallion into a gallop.

Blue water under the boat rippled gently toward the shoreline, and the deck beneath their feet rocked slightly. Colum lurched forward unsteadily and reached for Ingram's arms. "I didn't have me sea legs when I crossed before, and I don't have 'em now," he said, his voice flat. "Find us a seat somewhere, will you, knight?"

Ingram led his companion to a ladder that led below deck and helped the monk steady himself as he descended. Once they were safely seated inside the crowded cabin on a low bench, the monk sighed and closed his eyes. "'Tis better here," he said, crossing his arms across his belly. "Methinks I shall just spend the journey here, and not moving, if you take me meaning."

"Do as you will," Ingram replied. He glanced uncertainly at the monk, then dared to broach the subject he had been considering for two days. "Father, you knew my mother," he said. It was a statement, not a question.

Colum opened one eye. "Aye."

"Can you not tell me more of her? You gave me a birth date, and you told me to search for my parents—"

"No, that I never did." Both his eyes were open now, and a frown crossed his face. "I never did tell you to search. Some things are better left in the past."

"Why would I come to Ireland without searching? Why in God's name did you find me if not to return me to the place and people who gave me life?"

"I did it in God's name, me son. I will return you to the place of your birth, but you must consider the purpose of your birth, as well. You were given to God, a holy promise." The monk paused as if Ingram were supposed to make some sort of connection, and when he did not, Colum spoke again. "You should give yourself to God and keep the promise that was broken. I have done me part; I have brought you back."

"Give myself to God? I've already done that. God owns my life, and I serve him as a knight."

"Not as a knight." Father Colum waved the answer away. "Give yourself to the church."

"Become a monk?" Ingram felt as if the holy man had punched him in the stomach. A *monk*? Nothing could be farther from what Ingram was, what he had trained his entire life to do.

"You can't mean that. I'm a knight, Father. I fight for kings! I served God in the Holy Land for a time; I defend his anointed king; I uphold the king's and God's law—"

"If you are these things, if you have killed in God's name, the fault is mine." Colum sighed deeply. "Do you not think I have confessed my sin over and over? You were to be a monk, a holy man of God, given totally to God's service. I was, too, and in time God showed me the error of my ways. I came to show you."

"My ways are not in error. I follow God, and the path to which he has led me is that of a knight. As I fulfill his calling on my life, I serve and honor him."

"You are a man. You can be a monk."

"No." For one mad instant Ingram was tempted to stand up and demand that the boat return to England so he could leave this sorry, confused monk behind. But they were miles from shore; England lay far away. And if he never went to Ireland, he would never find the home he had always wanted.

He clenched his hands in impotent fury, wishing he could throttle the monk. What gave this man the right to enter Ingram's life and disparage all that he was? Why was serving God as a monk so much nobler than serving him as a knight?

Ingram felt his fury burning hotter and higher. To spare his fellow passengers an angry confrontation, he left the monk behind and climbed to the upper deck.

Ingram did not speak to Father Colum for the remainder of the journey, but when the shores of Ireland loomed into view, he found himself seeking the monk at the ship's rail. Despite his anger at the monk's deception, his pulse quickened at the sight of his birthplace. Ireland, with its emerald shores and unique culture, beckoned on the horizon, and Ingram was determined to explore the land of his birth.

Forget the monk, he told himself. If he knew the place of his birth, or even his mother's name, he could find his family himself. He could cooperate with the monk for as long as it took to find the answers he sought.

He started to ask Father Colum a question but stopped in surprise when he saw tears in the monk's eyes. "'The noblest share of earth,'" Colum said, his voice thick with nostalgia as he gazed across the water, "'is the far western world, whose name is written Scotia in the ancient books; rich in goods, in silver, jewels, cloth, and gold; benign to the body in air and mellow soil. With honey and with milk flow Ireland's lovely plains, with silk and arms, abundant fruit, with art and men. Worthy are the Irish to dwell in this their land, a race of men renowned in war, in peace, in faith.'"

The monk wiped his eyes with his sleeve. "When Donatus of Fiesole wrote that, he was away from his beloved Éireann, as I have been. She's a beautiful land, a jewel in the sea. 'Tis right that me bones should rest here when I die."

"You love this land," Ingram said, leaning his elbows on the smooth wood of the rail. "As you loved my mother."

"Aye," Colum agreed, not taking his eyes off the horizon. "Have you never known love, sir knight?"

Ingram nodded reluctantly. "Once."

"And did that love not bring you joy?"

"For a time. But she went away, and I was left with nothing."

"Aye, 'twas nearly the same with me." Father Colum turned tired eyes to Ingram. "She went away, but I was left with you. That's why I'm bringing you back. I was wrong to take you."

"I understand." Ingram forced a smile. "Where was I born, Father? I could go to the monastery there when we land and present myself to the priest."

Colum shook his head. "No, me lad. I don't know the state of the church in Ireland. When we land, I must present myself to the Archbishop of Cashel, the seat of the church. He will tell us what to do."

Ingram nodded and swallowed his impatience. "Fine, Father." He hated to beg, but there seemed no other way to gain what he wanted. He placed his hand on the monk's shoulder, forcing himself to be gentle. "Could you at least tell me my mother's name? If I knew her name, Father, I would understand more—"

Colum shook his head. "I never knew it meself."

❖ ❖ ❖

Ingram had expected Ireland to be another England, with an orderly class system and neat, walled houses. He entered Ireland at the port of Wexford and found himself in a universe of swarthy men in short trousers who called to each other in a tongue that resembled neither English, Latin, nor French. The port bustled with activity, and Ingram had to take long steps to keep up with Father Colum, who skittered off the ship like a rat scurrying for darkness.

"The horses," Ingram said, pointing toward the ship.

"Go on, get them," Colum answered before pausing to ask a question of a passing girl.

Ingram shook his head and went back to the dock to get the horses, noticing for the first time that curious glances were leveled at him. Did he look so out of place? As he led the horses down a wide gangplank, he realized that there were no men in armor to be seen. The other men were bareheaded and dressed in simple tunics or trousers with daggers gleaming in their belts. But no other man wore the mail and weapons of a knight.

For a moment he considered shedding his armor, but his pride in who and what he was sustained him. Let them stare. He had worked hard to become an honorable knight. God had called him to this life, and he would not take off his coat of mail merely to feel comfortable in a group of curious sailors and peasants. He lifted his chin and led the horses off the ship. If Wexford had never seen a knight, well, let him be the first.

He deliberately lifted his eyes above the curious glances around him and finally spied Father Colum in conversation with another monk. This monk, however, was like no priest Ingram had ever seen. Instead of the small bald spot at the crown of the head that all monks, young and old, wore in England and France, the Irish monk's head was shaved from forehead to crown, from ear to ear, his remaining hair hanging long over his shoulders. Instead of the dark brown robes favored by the holy men of England, the Irish monk wore a robe of white wool with a black cape. A hood of rough wool hung between his shoulder blades; a wooden cross dangled from a strip of leather about his neck.

Ingram ventured near and stood by while the monk conversed with Father Colum in the strange tongue that echoed around him. At last the Irish monk traced the sign of the cross on Father Colum's forehead, and they nodded solemnly to each other in farewell.

"We must go to Waterford," Colum told Ingram, moving to take the reins of the gelding. "The archbishop is in residence at the cathedral there."

"Waterford?" Ingram repeated, handing Colum the reins.

"A Norse city on the coast, to the west of this place," Colum answered, heaving his ungainly form over the gelding's broad back. "A ride of two days, if all goes well."

Ingram mounted and glanced up for a quick look at the sun. The day was yet young; west lay in the direction of his shadow.

SIX

Father Colum took his religious duties seriously once they reached Ireland. He began reciting the seven daily offices of the church at assigned hours through the day. Ingram ignored the monk's Latin prayers as best he could, certain that Father Colum's religious observances were less for his own benefit than for Ingram's conversion to the monastic life.

As they journeyed side by side, Ingram kept a wary eye on the narrow road. Father Colum pressed his hands together and closed his eyes to recite throughout the day the various offices of Tierce, Sext, None, and Vespers. When they stopped to sleep in the forest at nightfall, the monk recited Compline. In the dead of night, as darkness lay thick and congealed around them, the monk woke Ingram from a sound sleep with Matins and Lauds.

On the road Ingram did his best to block Colum's droning voice from his mind and marveled at the lay of the land before him. The low-lying coast of Wexford lay as flat as stretched cloth, but on the western horizon the land lifted and crumbled into highland masses and steep-sided valleys. Once they had left the shore and moved inland, Ingram noticed that the soil under his horse's hooves was gray, the good black earth washed away. Gray earth, Ingram knew, was good only for the scrubby fields of heather upon which cattle and sheep could be grazed.

When they passed a settlement of farmers, Ingram studied it carefully. The cluster of homes was enclosed by earthworks with a simple hedge growing round the top to keep out unwanted animals. The buildings themselves were shaped like beehives, made of wattle and daub and plastered over with dried mud. In the center of the group was another hive-shaped building, this one of stone. This structure was not much taller than a man and windowless.

Father Colum followed Ingram's gaze. "The stone building is the safest," he explained. "The head of the clan lives inside."

"This place is not defensible," Ingram said, scowling. "If I had to defend Lord Galbert in this place—"

"Your Lord Galbert is not in this place, so don't concern yourself," Father Colum answered. "You are in Ireland, or have you forgotten? Put aside thoughts of your sword and shield here, sir knight. You will find your destiny in another avenue of service."

The unspoken argument hung in the air between them, and Ingram spurred his horse into a canter so he would not have to talk.

The pasturelands soon yielded to virgin forest, rich woods in which oak, birch, and ash trees were covered in ferns and mosses. Wildlife was plentiful; Ingram's quick eye spotted an occasional fox and badger, and once he thought he spied the slinking form of a wolf. Overhead a peregrine falcon, one of the finest he had ever seen, flew untamed.

"Lord Galbert would truly covet that bird," he called to Colum, slowing his horse and interrupting the monk's prayers. He pointed to the falcon flying above. "He has an abundant collection of hawks and falcons."

"The Irish are not quick to ensnare animals," Colum answered, shading his eyes from the sun as he glanced upward.

"What are they quick to do?"

Colum shrugged and smiled slowly. "Tell tales. Mourn a death. Create new kings."

Ingram laughed. "Kings? Why can't they share one king, as England and Normandy do?"

"Because Ireland is not England," Colum answered, giving the knight a look of jaunty superiority. "You see, sir knight, before St. Patrick brought Christianity to us, Ireland was a Celtic country sprung from an unnamed race. The legends tell of one of the first leaders of Ireland—Ladhra, a man with sixteen wives. He was the first man to die in Ireland."

"From war?" Ingram guessed.

"No, from an excess of women," Colum answered, his dark eyes twinkling in secret amusement. "Ladhra's race was then destroyed in God's great flood, you see, and after him came Partholon. He created nine lakes, and in his time Ireland saw the first case of adultery, the first judicial ruling, and the first battle."

"Against whom?"

"A race of savages who came out of the sea to attack time and time again."

"Vikings?" Ingram asked, thinking of the strong seamen who had inhabited Wexford.

Colum shrugged. "Their forefathers, surely. Well, the Irish settled down to become a country of farmers, joined together in *tuatha*, what you would call kingdoms. The wealthier farmers became kings—the wealthiest became high kings."

Ingram slowed his horse. "It doesn't sound much different from our king and his lordly nobles."

Father Colum held up a finger. "Ah, but you don't understand, me boy. I've traveled in your country oft enough to see the heartbreak of those peasants who were enslaved, bought and sold with the land."

"The villeins," Ingram said.

The monk nodded. "Well, in Ireland, the unfree—slaves, laborers, workmen—do not have to remain so, for *is ferr fer a chiniud.*"

"What?" Ingram asked, annoyed that he couldn't understand.

"Gaelic. An old Irish maxim: 'A man is better than his birth.' By education, wealth, or accomplishment, even an unfree Irishman may rise to the aristocracy. Do you know an English villein who's been able to do the same?"

Ingram stared at the road ahead while he pondered this latest information. Such a concept was foreign in England, where a noble was born noble, a king was born to royalty, a villein remained a slave until he or she died or had the rare opportunity to marry a free woman or man.

"So, in Ireland, the son of a common man—"

"—might, by learning and good fortune, become a nobleman and sit at the king's table," Father Colum finished. "Doctors, monks, poets, the brehons who teach and uphold the law—all these are noble in Ireland, the *aes dana,* and any man may aspire to them."

"A man is better than his birth." Ingram repeated the words. What promise the old saying contained! But how did a man know if he had bettered himself until he knew into what station he had been born?

Riding at least a mile ahead of the plodding Father Colum, Ingram spied a clearing in the forest and reined in his horse so the steadier gelding could catch up. He had ridden ahead because the monk's constant prayers irritated him. Ingram had his own prayers to pray, and the monk's droning grated across the knight's nerves. The repetition was certainly designed to wear down his resistance to the idea of joining a monastery. But the idea of shaving his head in that ridiculous fashion and wearing rough wool repulsed Ingram. He was no monk—he was a knight. His knighthood was good enough for God; it should be enough for Colum.

Ingram allowed the stallion to ease into the leafy coolness of the clearing and nibble at a shrub. From deep in the woods at his right hand, a flock of startled birds rose to the air, the beating of their wings ominous in the quiet of the afternoon. No other sound disturbed the quiet of the forested road save the occasional breath of wind in the treetops. Ingram felt his scalp crawl as an intuitive fear gripped him. What had set the birds to flight? Did Irish robbers lurk in the trees like the Saxon thieves they had met earlier?

His stallion pawed the ground in nervous tension, and Ingram slipped from the saddle and led the horse to the shadow of an oak tree. There! Deep in the woods behind him, something moved. He stood still, peering through the thick greenery, and heard a woman's scream.

Bushes in the distance bent and bowed under some force, and Ingram reflexively flattened himself against a tree. If this was some civil war between petty kings, he did not want to become involved. But a woman had screamed, and a knight's sworn duty included aiding defenseless women. The rustling grew louder, and soon he heard the pounding of footsteps and a woman's frantic gasps for breath.

A fawnlike beauty burst into the clearing, her eyes wide with terror. She looked for a place to hide and darted behind a tree without spotting either Ingram or the horse. In a moment the bushes parted again, and a man appeared, a gangly youth with a face blotchy from exertion, limping slightly on one leg. He stopped in the clearing, panting.

"*Siùrach!*" he bellowed, his face purpling in anger. "*Striopach!*"

The youth was tall and could have been handsome had his features not been distorted by anger and hate. His brown hair shone golden in the afternoon sun, and Ingram saw that he carried only a dagger, which was still tucked securely into the handsome belt at his waist. His cloak was full and thick, his boots newly cobbled. Given his expensive clothing, he could have been a nobleman, Ingram guessed. So why was such a man chasing a woman through the forest as if for sport? Whatever his reasons, he had to be stopped.

Ingram slipped from behind the tree and stepped calmly into the clearing. "If you're looking for the young lady," he said, his tones clipped, "I don't think she wants your company, sir."

The young man blinked rapidly, then smiled in disbelief. "Pardon me," he said, his voice ringing with authority. "But the wench is mine."

"Is she your wife? Your sister?"

The youth threw back his head and laughed. "Me wife? I would not have such a one to wife."

Ingram took a step forward and flung his cloak over his shoulder so that his sword could not be missed. "If she is not your wife or your sister, then she is not yours," he said, placing his hand on the hilt of his sword. "And I do not believe that boys should harass helpless women. Go your way, my friend, and leave her alone."

"I am neither a boy nor your friend," the young man answered, lifting his chin. "I am Donal Kavanaugh of Leinster. You are in the Kingdom of Leinster, knight, and that sword will not shield your back in these woods."

"It shields me well enough," Ingram answered, lifting an eyebrow. "Now be gone from here, before I lose my patience."

Donal Kavanaugh drew his thin lips together in a tight smile and stepped back. "We shall meet again, knight," he called, a challenge in his voice. "On this field or some other, but we shall meet again."

Her heart had stopped when the knight first stepped into the clearing, but when she heard his words, Signe's pulse slowed. A defender! God be praised! But she had never expected to find a defender in these woods, nor such a handsome man on the face of the earth. He was Norman, certainly, by his tongue, though he spoke with a cultivated accent. A knight, by his dress, and most certainly out of place in the woods of Ireland. Why in heaven's name had he appeared to rescue her?

He stared down Donal Kavanaugh, the man of experience confronting the man of impunity, and the lesser man retreated into the woods. The knight watched him go without turning in her direction, and she hesitated in the silence that followed. She ought to thank him for his help, but how could she be sure he would not turn and attack her as Donal Kavanaugh had?

Unexpectedly, a solution to her quandary came from the road. "Hallo! Sir Ingram?" a man's voice called.

The knight smiled to himself and turned toward the sound. "Here I am," he answered, leaving the sanctuary and shade of the forest. "Wait there, Father."

Signe tiptoed carefully through the fallen leaves and low weeds to see what manner of men this Sir Ingram and his companion were. A balding monk rode up on a sturdy brown horse, sweat dripping from his hooked nose and the thin fringe of hair that lined his forehead. She stifled a nervous giggle.

"You disappeared," the monk said without surprise.

"I was needed," Ingram replied, loosing the bridle of a magnificent black stallion from an oak tree. He looped the reins over the high pommel of the saddle and pulled the animal back to the road. Could she let him leave? He would think her ungrateful.

"Excuse me, sir." She stepped out from behind the shelter of the forest and cringed inwardly when the monk gaped in surprise. "I owe you thanks."

The grooves beside the knight's mouth deepened into a full smile that was lazy, complacent, and smug. "A knight's duty is to uphold the peace and protect those who are weak," he replied, swinging easily into his saddle.

"Begging your pardon, sir . . . " She hesitated, raking her damp hair from her forehead. She squinted up at him. "I don't know how you do things wherever it is you come from, but the Irish don't call their women weak."

The monk clamped his mouth shut, and Sir Ingram leaned forward on his hands, grinning at her. She felt herself blushing.

"Not weak, then? I suppose you could have taken care of yourself there in the woods?"

"I had already escaped him once. I could have escaped his grasp again."

"How did you escape him?" There was mischief in his eyes but curiosity, too.

"I kicked him."

The knight clapped his hand to his face in mock horror. Signe felt her temper beginning to rise in earnest.

"That's right," Sir Ingram said, waving his hand at her. "The poor scoundrel was limping. You think you can step on a man's foot and escape with your life?"

"I didn't step on his foot." She shrugged impatiently. "Everyone knows Donal Kavanaugh has limped since birth. One of his legs is shorter than the other."

He chuckled. "Then how did you escape him?"

"I kicked him where a man hurts the most."

The monk colored and lowered his eyes, while the knight threw back his head and laughed. It was a deep, honest laugh, good-natured and sincere, so different from the irritating snickers of Donal Kavanaugh.

"Pardon me, then. You are not weak," he said finally, wiping tears of merriment from the corners of his blue eyes. "I suppose then, you will not want a ride into the city. Or perhaps you live here in the woods with the sprites and wood nymphs. . . ."

Signe brought herself up to her full height. "Do not mock me, sir. I live with my father in Waterford. He is a smith, the best in the city."

"Then adieu, madame. If we cannot be of service, we will leave you here alone. But of course, you have your considerable pride to keep you company."

He slapped the reins, and the stallion started forward while she blazed up at him: "You would leave me here? The sun falls; it will be dark soon!"

The knight turned his horse and gallantly removed his

helmet, bowing his head, a mass of golden curls. "Then let me be the first to offer you a ride, my lady."

She felt herself wavering. The man was insufferable—a cocky knight who doubtless would despise her and all things Irish, yet he was devilishly charming and handsome. He had sparred with her as if he enjoyed this kind of sweet warfare, and something in her savored it, too.

But her legs were still trembling from the rush of adrenaline that had spurred her through the woods and away from Donal Kavanaugh. "I'll take that ride, thank you," she said, nodding primly in the knight's direction. "But I'll ride only behind the good father here."

Donal Kavanaugh crept into his camp, anger reddening his cheeks even more than usual. "There's a cursed knight on the road to Waterford!" he told the three rough-featured men who sat around a smoldering fire. "English, or French, but who cares? The peasant thinks he owns the forest!"

"He insulted you?" one of the men asked, his eyes burning with eagerness.

"Aye," Kavanaugh replied. "As he will insult all of us. He rides boldly through Leinster lands with an eye for our Irish colleens."

"Och, then why are we sitting here?" another man replied, kicking sand onto the fire. "We can cut through the forest and meet him on the road ahead."

"Let's ride," said the other, reaching for his crossbow.

In deference to the monk's discomfort in the saddle, Ingram usually let the horses canter or walk on the road, but once the girl had climbed onto the gelding's back, he urged the stallion into a jerky trot. Glancing back in perverse pleasure, he watched the jolting monk and his passenger. The monk did not know how to ride comfortably, and the girl had no stirrups with which to brace herself on the jostling horse.

Well, Ingram reasoned, ignoring the twinge of guilt that pricked him and turning again to the road, they deserved a little discomfort. Both of them.

Still, Ingram had to admit, looking at the girl was a pleasure. In the forest she had reminded him of a flaming-haired nymph; in the road, with her lovely head cocked back and her hands on her slim hips, she had been a spitfire. It had been a long time since a woman had regarded him with a challenge in her eyes, and longer still since he had so carefully regarded a woman.

What was her name, and what had she been doing in the forest? He was dying to ask these questions, but he would not give her the pleasure of measuring his interest. Better for her to think him aloof than to know the simple truth: In the moment he first saw her, Ingram decided that if Ireland teemed with women like this one, life in England could easily be forfeited.

The road rose slightly, and as he passed the crest, Ingram saw two men on horseback waiting at the edge of the forest. A third horse was riderless, and all three faced into the trees. Ingram did not slow his pace, reasoning that they were merely resting from their journey, or perhaps the third rider was relieving himself in the woods. He scanned them quickly, then dropped his eyes, not wanting to offend.

The two mounted riders nodded slowly as he passed. Ingram was about to turn and smile at his pouting companions when a slender missile hissed through the air from behind him. An arrow narrowly missed his shoulder, and Ingram grabbed his shield, threw his leg over his saddle, and hit the ground running. He heard the gelding whinny behind him, saw the animal rear and turn, and watched in horror as another arrow was discharged. This one found its mark, striking Father Colum squarely in the heart.

Without a word, the old monk tilted sideways and fell from the saddle, while the girl's eyes widened and her hands rose at her sides as if to grasp the monk who no longer rode in front of her. "Quick!" Ingram called, rushing to her. He flung an arm about her waist, pulled her from the saddle, and sheltered her behind his shield.

The spooked stallion broke into a gallop and ran for the woods as the gelding followed. Ingram and the girl stood alone in the road, with only a shield and sword for protection and defense.

Signe sank to her knees and groaned behind the narrow defense of the knight's shield. She should have known something like this would happen! This foolish knight had taunted and bested Donal Kavanaugh, and the Irish did not take well to haughty invaders from across the sea. The handsome knight would be dispatched quickly, and she would be the unfortunate cause of it all.

"Get on your feet," the knight said, the calm and coaxing timbre of his voice cutting through her fear. "I'm going to walk you to the trees; you can hide there."

She could only nod dumbly and quietly pushed herself up until she wavered on her feet. She pressed her body into the knight's, willing herself to be thin enough to hide behind the shadow of the narrow shield, and as one being they darted toward the safety of the forest.

"Don't leave, my friend." Kavanaugh's mocking voice called from the other side of the road. Ingram's head jerked toward the sound.

"Donal Kavanaugh," she whispered. "He will cut you down unless you stay here with me. I know the woods; if you follow me, I can get us out of here."

"I cannot leave."

"What, your horse? Forget the horses—my father will buy you a new one. And the monk . . . we'll send someone to bury him later."

"I cannot leave. It would not be right."

Surely he had lost his senses. Yet there was no fear in his eyes, only concentration and a mild curiosity. He kept the shield before her until she was safely ensconced behind a wide oak, then he withdrew it and gripped his sword more firmly.

"That suit of mail is no match for a pointed arrow."

He jerked his head toward her, acknowledging her voice without hearing her words; then he nodded in the direction of the road. "How many men has he? Are there only those three?"

"I don't know." She gripped the gnarled bark of the tree in panic. "This morning I saw only Donal Kavanaugh. I was setting traps along the river, and he came upon me."

The knight took a deep breath and kept his eyes on the road. "Is this Donal Kavanaugh an honorable man?"

She covered her mouth with her hand to keep from laughing. Donal Kavanaugh, honorable? A man who would attack a woman in the woods—what was honor in England, anyway?

The knight waited for her answer. "No, he's not an honorable man," she said finally. "He will kill you. He does not forgive easily."

"But will he fight fairly? Are the laws of God and chivalry known in these parts, and does he abide by them?"

This time she did laugh. With no regard for her words, the knight stepped out from the safety of the forest to challenge Donal Kavanaugh, and Signe's laughter turned to sobbing.

SEVEN

"You have killed an innocent monk today," Ingram called, steadily eyeing Kavanaugh and the two men at his side. "Surely God will hold you to account for this murder."

"'Tis not murder to kill a kidnapper," Kavanaugh stated, stepping boldly forward. A battle-ax glinted in his hand.

"A kidnapper?"

"You took one of our women. The 'monk,' as you call him, looks like no monk I've ever seen. 'Tis a poor disguise."

"I see God's truth has no bearing in this matter," Ingram spoke slowly, feeling his way.

"Nothing matters here but your death," Kavanaugh answered, smiling with cruel confidence. "So come forward and meet my blade, knight."

"I am prepared to die wherever God wills, but 'twill not be today. Perhaps, fellow, it is your day to die."

Ingram unsheathed his sword.

From her hiding place in the forest, Signe watched as Ingram strode to meet Kavanaugh and his men as casually as if he were inviting them to dinner. The two men at Kavanaugh's side rushed the knight immediately, but quick on his feet, Sir Ingram whirled and cut both of them with his sword. He left them lying in the dark dust of the road.

Now Ingram faced Kavanaugh alone, and Signe held

her breath, certain the bold Irishman's luck had run out. "Would you like to offer a prayer before I dispatch you to heaven?" Ingram asked, pausing a stone's throw away from Kavanaugh, his bloody sword flashing in the late afternoon sun.

"God knows I have no need of prayer now," Kavanaugh answered, lifting the battle-ax as if he would charge. "But I'll say a prayer for you tonight, knight, when your soul wanders into hell." Kavanaugh thrust the blade of the axe down at his side. In the next instant an arrow flashed through the stillness and pierced Sir Ingram squarely between the shoulder blades.

Signe screamed.

The knight spun around in surprise, dropping his sword as he grappled helplessly for the arrow in his back. A few feet down the road, a screen of shrubs parted, and a fourth Irishman sauntered forth, a crossbow in his hand and a jaunty smile on his face.

The knight coughed, wheezed for breath, then dropped his hand to reach behind his shield. In one quick movement he flung forth a dagger, which flew end over end through the air and struck home with a quiet thud in the breast of the archer. The man fell, face forward, into the soft dirt of the road.

As Kavanaugh advanced, the axe in his hand, Ingram staggered toward the shelter of the forest and collapsed a few feet from Signe's feet.

With a frantic prayer for help, she burst from her hiding place and flew toward Donal Kavanaugh and the abandoned sword. Kavanaugh was within striking distance when she reached it; she could smell his rancid sweat as she hefted the heavy sword with both hands and held it before his throat.

"Come forward," she challenged, the point of the sword wavering as she trembled in Kavanaugh's path. "Come finish what you have begun."

Kavanaugh hesitated and lowered the battle-ax in his hand. He could easily strike the woman and behead the knight, leaving the bodies behind as a warning to other interlopers in Leinster lands. But the woman was too lovely a prize to kill immediately, and if he struck the knight while the crazed woman was still waving the sword, she might land a blow.

There was nothing to do, then, but kill the woman.

He pulled his weak leg forward, feeling the muscles knot as they always did when he was nervous. Just two steps and he would have her, as long as the wench didn't strike first.

But what if she did?

What if his leg gave out?

Serious considerations. He felt his weak leg begin to tremble. Chances are she would get to him first, and then he would die—or face the shame of being bested by a woman.

Donal Kavanaugh forced a snarl to his lips. "I will not kill you today, my pretty colleen," he said, his voice cracking against his will. "The knight will die. It is enough."

Never taking his eyes from the sword in her hand, he backed carefully toward his horse, then mounted and rode away.

Signe kept the blade extended in front of her until Donal Kavanaugh vanished in a cloud of dust, then she dropped the bloodstained sword in the road and shuddered. What had she done? Would Kavanaugh be back?

She wanted to wrap her arms around herself and curl up in silence until the horror had passed, but the ragged wheezing of the knight reminded her that she was not alone. The monk was dead; his eyes were glassy, and he had not moved since hitting the ground. Kavanaugh's three companions also lay like dead dogs in the soft dirt. But the knight lived!

She put her terror and apprehension aside and hurried to his side. He lay face down in the road, his head slightly turned. She could hear the rumble of fluid echoing in his chest. The arrow protruded from his back, but thankfully, as she lifted the knight's shoulder, she could see it hadn't completely pierced him through. Perhaps this silver armor was useful after all.

Signe closed her eyes and pressed her lips together. If she did nothing, he would certainly die here in the dust. Nothing she could do would make things worse.

"If you can hear me, sir knight," she said, her voice steady with a calmness she did not feel, "I'm going to pull this arrow from you. Don't move, and don't fight me."

He did not stir, so she stepped over his prone body, placed both her hands on the shaft of the arrow, and gave a mighty tug upward. The arrow came out cleanly and easily, and she noticed with relief that the iron tip was not barbed but a simple leaf-shaped head. The small circle of red on the knight's tunic immediately began to spread at the point of the wound, and Signe pressed down on the wound with her palms.

What else could she do? If she rode for help, he would bleed to death, and if she stayed, she could do little more than drag him from the road. "Jesus, holy Son of God," she said, lifting her eyes to the sky. "I'm not sure how long this knight will be living, but help me do what I can. 'Twould be terrible to have him die here on the road at the hands of our enemies."

As if in answer to her prayer, the knight moved his hand and moaned. His labored breathing seemed to ease a bit. There was life in him yet, and he was a fighter. Without further deliberation, she ripped the beautiful surcoat from the knight's back and struggled to pull the coat of silver mesh over his head.

It took her the better part of an hour to remove the knight's armor and tend to his wound, and the sun slipped behind the western hills while she worked. No traveler had come down the road to aid her, and Signe doubted if any would, for law-abiding citizens did not travel after dark. But when she was done, the knight lay in a bed of soft grass under an oak tree, his wound packed with a strip of linen torn from Signe's tunic. His bleeding had lessened, his breathing steadied.

She picked up the embroidered surcoat, now torn and bloody, but still whole enough to cover him. She laid it across his broad, bare back and marveled at its beauty. Someone thought a great deal of this knight, whoever he was. Had some noble lady made the surcoat for him? Was he on her mission? And did he act out of love, duty, or both?

His sword, hauberk, and shield she placed in a clearing some distance from the knight. Fully aware of the dangers of the open road, she covered Ingram's belongings with leaves and branches so that no curious passersby would find them. The dead monk and the three villains still lay in the road, and it was likely, she guessed, that any scavengers who might happen upon the bodies would surmise that the victors had ridden away with whatever loot there was to be had. No one would comb the bushes in the dark looking for a wounded survivor. Even if they did find the knight, he looked merely like a wounded man, not an important warrior. . . .

The rising moon shone dimly upon the road as she set out for home, and Signe was surprised to see something in the road reflect the moon's pale light. An object shone from the place where the knight had fallen, and she stooped and picked up a lovely brooch, one as distinctively Irish as she. How had the knight come to possess it? The twin ruby eyes of the animal's head winked at her in the dark, and without hesitating she blew the dirt away from the carving and slipped it into the fabric of her own cloak.

"Men would kill for such a brooch," she explained, calling over her shoulder to the unconscious knight. "I will keep it for you, so no one will be tempted."

She thought he moved, so she walked over to the clearing to examine him once again. Lying there in the moonlight, his bare shoulders not quite covered by the fabric of his surcoat, he looked as if he were merely sleeping.

"Sweet Jesus, place your hand of protection on him and spare his life," she whispered, studying the still face.

He was disturbingly attractive, even now, and she suddenly wondered what it would be like to stroke that smooth skin, to caress the golden beard upon his cheeks.

Signe gave herself a stern mental shake and moved ahead on the road, determined not to look at the dead bodies that stiffened in the moonlight. On an impulse, she whistled and was rewarded with a whinny and a frantic rustle in the woods. Her instincts had proved right. At least one horse had fled into the trees and snagged his bridle on the undergrowth. She quickened her steps toward the thrashing limbs.

When he felt earth and leaves under his hands, Ingram's first thought was that he would surely be bitten by a viper.

Father Colum's voice echoed through the fog in his head. "Don't you remember me telling you that Saint Patrick banished all snakes from Ireland?" Ingram smiled at the memory. "This is my first wound, you know," the monk said, pointing with pride to the bandage on his arm.

"No, you've had two wounds now," Ingram answered, his brain struggling to make sense of where he and Colum were. "Don't you remember what happened on the road to Waterford?"

What had happened? There had been a man with a limp, a nasal voice, and a belligerent attitude. And there was a girl with flaming red hair—or was she part of his delirium, too?

He clenched his fists, trying to throw off the lingering wisps of his dream. With the stab of burning pain in his back, awareness hit. He was wounded, and he lay in the grass. Something covered him, and as he glanced at his shoulder, he saw the embroidered eagle of Southwick. His own surcoat, now brown with dried blood. The confrontation in the road. *He* was wounded, not the monk. Colum was dead . . . he had found his way home to God at last.

Pain gripped Ingram's muscled back; he tried to take a deep breath but couldn't. He raised his head, an effort that required all his strength, and peered through the undergrowth for a sign of his horse or the girl. But all was quiet in the woods; nothing moved but his own feeble fingers, which tugged at his hair in response to the pain that racked his body.

"Holy God, help me . . . ," he prayed through clenched teeth, struggling to hold on to consciousness.

He grew aware that someone had moved him from the road, stripped him of his surcoat and hauberk, placed a bundle of soft grass under his head for a pillow. The girl, surely. But where had she gone? He waited a few moments, breathing as quietly as he could, and listened for the sound of movement in the bushes beyond. Nothing.

She had left him. The wench had pulled him off the road, taken his horse, sword, and—what else? He turned his head and saw the empty corner of his tunic where he had fastened the brooch. So she had taken it, too. He had nothing. No monk to guide him in his search for answers, no brooch to finance his journey through the country, no horse.

He pressed his hands to the ground at his side and tried to push up from the ground. Flashes of fire shot through his arms, a warm sticky wetness spilled from a pain center in his back, and his legs would not obey when he told them to move. *God, please, don't let it end like this!*

Waves of grayness passed over him, and Ingram fell back to the earth in a faint.

EIGHT

Signe wiped Ingram's golden brow with a damp cloth, a gesture she had repeated hundreds of times in the two weeks he had lain in her cot. His wound would heal, the doctor assured her, but the fever that had gripped him since his arrival at their house might yet sap his strength to the point of death. So she spent her days urging the semiconscious knight to drink of the broth she offered; she spent most of her nights sponging his rapidly thinning body. The fever that gripped him led him to ramble, and she caught women's names: "Lady Wynne" and once or twice, "Adele." But most of the time he muttered dark phrases in French, a tongue she didn't understand.

"Heal yourself," she urged him one night, speaking to his closed eyes with all the intensity she could muster. "I'll be wanting to sleep in me own cot soon, and you'll have to get out of it first."

The knight didn't answer, but his lips seemed to curve in a smile. Signe attributed the smirk to his lowered fever. "I know you're only thinking of your women, after all," she said, wringing a cloth in the bowl of fresh water at her side. "And sure, don't I know you'll be wanting to return to them? So get well, sir knight, and leave me cot. I'm growing weary of sleeping on the floor."

She smoothed the wet cloth and placed it on his forehead, wondering for a moment what he would look like without his rough beard. He had a pleasant face even with a beard, but sometimes a beard made a man appear old. And she wondered if she was tending a mere child, someone as young and headstrong as Donal Kavanaugh. But no, that couldn't be. She'd seen the two of them face each other, and though they were of the same height and form, Ingram was nothing like Kavanaugh.

Humming gently, she smoothed the blanket up to his chest and pulled his arms out from under the covers. Personally, she liked sleeping with her arms out, for the rough wool of the blanket scratched terribly. Then a hand tightened around her wrist.

His blue eyes were open.

She caught her breath, then forced a smile. "Well, and it's about time you looked around," she said. He had a surprising store of strength still about him, for his grasp on her wrist was secure.

"Where am I?" he said, his voice low and cautious.

"You don't have to whisper," she answered, tugging on her wrist. "Don't you remember me, sir knight? On the road to Waterford?"

"I remember."

"Then you'll be pleased to learn you're in me father's house."

"And the man with the axe?"

She snorted a laugh. "Donal Kavanaugh won't come into Waterford, knight. It's a Norse city, and Kavanaugh's a warrior from Leinster. The earl of Waterford wouldn't allow him and his band of ruffians inside the city walls. Indeed, you won't find much of the Leinster Irish around here excepting, of course, for me."

His eyes were puzzled, and she laughed. "If you'll let me hand go, I'll explain everything. But if you're thinking that I'll stand here and let you fasten me like a slave, well . . ."

He loosened his grip on her wrist and seemed to relax against his pillow.

"Good. Me father is Erik Lombay and Norse, so you'd

call him an Ostman. Me mother was Leinster Irish, but she's dead, God rest her soul."

His smile softened. "And you?" he asked. "I don't know your name."

"Signe," she answered, suddenly feeling as self-concious as a girl with her first suitor. "Signe Lombay."

His eyes left her face and lingered on the small window at the front of the house. "Does anyone know I'm here, Signe?"

"Only me father, the doctor, and two of Father's friends. They helped me fetch you back here, and they buried the dead by the roadside. They've kept news of you quiet, for 'tisn't every day we see a knight in Ireland. Your sort rarely passes through this city."

"No knights in Ireland?" He turned his head as if he had difficulty hearing her.

"Of warriors, we have a plenty. Men of steel with hearts of iron. But knights—" she waved an arm toward a bench in the corner of the room where Ingram's sword, hauberk, shield, and dagger rested— "knights we have no use for. Our warriors fight when they're needed and farm when they're not. Our fighting men have families to feed."

"But you know what I am—you knew right away I was a knight."

She shrugged. "And would you be thinking we're a pack of eejits and *amadons*? Waterford is a seaport, sir knight, so we hear tales from all over the world, of all sorts of people and customs."

"You speak English—"

"And Gaelic, and a wee bit o' Latin—prayers, mostly." She raised an eyebrow and regarded Ingram carefully. "Why did you come to us, sir knight? Shall me father and me be in danger for sheltering you? Are you—" She removed the cloth from his forehead and took a quick step back. "You asked me this about Donal Kavanaugh, and now I'll be asking you the same question. Are you an honorable man, or not? What is your business here?"

His eyes squinted with amusement even through his fever. "As to my honor, didn't I save your precious hide back there in the forest?"

"Didn't I save your life in return? We are even, knight. I owe you nothing, but as I've cared for you these weeks, you owe me an answer."

"I showed you kindness—does it count for nothing?"

"Even a scoundrel can be kind."

"Even a beautiful woman can steal."

She frowned. "And what would you be meaning by that?"

"I had a valuable brooch. It was gone when I woke up in the woods." He made an unsuccessful effort to sit up. "When I woke up, you were gone, and so were my brooch, my horse, my sword—"

"You'll find all those things in this house, save for the horses. Both your stallion and the gelding are in the stable," she snapped, feeling herself flush to the roots of her hair. "And how, by the way, did you come by such a brooch? Sure, I took it from you, but to spare your life from any covetous highwayman that might have come upon your useless body. And that brooch is as Irish as me mother, so how did you—"

"It was a gift," the knight answered, his eyelids drooping in exhaustion.

A twinge of guilt struck her. Her guest, her rescuer, lay tired and sick, and yet she tormented him. Her father was right—she could wear a man out with her challenges. At eighteen, she should have been married, but though many men had approached her father about a possible union, none had stayed through her fits of temper to win it.

She forced a smile and tentatively placed her hand on his forehead. "Sleep now," she said, watching as his face relaxed in gratitude. "I'll not be bothering you anymore tonight."

❖ ❖ ❖

"You asked why I came to Ireland."

The girl's hand froze in midair between his mouth and the bowl of broth she was patiently feeding him, but after a moment she smiled and held the spoon to his lips.

"Aye, don't you think it's only reasonable to tell your hosts of your business? Especially since a knight on our shores is rather like a whale beaching himself in the center of Waterford Square."

Ingram frowned at the uncomplimentary comparison. "A whale?"

She shrugged. "Tell us or don't tell us, sir knight; it's really none of me business what you are doing here."

"So I've said. And I wish you'd stop calling me that. My name is Ingram. I'm from Southwick Castle, in the south of England, and was, until early autumn, in service to Lord Galbert, a vassal of His Royal Highness, the king."

She paused and let the spoon rest in the bowl. "Is that all you're going to say?"

"No." He shook his head. "The monk who rode with me on the road that day bore a terrible secret. Years before, apparently, he stole a child promised to an Irish monastery and fled with the child to England. I was that child. The monk wished to make reparation for his deed before he died. He intended that I should come with him to Ireland and join a monastery."

Her lips parted slightly; he could hear her gasp. "So are you? Planning to join a monastery?"

"No. My reason for coming to Ireland was to find my parents. I have always served God as a knight and imagined myself to be as English as the oaks surrounding Southwick Castle, but it would appear that God first created me an Irishman."

"Truly, is that so bad?"

Ingram clenched his fist, hoping she could understand what he was feeling. "I must find out who and what I am."

She stirred the soup slowly, then raised the spoon to his lips. "'Tis an admirable cause," she said, her clear green eyes smiling down at him. "To follow it, you must be strong. Stop talking now and eat."

Ingram endured several moments of true panic as he convalesced in the house of Erik Lombay. When his body had rid itself of the fever, Ingram discovered he had little feeling in his legs. His first attempt to climb out of the cot was a disaster, and he crumpled to the stone floor like an awkward colt, his legs pale and thin beneath him.

What if he never walked again? Ingram had heard horror stories of crippled knights, and he hid his face, afraid he'd blubber in fear before the smith and his daughter. He had to be strong. "God, you spared my life," he prayed, fighting the creeping desperation. "Surely you do not intend me to live that life in a cripple's cot. What good is a knight who cannot ride or run to the battlefield? Strengthen me that I may serve you again."

As though in answer, as his wound healed, the sensations in the lower half of his body returned. Soon he was able to move his toes, then his knees, and finally even his whole leg. Every day, under Signe's constant exhortation, he practiced simple movements, building his strength and will.

She was relentless in her coaching. "Move your knee, sir knight," she'd say, tossing the blanket from his legs. She'd hold a dripping sea sponge over his head, and if he didn't comply with her forceful instructions, she'd allow the freezing water to drip on his shoulders while profusely apologizing for her sloppiness. If he did move, she would swab his knee or foot with the sponge, pretending that a simple bath was all she had in mind from the first. After a day or two of success, she'd think of something harder: "Bend your knee, knight, and kick the blanket from your legs. Are you thinking you're going to spend the rest of your life in me house?"

One day she came to him without the sponge. Her eyes

glinted in determination, and she threw off the blanket with her usual abruptness. "Swing your legs down, knight, for I've an idea that I'd like to sleep in me own cot tonight. Walk across the floor, and I'll make you a pallet by the fire."

The hard knot of fear twisted in his stomach. What if he could not do as she asked? Was this the day he would shame himself beyond redemption?

He bent his knees and pulled them off the cot. The soles of his feet touched the floor; the coolness of the stone tingled his toes. He pressed his hands on the straw mattress and took a deep breath. "Not like that," Signe said suddenly. She rushed to his side, her green eyes wide. Did she guess how badly he was frightened? She sat next to him and draped his arm about her shoulder. "We'll do it together."

With her strength under his arm, Ingram managed to stand and take a slow first step. He took another, leaning heavily upon her. Sweat glistened on his brow and ran down his legs and chest under his tunic; he could never recall making such an effort to do anything in his life. Together they walked three more steps, then Signe turned him around and helped him make his way back to the cot.

They both fell, exhausted, onto the narrow mattress, and Signe extracted herself from under his arm. "Well, I guess I don't mind sleeping on the floor a bit longer," she said, her face flushed. "But I'll be counting the days, sir knight, until I've kicked you out of me cot once and for all."

Ingram fell back upon the bed and closed his eyes. Though he was drenched with sweat and more tired than he had ever been in his life, he felt *good*. He would walk again. His body needed time to repair itself, but soon he'd be the knight he had always been, Ingram of Southwick, the champion of southern England.

Confident of his powers, he smiled and opened one eye. Signe stood over him, obviously concerned at his silence, and he managed a teasing smile. "What if I don't want to leave your cot?" he said.

"Sure, and I'll force you," she said, all concern leaving

her face. She picked up her broom and gave the floor an ineffective swipe. "'Tis me cot, 'tis me house, and you'll be well to be on your way."

"Why? With that tart tongue of yours, 'tis certain no other man is clamoring to get in your door."

The rough straw bristles of the broom swung through the air, and the wooden handle cracked across his jaw before Ingram had time to react. Stung, he let his head fall back on the mattress.

"How dare you insult the hospitality of this house!" she said, her face a mask of rage. The words were sudden and raw and very angry. "I'm going to forget that you said such a thing and not tell me father of your insult. But you will never, *ever* speak so again, or, by all that is holy, I'll drag you out onto the street and leave you for the dogs!"

She whirled and ran from the room; her broom clattered on the floor as she abandoned it. Ingram sighed and rubbed his throbbing jaw.

Though his words had been careless teasing and he had meant no offense, he was significantly more humble when she returned later that day with her father. Ingram had spent the afternoon in severe self-reproach for his careless words, determined not to waste any further time in romantic infatuation when his body needed to concentrate on healing. He would recover his strength, thank these people appropriately, and leave to find his parents.

But it would be important to know something of Ireland before he ventured alone into the countryside. So after supper in the weeks that followed, Ingram asked Erik Lombay about the city, the country, and the people. He learned that Waterford, with Wexford, Cork, Limerick, and Dublin, were cities composed of Ostmen—Norse Vikings whose ancestors had visited the Emerald Isle and found it good. "You can always find the Norse," Erik Lombay told him. "Just look for the water. The Irish love the land, the drumlins, the mountains, the bogs. The Ostmen love the sea."

"And you, Signe, what do you love?" Ingram asked, daring to tease her.

"Certainly not the water," she replied with a saucy toss of her long red hair. "For across it come bold knights who bring more trouble than they are worth." She looked up at him, her eyes like chipped emeralds in the dim light of the fire, and for a moment his throat constricted and he could not speak.

In the past few days, he had come to believe that Signe Lombay was the most entrancing creature he had ever known. Part of her charm lay in the simple fact that she was nothing like the women he had been taught to court by the rules of love. In Ingram's world noble ladies did not argue with men. They were not bold or boisterous, and they never openly contradicted their lords, masters, or lovers. In England noble women were continuously guarded or confined strictly to their castle chambers and workrooms. Men did men's work; women tended to the castle, the food, and their hours of sewing in the garden.

Signe, apparently, knew no boundaries, physical or social. She never hesitated to refute his word or challenge his thoughts, and she even rebuked her jovial father when he had, as he put it, "a wee drop too much of the drink." She spent as much time at the smithy as she did at home, and once he heard her arguing loudly with a group of men outside the house. Lady Wynne would have turned pale at the thought of such a public confrontation.

But Signe fascinated him. Pretending to be asleep, he studied her as she washed her hair and combed through the wet, red mane, sewed her father's clothes, and stirred the cauldron over the fire. She had a talent with music, and more than once he fell asleep to her gentle tunes and the quiet strumming of her lute. For the first time in his life, he was in close daily contact with a woman, and he could not believe the comfort her presence brought him.

76

Her little acts demystified some things he had always wondered about women. Once he caught her pinching her cheeks to make them red. Another time he watched her insert red-hot needles into the hair follicles under her sloping eyebrows, then dab sticky pitch to the delicate skin to remove stray hairs. But though he began to observe and understand *how* women accomplished the things that set them apart from men, he still had no idea *why* women did such things. Why did Signe take such pains with her appearance if she didn't want to love the man who openly admired her beauty? Why did she strive so hard to appear feminine if she walked, talked, and behaved like a man? Above all, why did she give so much of herself to help him if she didn't—and wouldn't— love him?

For despite his humility and his circumspect behavior, she kept her distance, growing more removed and careful as he grew stronger. Her conversations in the morning became sharper and shorter as the days passed. She more often handed him his bowl than sat by his side to watch him eat. She gave every indication that his presence was hard to bear, even an affront, and Ingram wished he had lost his voice as well as the use of his legs. If he had never spoken that cruel jest, she would never have been offended.

He kept his musings to himself and talked of Ireland with the father while remaining religiously circumspect with the daughter. He behaved like a monk—better than a monk, actually, he thought as he recalled Father Colum's bizarre tales. He never allowed his hands to caress or linger on the soft supporting shoulder that was offered to him daily as they walked through the room together. He tried to dismiss the smell of her hair, the glow of her smile, and the quick brightness in her voice.

But he could not.

You're going soft, he told himself one day after sighing in disappointment when Signe left the house. *You'll soon be good for nothing but playing the lute and singing witless love songs. Get up, get out of here, get on with your task.*

And so, very gingerly, he lowered his feet to the floor and crossed the room to the chair where his new tunic and mended hauberk lay.

NINE

Erik Lombay raised a cup of Christmas ale and nodded gravely at Ingram. "Here's to your health, young knight, and to your children," he cried, his voice heavy with the effect of his earlier toasts.

"To my children," Ingram echoed, laughing. Erik was in an uncommonly good mood today, probably having more to do with the fact that Ingram had walked all the way to the smithy and back than with the Christmas season. *He's eager to be rid of his houseguest,* Ingram thought, his eyes meeting Signe's over the rim of his cup. *And is the daughter likewise glad?*

"Here's to the nativity of our blessed Lord," Signe offered, raising her cup as well. "Happy Christmas to all."

"Amen," her father said, tipping his head back in a neat, practiced gesture as he drank.

Their cups lowered, and Ingram felt their eyes upon him as he searched for the proper salute. "To a hardworking father and loving daughter . . . my gracious hosts," Ingram said, raising his cup. "May this new year be one of prosperity."

"A wise man," Erik observed, raising his cup with enthusiasm. Signe nodded silently and sipped from her cup. She hesitated to meet Ingram's eyes, and for a moment he wondered if she would miss him when he had gone. For three months he had been a burdensome house guest, and now that he was well and his horse fit, he was prepared to ride forth and begin his quest.

A keening wind rattled the door and window of the small house, but all was cozy inside. Erik's eyes twinkled as he raised his cup again. "To health, home, and happiness," he said, "and to me daughter's new husband. May their children be as numerous as the sand of the sea."

He threw back his head and guzzled deeply, and Ingram turned quickly to Signe. Her eyes were wide with horror.

"New husband?" Ingram asked, trying to appear merely polite. "Have you been keeping a secret from us, Erik Lombay?"

The smith wiped his mouth with his sleeve and turned a wide grin upon Ingram. "Why, 'tis no secret, me friend. Surely you don't think you could be saving me daughter's life without me offering her to you as a bride? And since you're well and all, 'tis only natural that there should be a wedding, and soon." He leaned forward and winked conspiratorially at Signe, who blushed to the roots of her flaming hair. "I know me daughter, sir knight, and I know she fancies you better than any of the lads in the city."

He raised his glass again. "So I'll be drinking to the wedding. And to your happiness."

Erik tilted his glass, but Ingram put his hand on the man's arm. "Erik, my friend, this is a tremendous honor, but I'm afraid I'd be doing you and your daughter a great injustice if I agreed to this marriage."

Erik blinked slowly. "Can me ears be hearing right? What are you saying?"

Ingram cleared his throat, careful not to look at Signe as he searched for words to extricate himself from the awkward situation. "I'm not unaware of the honor you're bestowing on me, Erik. But I'm a knight, and I am out of place in Ireland. I have nothing to offer your daughter."

Erik grinned and waved Ingram's words away. "Your character is enough, me lad. You're a good man. I can see it in your face. I can train you to work at the smithy—"

"But I'm a knight, not a smith. I fight for kings."

Ingram bit his lip, realizing too late that his words sounded hopelessly pompous and egotistical. He searched for a new tactic: "Your daughter has a mind of her own, and she doesn't like me."

"He's right. I don't." Her words were clipped.

"Aye, she does, for I know me own daughter." Erik turned to Signe. "You do like him, for I see it—"

Signe slammed her cup on the table. "Father, I cannot marry him. He's rude—"

"She's loud." Ingram cringed inwardly at his boldness, but Erik seemed to take no offense.

"He's arrogant." It was a throwaway accusation, but her words stung nevertheless.

"She talks too much." He couldn't help himself. The abrupt declaration of war between them stirred his fighting instincts, and it was suddenly very important that Signe not win this battle. Couldn't she see he was trying to spare her?

Signe closed her eyes, then patted her father gently on the arm. "Don't ask me to do this, Father. He does not want to stay here."

Ingram had no counterattack for her last blow, for, unlike the others, her last statement was true. He could feel the power of her gaze upon him as she waited for his reply, and he felt strangely ashamed of his unwillingness to stay and make a home with the good people who had saved his life. "Signe is right," he said finally. "I must be going soon. I cannot rest until I find my family. . . ."

"Where are you going, son?" Erik asked, his shaky hand coming to rest almost tenderly on Ingram's own.

"I don't know."

Signe held her head high and knotted her mane of hair at the back of her neck. Ingram had thanked her for dinner and was now outside with her father, packing his saddle with provisions for his journey. He meant to leave after all. Though part of her admired him for setting a goal and having the determination to follow it through, another part of her wanted desperately for him to remain in Waterford.

He wore a curious blend of clothing: the Norman knight's helmet and hauberk and, over the armor, a distinctively Irish tunic embroidered with shamrocks. His sword gleamed in the winter sunlight from its place at his side; his shield hung from the stallion's saddle. Over his shoulder, fastened by his unique brooch, hung a thick woolen cloak, Signe's last gift to him. "You'll need this, for winter's winds are harsh," she had said last night as she gave it to him.

"It is beautiful and very fitting," he answered softly, running his hands over the soft wool. "Do you know what tomorrow is?"

"The sixth of January?" she asked, raising an eyebrow. "The holy day of Epiphany?"

"My first birthday," he whispered, staring absently at his hand on the cloak. "The first time I've ever observed a birthday, did you know that?"

"No."

She shook her head, and he gazed up at her with eyes that were suddenly bright. "I have a birthday, Signe, and somewhere out there, perhaps not far from here, some man and woman may think of me tomorrow and mark the day as I will. . . ."

She had left the folded garment in his hands, and her fingers touched his as the cloak passed between them. She wondered if he felt the same sense of tingling delight at their touch that she did, then decided that he did not. If he had, he would not be leaving.

Through the small front window, she watched him mount the stallion. She drew her shawl closer about her and stepped outside for a last word. Turning the skittish horse, he gave her a smart salute, and she felt the magnetic pull of his gaze threaten to tear her from the doorway where she lingered.

"Take care," she said, hoping her voice did not betray the emotion she felt. "Keep warm. And beware of the

Leinster men—they are in league with Donal Kavanaugh, and he carries a grudge longer than most."

"Ah, sure, and why would you be worrying about him?" Erik said, slapping Ingram's leg affectionately. "You're a tough lad, or I'm not the finest smith in Waterford. You can handle Kavanaugh any day, should you be running into him."

"I hadn't planned to look for him," Ingram answered, his eyes traveling up and down Signe though he spoke to her father. For a moment her breath caught in her throat—it almost seemed as though he strove to imprint her image on his mind. But surely that was impossible.

"Where will you go?" she asked in a strangled voice.

"Cashel," Ingram replied. "Father Colum spoke of a large monastery there. From there I'll ask the monks where I ought to go, until I've visited every house of God in Ireland or found my parents."

"The River Suir will lead you to the monastery at Cashel," Erik said, patting the stallion's neck absently. "Godspeed, Sir Ingram. You will always be welcome in the house of Erik Lombay."

"Thank you." Ingram turned his eyes toward Signe, and she was aware that he waited for her to say good-bye. How could she simply wish him well and watch him ride away?

She forced her feet to carry her to his horse, but she could not make her eyes look up to the man on the saddle.

The stallion snorted impatiently, anxious to be off.

Ingram spoke first. "I've left the gelding for you in the stable. He's a good horse and will serve you well."

"Thank you."

"'Tis the least I can do. You've done so much for me."

"You saved me first, remember?"

"Look at me, Signe."

His words compelled her to obey, and she studied him silently, his cool blue eyes holding her against her will. "You know why I could not marry you?"

"I know."

"It's not that I have no feeling for you. Indeed, I owe you everything."

"I know." A sob escaped her; she pressed her lips together as tears spilled from her rebellious eyes.

Without warning, he bent low, placed his fingers under her chin, and lifted her mouth to his. The whisper-light contact of their lips acted as a spark to kindling; the repressed emotion she had hidden burst into flame, burning her cheeks with its heat.

He must have felt the fire of her soul, for he suddenly pulled away. "I must go," he said, and then she felt only the whisper of his breath against her closed eyes. "But I leave you with this, as an inadequate payment for all you have given me."

He pressed something cold and round into her hand; when she opened her eyes, she held the bronze brooch. Ingram gathered his reins and turned to her father. "Farewell, Erik Lombay," the knight called, turning the stallion out of the courtyard of their house. "May God be with you until we meet again."

With the touch of a spur, he was gone. Signe stood, motionless, until she felt her father's strong arm about her. "He was a grand one," Erik commented. "Do you suppose he'll be back?"

"No, he won't," she answered. *Please, God,* she prayed silently, *don't let him come back. If he doesn't love me enough to stay now, he never will, and I could not bear seeing him without loving him.*

But how could she enter her house again without seeing him on her cot, by her hearth, or at her table? Only one thing would take the memories from her mind; there was only one way to find peace. Clasping the brooch in her hand, she turned to her father. "I need to be married, Father. I think it's time I had a home of me own."

Erik blinked in surprise, then nodded enthusiastically. "Are you willing at last? By heaven, girl, I thought you'd chase every suitor in town out of the house before you'd agree to wed. Are you finally ready to be agreeable to your suitors?"

Signe nodded. "I'm ready. Find a son-in-law you'd like, Father, and urge him on. I'll be a spring bride, if you can find a man to have me."

She turned abruptly and went into the house as her father danced a self-congratulatory jig in the courtyard and called to his neighbors. "Haven't I said in time she'd make a lovely bride? They'll not see her like again in this place, nor her mother's like, either, but me daughter Signe will make a fine wife. . . ."

She closed the door behind her and leaned against the sturdy oak. Let him preen and celebrate. Let a man come, any man, and as long as he was decent, she'd marry him.

Her father was growing old, and he needed a son-in-law and grandchildren. What did it matter whom she married? She had waited all her life to find a man to love, and that man had just ridden away and would never return.

TIERNÁN O'ROURKE
1152

Even though you have ten thousand guardians in Christ,
you do not have many fathers.

1 CORINTHIANS 4:15

TEN

The stallion loped easily down the riverbank, and Ingram
forced himself to think of his journey, not the family he had
just left behind. Aside from his one ridiculous proposition, he
had never done anything to make Signe believe he loved her,
though it was obvious from her face at their departure that
she had come to love him. Well, he had done what he could.
He left her with a valuable horse and brooch, and she was still
untouched, a perfect virgin bride for some lucky Ostman who
wouldn't mind being contradicted with her every breath.

A larger task awaited Ingram, and he intended to fulfill
it as quickly as possible. Today was his birthday, and he was
setting out to find the family he had never known. Large
monasteries existed at Cashel, Armagh, Clonard, Cork, and
Kildare, and he trusted that the goodness of the monks of
each diocese would compel them to give him further aid for
his journey. As he rode he prayed that God would lead him
to find his parents, if they were living, or record of them,
if they were dead. Perhaps he would find brothers, sisters,
cousins, and a geographical place to call home. And when
he finally knew who and what he was, he would be free to
search for the meaning of his life.

He followed the River Suir west out of Waterford and found
by day's end that the river turned to the north. As the sun
sank low at his left hand, Ingram grew hungry. The loaf of

bread from Signe's hearth had been a meager dinner, and after the exertion of his long ride, Ingram was ravenous.

Ahead on the bank of the river, two men were fishing. Ingram slowed his horse to a walk and approached slowly. They seemed to be jovial fellows, casting circular nets into the water and laughing when the nets came up empty. They worked together with easy familiarity, and Ingram noticed a marked similarity between them. Surely they were brothers. Ten feet from the men, Ingram stopped his horse. The two fishermen looked up at him, their hands automatically hovering over the daggers at their belts.

"Good evening and good fishing to you," Ingram called, bowing his head in exaggerated politeness.

"Good evening," the tall blond man replied, his eyes darting to his companion for assurance. "What is your business here? You are a knight, are you not?"

"A knight of England, but a son of Ireland," Ingram replied easily, folding his hands carelessly in plain sight. The brothers seemed to relax. "I'm searching for record of my birth, which I believe may be in the monastery at Cashel. Is it far from this place?"

"Another hour's ride," the second man answered. He was stockier than the first but with the same fair hair and striking blue eyes. "But the sun is nearly set, and only a fool travels in darkness along this river."

"I agree. I thank you for the information, but, my friends, what I really need now is a good supper. I've been traveling all day, and I'm starving."

The two men looked at each other, shrugged, then turned back to Ingram. He smiled and patted the flank of his horse. "I wonder if you'd be interested in a little wager? I'd be willing to bet neither of you can ride my horse for the length of, say, the Paternoster or the Miserere? If you can, I'll leave the beast with you. If you cannot ride, well . . ." He shrugged. "I'd expect a good supper of fish."

The men looked at each other and nodded. "So be it!" the shorter man answered, dropping his net and stepping forward. "Me brother here will recite the prayer. You, sir, may kiss your horse good-bye."

"Ah, I think I'd better hold the beast first," Ingram said, dismounting. He held the bridle firmly until the young man had mounted. "Ready?" Ingram asked. He released the bridle and slapped the stallion's flank. "Ride!"

The taller man began reciting the Paternoster while his brother attempted to urge the animal forward, but the stallion would have nothing to do with an unfamiliar rider. His ears flew back, his nostrils quivered, and he began to buck and kick. The tall brother had just finished "hallowed be thy name" when his companion flew off the horse and landed on his back in the rough pebbles of the riverbed.

"You *amadon!* I can do it," the taller one said, tossing his net aside and coming eagerly for the reins. "Let me at him, knight. Me brother knows nothing about riding. You have to treat a horse gentle, like a pretty colleen."

Ingram steadied the stallion while the defeated brother stood and brushed sand from his shoulders. The short one scowled but nodded and began reciting the common prayer as Ingram released the reins. The stallion hesitated, sensing a new, gentler individual on his back, but after a moment he shook his head and promptly threw the second rider.

As the brothers adjusted their dignity and went to fetch the prize, Ingram led the stallion to water and smiled at his new acquaintances. "There are too many fish here to feed one man," he said, taking the bucket with one hand and extending the other. "I am Ingram of Southwick, and I'd be pleased to share this supper with you."

The brothers grinned and took Ingram's hand in friendship.

Over a dinner of fish and brown bread, Ingram learned that his companions were Donnan and Ailean, two brothers who rode as warriors for Tiernán O'Rourke of Breifne, a small principality within the Kingdom of Connacht.

Donnan, the elder of the brothers, was short and hulking, "the image of me father," he told Ingram proudly. Ailean stood taller than his brother and slimmer, with the same blond hair and blue eyes but with more delicate features. Of the two, Ingram noticed, Ailean was the first to speak, Donnan, the first to act.

"What brings you this far south?" Ingram asked, trying to remember the lay of the land as Erik had described it to him. "Isn't Connacht far to the north of us?"

"Sure, and we're far from the others we're riding with," Ailean said, sliding a spit into a small fish. He held the fish over the coals of their fire. "But me brother and I wanted to get away for a day, so we rode out last night. The other lads won't mind a bit, our taking off. They understand it's only natural that a man needs time to get away from *her.*"

"Her?" Ingram asked, thinking suddenly of Signe. "A woman rides with you?"

"O'Rourke's wife," Donnan explained, looking slowly up from the fire. "She wanted to go to Cashel to make an offering to ensure the master's place in heaven. It's slow traveling, for she won't let the horses move faster than a walk—"

"'Tis nerve-wracking," Ailean interrupted. "And she talks constantly, about things only an eejit would imagine, mind you. She complains about the weather, about her husband, her horse . . ."

He lifted the smoking fish from the fire and took a hearty bite. With his mouth full, he mumbled, "So we left, you see. We're to meet them tomorrow outside Cashel. I doubt Dervorgilla will even notice that two of her men were gone."

"Dervorgilla," Ingram repeated, impaling another of the small fish upon his spit. "Surely your master's lady is a beauty. Could you not close your ears to her clamoring and feast upon the sight of her?"

The two brothers looked at each other, then laughed aloud. "A beauty? No," Ailean said, nearly choking on his laughter. "She's a Meath princess, she is, that's why O'Rourke married her. Meath lies between the kingdoms of Leinster and Breifne—"

"And Tiernán O'Rourke hates no one as much as Dermot MacMurrough of Leinster," Donnan added. "So he wooed, flattered, and married the lady before MacMurrough ever got wind of the prize."

"And the master's life has been nothing but merry mischief since," Ailean said, wiping his mouth on his sleeve. "Why don't you ride with us tomorrow? We're going to Cashel, the same as you."

"And 'tisn't safe to travel alone," Donnan added. "Come, Ingram, you seem a pleasant enough sort."

"I can see the Irish in you," Ailean said, grinning. "Ride with us to Cashel, and from there you can decide what to do."

"The men will be pleased that we've brought them an honest-to-goodness knight," Donnan said, his blue eyes merry. "They're forever jesting that Dermot MacMurrough will see the error of his ways and steal Dervorgilla away."

The idea of such a kidnapping set the brothers to laughing, and Ingram shook his head even as he laughed with them. They did have a point. Travel was safer in a company of men, and since they were going to Cashel . . .

"Let us get some sleep then," Ingram said, nodding toward the horizon where the sun had disappeared, leaving a pink-fringed twilight sky. "We'll join your fellows at sunrise."

"Sure, and didn't I know he was a natural-born leader?" Ailean joked, elbowing Donnan in the stomach. "Dervorgilla will love us for bringing her a knight."

In the dim light of dawn, Ingram again surveyed his companions. Mounted, the two brothers looked less like warriors than farmers with battle-axes slung over their saddles. Their horses were strong, sturdy farm animals, probably more at home behind a plow than charging into battle.

They nodded cheerfully to Ingram as they set out and followed the river northward.

They reached Cashel just after sunrise and trotted purposefully past the massive monastery that stood behind a thick stone wall. "We'll be back here soon enough," Donnan promised, pulling his horse abreast with Ingram's. "Dervorgilla, for all her walking the animals, seemed determined to reach Cashel soon. I'll wager they're just up the river."

"I'd think twice about wagering anything if I were you," Ingram answered, teasingly.

Donnan stiffened for a moment, then his expression melted into chagrin. "You're right, knight," Donnan answered, smiling broadly. He tossed the thick winter cloak from his shoulders so that the sun shone on his brawny arms. "But even a brute such as I can't ride an animal that's bewitched."

"He's not bewitched," Ingram answered, purposefully urging the stallion to pick up his pace and leave the farm mares in the dust. "He's the fine horse of a knight, bred from the stallions of the Holy Land."

"Still, I wouldn't hurry forward, if you take me meaning," Ailean called as Ingram passed him on the riverbank. "There's nothing ahead but Dervorgilla."

Ingram spotted the party of men and horses within the hour. He stopped the stallion and waited until Donnan and Ailean joined him at the riverbank. "Aye, that's her," Ailean said, looking ahead. He pretended to shudder at the sight. "Stay quiet, knight. If you're lucky today, the lady will not see you, and you can slip into the company unnoticed."

"Why shouldn't I be noticed?" Ingram asked, his pride injured. "In England 'twas my God-given duty to serve noble lords and their ladies. Why should it be different here in Ireland?"

Donnan closed his eyes and shook his head, and they waited in silence until the lady's party approached.

Dervorgilla pushed her heavy braid off her shoulder and silently cursed the sun. Even in the cool winter air, she'd be as brown as a chestnut before this ordeal was over, and she had taken such pains with her skin! She looked up, eager to snap at someone, when three mounted figures ahead caught her attention. Involuntarily, her hand clutched her throat. Surely it was not time yet!

"Coinneach, who are those men ahead?"

The man riding next to her craned his neck for a better view. "'Tis Donnan and Ailean, his brother," he said smoothly, twisting in the saddle to address the lady. "They are your husband's warriors."

"I know who they are," she snapped, giving him a killing look. "Who is with them? The one in armor?"

Coinneach shrugged. "I don't know."

"Go and find out. Let me know at once."

The warrior trotted forward to meet the trio on the riverbank, then led the three riders to meet the lady. "Donnan and Ailean you know," Coinneach said, his voice artificially pleasant. "This, mistress, is Ingram of Southwick, a knight in service to . . ."

He looked helplessly at the knight.

"The king of England and Lord Galbert of Southwick Castle," Ingram answered, bowing his head regally. "It is an honor to meet you, my lady."

In pleased surprise, Dervorgilla straightened in her saddle. How reverent the knight was, how young, . . . and how handsome! How in the world had those two dullards Donnan and Ailean managed to find him?

A blush rose to her cheeks as she nodded her head to return his greeting. "It is a pleasure to welcome you, Sir Ingram," she said, wishing she had dismounted so the knight could kiss her hand. She'd heard that knights were unusually gallant, and the thought of this handsome knight in attendance upon her was irresistible.

"Would you be so kind, Sir Ingram, to ride with us to Cashel?"

"My lady, it was my sincerest hope that you would allow me to join you."

She twittered, unused to such gallantry. Could it be that he found her attractive? She lowered her eyes demurely. "This may be very presumptuous of me, but would you be my personal escort inside the chapel? I have urgent personal business with the abbot at the monastery, and danger lurks in every corner when you are the wife of a king."

She gave him a helpless smile and waved her hands. Despite her affectations, she was honestly surprised when he nodded sincerely. "My lady, I would enjoy nothing more," the knight replied. "I myself have a request of the abbot at Cashel."

"Indeed." She smiled, wrapping herself in a warm bunting of imagination as she watched the knight. Coinneach finally broke the silence.

"Shall we go, or sit here all day?" he asked. Reluctantly, she gave the signal to move ahead.

❖ ❖ ❖

Ingram, Donnan, and Ailean fell in at the back of the procession. Snickering, Ailean ducked his head and called to Ingram, "How did you do it? She hasn't smiled since we left Breifne, has she, Brother?"

Donnan shook his head in bewilderment, and Ingram gave the brothers a knowing look. "You handle a spirited woman the same way you handle a spirited horse," he said, patting the stallion's neck affectionately. "Gently, but with respect and a healthy dose of flattery."

"Still, it has to be the right man handling her," Ailean said, his eyes glinting in amusement. "Or just like that stallion, a spirited woman's likely to leave you wishing you'd never tangled with her."

"Your lady seems harmless enough," Ingram said.

Donnan laughed. "You've only known her an hour, me friend."

The company of twenty warriors rode quietly through
the imposing walls of the huge monastery at Cashel, and
Ingram looked around with interest. The monks here were
attired as they had been in Wexford, in white and black,
and their heads were shaved from ear to ear in the peculiar
manner of the Irish. Still, he supposed, certain aspects of
religious devotion were the same throughout the world.
Whether in Ireland or Normandy, the grounds of a monastery were holy, its buildings a place of safety and refuge.
Inside the walls of the monastery, at least, the warriors of
Tiernán O'Rourke could relax.

Coinneach helped Dervorgilla dismount, and Ingram
felt twenty pairs of eyes fasten on him when the lady announced that Sir Ingram alone would accompany her into
the chapel. "I will pray first," she announced, as if the men
should care about her every movement, "and then I will
have a meeting with the abbot. You men may pray or visit,
but be forewarned that I shall take a great deal of time.
Coinneach, water the horses and remove their saddles. They
are tired from the journey."

The hapless Coinneach rolled his eyes and obeyed his mistress's bidding, and Ingram saw that a clear path had opened
for him to approach Dervorgilla. As he came closer, he found
the lady's eyes too hard for beauty and her mouth drawn up
into a tight knot, but she lifted her arm in the unmistakable
attitude of a woman who expects her hand to be kissed.

Ingram gallantly took the challenge, walked forward,
and pressed his lips to the lady's hand as an audible groan
filtered through the men. Dervorgilla pretended not to hear,
and Ingram took her hand and led her into the chapel.

Once he had seated the lady in a pew, he walked through
the chapel until he found a monk. "Please, Father, I would
speak to the abbot," he asked.

The monk nodded without saying a word and motioned for Ingram to follow. Soon they stood at a low wooden door, and the monk rapped twice. "Come," a voice called. Ingram stepped through into the austere chamber of an elderly monk.

"What can I do for you, sir knight?" the abbot asked, taking Ingram's measure in one quick glance.

"Please." Ingram's voice cracked. "Twenty-seven years ago, January 6, 1125, a baby boy was born and promised to God. A monk spirited him away, though, before the child was professed. Please, Father, I need to know—was the babe stolen from this monastery?"

The old man's face creased in a puzzled frown. "What has this matter to do with you, my son?"

"I am that babe," Ingram answered, fumbling awkwardly with his hands. "I am searching for my family, Abbot, and would know who I am. . . ."

The abbot nodded thoughtfully. "I understand. Take a seat in the chapel, my son, and I will search through the archives to see what can be found."

❖ ❖ ❖

Dervorgilla couldn't stop fidgeting with her hands. Would he come, or wouldn't he? And would having this handsome knight in attendance help or hurt her? She had thought Ingram a delightful last-minute addition to her plan, another proof that she had been well guarded. Her husband would have no idea of the truth, so if something went wrong, she could yet escape with her reputation.

She glanced around and sighed in relief when she spied Ingram coming back into the chapel. Where on earth had the knight gone? She wanted him close enough to observe but not close enough to hinder her plan. The other idiots were in the courtyard, doubtless lounging on their lazy behinds, never realizing that today was the appointed day, that all had been arranged in frantic, secret letters between Breifne and Leinster. . . .

A tall man entered the chapel through a side door, and Dervorgilla jerked upright at the sight of him. An oak of a man, he wore the voluminous red cloak of the aristocracy over a long tunic of white linen; a golden clasp gleamed at his shoulder. He ran his gray eyes over her for the briefest instant, then turned and genuflected before the altar.

She heard the knight stir in the pew behind her. When had he sat down? Had he noticed the man's interest?

"Sir Ingram," she said, bowing her head modestly as she turned to speak to him. "I thirst. I wonder if you could find a cup of water for me."

"My lady, I am not an errand boy."

His smooth pride rankled her. Her own men would never be so insolent. She thought for a moment about raking her long nails across his handsome face, but, reconsidering, she turned again and smiled. "Please?" She thrust out her lower lip in what she assumed to be a pretty pout. "I would be ever in your debt if you would bring me something to drink. I'm sure one of the monks would lead you to water, if only you would go."

"My lady, you asked me to vouchsafe you here in the chapel. If I wander from your side, how am I to protect you?"

"You wandered earlier without a thought for me."

"I told you I had an errand."

"And now I'm sending you on mine. For the last time, knight, *I thirst!*"

Her voice rose to a screech. The knight frowned and reluctantly rose to do her bidding. She turned to the altar again, folded her hands in prayer, and bowed her head. But she did not close her eyes. She waited, scarcely daring to breathe, until the tall man stood from where he knelt at the altar railing. Their eyes locked.

❖ ❖ ❖

Ingram silently cursed Dervorgilla O'Rourke as he returned with a dipper of water. Donnan and Ailean were right; the woman was an absolute shrew. He rounded the corner into the chapel just as the abbot approached from another hall. "Sir Ingram," the abbot said, pulling a thick volume from beneath his arm. "I have found the records of all oblates given to God in the year of our Lord eleven hundred and twenty-five."

Ingram drew in his breath. Did his answer lie in those yellowed pages of parchment?

A movement to his right caught his eye. Dervorgilla had risen and walked to the altar railing; a mere five feet separated her and a tall man in a scarlet cloak.

"Here are the listings for January," the abbot said, placing the book on a stand. He scanned the pages with a yellowed fingernail. "That was a fruitful month. We took in five boys for oblation, and three girls were presented to the nunnery. Another three boys were found in the fields of Munster and brought here to serve in the house of God. 'Tis an honorable occupation, after all, for as Hannah gave Samuel to the temple in the service of our God, so ought parents to consider it an honor to give their children to God."

"Aye, Father," Ingram said, wishing the abbot would hurry. Dervorgilla had lowered her head, but from here he could see that her hands fidgeted nervously. Why hadn't she remained in the pew to pray?

"If you were an oblate and did not serve God in your youth, it is not too late for you to remedy the mistake," the abbot said, his faded eyes searching Ingram's face. "Will you consider serving here, Sir Ingram, if your birth should be recorded in these pages?"

"I will pray for God's will," Ingram answered, his attention torn between the abbot's words and the activity in the front of the church. He was not fond of Dervorgilla, but he had promised to protect her. Now she stood close to a stranger, oblivious, probably, to all but her prayers. . . .

The abbot tapped his finger on the page. "Unfortunately, there is no record of any boy born on January sixth, nor of any male child who did not serve his lifetime in God's house," the abbot finished, shaking his head in regret. "I am sorry to say, Sir Ingram, that your answers do not lie in these parchments."

A short, shrill scream broke the stillness of the chapel. Ingram looked up to see Dervorgilla in the arms of the stranger as the man hurried to the side door of the chapel. "Quick!" Ingram said, pointing to the abbot. "Tell the men in the courtyard to saddle their horses! Our mistress has been kidnapped!"

The abbot gasped in stunned bewilderment as Ingram dropped the dipper of water and flew down the chapel aisle in pursuit of Dervorgilla and her unknown abductor.

ELEVEN

By the time Ingram reached the doorway, the stranger was riding through the monastery gate with Dervorgilla securely upon his saddle.

Ingram froze. What was this? Even if the man had the strength of ten men, it should have been difficult for him to lift an unwilling woman onto a single horse and carry her away. If he put her on the horse first, she could have slipped off; if he mounted first, she could have run to the safety of the chapel.

His knees turned to water as the truth hit him. Dervorgilla, wife of the mighty Tiernán O'Rourke, had arranged her own abduction. And she had chosen Ingram, a mighty knight of England, to guard her so that she might mock him in her escape!

His shame and humiliation quickly turned to rage. By all that was holy, she wouldn't win! No one, especially an aging queen with neither beauty nor charm to recommend her, would defeat Sir Ingram of Southwick. He turned and sprinted to the courtyard, where all the horses were in various stages of readiness, except his. The stallion had not been unsaddled.

"Join me, men," he shouted, leaping into the saddle. He jerked the stallion's head toward the open field now torn with the hoofprints of the stranger's escape. "We must fight to save your double-dealing mistress!"

"We'll need more motivation than that," Coinneach yelled, tossing his saddle on his mare.

"Then we must ride to save our honor!" Ingram answered, pulling his sword from its sheath.

He didn't know whether it was his reference to their collective pride or the gleam of his blade that convinced them, but the men energized their efforts. He tore across the field, and it was not long before he heard the thundering of hoofbeats behind him.

They rode until dark, fanning out across the green fields outside the monastery and angering more than one farmer who looked out of his hut to see tall horses stamping down his crops. When at nightfall they reconvened at the monastery gate, Ailean offered his report: "I saw nothing, but I met a peat cutter in the boglands who saw Dervorgilla. She was carried by Dermot MacMurrough. Curiously enough, our lady wasn't protesting as they passed through the boglands."

"What was she doing?" Ingram asked, his voice as cold as the winter wind that had chafed their faces all day.

"Kissing her captor," Ailean said, smirking. "MacMurrough joined a detachment of his own men just south of here, and they carried the lady through the boglands and toward Leinster."

"She arranged everything," Ingram said, looking from man to man to see if any doubted his word. Apparently none did. "She bade us unsaddle our horses—she only wanted one man inside with her. Once inside, she sent me on an errand to fetch her water."

"And you went?" Donnan asked, raising an eyebrow.

Ingram flushed. "Aye. And then she walked up to her lover, screamed, mounted his horse, and rode away. That's the story, gentlemen."

"How are we going to tell O'Rourke?" Coinneach asked. "Whose head will roll on this one?"

Ingram felt twenty pairs of eyes turn to him again. He stiffened. Very well, if these cowardly farmers were frightened to face the results of a plan instigated by a scheming woman, he'd do it. He'd tell O'Rourke what a worthless, faithless wife he had, and if someone had to die for it, well, it shouldn't be Ingram of Southwick. It should be O'Rourke, for being fool enough to marry a princess for her position and not for love.

"I'll tell O'Rourke," Ingram said, pulling his cloak around him. "I'll tell him everything."

The journey back to O'Rourke's castle was slow and cold, for no one was eager to face the king with news of Dervorgilla's abduction. Ingram put thoughts of that lady behind him and managed to enjoy the ride. Leaving behind the flat lands of the coast and the waters of the River Suir, they crossed breathtaking wintergreen mountains, rode through mossy bogs, and reached an unusual area that Coinneach called "drumlin land." These tightly packed small hills were low but quite steep and patched together by areas of bog or small lakes. Ingram never tired of reaching the crest of a forested hill and spying a crystal lake in the glen below.

No two Irish miles were exactly the same, and the only common denominator in the land itself was the emerald color of the grass, hills, and forest. He felt himself haunted by the color. Then he awoke from a deep sleep one night and realized why: Emerald was the color of Signe's eyes.

After a particularly cold and wet day's ride, the group rode out of the forest and crossed a stone-studded creek into a meadow. A small dirt road wound up through the verdant valley, and at the road's end the somber circle of a fortress rose from behind secure ramparts to challenge the bare stony hills that loomed in the distance. "Dromahair, the castle of O'Rourke," Donnan said, nodding at the cluster of buildings ahead. "He'll be expecting us."

Coinneach shouted a greeting to a man who stood on top of the outer wall, and the man waved them on. Ingram studied the fortress with some surprise. He had journeyed from England to the Holy Land and found all castles similar, but this fortress was markedly different from the design of noble homes in England and Normandy. Like the castle at Southwick, a tall wall surrounded the main house, but the fortress of O'Rourke was also skirted by two walls of earth and stone with a water-filled ditch between them.

Ingram guessed that the dry stone walls were at least thirteen feet thick and eighteen feet high, and they reinforced the strong impression of the castle's loneliness. Unlike the castles of England, where villeins lived outside the walls and farmed the lord's field or shepherded his cattle, not a single farm lay in sight of O'Rourke's fortress.

"Where are the people?" Ingram asked Ailean as they rode toward the fort. "O'Rourke's people, where do they live?"

"Some live inside," Ailean answered, nodding toward the fort. "Others live on farms in the country."

"Then how does he rule them? How does he exact his due?"

Ailean shook his head. "He doesn't *rule;* he protects. If the land is under attack, the people will come here. If we must defend ourselves, we leave our homes and ride out from the fort. But the farmers own their own land."

It was a radical idea and one that struck Ingram as being particularly liberating. To own the land! No wonder the farmers outside Cashel had reacted so violently when he rode his horse through their fields! The fields belonged to *them.*

"How do you judge a king's greatness, then," Ingram asked, unable to comprehend a system in which men served a lord freely rather than out of obligation, "if not by the number of estates he owns?"

"All freemen are landowners," Ailean explained. "A king is great according to how many men he provides for. The *saer cheili,* or free men, borrow cattle from their lord to stock their land. When the debt is repaid, they are no longer subject to him. The *aire tuise,* such as O'Rourke, are chiefs of a large group of freemen and responsible to represent the

tuath, or kingdom, in treaties. Only through his help can
a lesser man expect to recover damages or debts."

Ingram took in the information silently. "So this
O'Rourke, then, is an important man?"

Ailean nodded. "And a good warrior. But you will meet
him soon enough."

A cluster of stone buildings lay inside the castle walls, and
Coinneach led Ingram into the largest of these. Ingram
found himself in an expansive chamber richly decorated with
tapestries. A huge log roared in the fireplace, a sumptuous
banquet waited on a table, and upon the raised platform at
the head of the hall, a one-eyed man paced and scowled
impatiently at the returning warriors.

"I care not for your greeting, Coinneach," the man said,
his voice rumbling through the room. "What of my wife's
gift? Did the abbot assure her of my speedy advent to
heaven?"

"Your gold is still in my possession, my king,"
Coinneach said, stepping forward. He let a heavy pouch fall
to the floor at O'Rourke's feet.

"What's this?" O'Rourke growled. "Where's me wife?"

"That, sir, is the focus of a tale we must tell you,"
Coinneach said. "We met a knight on the road outside
Cashel, and—"

"I am the knight," Ingram said, stepping forward.
O'Rourke's mouth opened in surprise, then snapped shut.
They studied each other for a moment, and Ingram was
impressed with the rugged good sense evident in
O'Rourke's features. His hair, though thinning, was dark
and neatly combed, his face etched with intelligence and
hard-bitten strength. Most unusual, however, was the black
patch over one eye, and Ingram took pains to avoid staring
at it.

"The event at Cashel was my responsibility, and you may
do with me what you will, sir. I ask only that you keep in

mind that you, sir, chose to marry a woman who does not love you."

O'Rourke glared at Coinneach. "Who is this man? Why does he display the armor and speech of a foreigner? And why does he rebuke me for marrying my wife?"

Though his posture did not bend, Coinneach seemed to grovel. "He is a knight, sir, from England. Sir Ingram."

O'Rourke's good eye squinted as he took his seat and looked more closely at Ingram. "What say you of my wife, Sir Ingram?" he asked finally.

"She has been abducted, sir, by a man who snatched her from the monastery at Cashel. It is my belief—no, it is fact—that she arranged the abduction. A peat cutter saw them riding together and saw your wife kissing the man who abducted her."

Ingram braced himself for an onslaught from a distressed husband, but O'Rourke's expression did not change. "Abducted, then, you say? From the church?"

Ingram nodded. "Yes."

"And you gave pursuit?"

"She had sabotaged our efforts. The horses were unsaddled, and the men unprepared to give chase."

O'Rourke's single eye gleamed in sudden interest. "Did no one see this man up close?"

"I did, sir. He was tall, solid, and well dressed. The peat cutter later identified the man as Dermot MacMurrough of Leinster."

O'Rourke threw back his head and roared; the sound echoed for an eternity in the hall. Ingram stepped forward, afraid for a moment that the man had lost his senses.

"Get away from me, you ignorant fool!" The king's words shot out like a volley, thrusting Ingram back into the knot of men assembled in the room. "That man has wounded me, stabbed me in the heart! What I won from him, he has stolen from me. We shall not let him succeed!"

The furious king rose from his chair and stalked through the room, tearing tapestries from the walls, upending chairs, and tossing most of the waiting dishes upon his table to the floor. The servants who waited in the corner of the room wrung their hands and waited for his fury to cease.

Finally, O'Rourke stopped and stood before Ingram. With steel flashing in his eye, he shook his finger before the knight's face.

"What is it you do, knight?"

"I fight for kings, sir."

"What brought you out of England? Do you fight for Dermot MacMurrough?"

Ingram flinched. "No, I came to Ireland on a personal quest."

The king did not hesitate. "Then hear this: from this day forward, your personal quest is set aside. Since you fight for kings, you shall fight for me. You, Sir Ingram, have caused me untoward grief this day. I could have your head. But before God and these witnesses I command you to serve me until the day me wife is free from my dearest enemy, Dermot MacMurrough."

Still muttering, the one-eyed king stormed from the room.

The furious king's words contained such power that Ingram submitted to O'Rourke's demand without protest. The king was a true warrior at heart, and the man's feisty nature won Ingram's respect. He had a practical reason for submitting to O'Rourke, as well. In the king's service he would have a home base from which to ride and visit nearby monasteries; O'Rourke's "sentence" would hamper him very little, if at all.

What most surprised Ingram in his first few days at Dromahair was the counterbalance between O'Rourke's genuine anger at losing Dervorgilla and his equally genuine reluctance to bring the lady back. *He hates losing his wife,* Ingram thought one afternoon as O'Rourke launched into a tirade against Dermot MacMurrough at dinner, *but he misses her not at all. He only hates losing her to MacMurrough.*

Ingram had been certain that O'Rourke would immediately launch a war party to bring Dervorgilla back, but instead he sent most of his men home to their farms. The handful of men who lived at the fort were a quiet, unambitious lot, and when Ingram suggested strategies for winning the lady back, hoots and jeers met his plans.

"Leave her be," Ailean called, tossing a pair of dice in the courtyard one afternoon. "She wanted to go, so let her."

"But O'Rourke is crazed with anger."

"O'Rourke hates MacMurrough and always has," Donnan stated flatly, shaking a pair of dice in his hand. He blew on them for luck, then crossed himself for good measure. "This abduction is merely fuel to keep the hate alive."

"But I am kept here until the lady returns," Ingram finished, shaking his head.

"Would you rather be somewhere else?" Ailean answered, slapping Ingram on the back. "Here are the riches of the king's house: good food, good friends, and good gaming. You're free to come and go as you please. O'Rourke is a capable and fair master. What else are you thinking of wanting?"

For the briefest moment, Ingram thought of Signe. Softness melded with strength, intelligence with innocence, humor with wit. His life lacked the wonder of womanhood.

Ailean saw the gleam in his eye and laughed. "Ingram, me friend," he said, winking as he threw his arm around the knight, "if it's a wench you're wanting, any farmer's daughter in these parts would be happy to entertain you. Just ride down after supper one night—"

"Take a bath first," Donnan interjected, chewing on a piece of straw.

Ailean nodded. "Aye. Bathe, lather up, and visit a lady. With your good looks and that suit of armor, why, you could have any daughter in these parts."

Ingram smiled at their joke and scratched his beard as if in deep thought. But it wasn't a wench he wanted.

TWELVE

Winter passed into spring, and spring into summer. Ingram grew to know and respect the handful of professional warriors who dwelt at Dromahair, and he found that their skills, while different from those taught in his training for knighthood, were quite good. Like the squires of England, these warriors had served O'Rourke since the tender age of thirteen or fourteen. Several children trained at Dromahair, and Ingram enjoyed watching them. Through them he was able to relive much of his own youth.

In many ways, though, a warrior's training in Ireland differed greatly from the training Ingram had known at Southwick. Here the sons of noble families wore gold- and silver-embroidered silks in rich colors, while the humbler children under O'Rourke's fosterage wore black or white woolens. But though wealthy children were given better clothing, food, and equipment, Ingram noticed that all were level on the field of play.

"A raggy colt often makes a powerful horse," Donnan observed one afternoon while he and Ingram watched a game of hurling. A thin child, obviously poor, had just whisked the game ball from under the feet of a nobler child and courageously maneuvered it with his hurling stick to score for his team.

"Aye," Ingram agreed, enthusiastically applauding the boy's efforts. "The scrawny child may grow to be the best warrior of the lot."

After games the boys and men competed together in skill sports with the javelin and rope. Ingram marveled at the boys' athletic prowess as they leaped wide gorges, worked wonders with a rope and truss, and speared a moving target with ease. It was difficult for him to remember learning the same skills; it seemed he had known how to do these things all his life.

After dinner, however, while the squires of Southwick would have stayed in the great hall to hone their skills in dancing or composing poetry, the boys of Dromahair went to the barns and received lessons in animal husbandry, kiln drying, and wool combing. Ingram accompanied them only twice, disturbed when he saw that the young warriors were taught to handle lambs, kids, and pigs with ease. These lessons had not been a part of his education. In Norman knighthood a wide gulf existed between farmers and warriors.

After dark, when the men and boys of O'Rourke's force retired to the stone house that served as their garrison, Ingram lay on his straw mattress and listened with acute interest as his fellow warriors told tales. It was a distinctively Irish trait, he thought, this love of telling stories, and no evening was complete without at least an hour's recitation.

"The old warriors, the Celts, lived for battle." Ailean recited one night, the dim light from the fire exaggerating his features grotesquely as he glowered at the young boys. "They were fierce fighters, our fathers, and flung themselves naked into battle, wearing only their helmets, their neck torques, and belts. Their weapons were small bronze spears or short stabbing swords, and they were ready at any time or place to face danger. With nothing on their side but their own courage and wit, our fathers fought enemies and held this land for you, me lads."

"Did they learn at the king's house, like us?" a small voice piped up timidly from a dark corner of the room.

Ailean shook his head. "Some did; some did not. One young man was sent to live with Scathach, the Shadowy

One, a woman who lived on an island off the coast. From her he learned the feats of the sword edge and the sloped shield; the javelin and the rope; the heroic salmon-leap; the pole throw and the leap over a poisoned stroke; the noble chariot-fighter's crouch; the feat of the chariot wheel thrown on high and the feat of the shield rim; the snapping mouth and the hero's scream; the stroke of precision; stepping on a lance in flight and straightening erect on its point; and the trussing of a warrior on the points of spears."

All in the room were suitably impressed, and no one dared to breathe a word of contradiction to Ailean's tale. "What happened to him?" one brave boy finally asked.

"He became a king, of course," Ailean said, settling back onto his mattress. "Though he was not a prince and had no royal blood, he was skilled. He who serves his country well has no need of ancestors."

The room fell silent, and after a while Ingram drifted into sleep. He dreamed that night of battle and swords and a throne of his own.

When he wasn't helping train the boys, Ingram rode with his fellow warriors through the lands of Breifne to ensure the peace of O'Rourke's kingdom. Most of the villages based their livelihood upon farming, with cattle and sheep kept in the nearby fields. Aside from the occasional cattle raid between rival clans, the warriors had little to do but ride and enjoy the spectacular lay of the land. To the north and south of O'Rourke's castle, stony mountains rose majestically from green land stretched tight from peak to peak. Rushing rivers glinted silver in the sun as they traversed Breifne, and frequent rain watered the land like a loving mist.

At each village Ingram left his fellows and journeyed to the monastery. Many were small, with no more than five or six monks in residence, but he dared not pass up any possibility. Whether they greeted his request with curiosity, skepticism, or indifference, the monks never refused to answer his questions.

Ingram stared at their soil-stained hands and could barely disguise his contempt. Why would a man surrender himself to the church unless he had absolutely no other options? Certainly the church offered education and opportunity, but even the lowest child in Ireland could avail himself of a proper education through the monastery schools or fosterage.

And if a man became a monk to become closer to God, well, Father Colum had unwittingly proved the folly of that idea. Hadn't Colum been a monk for years while rebelling against the very thought of God? Wearing a humble woolen robe of white and black had nothing to do with the spiritual state of a man's soul. God demonstrated his presence more powerfully in the majestic expanse of nature, Ingram felt, than in a humble mud-and-timber chapel.

In his own life Ingram had never felt closer to God than when he had lain all night in vigil before the altar in preparation for the ceremony of knighthood. He had placed his life and sword in God's service and had felt assured that God heard and accepted his offering. Why then had Father Colum wanted him to serve God by donning a monk's cowl and shaving his head?

"You must be the holiest man I know," one of the warriors remarked when Ingram rejoined the group after one of his monastery visits. "You never let a church pass without stopping to pray. Doesn't God hear prayers as well from the fields?"

"Aye, I don't doubt that he does," Ingram answered, shifting his weight in the saddle.

"Well then, why do you go to the church?" The man laughed. "One would almost think you fancy yourself a monk, Sir Ingram."

Ingram turned and gave the man a quick, scathing glance. "Trust me, my friend," he said, placing his hand on the hilt of his sword. "There's not a man in the world less inclined to be a monk than Ingram of Southwick."

Dervorgilla jumped at the unfamiliar touch upon her shoulder.

"Sorry," a flat, nasal voice said. "I just wanted to see what my father brought home this time."

She turned. A young man of about twenty stood there, a man not unlike MacMurrough, with the same height and stature. But this man had thick golden-brown hair where MacMurrough had gray, and when he stepped forward, she noticed that he walked with a definite limp.

"You must be Niall," she said, forcing a smile. "Or perhaps you are Peadar? I've been waiting to meet Mac-Murrough's sons for such a long time."

"You'll not meet them at all, for they want nothing to do with any woman who is not their mother," the young man replied casually. "I, however, am the son of a harlot, so I don't care who sleeps with my father. I, Mistress Dervorgilla, am Donal Kavanaugh."

The name meant nothing to her; she was still reeling from the realization that MacMurrough had an illegitimate son. But she should not have been surprised. He was a lusty man, not confined by stringent morals, especially since his wife died. Perhaps she should not be surprised by anything.

The young man leaned toward her in a gentle, inquiring fashion. "Has my beautiful sister been here to see you?" he asked, his voice soft like velvet. "You'd like her. Eva is a mere child, but she is a charmer, and very ambitious, as you are. How long had you planned to leave your husband? How many letters did you send to my father, begging him to steal you away?"

"I did nothing of the sort," Dervorgilla lied, lifting her chin. "You father will tell you himself, we are—"

"I know he did not act so rashly because of your beauty," Donal Kavanaugh answered, sinking lazily into a chair. "You are as ugly as a threadbare carpet, lady, and surely about as comforting."

She choked on shame and humiliation, momentarily speechless. "You—," she cried, anger overriding her weakness. She stood and flung her arm toward the door. "Get out of here! I don't care who you are—if I see your face again, I'll have your head on a platter! I'll have your entrails served to the dogs!"

Kavanaugh stood slowly. "Don't be so harsh, lady," he said, smiling at her over his shoulder. "You may need a friend like me one day."

When she was sure he had gone, Dervorgilla collapsed on her bed in tears of rage.

Nothing had gone the way she had planned. MacMurrough had been solicitous at first, giving her the attention she craved, but once she was safely ensconced in his fortress at Ferns, he left her alone. And the one thing Dervorgilla could not stand was to be ignored.

She threatened the servants, ranted and raved, and utterly alienated MacMurrough's daughter, Eva. At last the young girl had left to live with a relative, telling her father that he could fetch her whenever "that woman" had gone. Dervorgilla had gloated in her triumph, convinced that MacMurrough's devotion to her (or at least to her lands, she reluctantly admitted) would outlast any ties to his children. But in the end MacMurrough spent less and less time at home, and Dervorgilla began to suspect that his attraction to her inheritance was not as strong as she had hoped.

"It's easy, Father," Eva MacMurrough assured the man who rode by her side. They were riding outside his fort at Ferns in the Kingdom of Leinster, and Eva had made it clear that these outings, too, would stop unless Dervorgilla disappeared from their home. "You can be rid of her next month, if you like. I know how it could be done."

"You are fourteen; what could you possibly know of such things?"

"Haven't I grown up in a king's house?" She fluttered her dark lashes briskly, knowing that the effect entranced her father. "I have learned strategy, dear Father, at the feet of the master."

"But O'Rourke would think me a fool and a dupe if we surrendered the woman," MacMurrough argued, stopping his horse. "I admit, taking Dervorgilla was folly, but how could I know she was the devil's own daughter? Eva, bonny child, if you can think of a plan to rid us of this evil, I'd be willing to hear it."

"Leave it to me," Eva replied smoothly, reaching out for her father's hand. She placed it tenderly on her cheek. "She'll be gone next week, and Niall, Peadar, and I will come home, Father. All will be as it should be in the house of Leinster."

❖ ❖ ❖

"A letter from Leinster!" Coinneach said, waving a parchment above his head. "Master, a woman writes from Leinster and says that your wife will be traveling to the church at Kildare in a month's time."

"Will MacMurrough be there?" O'Rourke snarled, his eye narrowing with distaste as he pronounced the name.

"Aye," Coinneach said, scanning the letter. "Is this not the opportunity to defeat MacMurrough and win your wife back to your side?"

O'Rourke scratched his scraggly beard thoughtfully, then nodded to Ingram. "Take you, Sir Ingram, twenty—no, thirty—of me best men, and ride at once to Kildare. Do whatever you must, but kill MacMurrough and bring me wife back."

"Aye," Ingram answered, inwardly rejoicing at the news. Not only would he have his chance to redeem his honor, but he had yet to visit the monastery at Kildare, deep in Leinster lands. Perhaps this would be the monastery for which he had been searching.

Ingram and his men arrived in the village of Kildare nearly a week before MacMurrough and Dervorgilla, and they took great pains to hide themselves so that MacMurrough would not be alerted to their presence. While at Kildare, Ingram crept away one afternoon to the monastery. With the help of an aged monk, he searched through the monastery's extensive archives to find only that there had been no baby boys placed in oblation in January 1125. Not only that, the old monk pointed out, but there were no baby boys even born in Kildare during that month.

Now, as he stood hidden in the forest outside the monastery, Ingram tried to forget the bitter disappointment that grew with every failed attempt to find a record of his birth.

Lord God, how much longer will it take?

He shifted restlessly in the shrubbery, but no heavenly answer was forthcoming. Apparently God had no intention of responding. Well, no matter, for now, at least. For though he had failed on one mission at Kildare, he was determined to succeed at another. MacMurrough would be vanquished, Dervorgilla restored to her home, and Ingram would be free to continue his search throughout Ireland. Today would bring at least one victory.

They had learned that morning that MacMurrough and Dervorgilla would definitely ride to the monastery today. The news had been easy to gather—almost too easy. Ingram shrugged off the coincidence. MacMurrough might be a great king, he told himself, but he was no military strategist. No knight or Norman lord would ever come openly on the road without defensive cover, especially if a sworn enemy stood likely to take revenge on a year-old vendetta.

The rumble of hoofbeats alerted him, and Ingram signaled the men who waited in the woods behind him. The archer to his right took careful aim at the cloaked figure who rode next to the lady. Ingram nodded; the archer released the bowstring. After the deadly hiss of a flying arrow, the man toppled to the ground. The lady screamed, Ingram spurred his horse, and the skirmish began.

The fight ended abruptly. The riders behind the lady panicked and fled down the road from which they had come, and Ingram himself easily grabbed the reins of the lady's horse and led the animal swiftly on the road back to the Kingdom of Breifne. He and his men would be safely inside the Kingdom of Meath in an hour, and before the sun set they would stand before O'Rourke and present him with his wife. It had been a perfect ambush.

Too perfect. A doubt lingered in the back of Ingram's mind. The man in the red cloak only faintly resembled the gray-haired man Ingram dimly remembered from the church at Cashel.

Dervorgilla stood before her husband, her hands folded calmly in front of her. He spared her only a brief glance, then asked the question foremost in his mind: "Is MacMurrough dead?"

Ingram took a step forward before Coinneach could accept the blame. "We killed the lady's escort and scattered the retinue, sir, but the man who lay dead in the road was not Dermot MacMurrough. We learned later that he had sent a proxy."

O'Rourke actually smiled, but he quickly wiped the grin from his face with his hand. "So the monster still lives? How clever of him. And how clever to send me wife home without her knowing she was being handed back like an unsavory dish at dinner. What did he tell you, my dear—that he had a headache and preferred to stay behind? Surely you must have noticed that he didn't care much for the man who rode at your side. That poor fool must have been expendable."

"I hate you," Dervorgilla said, glaring up at her husband.

"And MacMurrough, lady, hated you more, else he would not have sent you back," O'Rourke answered. "He bears me such great hatred that he would have kept you had you been the least bit amiable. But you poisoned him far beyond his hate for me. I think now that instead of his hate, I have his pity." He propped one hand across his mouth and stroked his jaw, regarding her evenly.

She spat at him. The spittle landed squarely on the hand at his mouth, and O'Rourke calmly wiped his hand upon his cloak, his steadfast eye not even blinking. "Take her to the small house at the back of the fort," he told Coinneach. "Have her kept there, under guard. She shall not escape to humiliate me again."

As Dervorgilla was led away, O'Rourke turned to Ingram. "And you, Sir Ingram, have proved yourself brave and faithful, even to a king whose favor you did not have to win."

"I found you fair and reasonable," Ingram said, bowing. "I only did my duty, sir, to God and to you."

"And now you are ready to depart my service? I cannot implore you to stay?"

"I may return, sir, but I have a personal—"

"Quest," O'Rourke finished for him. "I remember your words clearly. Well, Sir Ingram, since you are determined to go, I shall not stop you. Remember you are always welcome here, in my fortress and in my house. And as you go, I shall provide for your safety. I cannot send Ailean and Donnan, as much as they would like to accompany you, but I shall send you out tomorrow with two new companions. They bear no loyalty to any one king, but to all, and you can travel safely throughout any kingdom in Ireland as long as you travel in their steps."

Ingram bowed, uncertain of the king's meaning.

"Tomorrow, my friend, you shall meet Cathal, a brehon of Ireland, and his student, Griogair. You have taught my men much in the time you have been with them; now it is time for you to learn."

DONNCHAD
AND
AFRECCA
1153

There is a way that seems right to a man.

PROVERBS 14:12

Thirteen

When he entered O'Rourke's great hall the next morning, Ingram was startled to see that the mighty O'Rourke shared his raised dais with two men in blue tunics. Ingram knew that brehons were among the nobility, but was their stature so elevated that they received the reverence usually reserved for kings? Unsure of the proper protocol, Ingram followed Coinneach's lead and bowed deeply to all three men on the platform.

The stooped older man in blue lifted his leathery face slightly and pointed a long, bony finger in Ingram's direction. "This is the man?" he asked O'Rourke.

"Aye, 'tis the knight," O'Rourke answered. "He has served me well and will be a worthy companion for you and your student. In his manner and with his sword, he has brought honor to Dromahair."

"I have no need of a sword, only of a willing mind," the man answered, folding his aged hands at his breast. His eyes, which surely had once been dark, had faded to a soft gray, and his face was tanned and tough from a lifetime spent outdoors. He spoke slowly and thoughtfully, but his voice rang with authority. "Step forward, friend Ingram, so that I may have a better look at you. My eyes fail me."

Ingram stepped within an arm's reach of the man and stood at attention under the elder brehon's scrutiny. Keeping his eyes steadfastly upon the brehon, he studied the web of wrinkles that encompassed the man's face.

O'Rourke broke the silence. "Ingram, before you stands Cathal, one of Ireland's most learned brehons and equal to any king in the land." O'Rourke nodded deferentially to the old man. "He and his student, Griogiar, have given you leave to accompany them throughout Éireann until you have found what you seek."

"I will be pleased to serve and guard them," Ingram answered, lifting his chin. "If they are national treasures, as I have heard, they will be safe with me."

"We need no guard," Cathal said, his iron voice cutting through the stillness of the room. "I have walked the forests and roads of Ireland for more years than you have drawn breath, my friend, and never has a blade or blow bruised my skin. I am the walking law, and Ireland respects her brehons."

"I beg your pardon," Ingram answered, bowing in apology. "I meant no offense. But I have been a knight since my childhood, and I know something of the evil nature of men. Shortly after I landed here, I saw clearly that some Irish do not respect anything. My companion, a monk, surely a brehon's equal, was toppled from his horse by a coward's arrow—"

O'Rourke held up his hand. "You are not accompanying these men for their safety, Ingram, but for your learning and your safe passage. Brehons are the only men allowed to journey freely through the kingdoms of our island home. And though I have no doubt you will perform according to your nature, still, these men can and will teach you much, if you are willing to learn. Go with them, walk slowly, and listen carefully."

The king lowered his hand and offered Ingram a casual smile. "Of course, you are welcome to rejoin our ranks if and when you may, but if destiny calls you elsewhere, we wish you Godspeed and all success."

Ingram bowed on one knee before O'Rourke. "My king, I vow my loyalty to you and your cause should you have need of my sword. You have but to send word, and I will come to aid you."

O'Rourke's good eye gleamed in appreciation. "Your vow is accepted gratefully. Now go, my fearless friend, and we pray you will find the answers to your questions."

Ingram said his good-byes to Dromahair and Tiernán O'Rourke on a bright winter morning in March 1153. Ingram bade farewell to the boys in O'Rourke's fosterage and his fellow warriors, and then he fondly embraced Donnan and Ailean. "Promise you'll come back for a wee talk sometime," Ailean said, slapping Ingram on the back. "Dromahair won't be the same without you."

Ingram nodded wordlessly and took the reins of his waiting horse. Cathal began walking for the road without hesitation or comment, but Griogiar nodded in friendliness and held the stallion's bridle as Ingram mounted. Dressed like his master in a simple blue tunic with a thick woolen cloak of a deeper blue, the younger man shared Cathal's weather-beaten skin and lean form. But he still carried the sparkle of youth about him, and the dark blue eyes he turned upon Ingram were friendly.

Once they were past the gates of Dromahair, Cathal and Griogiar walked side by side on the road while Ingram rode his stallion behind them. Cathal took a brief moment to explain that their route would be circuitous—they would leave Breifne and travel up through the kingdoms of Oriel and Ulidia. "Then the kingdoms of the north," Cathal said, ticking off the names on his fingers, "Dalriada, Tir Eoghain, Tirconaill. Then we will change our direction southward to the Kingdom of Connacht and the Kingdom of Munster. Eastward, then, to the Kingdom of Leinster, and north to the Kingdom of Meath. Do you understand, friend Ingram?"

Ingram nodded, feeling oddly that he was expected to memorize their route in preparation for some sort of test. Perhaps he would next be asked to repeat every destination back.

But Cathal merely nodded. "After Meath, we shall arrive back in Breifne, and again enjoy the hospitality of Tiernán O'Rourke. If you have not found the answers you are seeking, perhaps you will join his men again?"

Ingram shook his head. "I must have success, Cathal. I have come too far to give up on my task."

"Can you not live without this success?" The brehon paused and seemed to weigh his words. "O'Rourke told me that you search for your parents. But consider, friend Ingram, are there not other ways to judge your worth?"

Ingram bit his lip. Over and over he had asked himself the same question. Why couldn't he be satisfied with being a knight? Why wasn't it enough that he was loyal and courteous and feared God—surely such a man could find honor in himself and his actions.

But the revelations of the past two years had caused him to question all he had assumed before. He was an Irishman, and Irishmen had no use for knights. He was born of Irish parents, and a man's parents formed him; they determined who he was and what he would become. In Norman England a man's birth shaped his destiny, and from what he had seen in Ireland, it was much the same. Occasionally, a boy did break out of the mold, but more often men followed in the footsteps of their fathers.

Cathal nodded slowly, sensing Ingram's distress. "Suppose, me new friend, I told you of a man whose ancestors include one who slept with his harlot daughter-in-law, a murdering king, an adulterer, and an idol worshiper. Suppose this man was conceived months before his mother's marriage to a poor man who was not the child's father." Cathal paused and turned his gray eyes upon Ingram. "What would you say of such a man?"

Ingram searched for a hidden meaning in the brehon's words, but could find none. "I would hate to be that man," he said finally, his voice flat on the morning air.

"Ah, and would you now?" Cathal answered, folding his hands behind his back. "'Tis a pity indeed, for the man I described was our blessed Lord himself. But Jesus' ancestry did not keep him from God's calling or from doing what God asked of him. Rather, it was all a part of being what God intended he should be. For if the Lord had descended only from nobility, how could he have understood the pain and struggle of common man? And if this is true of the Lord, that God uses all of who he is, past and present, can't it be true as well of a knight from England?"

Ingram felt his face empty of expression as the words rang over the trail where they walked. The brehon wasn't fair. The Son of God was one man; Ingram the knight was someone altogether different.

Cathal nodded in understanding when Ingram did not speak. "This is the reason we brehons memorize genealogies," he said softly, looking down at the ground as he walked. "Kings must know their ancestors throughout five hundred years; no less is the desire of the peasant farmer in the smallest village to know from whence he came. Search, friend Ingram. I pray you will find what you desire."

Life with the brehons was unlike anything Ingram had ever experienced. Each morning the three men rose from their campsite or from the house where they had slept, bid a courteous farewell to any who had hosted them, and set out upon the narrow winding roads or followed the riverbanks. After a time of meditation, during which they walked without speaking, Cathal's instruction began. He expounded on elements of Irish law while Griogiar listened, or Cathal walked silently as the younger man recited a lesson already learned.

Ingram was amazed at the depth of their knowledge. After a month of traveling with them, Ingram marveled that he had not heard a single lesson twice, nor had Griogiar made a single error in word or deed.

One afternoon as they rested by the side of a stream, Griogiar told Ingram that he had been Cathal's student for nearly fourteen years. "At first, I only listened while the master spoke," Griogiar said, leaning back on a broad tree trunk. He chuckled. "For a year, I listened without saying a word. Then Cathal began to question me not only of the things I had heard, but also about the things I had observed. Within five years I had learned three hundred stories, the set of metric forms, and the entire body of brehon law. For the last ten years I've been learning the genealogies of the kings and chief families and the long list of prerogatives, rights, duties, restrictions, and tributes of kings."

"This body of law," Ingram said, leaning forward in his eagerness. "Don't the kings decree their own laws? What is a king, if not the one who decrees law for his people?"

Griogiar shook his head. "The king is subject to the law, as are his people," he said. "The law is the law of nature, and Christ's law has been added to it. Nature teaches us that killing is wrong, for everything on the earth strives to live. Christ's teachings tell us not only that killing is wrong, but that we are to love our enemies and show mercy to them. Did not Christ himself say that he came not to destroy the law, but to fulfill it?"

"So the brehon law is Christian?"

Griogiar nodded. "It is also the law of the land. It contains tracts on beekeeping and water mills, fasting, marriage, women, and the fosterage of children. The law, not the king, is the final authority in any dispute."

Ingram soon saw just how extensive brehon law was. When they entered a *rath*, or farming community, the villagers welcomed Cathal and Griogiar with the enthusiasm and reverence due a visiting king. They were bedded in the finest house and given the best food and the choicest seats at the dinner table.

The next morning, after the brehons had slept well, an assortment of men and women would stand before Cathal and present their problems with their neighbors. Like an oracle, Cathal would recite the article of brehon law that remedied the situation, and the defendant and plaintiff would accept his judgment without argument.

Cathal's judgment was rarely subjective, Ingram noticed, for brehon law addressed nearly every facet of daily life. A man of Downpatrick died with no heirs; what was to be done with his farm? "Divide it evenly among the *deirbfhine*," Cathal intoned, while Griogiar explained to Ingram that the *deirbfhine* was the man's extended family up to and including his first cousins of four generations.

Barrenness plagued a woman of Bangor. Cathal muttered an incantation while waving his hands over the woman's head. She was sent home with instructions to sleep with her husband only when the moon shone full and to keep her life and thoughts pure.

During these sessions of law, Ingram began to understand the complex structure of Irish families. No law of primogeniture existed in Ireland; the land and possessions involved in an inheritance passed equally to brothers, regardless of their place in the birth order. Women did not inherit, but they did maintain an interest in the family's land so a woman's sons might inherit.

The men who usually represented family matters before Cathal were aged. Each was a *cenn fine,* the senior member of the immediate family clan, the *geilfhine.* Composed of five generations, the *geilfhine* consisted of a man, his brothers and sons, his father's brothers, his grandfather's brothers, and even his great-grandfather and his brothers. This family unit bore the responsibility and honor of the collective family.

In Rathlin, a stony point of north Ireland, two stooped *cenn fine* stood before Cathal and told the story of two friends, one of whom accidentally killed the other. The slain man's family wanted blood for revenge; the hapless survivor's family wanted mercy. What did the law say about such a matter?

Cathal listened without emotion. "The *fine,*" he said, pointing to the old man who stood as the head of the survivor's family, "is responsible for the misdeeds of its members. It is your duty to offer blood or the *eraic* to the dead man's *fine*. So says the law, and so you must obey."

Ingram glanced at Griogiar, and his brows lifted.

"The *eraic*," Griogiar whispered, "is a payment of blood money, equal to the dead man's worth."

The *cenn fine* from the slayer's family nodded gravely. "We will pay the dead man's honor price," he said. "The man had land worth thrice seven *sets*. Twenty-seven heifers will be led to the dead man's *geilfhine*."

The other family nodded in agreement and relief. The issue was settled without bloodshed, and Ingram felt a flash of respect for an old law that divided land equally, gave men the chance to rise above their circumstances, and allowed restitution to be made without bloodshed. Though he had originally thought Ireland barbaric, the place now seemed more civilized than the bloodthirsty and treacherous courts of Norman England.

Even on the road, where they were subject to the vagaries of weather and chance, life fell into a particular pattern. When they arrived in a village, Cathal and Griogiar made arrangements to hear the villagers' pleas while Ingram rode off in search of the nearest monastery. While at Dromahair he had visited most of the monasteries of Breifne, and now he was glad to have the opportunity to extend his search throughout Ireland. Time after time, however, even as he prayed that his journey would soon end, he was disappointed. Thus far, no abbot had been able to produce proof of a baby boy's oblation in January 1125.

He always returned to his companions in the midst of Cathal's discourse to the village. When the brehon had heard and decided every appeal in the community, the three men would eat dinner. Afterward Cathal would bless the elders of the gathering and lead his companions to the road.

They always walked in formation, the two scholars in

front, side by side, with Ingram behind on his impatient stallion. With every passing day Griogiar recited longer and more involved passages of the law, and Cathal spoke less and less. Ingram often wondered if the older man listened at all, for his vacant eyes would fix on some distant point ahead and his feet shuffled woodenly as if his mind had completely left his body.

When they stopped for water or to rest, Cathal always left the two younger men alone. "I don't think your master likes me," Ingram confided to Griogiar one afternoon as they stretched out in the grass to enjoy the warm spring sun. "He rarely speaks directly to me, have you noticed? He tells you what he wants me to hear."

Griogiar shrugged. "When I first joined him, I felt the same way. He would talk for hours, never allowing me to say a word, but punishing me severely if I missed a single truth or question. In time, I came to understand that when he is not teaching, Cathal prefers thinking to talking. In thought and in words, he is consistent, coherent, and curious. When I recite my lessons, I know he is hearing me with one part of his mind and wondering about some mystery of nature with another."

"It must have been hard to leave your family for such a master."

"Not really." Griogiar shook his head. "It is an honor to be tutored by a brehon. I was fifteen when we exchanged the vows contained in the laws, and we have learned to live with each other since that day."

"What vows?" Ingram asked, propping his head on his elbow.

Griogiar fixed his eyes on the bowl of blue sky above. "Cathal swore to give instruction without reservation, correction without harshness, and to feed and clothe me during the time I was at my learning. In return, I swore to support him against the threat of poverty and to sustain him in his old age."

"So you are bound for life?"

"Aye."

"And you will spend your life walking throughout these kingdoms, giving answers to peasants—"

"And kings," Griogiar interrupted. "You can't be forgetting that we are all under the law."

Ingram chewed on a stalk of grass. "It still seems a dull life. And when Cathal dies, will you take on a student?"

"Certainly, when the time is right."

"Why? It seems a tremendous amount of trouble."

"Because, me friend, two shorten the road."

One afternoon Ingram stood with his two companions on the green edge of a cliff at Inishowen. Far below, emerald moss clung stubbornly to the hollows and hidden places in the rocks, while waves tumbled lazily forward at the base of the bluff. Behind him a level plain of green stretched as far as he could see, and the stallion grazed on the grass.

"'Tis in such beauty that I see the creative power of God," Ingram offered, turning his face to the sea.

"Sure, and it reminds me of the hunger of man," Cathal answered, his smile faintly twisted. "See how the waves are never appeased? They wear away at the rock, never satisfied, never still."

The brehon turned to his pupil. "Have I told you, Griogiar, the story of the Grail quest and the king of Tara?" Cathal asked, his eyes on the watery horizon to the north.

Griogiar tilted his head and struggled to remember. "I don't think so, master."

"Then I'll be wanting to tell you now. Long ago, Airt Mac Con, a favored king, heard of the Holy Grail and dedicated himself to pursue it. He left his kingdom and spent his fortune as he battled infidels and searched the world to find the precious Holy Grail. At home, his son caught a fever and died; his wife followed soon after, dying of loneliness and a broken heart."

The brehon paused as a strong wind flapped their cloaks

in the wind. "In time, though, wouldn't you know," Cathal continued, "Airt Mac Con found the Grail—and the sorceress who guarded it. The woman was called Delvacheem. To gain the Grail, the king had to bring both Delvacheem and the Grail back to his home at Tara."

Griogiar waited expectantly and caught Ingram's eye over Cathal's head. Cathal never did anything without a purpose, but if a lesson existed in this story, it had been cleverly hidden.

Cathal turned to his pupil. "Do you not understand?" he asked, corking his spindly hands into the sleeves of his tunic. The wind hooted around them as he waited.

"The prize was worth the effort?" Griogiar suggested.

Cathal shook his head. "Airt Mac Con found what he sought, but he paid for it with everything he possessed and held dear. In owning his prize, he continued to pay. He had to live with Delvacheem, and didn't he learn his lesson? Her wicked beauty was a poor substitute for peace, for the loving wife and son he had left behind."

Cathal withdrew his hands and held them out toward the sea. "When we seek something of great value, my student, its attainment will bring us pain as well as joy, if you take me meaning. And the story does not end when we find what we seek. A man's quest ends only when his earthly life is done. Like the waves below, we go on searching, finding, wanting."

Ingram grinned in appreciation for the brehon's wit and looked across the water. The touch of a wizened hand on his arm, however, startled him. Cathal stared at him, his face alert. "I'll be wanting to know what you're thinking, friend Ingram. Was Airt Mac Con's prize worth the quest?"

Ingram had no answer.

In his dream, Ingram was seven again, and he sat at the feet of Lady Wynne. "Do you really wish to become a knight?" she asked, her dark eyes glowing in the fullness of her face.

"It won't be easy, Ingram. When we seek something of great value, my little friend, the prize will bring us pain as well as joy."

He nodded stupidly, eagerly. Yes, he wished to be a knight more than anything. Lady Wynne smiled, waved her hand, and suddenly he was fourteen, a squire of the chief knight of Southwick. The knight's armor hung on a wooden dummy in front of him, and it was Ingram's job to polish and mend the rings of metal mesh, to sharpen the sword, to carry weapons, feed horses, shovel the stalls without complaint. "For if you seek to be a knight," Sir Goscelin's gruff voice echoed in his memory, "the prize must bring you pain."

Suddenly he was sixteen, his arms strong from training, his legs toughened by hours of riding the fields of practice and contest. He wore a white robe and lay on the cool wooden floor of the chapel at Southwick Castle as he tented his fingers for a night-long vigil of prayer. "Please, God," he prayed, forsaking the familiar Latin prayers for one more personal and heartfelt, "I seek to be a knight, and I will take whatever pain is necessary to be a servant in your holy name. . . ."

The scene changed again; dressed in his armor, he stood before the assembled community of Southwick, his fingers wrapped about his sword. The chaplain blessed the sword; Ingram kissed the hilt, then placed it in the sheath at his side. He braced himself for the colée, the traditional blow, and barely winced as Lord Galbert's heavy hand hit his jaw. *If I would be a knight, I must suffer the pain . . . ,* his mind repeated as he heard Lord Galbert's words: "Go now, fair son of Southwick, be brave and upright, that God may love thee. . . ."

He led his lord and lady to the chapel, where he laid his sword on the altar and dedicated his knighthood to God. Before God and the people of his world, he vowed to exhibit the knightly qualities of prowess, loyalty, largess, and courtesy. He would be faithful to his king,

defend the Christian faith and the church, protect widows
and orphans, the old and the weak. . . .

He knelt before Lord Galbert again, and the man held
out his palms while Ingram curled his young hands inside
his master's. "Do you wish, without reservation, to become
my man?"

"I wish it."

Ingram looked up. The man who stood before him
was not Lord Galbert but Cathal. His face and neck were
wrinkled as crêpe. His old hands held Ingram's, and no
matter how Ingram struggled, he would not relax his grasp.
"Do you wish, without reservation, to pursue the prize?"

"I wish it," Ingram insisted, struggling to free himself.

Cathal's eyes grew dark and blank as his mouth drew up
into a disapproving knot. "Then you must bear the pain."

For more than three years Ingram traveled with the brehons,
and in that time he learned much about the country, the language, and the people of Ireland. O'Rourke had been wise to
arrange for his journey with brehons, Ingram realized. As
long as he traveled with Cathal and Griogiar, he was greeted
with *céad míle fáilte*, a hundred thousand welcomes. And
though the Irishmen of different kingdoms glanced curiously
at Ingram in his hauberk and helmet, they seemed to accept
him. After all, if the brehons, in their unfathomable wisdom,
had accepted a knight's company, why shouldn't he be freely
welcomed?

And so Ingram fell in love with the beauty and unpre-
dictability of Ireland and her people. England had been
lovely and cultivated, the steady Norman influence ever
present in the organized fields and the castles of the
nobles. But Ireland was a bit like a man with a strong shot
of liquor in him. Ingram never knew what lay beyond the
neighboring knoll, how the weather would change from
one hour to the next, or what an Irish man or woman
might do in any given circumstance.

Once Griogiar or Cathal had introduced Ingram to a community, he was inevitably drawn into the villagers' circle of conversation and peppered with a thousand questions. The Irish loved to talk, and he found himself treated to tales of love, treachery, and intrigue from the shores of northern Greencastle to the southern inland waterways of Cork.

While they were in Cork, he began to dream again of Signe. Much of the city reminded him of her, for Cork, like Waterford, had been founded by the Ostmen, and every stout and strong worker on the street reminded him of Erik Lombay. The houses in Cork were close together and square, quite unlike the stone beehives of the rural Gaelic Irish, and the city buzzed with a prosperous, efficient economy that also reminded him of the green-eyed girl. Four years had passed since he had last seen her, and he wondered if she was still bossing her father and managing his house. Had she rescued some other stranded wayfarer? Had Donal Kavanaugh found a way to exact vengeance upon her?

In his dreams she scolded him, laughed at him, and sang the quiet melodic songs that haunted his memory. He found himself waking in a sweat on hot summer nights, and he prayed that they would leave Cork for a cooler city somewhere in the mountains. But Cork was large, and the brehons were busy.

Ingram breathed a sigh of relief when they finally left Cork, but he felt his stomach churn when Cathal announced that they would journey through several smaller villages before reaching Waterford. Ingram knew that if he went into Waterford, he would have to visit Signe and her father. To ignore them would be a terrible breach of hospitality and an insult to their kindness. But if he saw her, what could he do?

He tried to pray, to seek God's peace and guidance. But his uncertainties overwhelmed and distracted him.

Though he dreamed of Signe and had never met a more desirable and fascinating woman, yet he still could not marry her. He was no closer to finding his personal answers now than he had been on the day they parted. And if she came to him with the same look of longing in her eyes that he had seen on that morning, he knew he would be drawn to her like a moth to flame. He was too lonely to avoid her if she was near, but too determined to find his answers to seek her out.

"Please, excuse me from this venture," Ingram pleaded as they neared Waterford. He noticed a gleam of curiosity in Cathal's gray eyes and hastily looked away. "I cannot go into Waterford."

Cathal seemed to weigh the hidden motivation behind Ingram's plea and finally nodded. "Perhaps it is best, then, that you leave us," he said, motioning to Griogiar that they should continue to walk. "We will meet you in three days time at Dunbrody in Leinster. You'll find the city on the banks of the River Barrow, east of Waterford."

"Thank you." Ingram sighed in relief. "In three days, then."

"Ingram," Griogiar called as Ingram nudged the horse to move ahead of them on the road. "Is there anyone in Waterford we should speak to for you?"

"No one," Ingram answered, ignoring the gentle urging in his heart to speak her name. He pressed gently with his thighs to urge the stallion forward. "No one at all."

FOURTEEN

Ingram rejoined his traveling companions three days later at
Dunbrody and grinned when Griogiar's face lit up in sincere
pleasure at the sight of him. The young man had become a
friend, and Ingram could not recall having a closer one. At
Southwick the barrier of rank had stood between him and
the knights who served under him; likewise, Lord Galbert,
who called himself lord and friend, was truly a friend in
name only. Even Father Colum had treated Ingram more as
an object of duty than a confidant.

After the village convocation at Dunbrody, they journeyed into the woods. When they paused from their walk at
sunset, Ingram helped Griogiar build a fire. Cathal withdrew
from them as he always did, too accustomed to deference to
be close to any man, even in sleep. Ingram and Griogiar
spread blankets on opposite sides of the campfire. As Ingram
lay on the ground listening to night noises, he thought
again of Signe. She was close, even tonight, no more than a
day's ride, and if he could find the courage, he might ride
and see her. But though he would not hesitate to do battle
or face a tyrant with only his sword, his courage failed at the
thought of facing her.

"Do you never dream of her?" Griogiar's voice broke
the stillness.

"What?" Had Griogiar read his mind?

"The mother you search for. Do you never imagine
what she must look like? Have you no memories of her?"

Ingram drew in a quick breath; he still kept his secret. "No, no memories," he said. A stout limb snapped in the fire, and he studied the dancing flame. "And yes, I think of her and my father. I knew a lady in England, Lady Wynne, who acted as mother to me for a time. She was a refined lady of position, with dark hair and eyes, a lovely figure, very accomplished. . . ."

"She sounds very *Norman.*"

Ingram winced at the implied insult. Few Normans had visited Ireland, but those who had come had left an unsavory impression upon the Irish and Ostmen.

"All the English nobles are Norman," Ingram tried to explain. "Since William the Conqueror took the lands from the Saxon chiefs and awarded manors to his nobles, the Normans have managed the lands in the name of the king. A man cannot buy from them; even a second son has no right of inheritance."

"And you, as a knight? What was your place?"

Ingram rolled onto his side to better see Griogiar. "I did only what was expected of me. I pledged my life in service to my lord and king. I might have married, I suppose, and Lord Galbert might have given us a little house on the estate."

"And your children?"

"My son would have become a knight, as well," Ingram said, staring at the fire again. "My daughter would have married a knight or served the lady of the castle as a maid. 'Twould be a worthy and honorable calling."

Griogiar shook his head. "'Tis different in Éireann. I am the son of a farmer, and my grandfather was unfree. But me father's father learned a trade; he became a harper and served a king. He rose from slavery, and his son, me father, became a *boaire,* a higher grade of freeman than his father."

"A noble?"

Griogiar's smile was rueful. "Not quite. But he was determined to have a son in the *aes dana,* so an arrangement was made with Cathal. If I proved to be quick, and sharp-witted, I might become a brehon." He sighed. "Finally, my father has a son in the learned class. Now, when my father's king holds the regular public assembly, my father sits at the king's table in the banquet hall." Griogiar paused, his voice heavy with loneliness. "Now my father can be proud."

Cathal's story of the Grail quest flashed through Ingram's mind. Griogiar's father had sought a learned and noble son and paid for his goal by sending his son away forever. Was pride worth such pain?

"Such a thing would never come to pass in England," Ingram said, hoping to steer Griogiar's thoughts to a less painful topic. "A man is who his father is, and his father before him. So it has always been."

"And so you search, my friend," Griogiar answered. "I understand more than you think."

As Ingram and the brehons traveled through the Kingdom of Leinster, Ingram thought of his chance meeting with Dermot MacMurrough and wondered if the king would recognize him if they should meet. The scene with Dervorgilla in the chapel four years before had been brief, but a knight in Ireland was rare. Would the king know him, and if he did, would he care that Ingram had once ridden with Tiernán O'Rourke?

After some consideration Ingram decided that Dermot MacMurrough's opinions would not matter. As an independent man, Ingram owed service to none but the two brehons who walked as his companions.

His own feelings for the king of Leinster were poorly defined. On one hand, he held a grudging respect for the man who had managed to send the quarrelsome Dervorgilla back without risking his life or his reputation; on the other hand, he knew Tiernán O'Rourke would not despise a man without good reason. O'Rourke did not bear ill will toward the other Irish kings whose kingdoms lay outside his own, so something in MacMurrough's character or past actions had upset O'Rourke deeply. Ingram felt enough loyalty to O'Rourke to be suspicious of MacMurrough.

They visited several villages in Leinster without incident and without seeing the king. In fact, when the brehons paused outside the king's stone castle at Ferns, they were given a bag of gold and told that Dermot MacMurrough did not require their services.

The monastery outside the village of Glendalough rose from the top of a mountain, barely visible through the thick barrier of forest that separated the house of God from the rest of the world. One single steep field had been cleared at the monastery's entrance, and as Ingram rode up the narrow path, he could see several young boys sitting in the grass. A lone monk stood in the center of the group and read from a leather-bound book.

The monk did not lift his gaze from the book as Ingram approached; several of the students did and were swiftly rebuked by a sharp snap from the monk's fingers.

Ingram dismounted inside the courtyard. The monastic buildings within the stone walls were fabrications of poles interwoven with slender branches and daubed with dark dried clay. Just inside the gate, a small chapel had been built of oak planks, and as Ingram walked into the chapel, he noticed that the stone altar had been ornately carved. Despite this monastery's seclusion, it had obviously received more than its share of talent.

A young monk spied him and hurried forward, his hands secreted in his wide sleeves, and Ingram bowed when the monk reached his side. "I would like to see your abbot," Ingram said, smiling openly. "Is he available for conversation with a weary traveler?"

"Abbot Steaphan is praying in his chamber," the young monk answered, his voice so low Ingram had to strain to hear. "I will call him for you soon. Would you like to wait?"

The monk extended his hand toward the rough benches

in the chapel, but Ingram shook his head. "I'll walk around, if you don't mind," he said, taking a step backward. "But I won't leave without seeing your abbot."

❖ ❖ ❖

No other abbot had forced him to wait so long. This Abbot Steaphan had to be either very pious or very pompous, for most came scurrying to Ingram's assistance merely out of curiosity.

He was peering through the open window of the forge when the young monk from the chapel tugged on his sleeve. Ingram was quick to follow him. "You are very busy here," Ingram said, indicating with his hand the work going on in the mill, lime kiln, forge, and barn.

"Pray daily, fast daily, study daily, work daily," the monk replied in a dull monotone. "That's what we do, sir knight." He paused before the doorway of the single stone building on the premises and turned so Ingram could enter first. "The abbot waits inside."

Ingram found himself inside a large, windowless room full of books. Wide tables lined the walls with open books displayed upon them, and satchels hung on leather straps from the walls. One wall was dedicated to shelving, where an ample supply of waxed tablets, parchments, quills, and inkhorns awaited use.

A silent, elfin man waited expectantly in the corner of the room. Abbot Steaphan.

"I trust you have not been waiting long, Sir Ingram," the abbot said, his voice pitched to reach Ingram and not a breath beyond. "I am glad God has brought you safely to us."

"You know my name?" Ingram asked, surprised. "How?"

The abbot chuckled. "If I were trying to impress you with my intimacy with God, I would say that he revealed it to me. But 'twould be a lie, and no man who lies is intimate with God." The abbot lifted a busy brow. "Truth be told, sir knight, I am recently come from Armagh. I was vice-abbot of the monastery there when you and the brehons visited last year."

"So you know the purpose for my visit." Ingram braced himself for disappointment. The abbot would surely tell him that he had already checked the records, that no baby boys were born in this area in January 1125 . . .

"I know that you search for your parents," Abbot Steaphan replied. "But I had no idea you'd visit today. While you were waiting, I had Father Sachairi pull the records of our oblations. We can search the parchments together, if you'd like."

"Of course. We should begin our search in January, 1125." Ingram removed his helmet. Running his hands through his hair, he walked to a table where the abbot opened a large book and flipped rapidly through the pages. He stopped on a page marked *1125*.

On that sheet a careful monk's hand had recorded all offerings to the church, from the solid gold bracelet given by a relative of the king to the pound of beans offered by a poor widow.

"Ah, what have we here?" the abbot asked, his finger pausing on an entry dated January 10, 1125. "One infant son, given to God by his parents, Donnchad and Afrecca of Glendalough, in thanksgiving to God for his goodness and faithfulness. The infant joins the twenty-eight consecrated souls at this house of God. To the Almighty be all the glory, honor, and praise."

The abbot looked up at Ingram. "Could this be the information for which you are searching?"

Ingram felt the room swirl about him; he reached for the table to steady himself. "What became of the child?" he asked, his voice hoarse with checked emotion. "Was he given a name? Does he still serve in this house of God?"

The abbot frowned and flipped the page. "Well, this is odd," he said, scanning the parchment. "In March of that year, another baby was given as an oblation, and the same

entry is recorded: 'The infant joins the twenty-eight consecrated souls at this house of God.'"

Abbot Steaphan looked up at Ingram. "There should
have been twenty-nine souls in this house."

"Yet there were only twenty-eight," Ingram whispered.
He sank abruptly onto a bench behind the table. *Dear God,
could it be . . . ?* "Is it likely . . . is it *possible* that the baby did
not remain here? Could he have been abducted?"

The abbot searched quickly through additional pages,
then closed the book. "Unfortunately, there are no further
mentions of the child of Donnchad and Afrecca, but there
are no deaths of an infant recorded, either. I am at a loss to
explain the record, Sir Ingram."

Ingram sat silently, the facts of the record buzzing in his
head. "What do I do now?" he muttered, more to himself
than to the abbot.

"I suggest," the abbot said, a self-satisfied smile upon
his face, "that we visit Donnchad and Afrecca."

"They are still living?"

"Aye, and not far from here. Come, sir knight, and I'll
take you there."

FIFTEEN

The abbot's tongue loosened once they left the monastery. Ingram thought the man strangely talkative for a monk, even an Irish one. Ingram let the man ramble on about his ambition and the archbishop as they rode up a narrow trail that led through the mountains. The words fell uselessly on his ears, for his mind buzzed with the realization that the mountain road could lead to his home and the parents for which he had been searching.

The monks had no horses for pleasure riding, preferring to walk as a sign of their sworn poverty, but the abbot had not hesitated to ride behind Ingram when he saw the magnificent stallion. "That animal won't fit in at all with Donnchad and Afrecca," he was saying now, sinking easily into the horse's gentle canter. "Oh no, sir knight, they'll have him pulling a plow within a fortnight. 'Tis a shame."

"They are farmers?"

"Of course. The few families who live in these forsaken mountains are all farmers," the abbot answered, waving his hand languidly at the forest. "Despite the stony terrain and the trees, they eke out a living as best they can. They do well to feed their families, for though they are poor in material possessions, they are rich in children. We take in a dozen oblates every year."

Ingram shook his head in wonder and tried to steady his hands as he held the reins. He had left England and the only home he had ever known for this moment, and before the sun set, he would see the result of six years' effort.

Would it be worth it? Would his parents, this Donnchad and Afrecca, be glad to see a grown son they had surely presumed dead? Would Afrecca, this woman Father Colum claimed to love, be strong like Signe, or gentle like Lady Wynne? Would Donnchad be proud of him? Would he see himself in Ingram?

Go to them.

The startling words rang deep within him and he nearly missed the turn onto the narrow boreen through the forest when the abbot tugged on his sleeve. Focusing his attention, he maneuvered the stallion through the small path and held the animal to the trail that led, the abbot assured him, to the community where Donnchad and Afrecca lived with their *fine*.

When the wooden gate and walled enclosure came into view, Ingram was gripped by a crazy notion to spur the horse and flee through the woods. He struggled to keep his facial muscles under control as the abbot hailed the family at the gate. Slowly, as if in a dream, the gate swung open, and from behind him Ingram felt the eager kick of the abbot's legs urging the stallion through the opening.

A teenage boy stood behind the gate, his dull eyes regarding Ingram and the monk without the faintest flicker of interest. The scent of roasting meat filled the air, and two small brown carcasses hung on a spit over an open fire. A young girl stood at the fire and eyed Ingram suspiciously until the abbot murmured something in a heavily accented Gaelic. Ingram had learned to converse in the Irish language while traveling with the brehons, but in his present dazed condition, he wasn't able to follow the conversation and had no idea what the abbot told the girl. But she scampered off toward one of the huts that lined the perimeter of the compound, and a pair of men from another hut leaned on their spears and regarded Ingram with dark eyes.

He swallowed. He hadn't counted on meeting his par-

ents before an audience, but since the abbot's greeting, at
least twenty people had appeared within the enclosure: men,
women, and children. They stood silently, regarding Ingram
and the abbot alike with expressionless eyes, until finally an
aged, balding man came forward and stood before the
abbot, his cap in his hand.

"Donnchad of Glendalough," the abbot said, slipping
from the horse. He walked forward and clasped the old
man's hand. "Joy to you, my friend. I bring you good
news."

The way the old man blinked reminded Ingram of a
watchful hawk.

The monk looked at the dour faces around him and
tried another approach. "Afrecca of Glendalough, wife of
Donnchad," he said, reaching for the age-spotted, worn
hand of a tiny woman in a dingy tunic. "Thirty-one years
ago you gave birth to a baby boy and placed him in the
house of God. It was an oblation, a *gibht*. Do you remember?"

Afrecca nodded slowly. Her free hand moved to clasp
the abbot's.

"Have you seen your child since that day?" the abbot
asked, looking from the face of Donnchad to Afrecca.
"Have you seen him at the monastery?"

The old woman's eyes filled with tears, and she clung
tightly to the abbot's hands as she shook her head.

"Then God has smiled on you today. He has revealed to
me, Afrecca, that your son lives. The man on the horse, the
knight, is the child you bore so long ago."

She shook her head, uncomprehending. The old man
wore a puzzled look.

"Do you understand?" the abbot asked, raising his
voice. "This knight, this *ridirich* . . . you are his *máthair*.
And you, Donnchad, you are the knight's *athair*."

The woman trembled and staggered backward; the collected audience murmured among themselves. Donnchad
regarded the abbot with open disbelief, but Afrecca pulled

herself from the supporting arms that held her and walked to the stallion. Looking up, she placed her hand on Ingram's foot. He looked down at her.

"Mac," she said simply, and Ingram recognized the word: *son.*

Ingram's mind reeled. He had wished for this day, prayed for it. And now, apparently, God had answered his prayers. Why, then, did his stomach knot with apprehension?

How could these people possibly be the family he had longed for, searched for? Father Colum had said he loved the woman who was Ingram's mother. But this woman was not at all the kind of mother Ingram had expected. These people were peasants, not nobles.

He glanced at the man called Donnchad. *Holy God, can this man truly be my father, this hawk-faced man with the blank stare?* Then his eyes returned to the woman called Afrecca, and he saw the pain and helplessness in her face.

He was a knight, sworn to protect the innocent and honor God. And God, for whatever reason, had led him here. He had to put his doubts aside and accept this new life. He had to believe that he had, at last, come home.

He dismounted and turned to Afrecca, and the frail woman buried herself in his arms. He stroked her gray hair silently, still wondering if he could truly have come from such a tiny, frail woman.

Donnchad was not convinced. He argued loudly with the abbot in Gaelic, and Ingram could not understand all of the conversation. The abbot declared over and over that God had willed this reunion, and finally the little woman pulled herself from Ingram's arms and scurried inside the stone hut. In a moment, as the men continued to argue, she returned, holding something in her hand.

It was a lock of fine hair, tied with a thin sliver of faded ribbon, and she held it aloft to the crowd, shouting something Ingram couldn't understand. At her words Donnchad ceased to argue, and the other women babbled excitedly, gathering her into their arms in celebratory embraces.

"She is holding a lock of her baby's hair," the abbot said, turning to Ingram. "The hair is the same golden color as yours, my friend. It would appear that you have at last come home to stay."

After a bland supper of boiled beans and rabbit, Ingram sat in the stone hut of Donnchad and Afrecca with Abbot Steaphan by his side. Accustomed to the heavy accented Gaelic of the mountain Irish, the abbot was able to interpret most of the conversation for Ingram.

"Afrecca says you have two brothers," the abbot said, wiping his mouth delicately with a square of linen from a pocket in his robe. "Pádruig would have been forty-six this year, but he died five years ago. A pack of wolves caught him in the forest."

The abbot listened closely to the story of the second brother, while Ingram looked around him. The interior of the hut was close and damp; the smoke from the tiny fire drifted lazily toward a fist-sized opening in the roof. There were no windows, no tapestries, and no furnishings save a pile of straw in one dark recess of the room. Ingram could never recall having seen such poverty.

"Your other brother, Philip, lives here," the abbot explained, turning again to Ingram. "He is forty-three years of age and has a wife who has borne ten children. Three of them remain."

"I am the youngest son?" Ingram asked, thinking that Afrecca looked to be at least sixty, and Donnchad even older.

"Aye. You are the *iochtar*, or youngest child. That's the way it always is," the abbot answered, discreetly lowering his voice. "They can't afford to feed the later arrivals, so the children are given as an oblation. Count yourself lucky to have survived, my friend. Food was no doubt scarce in the winter of your birth. This hut would be covering your bones now if your parents had not brought you to God."

The abbot turned again to their host and hostess, and

Ingram shivered as he imagined the probable end for a poor newborn baby in this desolate place. Afrecca stirred from her place by the fire and came to stand behind Ingram. After a moment, she placed her hands on his shoulders. She murmured something, and Donnchad's face reddened while the abbot laughed.

"What?" Ingram asked, leaning toward the abbot. "What did she say?"

"She says," the abbot paused and made a gallant effort to clear his face, "that when the babe was born, the family members thought it suffered from *amadanachd.*"

"Which is?" Ingram demanded.

"Idiotism. The others urged her to be rid of the child," the abbot finished. "Afrecca boasts that all idiots should turn out as well as you!"

Ingram smiled, and the smoky haze of the room seemed to act as a veil that separated him from reality. Had he searched the entire of Ireland for this? To find a frail, sparrow-like mother and a sullen father who had not ceased to glare at him from the time he entered the compound?

Afrecca murmured something to the abbot, who smiled and nodded at Ingram. "She says you are welcome to spend the night here with them. Tomorrow, the *fine* will help you build a hut of your own, and in time, you may take a wife." The abbot colored slightly as he added: "She says she cannot believe you are hers. Her womb has never before produced such a handsome man."

Ingram smiled and nodded pleasantly toward Afrecca. God had restored him to his mother, and she deserved his respect no matter how far removed she was from the noble, wealthy mother of his imagination.

Later, in his spacious chamber at the monastery, Abbot Steaphan smoothed the supple fabric of his tunic and smiled. The knight called Sir Ingram had tried to hide his disappointment, but it was obvious that the noble knight felt like a lion in a den of kittens. Why wouldn't he? Educated, skilled, and handsome, the knight clearly did not belong on a poor farm atop a Wicklow mountain. Donnchad and Afrecca's family were common, hardworking people who had never had more than a day's meat in storage and whose crops never resulted in a harvest great enough to last through the harsh winters. The knight had nothing in common with them; their social and temperamental characteristics differed as vastly as winter and summer.

Even the physical resemblance was slight. "Aye, two eyes, a nose, and a mouth," the abbot muttered to himself. "Upon my soul, with such in common, they are bound to be related by blood." Still, he mused, the knight's character had to be commended. It had required nerves of steel to face that hostile crowd—and even greater courage to remain behind.

The abbot leaned back in his chair, his chin in his hand. Why should Donnchad and Afrecca have custody of such a man? If the child had been promised to God as an oblate, that vow held still! Ingram rightfully belonged at the monastery, where his intelligence, faithfulness, and loyalty would be appreciated. Undoubtedly literate, the knight could probably speak several languages. . . .

Steaphan's hand trembled with suppressed excitement as he reached for a quill and his inkhorn. He would write to the archbishop in Armagh immediately and request permission to bring Ingram to the monastery. The archbishop would be truly impressed that the young, untried abbot at Glendalough had arranged such a coup. Perhaps he would be impressed enough to ensure a promotion for Steaphan, a way out of the mountains and this poor, timbered monastery.

Steaphan hesitated for only a moment, tapping the quill on his desk as he searched for the right words. Something humble, something soothing . . .

"Your Eminence," he began to write.

Two days later, Cathal and Griogiar stood in the family compound of Donnchad and Afrecca. Cathal surveyed all with his impassive gray eyes while Griogiar gaped in utter amazement. "Did you ever imagine your home to be like this?" Griogiar said, pointing to a pigsty behind one of the mud huts. "Somehow, my friend, I imagined that you sprang from finer stock."

Ingram felt himself flushing with embarrassment. "I am what I am," he said, jerking his chin upward. "I do not apologize for these people."

"I meant no offense." Griogiar's tone softened. "True, a man can rise above his situation, as you have certainly done. But most men rise a single level in a lifetime, and from this to knighthood—" he opened his arms wide— "'tis a vast ocean of difference."

"How are you faring with these people?" Cathal interrupted. "Well enough," Ingram answered, surprised that Cathal had spoken. "Though I struggle to speak their language, for their accent is heavy. But we manage."

"And the *geilfhine*?" Cathal pressed. "How have the others received you?"

Ingram hesitated, thinking of the curious stares and doubtful glances cast his way at meal times. "I think they respect my mother and father too much to upbraid me," he said. "Time will mend all that time has broken."

"Well said," Griogiar said.

"Well enough," Cathal agreed.

Cathal sat before the thirty-five members of Ingram's new family as a brehon and answered their questions. Ingram was not surprised that many of their questions concerned him and his role in the *geilfhine*.

"The newcomer is of blood birth," Cathal said, in answer to a question put by Philip, the short, solid man

Afrecca had introduced as Ingram's brother. "He shall share equally in the inheritances and obligations of the *fine*, as shall any children he brings to the *geilfhine*."

Another man asked a question, and Cathal inclined his head slightly as he answered. "He is of the same status as you, my friend. He owns nothing but his share of this land, his armor, sword, and horse. I know him personally, and he is not hoarding treasure in another place. All he has, he brings to the *fine*. All you have must be shared with him."

An idea formed in Ingram's mind, born of necessity and desperation. If God had truly led him here, he had no choice but to demonstrate—to God and to them all—that he accepted this strange turn of fate. He stepped forward and waited for Cathal to recognize him. "Let all who hear mark this day," he said carefully in Gaelic, after the old man nodded his permission for Ingram to speak. "I, formerly known as Sir Ingram of Southwick, do pledge my allegiance to this family and to Donnchad and Afrecca, as my parents. I shall take off my armor, my sword, and helmet. I willingly lay aside my shield, to pick it up again only if this family is threatened. And my horse—"

Every eye in the place turned to the fence where the handsome animal fluttered his ears at the sound of Ingram's voice.

"My horse will be sold, and the proceeds divided equally among the *fine*, according to the law and word of the brehon," he finished. A ripple of satisfaction ran through the crowd. Afrecca clasped her hands together and beamed at him in maternal pride, and Ingram smiled at her even as his heart sank. The stallion had been a gift from Lord Galbert; the horse was the one living thing that had ever belonged to him.

"So be it," Cathal said, rising from his place.

Ingram patted the stallion's neck affectionately as Griogiar took the horse's bridle. "Are you sure of this?" Griogiar asked. "He has carried you alone; no other man will be able to ride him."

"Another man will," Ingram said, hardening his resolve as he turned from the animal. "After his will is broken. He was too much a prideful destrier, a battle horse, and now he must find a new role."

"You sound as if you regret coming here."

"Do I?" Ingram looked up at his friend and forced a smile. "I found what I sought. But a way of life for me has ended, and I'm not sure who Ingram of Glendalough is."

"Sir Ingram of Southwick was a fine man."

"A fine *knight*," Ingram corrected him. "There is no need for knights here on this mountain. And time will tell what sort of man I really am."

"I wish you God's best, then," Griogiar said, leading the stallion toward the gate. "I will send whatever silver the horse brings by a trusted courier."

"Thank you, and farewell," Ingram answered, lifting a hand in salute. He watched as Cathal, Griogiar, and the stallion moved through the gate and into the forest, then he walked slowly to the mud hut where his hauberk, sword, helmet, and shield lay buried like dead things in the soft earthen floor.

Ingram swore in impotent fury and sank to the ground as the cow trotted steadily toward the rough stall where she knew food waited. He had a nagging suspicion that the others were laughing at him, for he had already overheard the rumor that Donnchad and Afrecca's new son was worthless. "Perhaps we should put him on a shelf," Donnchad's sister remarked carelessly in Ingram's hearing. "He is pretty to look at, but of no earthly use."

He had wandered freely during his first week with his family and struggled to learn who lived in which hut and with which other family members. Donnchad and Afrecca lived in the largest hut of stone; Philip and his wife, Eamhair, occupied another hut with two nearly grown children. Philip's eldest son and his new wife lived in yet another, and

Pádruig's widow lived in another with her four children. On the other side of the compound stood yet another group of huts where Donnchad's sister and her children lived. Her five sons all had wives and children of their own.

After a week, Ingram despaired of learning every name, particularly since there were so many children similar in age and appearance. He begged Donnchad for work to do. Donnchad suggested that Ingram join Philip and the other men in the field outside the wall of the *rath*, and Ingram set out to work with high hopes that he would enjoy his work and the company.

The other men had immediately set their shoulders to rough-hewn plows, but Ingram would have none of that. He brought the family's one cow to the field, a cantankerous beast that looked to be at least fifteen years old, and attempted to harness the plow to the animal. "It will work," he told Philip, who looked skeptical. "In England, the villeins plow with oxen in every field. Just watch."

And so he had hit the animal's bony rump with a switch. The old cow merely bawled, lowered her head, and trotted back to the safety of her stall with surprising speed. "Och, and if she doesn't give milk tomorrow, you'll pay for this, *coimheach*," Philip had snarled.

Coimheach? Suddenly he remembered. *Foreigner.* Regardless of Afrecca's affectionate reassurance, he was not part of the family. He was still a foreigner, an outsider.

In the days and weeks ahead, he attempted plowing by hand, planting, and even cooking. In no area could he find success. Finally, Donnchad set Ingram to work on the perimeter of the field. "See these?" he said, pointing to tiny saplings growing among the plowed clods. "They must be pulled out and thrown away. We worked hard to clear this field, and the forest threatens continually to take it back."

A child could have done it, but Ingram swallowed his pride and bent to perform the menial labor. As he worked, dirt flew into his face, bugs buzzed around his ears, and nettles stung his unprotected arms. Ingram found himself wishing that someone would ride up to the gate and threaten his family. Then, at least, he could withdraw his sword and prove to them that he was worth something.

The family gathered around a bubbling cauldron for supper and ate stew from rough bowls hewn from dark wood. Ingram accepted his bowl and his portion gratefully, and he sat alone in the shade of a hut to eat. The other adults studiously avoided him; their laughter and conversation excluded him. Only the children sought out his company.

I am an oddity, he thought suddenly, as a little girl perched on a log nearby and smiled up at him. *The children work at my side because I am the big, bumbling fool who cannot complete a man's job. I thought these people low and slow, but I cannot accomplish even their mundane tasks. Dear God, I entreat you, show me what I have to offer these people.*

The little girl came closer and shyly smiled, her eyes large and dark beneath the widow's peak of her hairline. He offered a bit of his bread to her, and she reached out and took it, stuffing it into her mouth while she giggled at him.

The mischievous gleam in the girl's eye reminded him of Signe, and the thought made him laugh. He had left her to search for his noble family, certain in his heart that his station would prove to be far above the daughter of a mere blacksmith! His smile flattened as he thought of the bitter irony brought by the fulfillment of his dream.

Tears of remorse filled his eyes, and the little girl tilted her head and looked at him. He wiped his face with his sleeve and tried to smile, but she recognized his emotion and patted him gently on the shoulder. "Poor man," she said quietly, the strangely lyrical Gaelic lilting on her tongue. "Poor, pretty man."

SIXTEEN

Though he proved to be as ineffectual at harvesting as he was at planting and plowing, in time Ingram learned to be a passable farmer. The others no longer mocked him openly, but he remained the focus of their jokes. His brother Philip still brought in four bushels of wheat for every one of Ingram's and still plowed ten furrows in the time it took Ingram to complete one.

But in one area, at least, Ingram managed to equal the men of his *fine*. If meat was to be had at dinner, it must be hunted, and though Ingram's weapon of choice had always been his sword, his knightly training had required skill with the javelin and dagger, too. The other men preferred to hunt with crossbows, but Ingram disdained that weapon. Only hired mercenary warriors had used the crossbow in England. Knights were masters of the sword, lance, and mace, and though neither the sword nor the mace was very useful in hunting, Ingram quickly learned to turn his skill with a jousting lance into deadly aim with a hunting spear.

The first time he killed a rabbit with a spear, his brother and cousins laughed, for he did not toss it blindly into the fields as they did, but ran toward his quarry with the spear extended, the way he would have rammed an opponent in the jousting arena. They stopped laughing when Ingram pressed his height advantage and hurled the spear beyond their capabilities, spearing the rabbit against a tree. Though he ran farther and harder than they did when hunting, his method proved to be far more accurate and ultimately resulted in more meat in the family's dinner cauldron.

With his confidence boosted by his success in the field, Ingram endeavored to improve the family's lot. He encouraged Donnchad to send the young children to school at the monastery, but his father vetoed the idea, saying that the road was not safe for children and they could not spare an adult to convey them to and from the monastery each day. Ingram then endeavored to teach the children himself. He began with lessons in French, but the children found that tongue laughably strange.

"Le sort fait les parents; le choix fait les amis," he recited, remembering the old maxim from his childhood. (Fate chooses our relatives; we choose our friends.) "Repeat after me, children. *Le sort fait les parents; . . ."*

The children dissolved into giggles, and the noise brought Philip's wife, Eamhair, over to survey the informal French class.

"Ah, sure, and what good will French do them?" Eamhair said, pulling her daughter out of the circle of children at Ingram's feet. "Better you teach them how to plow, plant, and mend, Ingram. There is work to be done, and we have no time for this foolishness."

Ingram sat in silence as the implication of Eamhair's words echoed in the small circle. Everyone knew that Ingram's weakness lay in plowing, planting, and mending, the very skills the family needed for survival.

He shooed the children away. Laughing, they ran to their chores while he put his chin in his hand. As a child he had spent hours learning the aristocratic dances, the language of courtly love, and how to tilt at the quintain. His chores had involved cleaning stables, currying horses, and assembling armor for the elder knights. He had become expert with a sword, shield, and lance. But what good were those skills to him now? There were no horses in his *rath*, no armor, no knights, no dances.

The knightly virtues of prowess, loyalty, largess, courtesy, and good birth he had always thought he had possessed in abundance, but reality had proved those qualities false. Better to do a lowly job well, he supposed, than to parade attitudes and abilities that had no place on the mountains of Glendalough.

And so, after many months, Ingram found his place in the family. He became the preferred uncle, a playmate for the children, a devoted helper for Afrecca, and too often the butt of the men's jokes. He bore their insults patiently, feeling partially that he was to blame for his own downfall. If he hadn't been so intent on claiming his rightful place as an Irish nobleman's son, he would never have discovered his true place among the common people. He would never have known that Sir Ingram the knight had been a mere figment of imagination; for in reality Ingram was only a clumsy farmer whose single claim to greatness was his unparalleled ability to spear a rabbit.

"Ingram," Afrecca's voice crackled at his door. "Abbot Steaphan is here to see you."

Ingram stuck his head out of the mud-and-timber hut he now called home. The abbot stood outside, as elfin as ever, wearing a spotless white robe and a satisfied smile.

"Good day, Abbot," Ingram said, removing the rough woolen cap he wore to keep lice from his hair. "What brings you here today?"

"News, Sir Ingram."

"Please." He held up a dirt-stained hand. "I'm just Ingram, Father."

"All right, Ingram." The monk perched on a low stool in the yard and motioned for Ingram to sit as well. When Ingram had taken a seat on the ground, the monk pulled a sheaf of paper from a fold in his robe. "I've a letter from the archbishop at Armagh. I wrote him about your situation, and I have just received a reply."

"You wrote about me?"

"Yes. Your story was most unusual, don't you agree? Anyway, I wrote him some months ago, and the archbishop has an answer for us."

Ingram scratched his head. "I don't recall asking a question."

The abbot burst into a grin. "I like that about you, Sir— I mean—Ingram. You're quick. I wrote the archbishop, told him your entire story, and he said you belong to me now. I thought his timing was ideal. The harvest is in, the family's had a good look at you, and, knowing you and your background, you're probably ready to be rid of this place. Am I right?"

The abbot smiled in calm assurance while Ingram listened with a vague sense of unreality. Leave this place? And go where? To the monastery? The scenario became immediately clear: Like Father Colum, the abbot was trying to enslave him. Ingram stood and looked down at Abbot Steaphan.

"I don't belong to you."

"Of course not; a bad choice of words on my part. You belong to God. Donnchad and Afrecca gave you to God over thirty years ago, and that kind of vow cannot be broken. Your oblation is entered in the register—you belong to the monastery! With your skill and education, you'll be an invaluable tool for God, Ingram. No more dirt and digging, not with your knowledge. You'll be a scribe; I will see to it personally. Perhaps even vice-abbot within a year. Then if I move on, we shall see—"

"You don't understand, Father. I have spent several years following God, trying to find my place, and this is where he led me. Here." He stamped his foot into the dark black earth and opened his hand to the crude hut. "This is my house, my land, my family. I have nothing else; I want nothing else."

"Ah, but you're wrong." The abbot stood and met Ingram's gaze with defiance. Every trace of his smile vanished. "You've lasted a year, but how much longer can you take this existence, Ingram of Southwick? I know you and your sort. The monastery would be difficult, but less so than this hand-to-mouth existence."

"Thank you, Father, but I will remain here."

"It isn't that simple, you know. I will write to the archbishop, who will write the pope for a papal interdict. If you do not obey then, you will be excommunicated and your soul doomed to an eternity in hell."

"Let him write," Ingram said, dismissing the abbot with a wave of his hand. "If the pope wants me, he will have to come get me."

Two years passed. Babies were born, another of Philip's sons married, another hut rose in the compound. Abbot Steaphan journeyed to the family *rath* every season with the same plea: Ingram should return to the monastery, for God's claim on his soul took precedence over that of Donnchad and Afrecca. When the abbot made no progress with Ingram, he turned to Donnchad, who would have easily agreed to send Ingram away except for the stubborn intervention of Afrecca. "God brought my son back to me," she told the abbot, her voice and hands quivering with the palsy of the aged. "And he has given me these years to know my son. You will not take him away."

One summer afternoon, Ingram spied another solitary figure walking up the narrow trail to the family home, and he stiffened in annoyance that the abbot should try yet again to lure him away. But as the figure drew closer, he realized the man did not wear a monk's robes. Instead, he wore the blue tunic and cloak of a brehon. Griogiar!

Ingram shouted a greeting and bounded through the woods to meet his friend. They embraced on the trail. "Where is Cathal?" Ingram asked, looking down the path. "Surely he travels with you?"

"Cathal died last spring," Griogiar said. His eyes were graver than they had been and filled with the wisdom of sorrow. Ingram steadied his tone and walked with his friend to a fallen tree where they could sit and talk.

"Ah, 'tis good to see you, my friend," Griogar said, studying Ingram's face. "Often God has brought you to my mind, and often I have asked him to care for you."

"I thank you, Griogiar. Do you come to visit my family today?" Ingram asked. "It has been a year since a brehon has visited."

"Do you have need of the law?" Griogiar asked, lifting an eyebrow. "Surely you have learned enough to settle any disputes that have arisen in your clan."

"Aye," Ingram agreed, finding himself strangely at a loss for words. "I am . . ." He struggled to find the right word; what he really felt was *resigned,* but he settled for what he thought he should feel. "I am content."

"Have you married?"

"No. I am a poor farmer, a fair hunter, but a wonderful companion for children. The women leave their babies with me."

"Your mother and father?"

"They are old, but well."

An awkward silence fell between them. "This is a wall," Griogiar said, indicating the forest around him. "Your family is secluded, Ingram. You should travel, find a wife."

"Perhaps." Ingram managed a pleasant laugh. "So tell me of things and people outside of . . . this." He waved his hand at the trees. "What's happening in the world?"

"Much." Griogiar smiled, but his eyes held no trace of merriment. "Ireland is a trembling sod, my friend. Do you remember when the high king Turloch O'Connor died? His son Rory succeeded him in Connacht."

"I remember," Ingram said, shrugging. "I was with you then."

"'Twas but the beginning of strife," Griogiar continued. "Rory O'Connor claimed the high kingship, but his claim has been thrust aside by Murcertach MacLochlainn of Ailech, in the north country. The land outside of this forest is engaged in endless campaigns, cattle raids, burnings, and atrocities. MacLochlainn is currently at war with Eochy MacDunlevy, king of Ulidia."

"Those are northern kingdoms," Ingram said, puzzled. "Why should they affect our people?"

"MacLochlainn is allied with Dermot MacMurrough," Griogiar said. "And your quiet homestead here is in the Kingdom of Leinster. MacMurrough is your own king, my friend. If he finds that a skilled knight lives among his own people—"

"Do you think he'd come looking for me?" Ingram threw his hands up in mock horror. "I guarantee he won't. I am a knight no longer, and my reputation in these parts would not interest a king." He wiped his dirty hands on his tunic and held his callused palms up before Griogiar. "These are not the hands of a knight, but a farmer. An unskilled farmer, at best."

"Still, I came to warn you of danger," Griogiar said. His blue eyes said, *Be wary; take care.*

Ingram laughed.

Two years later, in June of 1162, all Ireland acknowledged Murcertach MacLochlainn as high king, and Ingram finally conceded to his parents' wishes and left the family home to seek a wife. He did not inquire at the monastery for a suitable family, for Abbot Steaphan still insisted that Ingram belonged to God and that a papal interdict would soon attest to that fact.

Instead, Ingram traveled to Wicklow, a coastal town, and spent a week making discreet inquiries among the townspeople about which maidens were of marriageable age, had good temperaments, and "not unpleasant" faces. Over and over, one name surfaced. Ingram proceeded at once to confer with the girl's anxious father, a tired horse trader who explained that they were a poor family and had no dowry. Ingram replied that a dowry didn't matter; all he wanted was a bride.

Before the sun had set, Ingram found himself at the doorstep of a church where he married one Brenna of Wicklow. The moment he looked at his bride, he knew she was no Signe. Her brown eyes were calm and quiet, like a doe's. They would never flash with wit or gleam with feistiness. This girl would be quiet, yielding, and maternal—the perfect wife.

After they said their vows, he led her on the long walk home.

As they walked up the long road to Glendalough, he found himself regarding the silent girl curiously. He, a man who had brazenly scolded O'Rourke for marrying a woman who did not love him, had taken a bride he did not even know.

Why had he married her? For years his parents had been hinting that he should marry; Afrecca had taken to crying over supper about the fact that she had never cuddled one of Ingram's children. Ingram was also honest enough to admit that part of his reason for marrying undoubtedly had to do with the fact that Philip was married, and he felt a none-too-subtle pressure to perform at least as well as Philip in everything. When he had finally managed to equal Philip in the field and forest, he supposed it was time to match Philip in the matrimonial arena as well.

What would she be like, this girl? Unstylish and soft-looking, she carried herself easily, as though she were unaware of the gentle swing of her hips. Ingram slowed his pace so that she walked ahead of him for a moment, and he bit his lip as he studied her shape and form. It was hard to believe she was his, this girl. After years of celibacy and self-control, he would at last be free to indulge in a pleasure he had all but forsaken.

He whistled as he lengthened his stride and joined her on the road.

I love her, he told himself, stretching on the rough straw that had served as their marriage bed. Her flesh was sweet and smooth, her touch gentle, her yielding complete. She lay next to him, her brown hair tangled, her linen tunic rumpled. What did it matter that she would never challenge him, never thrill him when she came into the room, never engage in the tiny acts of vanity that women endured for beauty? Brenna, his wife, was of the earth: pure, simple, and good. He had been wise to marry her.

He resisted the urge to wake her and explore the joys of marriage again, for life stirred in the courtyard outside and he knew the entire family would be anxious to scrutinize his bride. "Brenna, it's time to wake," he said, his voice gentle and low.

She stirred and raked the hair from her eyes. "Morning so soon?" she asked, squinting toward the stream of daylight that filtered through the small vent in the roof. She shivered. "It's cold in here, Husband."

"Ingram." He stood over her, smiling at his successful victory over memories of Signe. "My name is Ingram."

She bit her lip and looked up in fear of his rebuke, and something in Ingram melted. "Don't worry," he said, kneeling on the straw pallet. "You'll learn my name soon enough." He pulled her up into his arms and pressed his lips gently to hers. "I will never hurt you," he whispered, trailing his lips from her mouth to her ear. "Never."

He felt her arms go around his neck, and she timidly pecked his cheek with a chaste kiss. He groaned, touched by her girlish trust and surrender, and placed his hand at her back, pulling her body to his as if they would never be parted.

She watched him go, proud and confident, and felt her smile fade as he left the little mud hut to which he had brought her. When she was certain he was gone, she hugged her

knees and cried. At sixteen, she had never been away from
the security of her village, and in two brief days she had
been married and transported to this *rath* on the top of a
mountain, where every person save her husband and a few
children wore the indelible stamp of solitude and hard work.

Who was this man, anyway? Her father had introduced
him merely as "Ingram of Glendalough, a worthy suitor,"
and Brenna had been handed over like a fish on a platter.
She had not dared to refuse, for her father had a fierce temper and would have beaten her until she could not show her
face.

Ingram, her husband, was strong and handsome and
seemed kind, for all that he did not speak much. On their
long walk from Wicklow, he had barely said twenty words
and had not asked her a single question. He seemed content
merely to have brought home a bride; after last night his
mood had improved dramatically.

"If that's what it takes to keep a husband happy . . . ,"
she whispered, looking around at the dismal, dark hut that
would be her home. At least *he* was attractive, even though
he was more than twice her age. And if she made him happy,
he wouldn't beat her.

She rose and dressed carefully to meet her new husband's clan.

In the bitter cold of December, six months after Ingram's
marriage, Donnchad died. Afrecca followed her husband
into eternity a day later, willing herself to die with her husband. While Eamhair and the other women wrapped the
bodies in linen, inserting into the shrouds the traditional
piece of candle, a coin, and a small bottle of wine, Ingram
and Philip dug trenches in the frozen earth. The bodies
were laid to rest side by side in a glen on the side of the
mountain.

These were the first deaths Ingram had closely observed
in Ireland. Despite the keening wails of sorrow during the

burying ritual, he was impressed by the survivors' conviction that life would triumph over death. After the burial the family gathered in the clearing for a celebratory dinner, and they joined around the evening fire with bold stories of Donnchad and Afrecca's youthful exploits.

With Donnchad's death, Philip became head of the family as *cenn fine,* and as such, he wore a new mantle of dignity that seemed to ease his bitter rivalry with Ingram. The issue of dominance was settled now, or so it seemed. They were brothers; each had his own family, and Philip, as the eldest, carried the authority.

Ingram conceded to Philip's authority and kept peace with his brother, because in the last few months, he had begun to feel the need of an ally. Brenna was pregnant, and Ingram could not stop worrying. Southwick Castle had midwives, and a doctor had been within a day's ride. Ladies did not give birth in the presence of men—or even within shouting distance. But, somehow, he knew the Irish way would be different.

It was. One dark morning in February, fully a month before her time, he felt Brenna stir beside him. "It begins," she said simply, the mound of her belly rising in the darkness beside him. "By all in heaven, Ingram, are you going to sit there and watch me die?"

He leaped from their bed and went to Philip's hut for help. Eamhair came out in the darkness and shushed his frantic fears as the wind howled in his ears. "So, the child is early. Babies are born every day," she said, laughing as she braced herself against the stiff wind. "Go back and hold your wife's hand, Ingram. Throw a log on the fire to keep the girl warm. I'll gather a blanket and some water. She'll be thirsty before long."

And so it had begun. He sat for hours, through the morning and midday, tossing logs on the fire until Brenna claimed he intended to roast her alive. But then she'd shiver and scream, and Ingram would grimace as though the pain were his own. "Say something!" she screamed at him once as the pain ripped through her. "Take me mind off this, you bloody fool!"

"Ladies shouldn't use such language," he reproved her gently. But he excused the insult and cast about in his mind for a topic of conversation. It occurred to him that his wife knew nothing about him apart from his life as a farmer, and he started to speak just as another spasm distorted Brenna's face.

She screamed loud enough to wake the eternal sleep of Donnchad and Afrecca. "Talk, you *mortair!*"

"Why, Brenna, should you call me a murderer?" he asked, trying to smile at her. "You'll be fine by supper time."

She screamed again, this time in fury, and Ingram took her clenched hand and patted it absently. "All right," he said, still patting her hand. "I'll tell you a true story. I grew up at Southwick Castle, in the south of England, and served a noble Norman lord and his lady. . . ."

Despite her pain, Brenna's eyes grew large in wonder and surprise, and Ingram smiled in satisfaction.

SEVENTEEN

His prophecy proved correct: By supper time that evening, Ingram held his newborn son in his arms. Philip patted him on the shoulder in congratulations as Ingram counted toes and fingers and beheld the small miracle of life.

"He's a lovely boy," Eamhair said as she brought a steaming bowl of soup into the hut. "Afrecca would be proud."

"He looks nothing like ye," Philip said, smiling at Ingram. "He's fortunate."

"He'll be fine as long as he doesn't look like you." Ingram couldn't stop the foolish grin that spread from one ear to the other. "His name will be Alden."

"Alden?" Eamhair frowned. "I've never heard the like. Where'd you dream up such a name?"

"It's English," Ingram answered, staring in amazement as his tiny son's fist closed around his finger. "It means 'wise protector.'"

"Bah! Who's the babe going to protect?" Philip said, laughing.

"He's not the protector; I am," Ingram answered. He lowered his face to the baby's and let the warmth of his breath cover the child's face. "At least for now. As long as I have breath, I will protect my son."

Brenna dozed for a while, then awoke and held her arms out for the baby. "He really is beautiful," she whispered, gathering the child into her arms. "My family has never had a babe so pretty."

"He has your eyes," Ingram volunteered.

"Perhaps," Brenna answered, adjusting the curve of her arm so the baby rested more securely. "But he doesn't look a thing like *them*."

"Like who, my love?"

"Them." She jerked her head toward the door. "Your clan. They all have a peaked hairline, or haven't you noticed? You are the only one who escaped that horrible fate, Ingram." She turned to him, and her smile went straight to his heart. "Sir Ingram."

"Don't call me that," he said, going to sit beside her on the pallet of straw. He put his arm behind her, and she leaned back on his strength, nestling against him as the baby nursed and the cold February wind howled outside.

❖ ❖ ❖

"Me husband has a habit that bothers me," Brenna complained to Eamhair one spring morning. The baby slept in her arms, and Brenna was grateful for a chance to step outside and enjoy the sunshine.

"What husband doesn't?" Eamhair said, picking up a pair of her son's leather boots to mend. She smiled at the younger girl. "Tell me about it, dearie. I might as well listen while I sew."

Brenna sat down on a bench near the table where Eamhair worked, careful not to disturb the baby. "It's the things he says to Alden. I know the baby's only weeks old, but Ingram says things like, 'No farming for you, me son. I'll send you to England, or perhaps you would like to learn a trade.' Isn't that foolishness?"

Eamhair paused a moment as she threaded her needle. "Ingram is not like the rest of us," she said finally. "He was not raised here, and he thinks differently. Perhaps he truly wishes these things for his son."

"But I don't want me son to do any of those things, and

why should Ingram? Isn't our life good enough for him? Isn't it good enough for our son?"

Eamhair tilted her head. "I can't say. But Ingram seems to be happy."

"He's not," Brenna replied, her voice flat. "I know me husband, and I know he doesn't love me. He loves someone else."

Eamhair made a small snorting noise. "Foolish girl! There are no women in his past; he's been here for years. Who do you think he's in love with, if not ye?"

"I don't know who she is, but I know for certain he doesn't like me. He's always comparing me to her. He tells me to lower my voice, to wear my hair in braids, to take smaller steps when I walk. He tried to teach me to sing; he wants to talk about kings and honor—"

The older woman laughed. "He is a dreamer. Abide with him, and this will pass."

"I think not." Brenna smoothed her hand over her baby's head and bent to kiss his closed eyes. She hummed softly for a moment, then turned to Eamhair again. "Sometimes I think that if I do all the things he says, I'll turn into the other woman, the woman he really wants. He'd be happy, but I'd be . . ."

"What?"

"Lost."

He was kind to her, Brenna thought when she left Eamhair, a good husband and gentle lover. When he had learned that she expected a child, he held her in his arms and tenderly stroked her belly for a long, long time. But her intuition told her he wasn't stroking *her* but the child, just as he didn't truly hold *her* in the darkness but someone else. He never spoke her name, never asked for her opinions, never told her what thoughts lay on his heart. And didn't a man who loved a woman love *all* of her, her heart as well as her body?

They had married on the sixteenth of June 1162, and on the
seventeenth of June the following year, Brenna stood in the
courtyard of the family compound and told them she was leaving. "According to brehon law, either marriage partner can
leave after a year and a day," she said, turning her face from
the sight of her baby in Ingram's arms. "It is my choice. I am
leaving this place, Ingram, and returning to me home in
Wicklow. Don't try to find me, for I'll marry another as soon
as I'm able."

"What are you doing?" Ingram handed the baby to
Eamhair and walked to Brenna. He placed his hands on her
shoulders and lowered his voice. "What in God's name—"

"'Tis in his name I go, for God alone knows that you
lie," she said, a deep sadness in her words. Her eyes met his;
he saw the pain but was helpless to understand it. "Ye do
not love me, Ingram, nor did you ever. I don't know who it
is who fills your mind, but 'tis not me."

"How can you say that?" He felt the sting of her words,
and his face flushed. The truth hurt, but how had she
known?

He tightened his hands on her shoulders. "I won't let
you go. My son needs his mother."

"I am free. The law has decreed it. You cannot stop me."

"Marriage is for life. I married you forever, Brenna, and
I intend to be true to you. A knight is faithful—"

He broke off, stunned by his own words. She nodded and
pulled away from him. "Always a knight, aren't you?" she
said, staring at the ground as if she were afraid to look at him
again. "I'm not able to be the wife of a knight. I'm a simple
girl. I wanted simple things, like a husband who loved me. And
children—" Her chin quivered, and she would not go on.

"You would leave your baby?"

Brenna pressed her lips together. "I can have other
babies. And though you don't love me, I know you love the
child. The baby is like you, you see—*noble.*"

Tears poured freely down her face, and her words broke through her reserve in a torrent. "I waited a year to tell you these things, Ingram, because you would not hear me otherwise. You want me to be what I am not, and by the law, I can leave today. So kill me or move aside, because I am going home."

Ingram stepped aside. *God, what else can I do?* he wondered brokenly. Brenna took a deep breath and stepped forward. Not once did she look back at her husband or her son as she walked through the gate.

Ingram saw the determined squaring of her shoulders and the lift of her head, and he waited until she had passed out of sight before turning to Caoidhean, one of his nephews. "Escort her safely to the Wicklow road," he said, waving his hand helplessly toward the gate. His voice broke in frustration. Cursed be these Irish laws! How could he have ever thought them liberating? Now he had no wife, no mother for his child. . . .

Caoidhean moved through the gate, and a moment later the boy called out, "Someone approaches!"

Ingram held his breath. Had she returned? He jogged slowly toward the gate and stopped short when he recognized Abbot Steaphan.

"Hallo, Ingram," the abbot called, his greeting falsely cheerful. "I met your wife in the way just now. Is all well here?"

"Well enough," Ingram answered, smiling woodenly. "What brings you to us, Father?"

"Only this." The abbot waved a piece of parchment. "The archbishop has received a letter from the pope. The pope hasn't made a final decision yet, mind you, but it's almost certain he'll issue an interdict soon and require all oblates to serve their full terms in the house of God. 'Tis a sacred vow, you know. Why, can you imagine what horrible things would have happened if Samuel had left the temple and returned to the world?"

"I imagine God had the situation firmly in hand,"

Ingram remarked dryly. "But it doesn't matter, Father. I won't return to the monastery. I've a wife and a child."

"I just spoke to Brenna, Ingram." The abbot's smile faded. "She told me she's left for good. The marriage is over, according to the law. The church will declare your marriage annulled." He smiled slyly. "The Holy Scriptures and the Irish law are both in agreement, Ingram. St. Paul said, 'If the unbelieving partner leaves, let her go; you are under no obligation.' So, you see, you are free from your marriage vows, free to fulfill the vow to the church. God works in mysterious ways, indeed."

Ingram grimaced. "And my child?"

"Doomed to perdition unless you have the babe baptized. And I'll not baptize him, for rightfully, he belongs to the church, too. He is your seed, Ingram, and your seed belongs to God, as do you."

The abbot tilted his head, and Ingram had an overwhelming impulse to smash his fist into the man's jaw and feel the bones give. He had given himself to God—once in the vows of his knighthood and again in his acceptance of this new life. What did God want from him, after all? Could this weasel-like monk possibly speak for God? His hand clenched, but Philip's shadow fell between them.

"We're in need of Ingram, Father," Philip called, firmly tugging on Ingram's bent elbow. "Farewell."

The weasel monk had the nerve to make the sign of the cross in Ingram's direction before he left.

For the next few weeks Ingram worked alone under a dark cloud of gloom. He left the care of the baby to the other women, who doted on Alden as a rare jewel, and Ingram hunted in the forest with a ferocity he had never known. Meat appeared on the table every night, more than they could eat, because Ingram charged every creature that moved with his lance.

Something was wrong with his life. Like the king who

had acquired the Holy Grail in his ill-fated quest, Ingram had met his goal and found it brought him more pain than pleasure. He had imagined that finding his parents would solve his questions, but life with Donnchad and Afrecca had only brought him face-to-face with his inadequacies and false pride. Destiny had brought him low. Even his young wife, a simple girl with scarcely an original thought in her head, had seen the falsity of his life. Brenna had known that he only played a role in Glendalough, and he did not play it well.

What was he? A farmer or a knight? The son of peasants or the foster child of nobility? He was all these things, and in that truth lay his trouble.

Abbot Steaphan added to his confusion, promising hellfire and eternal retribution if he didn't keep someone else's promise with his life. The abbot had even dared to threaten his son! Ingram didn't know what road Alden would choose to follow, but he determined that no one would make that choice for his son. Alden would be free, an educated landowner, and the world would open before him for the taking. . . .

But the boy would have to survive first—and grow up in a secure world, a better place than the collection of hovels Donnchad and Afrecca's *fine* called home. Ingram would have to improve his son's lot. But how could that be done?

He wished for an instant that Griogiar was near, or Signe, or even Tiernán O'Rourke. Any one of them would have definite advice. Griogiar would advise him according to the law, Signe would see through his pride and confusion, and O'Rourke's brave fearlessness would advise him to take action. Instead he was alone with only himself for guidance.

But which Ingram could guide him now? The farmer, the knight, the husband, or the father?

A verse sprang to mind, a snippet of Scripture learned in his lessons in the chapel of Southwick Castle: "What does God require of a man?" the chaplain had asked, his pale face floating even now on the mist in the forest. "His requirements are simple: a man must do justly and love mercy, and walk humbly with God."

How could he best pursue justice, love mercy, and walk humbly? Ingram knew only one way—the way he had been taught since childhood. The way of knighthood.

Always a knight, aren't you? Brenna's voice echoed in his memory. He *was* a knight, regardless of his parentage. The training was a part of his nature. As a knight his way was clear. His was the way of truth, honor, and battle. He would serve God as he had always intended, with his sword and shield. To be true to his calling, it was time to abandon the plow and the family he had come to know.

But not his son. He would never surrender his son.

Ingram drew back and launched the hunting spear in his hand with all his strength. It sailed through the air smoothly, then buried itself deep in the trunk of a young oak.

Ingram turned from the forest and walked back to the family compound.

His hauberk had lain in the ground for too many years. Rusted and stiff, it was useless, but his sword could be salvaged with sharpening. He would polish and grind the blemishes from the blade with pleasure. His shield and helmet were worthless and a pitiful sight, but he could procure new ones easily once he had agreed to serve a new master, an Irish king.

Griogiar had called the land a trembling sod, and Ingram knew that his skills would be in demand. He would take his rightful place among the warriors of the aristocracy, and in time, he would send for his son. Alden would grow up as a true son of Ireland, experiencing the best Ireland had to offer, and enjoy his liberty as a freeman and the son of a chieftain's warrior.

Philip stooped to enter Ingram's low door and paused when he saw the sword in Ingram's hand. His eyes flooded with understanding.

"Have you stopped to consider what our parents would

think?" he said finally, his eyes roving toward the empty stone hut no one had occupied in months. "To leave the *fine* . . ."

"'Tis what I must do to be true to myself," Ingram answered, relishing the weight of the sword's hilt in his hand. "How's your polishing arm, Philip? Will you help me in this?"

Philip pressed his lips together. "'Tis what I must do to be true to ye," he replied, extending his hand.

He was not the dashing knight of years past, and at thirty-eight he doubted he could still leap onto the back of a horse from a run. But as Ingram tucked his dagger in his belt and strapped on his sword, he felt invincible. He had no horse, no lance, no armor, and no shield, but for the first time in years, he felt confidence in himself.

Bless Donnchad and Afrecca, he prayed, walking out of the family compound. Bless old Father Colum, who had obviously taken one look at the frail Afrecca and felt pity for her poverty. He loved her compassionately and stole her offering to God, sending Ingram away to become a knight in God's service, not a monk. Ingram could not help but think that God's will had been accomplished nonetheless.

He stopped at the gate to kiss his son, tucked safely in Eamhair's arms. "Keep watch over him for me," Ingram said, his voice husky with emotion.

"I will," she answered, giving the baby her finger to suckle.

Ingram gave a final wave and turned his back on the family home. He knew where he had to go first. No matter how long it took him to reach the coast, his first formal visit would be to the house of Erik Lombay in Waterford.

DERMOT
MACMURROUGH
1163

There is deceit in the hearts of those who plot evil.

PROVERBS 12:20

Eighteen

Ingram walked west into the direction of the setting sun until he reached Castledermot, then followed the River Barrow southward. He knew the river would lead him straight to Waterford . . . and Signe Lombay. He did not know exactly why he was drawn to her, but something in him desperately longed for her beauty and no-nonsense efficiency. Once before she had brought him back to health. This time his spirit, not his body, needed a healing touch.

The cool, dispassionate voice of reason told him he had no reason to believe she would welcome him, for many years had passed since he had last seen her. But with every step toward Waterford, he grew more hopeful. She had been, after all, strong-willed and quarrelsome, and her father depended upon her. Perhaps she was unmarried, even after all this time.

And perhaps, an inner voice dared to whisper, *she loved you so much that she could not give herself to another and waits for you still.*

Ingram frowned at the thought. If Signe waited for him, he would disappoint her again. The years of humiliation at Glendalough had revealed hidden aspects of his character. One uncomfortable realization was that he did not marry Signe Lombay in Waterford primarily because the simple daughter of a blacksmith lay below his ambitions and desires.

The truth had come to him one day not long after his arrival in the family *fine*. He and Philip plowed together in a field, and Philip had been in an unusually talkative mood. Among other tales, he told Ingram the story of how he wooed and wed his wife, Eamhair. "She was the strongest girl in Dublin," Philip had said, deliberately slowing his pace so Ingram could hold the plow steady in the furrow. "Her lace brought top prices in the market."

"And her father?" Ingram had asked, thinking as always of family lineage.

"A skilled metalworker," Philip had answered, throwing Ingram a suspicious glance. "I worked hard to convince him that I was worthy of his daughter."

Ingram had chuckled to himself, imagining the rustic Philip persuading a Norse father that his daughter would be well served by life on a remote mountain. But Philip needed a strong and marketable girl to survive, whereas Ingram wanted a woman of beauty, sophistication, and nobility. . . .

He became aware that Philip had stopped and turned in the furrow, a frown darkening his face. "You *amadon*," Philip snarled, correctly reading the smug grin on Ingram's face. "Is it not me wife that cooks your dinner? Sews your clothes? Shears the lambs that give us wool?"

Ingram had stammered in confusion.

"Ye are a foolish shadow bird," Philip had said, his strength pulling the leather straps of the plow taut as he moved ahead with barely controlled fury. "Ye see your shadow on the mountain and think yourself far bigger and more important than other birds. But when the sun sets, me *brother*," he spat the word distastefully, "then you will see that you are smaller than the rest of us."

They had not spoken another word that day, but Philip's words had rung true. And now, as Ingram reconsidered them on the walk to Waterford, he realized that he had lied to Signe when he told her he could not marry her because he did not know his parents. In truth the shadow bird had lived then; he had imagined himself far above her. Now he knew himself to be small, far below Signe's station. But perhaps with Signe's healing touch, he could yet be restored to her.

He closed his eyes and let the warm summer sun caress his face. If God in heaven loved him, Signe would be waiting.

He traveled slowly through the warmth of July and the early days of August, sleeping under the stars when night fell. His muscles, strong from farming, grew even leaner from his vigorous walking; his skin darkened even more in the rays of the sun, and his hair, no longer covered by a cap, regained its golden cast. He left the forested mountains behind and descended into the plains, eating rabbits and plants and begging the occasional bowl of soup from small settlements he passed along the way.

When he unsheathed his sword and announced that he was of a Glendalough clan, the Gaelic Irish farmers welcomed him and pressed him for news of his journey. Had marauders attacked his family compound? Did the king of his *tuath* fare well? Had he a wife and children?

He answered every question as best he could and paused when a gray-haired elder asked why he had left his *fine*. "These are dangerous times," the old man said, his long gray hair trailing over his shoulders. "Did you leave your *fine* unprotected?"

"No," Ingram said, resting his elbows upon his crossed knees. "My family is large and well endowed with men to protect the *rath*. I left because I can best serve them if I go elsewhere. I am a warrior, and I want to do something more than merely defend them."

A younger man nodded in eager agreement, but the elder lifted a hand and quieted the gathering around the cauldron. "If you are truly a warrior, as a warrior you shall live and die. Godspeed, my friend, but take yourself from this peaceful place, and may heaven help the ones who truly love you."

For a moment Ingram squinted at the elder, unable to tell if his words were meant as a benediction or curse. The younger man flushed in embarrassment, and when no one

else spoke, Ingram brushed bread crumbs from his tunic
and bowed to the gathering before leaving.

His second journey to Waterford was nothing like his first,
for he and Father Colum had approached from the east, on
horseback, and flush in the excitement of discovery. Now
Ingram walked slowly southward and studied the city from a
different perspective. Tall oak doors stood open at the city
gates, and iron bars blocked the brick aqueduct that allowed
the flowing river water into the city. Well-built and well-forti-
fied, Waterford guarded her inhabitants well.

Behind the wall the thatched roofs of small, square
houses were visible, and Ingram's heart stirred within him.
In one of those houses, God willing, Signe lived. He picked
up his pace and lengthened his strides, eager now to see the
woman who had haunted his dreams for so long.

The gatekeepers raised their eyebrows at the sight of
Ingram's sword, but they allowed him to enter the city.
"Just remember," one stout guard called, "God watches evil-
doers, and the earl of Waterford will behead any man who
murders or plots mischief in the streets!"

The narrow streets bustled with trade; donkey-drawn
carts jostled one another as whips sang through the air and
urged the animals forward. Ingram savored the smells and
sounds of activity. He had been so long in the quiet solitude
of the mountains that the noise and bustle of the city
seemed delightfully new and exciting again. Foreign tongues
assailed his ears; men of all colors and varieties sauntered or
hurried by with wares on their shoulders.

Strangely invigorated, he stepped into a shop and asked
for directions to the smithy operated by Erik Lombay.

Erik straightened and dabbed his heavy apron at the stream
of perspiration on his face. Every night his body amplified its
protest against his continual bending, pounding, and sweat-

ing, but as a man he had no choice but to work until he died. If, God forbid, he lost his wits or his health, Signe would take care of him. But the girl had already spent a lifetime doing just that. 'Twouldn't be fair to ask her to continue caring for her father.

A stranger stepped into the darkness of the smithy, and Erik waved a greeting without looking up. "I'll be with you in a minute," he called, shifting a piece of iron in the fire. "Though it's nearly time for supper, and I'm about ready to go home."

He pulled off his heavy leather gloves and squinted up at the tall man who stood before him. "What can I do for you?"

"You've already done all that one man can do for another," the man said, his voice strangely familiar. "You saved my life once. I pray you can do it again."

"Sir Ingram?" Erik let the gloves drop to the ground. "Can it be you? Where on earth have you been hiding yourself? We thought you had vanished into the mist. We never heard a word of you for . . . how long has it been?"

"Eleven years," Ingram answered. "A very long time."

Erik stepped closer to have a look at his visitor. The knight had grown older; tiny creases lined his eyes and mouth, but his face still glowed with good looks. His hands were dark now and calloused from hard work, and his golden hair had lengthened considerably. He wore the simple trousers of the common farming class with a short jacket and cloak. A dagger hilt showed from the belt at his waist, and a sword hung by his side. But the armor, shield, helmet, and even the extraordinary stallion had disappeared.

"You know," Erik said, folding one arm and laying his finger aside his mouth, "even if you stood before me in armor, I still wouldn't know you. There's something very different about you, sir knight."

"I'm just Ingram now. Maybe that's the difference."

Erik lifted a brow and nodded in agreement. Gone was

the cocky pride that had so irritated Signe. The man's shoulders were stooped; he carried himself differently.

"Are you in trouble, me lad?" Erik asked. "You said something about me saving your life."

"I'm not exactly in trouble," Ingram answered, a weak smile flitting across his face. He opened his hands as if he would explain, then folded his arms defensively as a veil of tears crossed his eyes. Erik dropped his jaw in amazement. The man had surely been brought low, but what had done this?

Erik shuffled forward and pointed toward a bench. As Ingram took a seat, Erik perched on the edge of a stool and placed his hands on his knees. "What brings you to us, me boy? I've a right to be asking, don't you think? Did you find the father you went looking for?"

"Yes. I've been with him and my family for some time. But that's not why I'm here, Erik. I've come today because I've realized . . ."

"What?"

"I need to see your daughter. Of all the women in Ireland, she's the only one who can help me now. I should have married her eleven years ago, but now so much has happened. . . ." The knight shrugged. "I just had to come. She helped save my life once; I think now I need her to help save my soul."

Erik exhaled in a long, slow hiss and sat back upon the stool by the dying fire. "You're eleven years too late, man. Signe cannot help you now."

"Is she dead?" Flashes of worry darted into the knight's eyes, and Erik actually felt sorry for him. Eleven years ago he had wanted to beat this knight for breaking his daughter's heart, but now, with him being so broken and all . . .

"Signe lives. She's well, but she's married to a metalworker, a fellow called Ailbeart. She married right after you left us," Erik answered, tapping his fingers on his knees. "She has two children, a girl and a boy. There was another girl, too, a baby who died."

All emotion drained from the knight's face. Erik was tempted to offer his arm for support, for the man looked weak enough to fall off the bench and hurt himself.

"She's married," Ingram repeated at last, looking to Erik as if there were a possibility he had been mistaken.

"No doubt about it," Erik answered. He snapped his fingers as a thought came to mind. "Wait! I nearly forgot. I've got something for you."

Curiosity flickered in Ingram's eyes, and Erik turned to the locked wooden box behind him. Pulling a key from a chain around his neck, he unlocked the box, fumbled among the tools inside, and pulled out a square of silk.

"Signe gave this to me on the eve of her wedding," Erik explained, offering the silk to Ingram. "She made me promise that I should give it to you. She thought you might return, but I'm thinking she had no idea it would take you eleven years to come back."

Ingram unwrapped the square of silk and gently fingered the exquisite bronze brooch wrapped inside. "I had nearly forgotten about this," he said. "I wanted her to have it, to repay her for taking care of me."

"She didn't want your treasure," Erik said. He nearly added, *She wanted you instead,* but he decided that would be saying too much. What's done was done, and there was no sense in bringing up what could have been.

"She didn't want to be indebted to you," he said simply.

"Thank you, Erik. I won't bother you anymore," Ingram said, rewrapping the brooch and sliding it inside the pouch at his waist. He stood to leave, then paused. "Does she love him, this Ailbeart?" he asked over his shoulder, not looking at Erik.

Erik paused. Should he lie? If he told the truth, the knight might do something reckless, something that would hurt the children and destroy his daughter's security. And what did it matter that Signe felt no love for the man she lived with? They were content, they were stable, and that was enough.

"Aye, she loves him very much," Erik answered.

He sighed in relief when the knight nodded and continued through the doorway.

He knew he ought to find the nearest road out of Waterford and leave the city, but an overwhelming urge drove him to stop a group of women at a well and ask for the house of Ailbeart and Signe, the daughter of the blacksmith in the south of town. One of the women knew the house well, gave him directions, and continued to turn back and smile at him even as the group of housewives moved away.

Ingram found the small, square stone dwelling without much trouble. He leaned against the courtyard fence across the crowded street and took a moment to study the house. Smoke wafted lazily from the opening in the center of the thatched roof. Signe probably stood at the hearth, cooking a porridge for supper, perhaps. The squeal of bickering children came through the window, and the sound reminded him of Glendalough. He smiled.

The place was neat, tidy, and prosperous, just as he imagined Signe's home would be. Her husband would be along soon, leading a donkey or a wagon, perhaps, and he would meet his wife at the door, kiss her in greeting, and tousle the heads of the young ones.

"Are you going to stand there all day, or would you like to come inside?"

The chill shock of her voice turned his knees to water, and he turned in absolute surprise. Signe stood beside him on the road and regarded him with a look that forced his breath from his body. How lovely she was! Eleven years had done her nothing but good. Her body had ripened to a womanly fullness, a generous cloak billowed modestly around her feet, and her flaming red hair hung over her shoulder in an intricate braid.

Her eyes had not changed. They were still clear, green,

and challenging as she awaited his answer. For the first time
in his life, Ingram couldn't find words to fit his thoughts.

"Signe—you startled me. I didn't expect to see you."

"Liar." Her brows lifted at the word.

"I didn't know if I ought to see you. I'm only passing
through Waterford. . . ."

"You're lying again." Her eyes took in his poor dress,
his farmer's trousers, the dirt under his nails. When she saw
the sword at his side, her lips parted in a secret smile. "Still a
knight, Ingram?"

"No." He shook his head. "I don't know what I am any
longer. I hoped you could help me. But you—you're some-
body's wife."

"Ailbeart's."

"Congratulations."

"You're a few years too late, don't you think?"

"Yes." He whispered the admission. Why, God? Why
were they cutting each other with their words? He had
hoped for comfort and counsel, and if not that, then only
for a glimpse of her, a memory he could take with him for
the rest of his life. But she had ambushed him again and
caught him unprepared. Well, he would let her win this
battle. He wouldn't spar with her—that was Ailbeart's rightful place and duty.

"So what are you doing here?" she asked, shifting the
basket on her arm. "No one comes to Waterford unless they
have business here. And you—" she gave him another top-
to-toe glance— "you have no business here, I'll wager."

Ingram smiled and tried to be pleasant. "You're right.
I'm on my way to fight for Tiernán O'Rourke—"

She laughed softly, cutting him off. "O'Rourke's kingdom is in the north. You are as south as a man can come
without falling into the sea, Sir Ingram."

"Please—I'm just Ingram now. Ingram of Glendalough,
if you're interested. I found my parents. They are common
folk, farmers, and hunters."

She tapped her foot impatiently. "And you found brothers and sisters and cousins. Do you have children?"

"One son, Alden." He answered without thinking, and when she drew in a quick breath, he realized he'd fallen into a trap. Without asking, she'd wanted to know if he had taken a wife, and by mentioning his son, she knew he had.

"Well, Godspeed, old friend," she said, tossing her head curtly. "It was good to see you."

She moved to cross the road, and Ingram caught her arm and pulled her back just as a horse-drawn wagon barreled around the corner. They stood in silence until the wagon had passed.

"I suppose I should thank you again for saving my life, but I'm sure you'll be saying that's only what knights do," she said, pulling away. Ingram kept his hand on her arm. It had been so long since he had touched her.

"I was married," he volunteered, "but my wife left after a year and a day, as is the custom among the Irish."

"Don't tell me about the Irish," she snapped. Then she settled and faced him again. "So she discovered how horrible you truly are, did she now?"

"No. She told me, after a year and a day, that she couldn't stay . . . because I loved another."

She looked up now, fully, into his eyes, and he savored the moment, holding her in his gaze. Could she not see that he had changed? Couldn't she see how much he needed her?

"And who did you love?" she whispered finally, her eyes still fastened on his. "Yourself?"

If she had been in his arms, he would have shaken her; instead, he thrust her arm away and set his jaw. "Unlucky man, Ailbeart," he hissed, his face a mask of rage. "To come home and trade insults with you every night."

"You never could face the truth, could you?" she blazed back at him. "You want only to see honor and glory and battle for kings, but still you cannot see past your precious knightly chivalry! I don't know where you are, Ingram, but there's a real world out here, and I'm in it!"

"Stay in it!" he shouted, not caring who might hear. "Stay far away from me! And to think I used to dream of your face—I must have been insane, a complete *amadon!*"

She ran from him then but turned halfway across the road and continued to shout at him, even as she walked backward to her courtyard. "So you finally learned some Gaelic!" she said, laughing. "How noble of you to stoop to the language of the Irish! And how terrible your adventures must have been, if you were forced to dream of the likes of me!"

Two little faces peered through the window of her house, and Ingram watched her smooth her face and smile at them as she stepped through her doorway. In a moment the children darted away, and she leaned out the window, grasped the shutters, and closed them with a bang.

He stamped his foot in frustration. Always, always she frustrated him. And, despite his anger, never had he wanted her more.

Signe turned restlessly on her straw mattress as her husband snored gently beside her. How dare Ingram of the cursed knighthood show his face at her house! She had nearly forgotten him, nearly put thoughts of him totally from her mind.

Liar, her heart chided. *You have never forgotten, never ceased to pray for him, never stopped hoping he would one day return. . . .*

She turned her face to the roof above. *Dear God,* she prayed soundlessly. *Why did you bring him back into my life? Shall I pray for his health and success again? Once you led me to care for him, once I would have given him my heart, but you led him away. Why should I pray for angels to guard him? Why do you burden my heart for his care when he has married another?*

Tears ran from the corners of her eyes and dampened her hair. A rush of bitter remembrance overwhelmed her, days and nights of praying for the knight's journey for his parents, the unspoken fears that he would find his family and return for her.

But he had not come. And so she had married and borne children and prayed for the knight only when thoughts of him straggled across her mind . . . which was nearly every day. For she knew that, even if they were not to be together, God was calling her to prayer for this man who had hurt her so deeply.

Obediently, she lifted her heart and thoughts toward heaven once again and prayed that God would keep and guide Ingram to a place of love and rest.

He slept that night in the courtyard of the cathedral in Waterford. A fellow traveler who bedded down in the sanctuary courtyard spied his sword and told him that Dermot MacMurrough sought mercenaries to guard his castle at Ferns.

"I am no friend of MacMurrough," Ingram replied, folding his hands behind his head for a pillow. "I have fought in the past for Tiernán O'Rourke. I will go to Breifne."

"O'Rourke is a good man, but he does not have a lovely daughter like Eva. I hear she can teach the birds to sing, and men beg just for the sight of her face."

"Truly?" Ingram stirred to see the man better.

"Would I be inventing such a tale?" the man said, shrugging. "I'd be wanting to go see the lady meself, but I'm no warrior. Not much of a farmer, either."

"'Tis no shame; neither am I," Ingram said. They laughed together, then fell silent. ·

As Ingram considered the stars above him, he thought about this daughter of Dermot MacMurrough. A beautiful woman! If such tales of her beauty were true, perhaps she would have the power to drive thoughts of Signe from his mind.

"Where's the harm in a man fighting for Dermot Mac-

Murrough?" Ingram asked, turning to his companion once again. "Since I'm already so near to Leinster, 'twould be a shame not to see this lady for myself."

The man only snored in reply.

Nineteen

As Ingram made his way across the lower portion of the Kingdom of Leinster, he gradually became aware that his confrontation with Signe had, in a sense, helped him find himself. She had stirred him to anger, and for the first time in months, a strong emotion drove Ingram forward. He didn't need her, and he didn't need her disparaging comments about his knighthood. He could make it on his warrior's heart alone. The trappings of knighthood—largess, prowess, loyalty, courtesy, and high birth—those godly virtues, convenient in a civilized place and time, were totally expendable in the barbaric fortresses of Ireland. He had sought to serve God, and God had returned the favor by giving him a family where he didn't fit, a wife who left him, and an abbot intent upon enslaving him to the church. But he was a freeman. He could walk away, forget his vows, and serve himself. And from now on, that is exactly what he intended to do.

Ah, but the skills of knighthood he would use. He could still wield a sword with the best warrior, could still ride a horse and aim a deadly lance. His arms were tough and lean from hard work, his legs strong from miles of walking, his reflexes quick.

He walked faster as he formulated his plan. He would present himself at Dermot MacMurrough's castle as a warrior, without a word of his knightly status. He would no longer speak of Southwick Castle and would keep his birth and upbringing secret. From what he had heard, Ingram knew MacMurrough would value a quick sword more than a noble heart.

If, in Ireland, a man truly was better than his birth, then Ingram would prove himself a better man than those who had remained behind in Glendalough. In time he would regain the status he deserved. In time he would respect himself again.

The leaves had begun to exchange summer's green for autumn's golden palette when he approached Ferns, and Ingram was immediately impressed by the size and strength of Dermot MacMurrough's castle. Like Dromahair, Mac-Murrough's castle was enclosed by a double rampart with an outer ring of solid stone. But the inner ring stood taller than any Ingram had seen in Ireland. A large, open field surrounded the elevated castle and insured that the tower guards could see for miles in every direction. The structure appealed to Ingram's military sense, and he mentally congratulated MacMurrough on having the good judgment to build such a fortress.

He hailed the guard on duty at the castle gate and noticed that the man did not hurry to answer his summons. "What do you want?" the guard called down, leaning lazily on the skirt of the outer wall. "The king doesn't need whatever you have to sell."

Ingram tossed his short cloak over his shoulder and gripped the handle of his sword in a conspicuous gesture. "Perhaps he does, my friend," he answered, glaring up at the guard. "Tell him Ingram of Glendalough wishes to see him. I am a warrior, and I offer myself for MacMurrough's service."

The man hesitated, but when Ingram did not flinch or waver, he nodded. "Come in, then," the guard said, motioning to a servant to open the gate.

Ingram stepped into the courtyard of Dermot MacMurrough and tried to forget that he would soon present himself to the sworn enemy of Tiernán O'Rourke, one of the few friends he possessed. But loyalty, he reminded himself, was a quality best forgotten. Ingram of Glendalough had to put knighthood behind him.

Dermot MacMurrough sat at dinner when Ingram found him, and the guard who escorted Ingram into the king's banquet hall motioned for him to be seated on the floor near the door until the great king should find it convenient to look in his direction. The order pricked Ingram's pride until he reminded himself that he was only a farmer, so he sat obediently and waited.

While he waited, Ingram felt his pulse quickening. The king's banquet hall was plush, opulent, noble, and *familiar,* more like the castles of England than anything he had seen in Ireland. Beautiful embroidered tapestries hung on the walls; the guests wore fine silk robes of purple, red, and gold; and the sweet scent of Oriental incense flowed through the room. Tables laden with succulent dishes sagged under the bounty, and the guests dipped and dabbled casually in the rich sauces and meat dishes as if they had never known hunger. The room was *royal,* more richly decorated than anything in O'Rourke's castle, but that king had never given much attention to anything other than war. Dermot MacMurrough, it appeared, had a taste for the finer things of life.

Immediately beside the doorway where Ingram sat were four warriors, two on each side. Each guard wore an impressive gold-handled dagger at his belt, and each stood with folded arms, staring impassively at the commotion of the banquet before them. They were tall, broad-shouldered, and blond, and Ingram guessed that they were mercenaries, for they possessed neither the look nor the stance of the Irishmen he had come to know.

In another dark corner of the room, a band of jugglers

and pipers awaited the king's pleasure. Ingram felt a twinge
of pity for them, for the brass bands on their wrists indicated
that they were unfree and bound to do the king's bidding
for as long as they lived.

Not far from Ingram, eating at a low table, were the
king's hostages, easily identifiable by shackles on their
ankles. A chain of about a foot in length connected each
man's legs, so that movement was possible but escape
unlikely. Farther into the room were the king's guests; past
them were traveling poets in robes of blue and white; and
next to the poets, a group of harpers strummed delicate
music for the king's enjoyment.

The king's table stood at the farthest point of the room,
and Ingram could identify every man at the table by his station and clothing. Several important clients clustered at the
end of the table: sub-kings who ruled far corners of MacMurrough's expansive kingdom, then a brehon in blue, and
finally, a woman and the man wearing the crown. Ingram supposed the woman to be the king's wife, but then he remembered that Dermot MacMurrough had no wife. The woman
had to be the beautiful daughter, Eva.

Ingram lifted himself to his knees to see the beauty and
caught his breath at the sight of her. She had a narrow and
elegant face; her nose was slender and fine, her lips red and
full. She turned to her father and appeared to laugh, and
Ingram noticed the clear purity of her profile and the shining mass of dark hair gathered into a jeweled net at the back
of her head. He could not see the design of the robe she
wore, but it was sleeveless, despite autumn's chill, and pure
white.

She must have sensed his admiring gaze, for her striking
blue eyes fell on him. Ingram forgot every lesson he had ever
learned about proper deference and grinned boldly out of an
overflow of appreciation for her beauty. The lady dipped her
head and whispered something to her father. Then Dermot
MacMurrough stood and pointed in his direction.

"The man at the door! Bring him to me!" he called, his

voice hoarse. Two of the guards lifted Ingram to his feet and roughly escorted him to the king's table.

"Who are you?" MacMurrough growled, pursing his lips suspiciously. "Do I know you?"

"Not yet," Ingram replied, bowing. He chose his words carefully and spoke in Gaelic. "I am Ingram of Glendalough, a warrior."

"What brings you here?" the king snapped, glaring at the guards as if they had done wrong to let a mere peasant into the room.

"I repeat, I am a warrior. Glendalough is in Leinster, and you are my king. I heard that you might have use for a skilled sword and brave heart."

MacMurrough snorted. "From you? You, friend, are too old to run around the hills waving a sword. A man half your age would cut you to ribbons."

"Name one of them, sir, and I will prove my worth."

MacMurrough cocked his head as if he hadn't heard correctly. "Indeed?"

"Truly, sir. Thirty-eight is not so vast an age. The mind can compensate for what time diminishes."

The king signaled to one of the warriors who stood behind him at the table, and while the man slipped out of the room, MacMurrough folded his hands and regarded Ingram with a sly smile. "You speak as if you are not from this place."

"I have traveled a great deal. Three years I journeyed with Griogiar, the brehon, and Cathal, his teacher."

MacMurrough's brow lifted in mute appreciation, then he took the hand of the beauty next to him and waved an arm toward the assembled guests. "My captain, Bhaltair, is preparing in the courtyard," he announced, stepping from behind his dining table. "This Ingram of Glendalough has promised us entertainment. Harpers, put away your harps; we shall not be needing them today."

He paused before leaving the room. "Unless, Ingram of Glendalough, you would like them to play a funeral song while you are buried."

Ingram stepped into the large circle of faces and gripped his sword. Ordinarily, he would have knelt to pray and crossed himself before standing, but prayer was a knightly exercise. He was now a barbaric warrior.

His sword felt slippery in his clammy hand, and for a brief instant, he wondered if this challenge had been wise. Ingram of Southwick, the knight of yesteryear, could have defeated any man in Ireland, but Ingram the farmer had not hefted a sword in twelve years. Ingram of Southwick would have met defeat with honor and without regret, but Ingram of Glendalough had a son to protect and provide for.

He gripped his sword with two hands, crouched low, and waited for Bhaltair's attack. A solid man, nearly as broad as he was tall, Bhaltair had a shock of red hair and generously freckled skin. Heavily muscled legs protruded from his short warrior's tunic, and his arms hung like sides of butchered beef from his shoulders. In his thick hands he gripped the Irish battle-ax, and he smiled confidently as he approached Ingram.

For a full minute they circled each other like two wary cats, and Ingram realized too late that he had spoken truly when he told MacMurrough that his brain power, not his brawn, would insure victory. His reflexes could not be trusted, nor could his strength possibly be equal to this huge man's. His life depended on quick thinking and the form and skills learned a lifetime ago.

Bhaltair roared and charged, raising the axe, and Ingram froze, his pulse pounding, while his mind raced helplessly. At the last possible instant, he turned in sheer panic, and the brute's momentum carried him forward to the dusty ground. Ingram gently slapped the champion's behind with the flat side of his sword and cleared his throat. "Excuse me, my friend," he called, steadying his voice as it echoed in the courtyard. "But I am over here." Behind him, women giggled.

Bhaltair did not smile when he rose from the dust but

charged again, swinging the axe repeatedly over his head and across his body. Ingram dodged each blow until he found himself backed against the stone wall of the garrison. As Bhaltair prepared to raise the axe for a final, fatal blow, Ingram inserted his sword into the axe's upward path. The weapon fell from Bhaltair's hand and flew toward the crowd, and the onlookers screamed and scrambled as the blade tumbled uselessly into the dust.

Breathless and slightly giddy, Ingram turned to MacMurrough, sheathed his sword, and nodded curtly toward the king, waiting for some remark of commendation. MacMurrough gave Ingram a fixed and meaningless smile; then his eyes swiveled to a point behind Ingram's shoulder.

Ingram turned but too late. Colors exploded in his brain, and he staggered as Bhaltair backed away, his fist still clenched from the blow he had dealt.

Ingram struggled to stay on his feet as the brute lowered his red head and came again like a human battering ram. Forgetting his dignity, Ingram sprinted away, a rush of adrenaline clearing his mind. He felt his panic rising—how could he have forgotten the most basic rule of a knight's training? A knight never, *ever* turned his back on an enemy unless the enemy was dead or had admitted defeat. And a knight never left his opponent standing.

He could hear the soft puff of Bhaltair's footsteps in the dust behind him. As the crowd laughed at the spectacle of the chase, Ingram spun around and bestowed a front snap-kick to Bhaltair's groin. The blow hit home, for the Irish wore no armor of any kind, and the big brute gaped like a snagged fish and crumpled forward in pain.

Never leave a man standing. As Bhaltair bent before him, helpless, Ingram smashed his fist into the man's jaw and felt the bones in his hands give. Pain shot through his veins like cold needles, but the blow was enough to topple Bhaltair to the ground.

Ingram drew his sword, placed it at Bhaltair's neck, and

glared at Dermot MacMurrough. No one in the crowd stirred. "What do you say now, King?" he called.

"Spare my captain, and serve me in my force," MacMurrough answered, his expression smug. "And join me at my table tomorrow for dinner."

In twenty-four hours Ingram underwent a strange transformation. Stripped, bathed, bandaged, and massaged by MacMurrough's servants, Ingram took his new tunic, shield, and cloak from the hand of Bhaltair himself. The huge giant also offered a battle-ax.

"If you don't mind, I'd prefer to keep my sword," Ingram said. "An axe is unwieldy."

Ingram could tell immediately that he had offended MacMurrough's captain, for the battle-ax was every Irish warrior's weapon of choice. "It's not that I don't like an axe," Ingram hastened to say. "It's just that you're so quick with it, Bhaltair. I would never be able to keep pace with you. Let me keep my sword, and I will fight behind you."

Bhaltair grinned; this logic appealed to him. "Ye didn't get a scratch on me with that sword, did you now?" he asked, his face as innocent as a child's.

"No, I didn't," Ingram answered. "Though 'twas only luck and God's mercy that allowed me to win at all."

❖ ❖ ❖

Dermot MacMurrough hesitated before entering his banquet room, and he peered through the curtain at his private entrance to see that all were in their places. The new man, Ingram, sat at the king's table already, looking much more like a warrior than he had the day before. Who had known the man could wield a sword and dance circles around his best fighter? But though the man was a quick and intelligent warrior, his weak spot was already obvious. The man was practically salivating over Eva, who sat at the end of the table.

MacMurrough nodded in approval. His daughter ignored the newcomer, as was proper, but this attraction might prove useful.

He cleared his throat, the guards sprang to attention, and his guests rose from their seats. MacMurrough scowled at them all as he entered, and only after he had been seated did the guests relax and take their places.

As the guests and servants waited expectantly for his signal for dinner to begin, MacMurrough waved at the brehon who sat at Eva's right hand. "You, brehon," MacMurrough said, turning to the elder in disdain. "Go to the end of the table. Ingram will sit between me and my daughter today. I'll be wanting to talk to him."

The brehon stood, embarrassment and displeasure evident on his face, while Ingram took the seat that had been offered to him. MacMurrough signaled for the meal to be served, and as the servants scurried to bring out the food, the king folded his hands and looked steadily at Ingram. "Does my daughter please you?" he asked.

Ingram's smile was polite, his manner reserved. "She is very lovely. I heard reports of her beauty even in Waterford."

"Reports of her beauty have spread throughout the world," MacMurrough observed dryly. "Some have faulted me for keeping her unmarried so long, but twenty-five is not such a vast age, is it my dear?"

The girl colored, but she looked at Ingram as she answered. "It is a good age, Father."

"That is what I think," MacMurrough continued, leaning toward Ingram. "And so I'll keep her until I find a truly remarkable man, one who is willing to give me what I want and what I need. After all, if a father must give a daughter and a dowry, shouldn't he be getting something from the deal?"

A servant offered a basket of bread; the king took a large loaf and broke it, handing half to his newest warrior. The man nodded his thanks and took a bite, and then

MacMurrough asked, "Are you a remarkable man, Ingram of Glendalough?"

Ingram seemed to choke on his bread. When he had regained his composure and taken a sip of water, he shrugged. "Some would say that I am. Others would not agree. But if you want a man to help you attain what you want . . ." He looked pointedly at MacMurrough. "I suppose all would depend upon what you want to achieve."

The king smiled, impressed with the man's forthrightness. "Ah, sure, there's no secret in that. I want to be the *ard-ri*, the high king of all Ireland. 'Tis my due, after all. If you travel the whole of Ireland, my friend, you'll not find as wealthy a kingdom, as cultivated a court, or warriors as brave as mine. Why shouldn't I be high king?"

"Perhaps because there can only be one, and your friend, Murcertach MacLochlainn of Ailech, holds that title now."

"Ah, but can you be thinking that MacLochlainn will be high king forever? These are dangerous and uncertain times, me friend."

Ingram shrugged. "You speak the truth," he said simply, then he turned to smile at Eva.

MacMurrough turned his attention to his dinner. 'Twould do no harm to let the man fantasize awhile. If his daughter's beauty bound such an able warrior to his camp, then he was glad for such a daughter. Let all men be attracted to her, but only one would marry her—and only when all of Ireland was finally in the hands of Dermot Mac-Murrough.

TWENTY

"Ingram."

On his way to the garrison through the darkened court-yard, the new man paused. Eva laughed softly.

"Princess?" he asked, turning toward her in the shadows.

She extended her hand out of the darkness; her arm shone white and smooth in the moonlight. "Come here," she called again. "I've a present for you."

"You shouldn't be out here; it's chilly," he said, coming closer. *He fusses like a mother hen,* she thought, enjoying the attention. But when he stood directly before her, she drew in her breath and revised her opinion. At this close range, nothing fussy or feminine existed in the man called Ingram of Glendalough. His eyes gleamed like sapphires in the semi-darkness; his golden hair seemed to light the alcove where she stood. His broad shoulders blocked her path, and an unusually intricate, jeweled brooch gleamed in the fabric of his luxurious new cloak.

She shivered as she realized that she had managed to find him alone. Without the watchful eyes of her father hovering near, anything might happen in the magic of moonlight.

"They say fairies dance on nights like this," she said, rubbing her hands over her bare arms. "Have you heard of the *púca*, Ingram?"

"The fairy horse?" He laughed. "Surely you don't believe such tales, Princess. The priest would require a penance of you for saying so."

"The priests don't know everything." She allowed herself to shiver. "When they brought Christianity to this land, the ancient gods were driven underground. Leprechauns, *púcas,* fairies—I like to believe in all of them."

Flames of laughter lit in his eyes to match the glow of his smile in the moonlight. "I've certainly never seen a fairy."

She gave him a look of jaunty superiority. "Then I'm more privileged than you, sir."

His smile seemed to fade. "Perhaps you are."

He turned as if to go, and she caught the corner of his robe. "I am cold," she said, lifting the edge of his new cloak and snuggling against him.

He smiled in surprise and pleasure but neither resisted nor embraced her. "Princess, your father would kill me if he found us like this. Why don't you go inside? We can talk tomorrow."

"But I have a gift for you."

He chuckled. "I should be wary of such gifts."

She laughed softly, allowing her laughter to caress him in the darkness. "I give this with my father's permission. It's something very special, something every warrior needs."

His curiosity overcame his doubts, for he did not pull away when she took his hand and led him into the stable. The smell of hay and manure and horses blended in a pungent combination of earthy smells, a fragrance she loved, for it reminded her of her father and brothers.

"Here," she said, leading him to a stall. Inside stood a beautiful chestnut gelding with distinctive white stockings on the legs and a white blaze down the face. The animal's dark eyes studied Ingram, and he snorted gently as Ingram approached.

"For me?" Ingram asked. He leaped the gate into the stall, and in the glow of torchlight Eva watched him expertly run his hands over the animal's legs. "He's beautiful. You must thank your father for me."

"It's my gift. He was my horse."

"Then thank *you,* Princess."

He faced her, the gate of the stall between them, and more than anything she wished that he would touch her with the affection he had shown the horse. "Please call me Eva. I like to hear you say it."

"All right, Eva."

She put her hands on the gate and leaned back, smiling mischievously at him. "Tell me truly, Ingram, where *are* you from? Do you speak English?"

"Yes."

"I knew it!"

"And how do you know?"

He came to the gate, and she leaned forward until their faces were only inches apart. "Though your Gaelic is good, you don't use Irish speech patterns. English is your first language, true?"

"No. I spoke French first."

She gaped in wonder. French, then English, then Irish—who *was* this man?

He gave her a warning look. "I'd rather you didn't tell anyone about this, Eva. I've done nothing wrong, but the past is over, and I'd like to concentrate on the present."

"Perhaps I might be persuaded to keep the secrets of your past," she whispered, leaning closer and raising her lips to his. "If you concentrate on me in the present."

He hesitated only a moment before his lips touched hers. She swayed on her feet and fell against the gate, then wrapped her arms around his neck to steady herself. His kiss grew deeper and stronger; then he abruptly pulled himself away.

"To secrets, then," he said finally, gently removing her arms from his neck. "Mine of the past, and yours of the present."

"Ours, darling," Eva whispered, not willing to let him go. She twined her arms around his head again. "Ours."

A symmetry and rhythm of life existed even in the unruly castle of Dermot MacMurrough, and Ingram easily fell into his role as an Irish warrior. Most days were spent at the castle, practicing horsemanship, wrestling, or dueling, and Ingram introduced MacMurrough's warriors to lessons and practice in the unfamiliar arts of sword fighting and jousting.

But when it came to battle, MacMurrough's warriors wanted nothing to do with Ingram's long sword and lance. While adept with their short swords, they still preferred the battle-ax, and since the warriors wore no armor, the thought of facing a piercing lance on a charging horse chilled the blood of even the most courageous swordsman. "Give me a shield, an axe, and a sling," Bhaltair cried one afternoon after Ingram's padded lance knocked the giant from his horse and left him gasping for breath. "I've had enough of this jousting. If a man can run and throw an axe, to my way of thinking, he's a good enough warrior."

The real trouble with MacMurrough's ever-changing military force, Ingram realized, was that only a handful of the men were dedicated warriors. Unlike the knights of England, who were a social class unto themselves and owned no land, the Irish warriors were farmers, more concerned with raising a crop and feeding their families than learning to ride in battle. They came when MacMurrough summoned them; they fought bravely and with courage when required. But the only weapons they owned were slender hunting spears, an occasional short sword or axe, and slingshots. Not a single Irish farmer owned a hauberk, a decent shield, or an iron helmet.

After one particularly disappointing training session, Ingram left the ragtag group of men who served MacMurrough and disgustedly threw his dagger into the straw dummy he had made for sword practice. 'Twas a good thing the Irish fought only each other, for if they ever came face-to-face with the seasoned knights of a Norman army, Ireland's emerald hills would run red with the blood of her men.

Despite his army's shortcomings, Dermot MacMurrough loved waging war with his neighbors, and Ingram always groaned inwardly when the trumpet blew from the tower of the fortress at Ferns to summon the warriors to the garrison. Such-and-such a king had offended MacMurrough, so they were to steal fifty of the king's cattle. Or so-and-so of a sub-kingdom had entertained a rival king, so the warriors were to burn five farms within that rebellious noble's territory. It was petty tribal warfare, Ingram realized, and beneath a knight's honor. But he had disavowed his knighthood. He had agreed to be a hired warrior, and MacMurrough had more than met his price.

From the king Ingram received his horse, food, clothing, and lodging—all a warrior should expect. But Ingram had asked for one other thing: permission to visit his family every season. Permission had been reluctantly granted, for though MacMurrough was accustomed to losing men for extended periods of time, Ingram knew MacMurrough hated the thought of losing his most valued and unique warrior. Confident of his place in the king's estimation, Ingram pressed his case and rode home to Glendalough for a week every spring, summer, winter, and fall.

Ingram found that the *rath* itself never changed; it stood bare and bleak atop the mountain as it always had. But over the course of time the children grew like sturdy pines, the adults toughened and thinned. Philip's face lined with wrinkles; gray strands crept through Eamhair's black hair. Still the family members were always quick to welcome him and share the bounty he brought from Ferns. After a year Ingram thought that even baby Alden came to look forward to his visits.

"Do you think he knows who I am?" Ingram asked Eamhair one summer afternoon as the boy slipped from his arms and toddled off to play with his cousins.

"Aye, he knows you are his father," Eamhair answered, wiping a stray hair from her eyes as she stirred the big cauldron over the fire. "We tell him oft enough."

"But what does he think a father is?" Ingram whispered, more to himself than to his sister-in-law. "Someone who comes with presents a few times every year? Does he know I'd give my life to protect him?"

"I expect he'll understand that when he's older," Eamhair answered, her voice tired. She let go of the wooden plank she used to stir the pot and rubbed her arms. "Ye have to remember, Ingram, he's only a baby, barely a year old."

"Still, sometimes I wonder if I'm doing the right thing. Perhaps I should stay here so my son will be near me."

Eamhair put her hands on her hips and gave him a disapproving glance. "Ye are no farmer, Ingram, and you know it. The boy is loved here and cared for. You should do what you must and trust God to lead you to the right path for your son."

A few feet down the path, Alden slipped on a rock and fell onto his knees. Ingram leaped to his feet, but Eamhair's restraining arm kept him from rushing to the baby. "He's not hurt," she said softly, her dark eyes filling with pity for Ingram. "Leave the child alone. There are times when a lad must learn to do things for himself."

Ingram leaned against the pressure of her hand, ready to thrust her off if Alden even whimpered in pain. But though the baby's face screwed up as if he would cry, he pushed himself back onto his seat, wiped his hands on his shirt, and immediately began to concentrate again on standing to join the other children a few feet away.

Ingram relaxed and smiled up at Eamhair. "You know best," he said, squeezing her hand affectionately. "I know I shouldn't worry about him when I'm away."

Abruptly, he dropped her hand and pulled the jeweled brooch from his cloak. "Take this, Eamhair, and use it for the child," he said, pushing the brooch into her hand.

"No," she whispered, drawing away as if it would bite her. "It is too rich. We would have no use for such a thing."

"Please." Ingram pressed the brooch steadily in her hand. "If I'm not here, if the child needs something—food or a tunic—you could sell this in Dublin. . . ."

Slowly, her fingers curled around the brooch, and she gave him a doubtful glance. "Are you sure?"

"Aye." He grinned at her. "'Tis the only thing I have of value, and the least I can do for my son."

That night, as Alden lay sleeping in his arms, Ingram spoke the words closest to his heart. "I will always care for you," he whispered, studying the healthy glow of the child's soft skin. "I will always love you, and you will never have to wonder who your father is. One day, as soon as you are of a capable age, I will come for you, and we will make our way in the world together, you and I."

The boy snored softly, and Ingram kissed his son on the forehead.

As bittersweet as his visits to Glendalough were, Ingram always enjoyed his welcome at Ferns. As soon as his horse was spotted on the field, a trumpet blew in greeting, and the men inside the garrison flowed into the courtyard to hail Ingram. The serving women applauded his return with many shy smiles and a few forward winks, and on the evening of his homecoming Eva would fervently kiss him and assure him he had been missed.

Many nights Eva begged him to come to the stable. Once there, she held him close and teased him with her kisses until he tore himself away in frustration and left her laughing in the dark. Each time he swore he would never meet her again, but at dinner the next day, she would flash her icy blue eyes at him, touch his arm lightly with her hand, or curve her lips in the lovely sleepy-cat smile that entranced him. And that night he would wander to the stable again, hoping she would join him.

In the first few months of her attention, Ingram had convinced himself that Eva was the antidote necessary to vanquish Signe's memory. With the warm and exquisite Eva in his arms, how could he think of the quarrelsome, green-eyed witch of Waterford? But no matter how hard he tried,

Signe refused to be banished. Her memory lingered at the back of his mind, joined him in his reverie, surfaced in his dreams.

After two years of balancing Signe's memory with Eva's flirtations, Ingram decided that the answer to his predicament lay in having Eva as his wife. She was no ignorant country girl like Brenna. Eva was intelligent, quick to speak, and a temptress. If Eva was his, thoughts of Signe would vanish like morning mist in a hot sun.

But MacMurrough had made it clear that Eva's hand would not be won easily. No man would marry her until MacMurrough had been assured of the high kingship, and though Ingram didn't know how that could be won, he determined to do his best to please Dermot MacMurrough. If MacMurrough would give his daughter only to the man who could win the *ard-ri,* when the time came, Ingram would be that man.

Strange news awaited Ingram when he returned from Glendalough in the spring of 1166. He had scarcely dismounted from his horse when Bhaltair burst into the stable, waving his hands in excitement. "It begins," the big man said, his eyes burning with intensity. "The high king Murcertach MacLochlainn is dead."

Ingram led his horse into a stall and tried to contain his rising excitement. "So MacMurrough is happy." He smiled. "The high kingship will be his. When do we ride to claim it for our master?"

"It will not be our master's without a fight. MacLochlainn did not die naturally, Ingram. He took his enemy Eochy MacDunlevy prisoner—"

"They've been fighting for years," Ingram interrupted, picking up an empty bucket to bring water for the horse. "Each has been the prisoner of the other before."

"MacLochlainn had MacDunlevy's eyes put out," Bhaltair said, his freckled face stone somber. "Never has such a thing been done to an Irish king, not by another Irish king. The land shuddered when the deed was done."

Ingram froze, the bucket in his hand. This was unusual. While atrocities filled Ireland's history and had been faithfully recounted by the brehons, all such barbarism had been attributed to the Vikings or other warlike invaders. Never had such a thing been done by one Irishman to another.

"What happened?"

Bhaltair nodded. "Ye can imagine, can't ye? MacLochlainn's vassals revolted against him and persuaded Donnchad O'Crvall, king of Oriel, to lead them against MacLochlainn. The two war parties met at Leitir Luin. They say MacLochlainn was killed as easily as a common foot soldier. He was killed, don't you know, like Goliath, struck in the head by a pebble from a common farmer's slingshot."

"So who challenges MacMurrough for the high kingship? O'Crvall of Oriel?"

"Rory O'Connor has already claimed the circuit of the *ard-ri*," Bhaltair explained, looking dejectedly at the ground. "A brehon has come and told MacMurrough to abide by the law. Every kingdom supports O'Connor—"

"Every kingdom but Leinster," Ingram finished for him. "MacMurrough must be in a raging fit."

"Aye." The big man nodded. "I've been afraid to go into the hall. MacMurrough is mad with rage, and he waits to hear your plan."

"I'll see what can be done," Ingram said, handing the empty bucket to Bhaltair. "Water my horse, will you?" He took two steps, then turned for a final question. "This brehon—what is his name?"

"Griogiar," Bhaltair answered.

"Griogiar." Ingram pitched his voice to reach only the brehon, who stood just inside MacMurrough's bedchamber. Through the open door Ingram could see the king stretched out on his bed, his eyes closed, his countenance troubled.

Eva stood by his side, rubbing his temples, and she cast Ingram a worried look.

The brehon's eyes lit up when he saw Ingram. He slipped out of the room and embraced his friend in the hall. "It is good to see you, Ingram," he said, clasping him firmly by the shoulders. "I wondered what had become of you, but when I visited your *fine* months ago, your people said you served Dermot MacMurrough." He released Ingram and smiled. "Your son is a winsome child."

"Thank you." Ingram warmed to the praise. "You look good, Griogiar. Handsome and fit."

The brehon shrugged away the compliment. "I live well. It is a lonely life, but I am used to it."

Ingram gave a perfunctory nod toward MacMurrough's chamber. "How is Leinster's king faring?"

"Not well," Griogiar said, pulling Ingram away from the chamber. "His ambition will not die easily. He thought Ireland lay at his feet and has found instead that Ireland lunges for his throat."

Ingram dropped his voice. "Should he then be content with Leinster?"

Griogiar pulled away in surprise. "He will be fortunate to keep Leinster. His own people have turned against him and allied with the other kings. Even now, the northern Leinster tribes are set against MacMurrough and will revolt. They have not forgotten the raids, the burnings, the pillaging done by MacMurrough's men."

With terrible suddenness Ingram realized that he was one of the men who had engaged in raids and pillaging, and he lowered his head in embarrassment.

"These men operate on MacMurrough's order," he said, unable to meet Griogiar's gaze.

"MacMurrough is finished giving orders," Griogiar answered. "Now that his ally Murcertach MacLochlainn is gone, MacMurrough's atrocities will not be tolerated." He turned his face toward the window. "I've heard rumors that even now Tiernán O'Rourke is gathering an army to force MacMurrough from Ireland."

"But MacMurrough is the rightful ruler of this kingdom!" Ingram protested, honestly surprised. "What right has O'Rourke to intrude upon Leinster?"

"He comes to amend the injustices MacMurrough has committed over the years, including the abduction of his wife," Griogiar answered. "Perhaps you cannot see, Ingram, for your loyalty to your master blinds you. But Dermot Mac-Murrough is ruthless."

"Dervorgilla was not abducted; she arranged to leave O'Rourke."

"Still, what manner of king takes another's wife?"

"MacMurrough is hard, and often forbidding, but all kings are."

"He is more than hard—he is unjust."

"He seeks vengeance for the wrongs done to him."

"He injures innocent people on his own whims. Once he forced the abbess of Kildare to leave her convent and marry one of his own cousins, a lecherous fiend who admired her beauty. The woman threw herself off a cliff within a week of her marriage."

For this Ingram had no answer. Griogiar watched him for a moment, then took a seat on a nearby bench. "'Tis no matter, Ingram," he said, shrugging. "All will be settled soon regardless of what you or I do. Justice will prevail; the High King Rory O'Connor will see to it."

"Fine." Ingram dismissed the topic with a wave of his hand and sat on the bench beside the brehon. "And you are wrong, Griogiar, I am loyal no longer. I left knightly loyalty behind when I agreed to be hired by MacMurrough."

"I see," Griogiar whispered, nodding gravely. "I wondered how you could justify fighting for such a man."

"I have done nothing wrong."

"Then why is your face flushed with shame, me friend? Let us not lie to one another. No matter what you have told yourself, Ingram, the knightly virtues you say you have discarded are a part of you yet. Chivalry, loyalty, courtesy—"

"I am not that man, I tell you!" His words came suddenly, raw and angry, and Griogiar blanched and looked away.

Ingram forced a smile and shook his head. "I am not worthy of those ideals, Griogiar. I was not born to them. And speaking of birth, I have wanted to discuss something else with you. I hoped I might see you soon, for I have a plan."

The brehon looked skeptical. "I have learned to beware of the plans of warriors. They usually end in bloodshed or strife."

"This one will not," Ingram answered, smiling easily. "My son is now three years old. You will need a student, Griogiar, to care for you in your old age. Why not Alden? He can join you when he is old enough—"

"Ah." Griogiar lifted a hand, stopping Ingram. "I am sorry, my friend, but you have the wrong brehon. I would love to take your son, for he seems a bright child, and I do not doubt that he would be well suited for any sort of work he might undertake. But a child must be fifteen before undertaking this course and must study for fifteen years."

"So?" Ingram asked, not understanding Griogiar's reluctance.

"We are not immortal, me friend. I am forty-one, as are you. I will be fifty-three when your son is fifteen and would not complete his training until my sixty-eighth year."

Ingram stared at him blankly.

"I will not live that long. Few men do. And since you live by the way of the sword—" the brehon shrugged— "you will not live as long as I."

Ingram wanted to laugh. Did Griogiar now think himself a prophet? Ingram was not young, but he was strong, as close to invincible as a warrior could be. Still, he knew that he could not argue with Griogiar about Alden. The brehon, after all, represented the indisputable law.

Ingram stiffened. "Very well. Perhaps I shall find a younger brehon to teach my son."

Griogiar stood and led the way as they walked from the king's house. "Perhaps you shall. Until then, me friend Ingram, did you know Abbot Steaphan has sent scouts into the mountains of Wicklow to find you? He claims you are a runaway monk and says that the pope is willing to command you to a monastery."

"Faith," Ingram quipped, smiling at his friend. "The church must be desperate if they seek one such as I."

"Ah, sure, and haven't I said so?" Griogiar answered. "That's what I told the abbot."

Far beyond the plain outside Dermot MacMurrough's castle, Griogiar made his solitary way up a mountain path and turned to study the castle on the horizon. The lingering twilight embraced the stone structure like a tender lover, but Griogiar knew little love existed within the building's walls. Even Ingram, whose heart had once been pure, though confused, now lay under MacMurrough's dark spell.

"And, blessed Father God," the brehon prayed, the sound of his voice scattering a flock of roosting birds from a nearby tree, "if Ingram falls, what hope will there be for the dark days ahead? My departed master was right—power is a destroyer when married to ambition, and if Ingram is married to MacMurrough . . ."

A quiet voice, an unseen presence, brought a memory to mind: a golden-haired, sunny-faced child on a mountaintop. "Ah, yes, Lord," Griogiar whispered, smiling. "The child. Perchance the child will save the man."

Still smiling, the brehon turned in a whirl of dark blue and vanished into the deepening night.

TWENTY-ONE

A breathless courier burst into the king's banquet hall the next day, his face red and streaked with perspiration. "God save us all," he cried, falling prostrate before MacMurrough's feet. "The end is upon us!"

Ingram saw MacMurrough glare at the guards who stood by the door. "Who allowed this miscreant in?" he growled. "You are disturbing the peace of this dinner."

"Please sir, I alone am loyal to you from the northern tribes of Kildare, Bray, and Enniskerry. They are massing in the north, my king, with the warriors of O'Rourke and O'Melaghlin of Meath. The Ostmen of Wexford are prepared to march upon us from the south—"

"Enough!" MacMurrough slammed his hand down upon the table and stood. Next to her father, Eva paled slightly, and Ingram felt his whole body tighten. If Tiernán O'Rourke was truly advancing, what could he do? In his time at the castle of MacMurrough, he had justified his lack of loyalty to O'Rourke by reasoning that he had never lifted his sword against any of O'Rourke's men. To do so now would be a flagrant violation of the northern king's trust.

Dermot MacMurrough gestured to the guards, who lifted the frightened farmer by his arms and dragged him from the hall. "Eat, my guests; play, harpers," MacMurrough said in a soothing tone. He sat back down and, lowering his voice, leaned over Eva toward Ingram. "Go at once to the stable; have the horses saddled. We will call for all our able-bodied and strong men, and we will ride out tomorrow."

"Sire, you must know that I once took an oath—"

MacMurrough's eyes flashed. "Do as I say, fool," he said, motioning past Ingram to Bhaltair. "Both of you, go now and be quick about it."

Ingram paused only to give a reassuring glance to Eva, then hurried to the stables. MacMurrough would regret not hearing him out, for though Ingram had been hired to serve Leinster's king, another, earlier vow stood firm. He would not fight against Tiernán O'Rourke; he could not break that vow. Perhaps Griogiar was right. He had tried to reject his vow to God, but he could not evade his own nature. Too much of the knight still resided in him.

Horses were saddled, and couriers were sent throughout the countryside to gather warriors for the coming conflict. Ingram made sure all progressed well with the men; then he hurried toward the castle to find Eva. Her cool composure had been upset by the news at dinner, and Ingram looked forward to comforting her. Whether as a knight or a man, he had a duty to rescue and honor women, and with every step through the palace his jaw became firmer, his muscles tighter, his heart more eager. He yearned to protect her, to demonstrate his devotion.

He found her alone in her small chamber. Ignoring all protocol, he entered and swept her into his arms. "Your father would not let me speak, but I will tell you," he said, breathing in the delicious scent of her. "Tiernán O'Rourke is no enemy of mine, but a friend, and I will not fight against him. But I will defend you, Eva, though a thousand O'Rourkes come against you."

She stiffened in his grasp, then wriggled free. "What are you saying?" she said, pushing her hair back and glaring at him. "If you fight for my father, you will fight anyone who threatens us."

"Only if they threaten *you*, my lady," Ingram said. "You have never asked about my past, so you do not know that Tiernán O'Rourke acted as my friend when your father carried away his wife."

"That witch Dervorgilla?" She opened her eyes wide in amused disbelief. "Surely O'Rourke does not hate my father for that. He should have been glad to be rid of the woman."

"I stood guard on the day she was taken; I watched as she returned," Ingram said. "Your father planned a most devious strategy. A proxy died in his place that day."

"The strategy was mine," Eva answered, turning away from him. She smoothed her hair, then turned her face toward him. "Tell me more, Ingram, of this friendship between you and O'Rourke."

"'Tis not important. I came only to tell you that I will defend your life, but you must leave the palace with me immediately. We can find a cave in the hills and remain there until the fighting is over. You will be safe, and I will not have to break my vow of friendship."

"No, Ingram. I will not take you from my father's battle." She stepped toward him, her long hair swinging freely down her back. Her breath intoxicated him, as did the movement of her eyes as they swept into his. "If you would protect me, Ingram, if you would win me, you must stay and fight for my father." Her voice took on a teasing tone. "You do want me, don't you, Ingram?"

Flee.

The warning rang in his mind, but the torment of her presence dulled his thinking.

She laughed gently in response; her hand tugged at his tunic and pulled him to her. "You want me." Her words were not a question but a statement. "You know what it will take to win me. My father must have a victory, and you are the only man who can give it to him. Bhaltair is a strong warrior, but he is not a Norman knight."

He started in surprise at her words, and she laughed. "Oh, yes, Ingram, I know what you are. I don't know how you came to be here, or why you disguise the truth, but no dirt farmer from Glendalough speaks English and French as you do. Surely you didn't think I would love a common peasant as I love you? You're as Norman as I am royal, and let's not be hiding the truth any longer."

She gave him a heart-stopping smile. "You, Ingram, shall lead Dermot MacMurrough's troops against all who come against him. You will be victorious over them all. And then I will be yours."

His response was shameless, instant, and total. He pulled her to him and pressed his lips to her throat. He could feel the slow and steady pulse of her heart beneath his flesh as strong and vivid desires coursed through him. What, after all, did O'Rourke mean to him? The vow had been given more than a dozen years ago; he was not the same man he had been in those days. Perhaps even O'Rourke could excuse the vow if he saw and understood the unbelievably desirable woman in Ingram's arms. And Eva saw him not as a poor farmer but as a worthy and noble knight.

She held him tightly for a moment, then pressed her hands to his shoulders and gently pushed him away. He lifted his eyes to hers. "You see now that my way is best?" she whispered, taking his hand. She placed it over her heart, and he could feel the heat of her flesh beneath the silky fabric of her tunic.

He sighed. "Yes."

"Then go." Her voice was husky. "Win me, Sir Ingram, and I will be *completely* yours."

Scouts reported the advancing armies the next day, and Ingram went over his battle plan once again in the hall of MacMurrough's castle. Several warriors had been named captains over the men MacMurrough had been able to produce, and Ingram tried to ignore the hard knot of fear that twisted in his stomach. Hundreds of men, perhaps a thousand, were marching upon Ferns, and Ingram had only a hundred men to turn the battle.

"I must have absolute cooperation for this plan to work," he said, looking straight at MacMurrough. "Every man must do his part. Bhaltair will remain here at the castle with ten men, to guard Princess Eva." He nodded to the huge man who stood with his arms crossed. "I am sorry, my friend, for I know you love battle, but the princess must be protected. You are the man to do it."

Bhaltair nodded in response, his pride mollified. Ingram then turned to MacMurrough. "You and your warriors, sir, must ride south to the banks of the River Slaney. The Ostmen will certainly come along the banks, and with a careful ambush, you will be able to wipe out the advance guard and send the others scurrying back to Wexford. Take five of the best archers, ride quickly, and hide carefully."

MacMurrough nodded, his lined face showing signs of a restless night.

"The rest of you men will come with me now," Ingram said, pulling himself up to his full height. "Mount the fastest horses, sharpen your blades, collect shields from the garrison. We will meet the advancing army as they come over the mountains and startle them with our arrogance. They will believe that since we ride so bravely and so well, we are reinforced by an army of thousands, and perhaps—"

He glanced at Eva, who smiled in encouragement.

Ingram turned back to the men and thrust his fist into the air. "They will know not to advance upon the Kingdom of Leinster!"

Dermot MacMurrough waited until the cheering warriors had followed Ingram into the courtyard; then he walked to a window and watched the motley crew mount up. When at last they were organized into two lines, Ingram gave the signal. The trumpet blew, and the men tightened their clammy fists about their shields. The castle gate opened, and the double line rode out of the courtyard and into the countryside.

"They are impressive, are they not?" Eva asked, her soft voice cutting through MacMurrough's thoughts.

"Yes," he said, turning away from the window and to his daughter. "But they are too few. Take a last look, my daughter, for we will not see them again. The vultures from the north will be on them before the day is out. But if they fight well, they will buy us the time we need."

"But sire—" Bhaltair stepped forward, a puzzled look on his face— "Ingram said we could win this battle."

MacMurrough spat on the floor as if he considered the idea ridiculous. "That conceited fool thinks he can but wave his sword and everyone will fall at his feet. Ingram is an optimist, a dangerous and vile trait in a warrior. Soon he will be dead."

Eva pressed her hand upon Bhaltair's muscled arm. "Be glad, Bhaltair, that I asked Ingram to leave you here with me. We are leaving this place. A boat waits even now for us at the coast."

Bhaltair turned slowly to MacMurrough. "You are not going to the river with the archers?"

"By heaven, Bhaltair, you are more stupid than a rock," MacMurrough said, moving rapidly through the remaining men. "You, archers, make sure there are twenty horses made ready. We're going east to the shore. Mount quickly, for we ride at once."

The chestnut gelding covered the miles effortlessly, and despite the deadly seriousness of his journey, Ingram exulted in the feeling of leading warriors into conflict. This was what he had trained to do, regardless of his breeding and birth, and if it should prove to be his last battle, he would do honor to himself and all knights before him. Only one thought troubled him—if he died today, he might never see his son again. But all would hear of the tale and know that he had done his job and done it well.

Look, Éireann, he thought, as the horses behind him thundered over the soft green earth, *a knight of England rides today, making war for love and glory. Though the odds be a hundred to one, righteousness will prevail, and God's will be done.*

A light rain began to fall as they rode, and Ingram felt strangely naked as the rain hit his skin, for he wore only the short, light tunic of the Irish warrior. A dagger hung by his belt, his sword by his side. The round Irish shield he carried was nothing at all like the narrow kite-shaped Norman shield that could effectively cover a man in the thick of battle.

His pulse quickened as he crested the next hill, and he pulled back on his reins so suddenly that his horse reared, the animal's mighty hooves cleaving the air. Before them, at the crest of the next sloping hill, another army advanced through the mist: the combined forces of Meath, Connacht, Oriel, Breifne, and the northern tribes of Leinster. They were spread out across the gray horizon, an advancing force of thousands.

Ingram motioned for his warriors to fan out behind him.

"Adhamh," he said, speaking to the sword-thin man who rode beside him, a farmer with ten children. "Do you know the Holy Scriptures?"

"Aye," Adhamh answered, his eyes, like Ingram's, fixed on the steadily advancing sea of men on the next hill.

"Would you say this is how David felt before Goliath?"

"Ah, no," the man answered, leaning companionably toward Ingram as if he would share a joke. "David had an army behind him. We got nothing but God's own green field, not even a tree to hide behind."

Only an Irishman, Ingram thought, *could look into the face of doom and laugh.*

TWENTY-TWO

The advancing army halted and spread its line even further. It looked like an ever-growing caterpillar with prickly, shining spines along its back. Ingram strove to spot O'Rourke in the crowd, but the faces of the enemy seemed strangely alike at this distance, all stern and implacable and determined to rid the land of the evil of Dermot MacMurrough.

Ingram drew in his breath. But for Eva, he would not be here. Because of Eva, he would fight and break an unchangeable vow.

He raised his hand through the rain, gave a terrible yell, and spurred his horse. The animal leaped ahead, and Ingram drew his sword, prepared to do battle.

The silent torrent of arrows from the enemy archers fell upon Ingram's charging line even before the two armies met, and Ingram dared not look behind to see how many of his men had fallen. Before the archers had time to fire a second volley, the two lines crashed together with the ring of sword against shield. Warriors cried, horses screamed as they fell in the press and clamor of battle, and black mud from the wounded earth beneath their feet claimed man and beast alike as they fought in the muck.

Ingram fought with the valor of a man who has nothing to lose. His sword, longer than most, darted in and out of the fray with an almost poetic grace, and his small shield proved more than adequate to fend off approaching blows. He had not fought like this since his journey to the Holy Land.

He dueled until he thought his arms would drop from his shoulders, and only when the sounds of conflict quieted around him did he realize that most of the fighting had ended. Few of his men remained on their feet, and when a knot of enemy warriors pinned him against a tree, he realized the battle was completely and soundly lost.

"Say your prayers, for in this hour you die," a man snarled in Gaelic, his short sword at Ingram's throat. Ingram panted against the tree. Blood streamed from a cut on his forehead; when had that happened? He paused to wipe blood from his eye and held up his hand for a moment's peace. For the first time in his life, he had been defeated.

"Kill me, then," he said, his head falling back onto the rough bark of the tree. He closed his eyes, heard the man's swift intake of breath, and steeled himself for the blade across his throat.

"Don't kill this one," a gruff voice called. Ingram opened his eyes. A man with wild blond hair, broad shoulders, and tree-trunk legs had stopped the executioner's sword.

"Donnan." Ingram smiled weakly but did not lift his head. Part of him wanted to die of shame in that moment. He had done the unthinkable, lifting his hand and sword not only against the king he had promised to serve but also against his friends.

"I surrender to you," he whispered, and a dozen hands pulled him into custody.

"Bind him closely," called another husky, familiar voice, and as his hands were forced behind him, Ingram looked up. Before him stood Tiernán O'Rourke, his one eye glaring hotly even in the soft drizzle of the rain. "We shall have much to say to that one."

His hands bound, Ingram avoided the curious stares of O'Rourke's men as he was herded into a knot of other prisoners and forced to follow the mounted army south to Ferns. Not only did Donnan and Ailean ride with O'Rourke, but it was likely that several of these mounted men were the boys Ingram himself had helped train at Dromahair. Disgrace threatened to engulf him; only pride and the hope that Eva still survived allowed Ingram to hold his head high and remain on his weary legs.

They won't like what they find at Ferns, he thought, gazing boldly ahead. *With ten men mounted on the castle walls, Bhaltair could hold the castle for a week, maybe longer.*

O'Rourke's army moved at an almost leisurely pace. When they stood at last on the plain surrounding MacMurrough's castle, Ingram took a quick breath. Something was not right! No smoke lifted from the chimneys; no guards walked the ramparts. What was Bhaltair doing?

A burly warrior came to fetch Ingram from the group of prisoners and pushed him forward until he stood next to O'Rourke. The one-eyed king leaned down from his horse and pointed lazily at the castle. "How inconvenient for us," O'Rourke drawled, speaking slowly. "My scouts report that Dermot MacMurrough is not home. Where has he gone, Sir Ingram?"

"Why should he be home?" Ingram answered, lifting his chin. "Surely he is out defending his rightful kingdom and throne."

"No." O'Rourke looked toward the walls and tightened his grip on his reins. "Dermot MacMurrough is a coward. A frightened servant told us that MacMurrough, his daughter, and a handful of men rode east hours ago. They have gone to the coast, and probably from there on to England."

The news chilled Ingram to the marrow. Could it be true? Had MacMurrough risked the lives of a hundred men in order to turn and run?

O'Rourke studied Ingram's face carefully, then nodded with understanding. "You were used, my friend," he said simply. He turned to his men. "Ride freely into the castle of Dermot MacMurrough," he called. "Tonight we feast on everything good we find there; tomorrow we shall burn the place to the ground."

The men roared in appreciation and streamed through the defenseless gate into the castle.

Ingram's bonds were removed once they were inside, and while the army invaded MacMurrough's stores of food, clothing, furs, and livestock, O'Rourke took Ingram aside and pushed a plate of food in his direction.

"Eat," he urged, chewing on a hunk of the Leinster king's white bread. "And tell me what Dermot MacMurrough could have said to induce you to break the vow of service between us."

"'Twas not MacMurrough," Ingram admitted, feeling like a scolded child. "'Twas his daughter."

"Ah." O'Rourke lifted his brows in comprehension. "I have never seen the lady but have heard of her beauty."

"She is beautiful, and more," Ingram said, staring at the full plate but feeling no appetite. "I told her I would not fight you, but she . . ."

He felt himself blushing. How ridiculous! He was a man grown, not an adolescent boy, yet the memory of Eva's persuasion still embarrassed him. She had played him like a lute, knowing that his infatuation for her would lead him to forget his honor, break his vow, and betray his friend.

"I apologize," Ingram said, pushing the food away. "My life is forfeit to you. I am not worthy to be your friend."

"Dermot MacMurrough is the man not worthy," O'Rourke said. "I shall not claim your life, Sir Ingram, for like Adam in the Garden, you have sinned, but you were deceived by a woman. A curious race, women. 'Tis a bit strange, don't you think, that God put them here to torment us?"

"Aye."

"Then let us drink to them, me friend." O'Rourke stood to his feet and lifted a generous cup of Dermot MacMurrough's ale. "To women, who break us and yet make us what we are."

The men around lifted their cups in a noisy toast. "To women," they cheered. Ingram lifted his cup, too, and drank deeply of the sour ale.

Donal Kavanaugh watched as the last barrel of his father's hastily packed belongings was put aboard the ship that would take Dermot MacMurrough across the Irish Sea. He had come alone to respond to his father's summons, leaving behind his band of thieves and troublemakers. Let them prey on hapless travelers and feast on poached venison without him, for Donal Kavanaugh would answer the call of his father's voice. In it, he knew, lay his destiny.

"Are you sure you should go?" he asked, studying his father's face carefully. The vein in Dermot MacMurrough's forehead had swelled like a thick, black snake; the flight from Ferns had taken its toll on the proud man's appearance.

"This must be done," his father answered, his voice hoarse from shouting commands to the sailors who had worked like dogs to ready the king's ship. "I've always done what I had to do. It is the only way, Donal. I will rely on you to stay behind and represent me in this land of ours."

Donal Kavanaugh blinked as a wave of admiration and fear swept over him. The man before him, who seemed almost weak in his weariness, could not be ignored. He had, Donal knew, gained the throne of Leinster by killing two rival princes and blinding a third. Now MacMurrough was determined to regain his throne by bringing in foreigners who would teach lessons in bloodshed to the Irish who had cast him out.

"You, Donal," his father said, placing a heavy hand upon his shoulder. "As I love you, remain here and guard me interests. Do nothing openly, but watch and listen. Keep your ear to the ground and your face to the wind. Learn what plans me enemies have laid for me so that revenge will be all the sweeter when I return."

"Yes, Father." Donal paused, searching for words that would prolong the bittersweet farewell. "Do any of our men remain at Ferns?"

MacMurrough shook his head. "I doubt it. I sent all the able-bodied men near Ferns to certain death. 'Twill rid the land of any who might join with our enemies in our absence, so our return will be safer. Ingram led them into battle."

"Ingram?"

The king shrugged. "A mighty warrior who has served me for some time. Despite Ingram's considerable ingenuity, I fear they are all captured or have perished."

Donal searched his memory; the name still did not register. "Have I met this Ingram?"

"No." MacMurrough's eyes flitted carefully over Donal's face; then his face erupted into a grin. "I know you are a jealous sort, Donal, so I kept him from you. He was much like you—dedicated, handsome, skillful to a fault." He clapped his heavy hand on his son's shoulder. "But never you worry, me son, he's probably dead. Led the charge, he did, and I don't think we'll be seeing him again."

Donal grinned through clenched teeth as his father turned toward the boat. "There's nothing to worry about. I am not truly jealous, Father."

MacMurrough turned over his shoulder and lifted a warning finger. "Don't call me that." He lowered his voice. "Though you are me favorite son, none must know it now. Wait, Donal, until I sit on the throne of the *ard-ri;* then you shall broadcast it to the world."

Donal Kavanaugh nodded in reply and stepped back into the shadows as his father stepped gingerly over the small gangplank that led aboard the small ship. His half brothers and half sister were already aboard with a handful of his father's warriors. Donal could do nothing but wait and follow his father's commands.

As the ship prepared to embark, a dark thundercloud moved over the water, and lightning cracked the skies. Dermot MacMurrough lifted his hand in a final farewell. Niall and Peadar, who stood by their father's side, did not salute him but stared coldly over the stern of the boat. Very well. Even though they carried their father's name, it would be he, Donal Kavanaugh, who followed Dermot MacMurrough into greatness.

By torchlight that night the assembled kings of Ireland met at the conquered castle with Rory O'Connor, the *ard-ri,* and listened with respect as he divided the land. "Our thanks to Tiernán O'Rourke for ridding Ireland of this difficult king," O'Connor said, nodding to O'Rourke. "From this day forward this island shall be whole and complete. Her princes shall rule her kingdoms: Munster shall be ruled by Dermot MacCarthy and Donal Mór O'Brien; Meath by Tiernán O'Rourke and Dermot O'Melaghlin; Leinster by Donal MacGillapatric of Ossory and the rebel king's brother, Merchad MacMurrough; the kingdoms of the north by Niall Murcertach and Aedh O'Neill. Let us, one month from today, celebrate the Tailten games at the ancient hill of Tara, and let there be no more war between us."

The kings nodded in agreement, and the assembled men roared their approval. But from where he sat between Donnan and Ailean, Ingram scarcely heard O'Connor's words. He had much on his mind: why—and if—Eva had betrayed him.

HENRY II
1166

For I, the LORD your God, am a jealous God,
punishing the children for the sin of the fathers
to the third and fourth generation of those who hate me,
but showing love to a thousand generations of
those who love me and keep my commandments.

EXODUS 20:5-6

Twenty-three

The sea swelled gently under the bow of the ship, and a warm spring breeze teased Eva's long, dark hair as she searched the cloudless horizon for some sight of land. Before the day ended, she would be in the domain of Henry II, King of England, Normandy, Toulouse, Wales, and Scotland.

What would this king require of them? She knew full well that her father would not rest until he had procured Henry's aid in regaining the throne from which he had been so thoroughly displaced. But her father had nothing to offer but his loyalty—and *her*.

The sea captain's young daughter whimpered behind her, and Eva turned to see the girl's mother gather the tired child into her arms. A tiny thread of jealousy wound itself around her heart. She had never known a mother's loving arms, for her mother had died while Eva was yet a baby.

What would it be like, she wondered, to creep into a tender embrace and find comfort, to know that nothing and no one could disturb your peace and rest? She had known something of that peace in her flirtatious rendezvous with Ingram, for no matter how she teased him, something in his steadfast nature made her feel safe, secure, and protected.

Her face hardened as she turned back to the sea. Though she had not known a mother, she had learned to endure as a woman. She knew the rules of survival. The first, a precept she had learned by herself, was that the weapon of beauty

233

could not be underestimated. The second, which her father had taught her, was that success could be found in knowing the strengths of an enemy and the weaknesses of a friend.

Dermot MacMurrough had taken pains to insure he would not arrive in England penniless. For more than a year he had been safeguarding his future, sending gold and silver to a certain steward in Bristol, and even now the man bobbed before him, bowing and flourishing a ridiculous feathered cap. "All is in readiness, my king," the man said, his boarish eyes squinting at Eva even as he bowed before her father.

"None of that," MacMurrough snapped, jerking the man upright as he passed. "No bowing to me in this land of Henry's, and don't call me king. None is king here but Henry, and I won't have it said that I've been forgetting that."

"Of course not, sir." The steward stood stiffly upright and smoothed the fawning expression from his face. "All is in readiness, as I said. The house has been procured, the horses arranged—"

"Good." MacMurrough moved swiftly away from the docks. "We are fifteen in number. Make haste, man, and show us the way, for there is not a moment to be wasted."

The steward, Bert, had arranged for MacMurrough and his party to headquarter in a large house in Bristol. Eva hated it the moment they arrived. How different it was from the stone palace in Leinster! Unlike the spacious emerald fields of Ferns, Bristol's narrow streets roared with noisy life. The houses squatted behind tiny, muddy garden plots, each not more than a stone's throw from its neighbor. Why, not even the busy Norse cities in Ireland were this shabby!

As Eva alighted from the mare Bert had provided, she reached out for the arm of her father. "I hope our stay here will not be long. I don't know how long I can endure this."

MacMurrough gave her a reassuring smile and drew her arm through his as they walked through the cheerless courtyard. "Not long at all, my dear; haven't I said so? Bert's wife will be your maid and companion while the men and I ride in search of Henry. As soon as we receive his help, we will return to our own land with the full honor we deserve."

"Can't I go along? Is there anything I can do?"

MacMurrough patted her hand. "You know, my dear, that I do this for you. I would see you properly wed, with a valiant husband who will love you as you ought to be loved. I would see your children ruling the land that is rightfully ours, by the ancient laws of the *ard-ri.* . . ."

He drifted away on the ocean of his ambition; she cleared her throat to regain his attention. "Still, Father, I could help you. Remember my plan for Dervorgilla? And how I helped rid you of the troublesome Loaghair?"

Her father's face softened in a smile. "Yes, my lamb; there is no one like you for strategy."

"So if I can help you now, tell me your problem, the entire truth, so that I may see our situation clearly."

They paused at the imposing door of the house, and Bert sprinted forward to open it. Eva did not look up but kept her eyes on her father's face until he answered. "If you would aid our suit, Eva, then remain pure and beautiful. Think always of yourself as a bride worth winning. In time, our plans shall come to fruition."

They stepped into a long corridor, and Bert shuffled forward and bowed again. "If you please, my lord, my wife has prepared a dinner for you and your guests."

"Very well, then," MacMurrough said, dropping Eva's arm as he raised his hand for all to follow. "To the banquet hall! Let us partake of the goodness of England and drink to her king!"

The men roared in salute, and Eva followed, hoping Henry would prove to be all her father thought he was.

The warriors in Dermot's banquet hall ate and drank with more abandon than usual, Bhaltair thought, probably because they drank to forget that they had left other comrades behind on a battlefield and almost certainly had consigned them to death. Peadar and Niall sat across from their father, enjoying his uncharacteristic good humor and undemanding attention, while Eva ate slowly, spooning delicate mouthfuls of a savory pottage without compliment or complaint. Gladys and Bert hovered nervously in the background, taking care that bowls and cups were kept filled and that the master's bread was warm from the oven.

Only Bhaltair had no appetite. He tried to keep pace with his fellow warriors at his table, raising his cup with them and cheering the victory that had been promised, but he felt anything but victorious. He could not forget that he had pledged to support Ingram on the field of battle, and instead he had followed his master and fled to England. Ingram, Bhaltair knew, would never have done such a thing.

In the three years he had known Ingram, Bhaltair had observed that Ingram was distinctly different from other warriors. As a skilled fighter, Ingram had no peer, but the warrior from Glendalough fought by an invisible code that Bhaltair could not grasp. Commanded to punish a guilty rebel, Ingram complied, but he would quietly spare the man's wife and children. If charged to burn a rebellious village, Ingram obeyed, but he would not allow a torch inside the village walls until he had cleared the place of every man, woman, child, and domestic animal.

Before Ingram's arrival Bhaltair had engaged in ruthless destruction, never considering anything but his master's ultimate authority and his own pleasure in brute force. But Ingram had demonstrated power under control, gentleness in strength, and conditional obedience that seemed to acknowledge a master far above Dermot MacMurrough.

Bhaltair remembered a day when he and Ingram had

found a little girl lost in the drumlins of Leinster. Days before, MacMurrough had commanded a rebellious family's *rath* to be burned, and Ingram had ordered the family to flee before he allowed his men to set fire to the buildings. Bhaltair knew that the little girl had probably been lost in the haste and confusion as the family had fled with their meager belongings.

The little girl had just stood there while the two men approached, her eyes wide with fear. "It's best we leave her," Bhaltair said, steadying his stallion. "She's already perishing with the hunger; she won't live long."

Ingram had glared at him in disbelief. "We won't leave her," he declared, dismounting from his horse. He gathered the dirty child into his arms and smoothed her tousled hair. "We'll find someone to feed her and charge them to search for her parents. I'll give my last ounce of gold to make sure she finds her family again."

"MacMurrough won't like it," Bhaltair had pointed out. "She's only a peasant's child and such a wee thing as not to be bothered with."

"She'll be bothered with, and the devil take MacMurrough," Ingram had answered, remounting with the child in his arms. "There are authorities, Bhaltair, higher than the king of Leinster."

Though he never spoke specifically of his "higher authority," still Ingram behaved as though someone else watched and judged him, a great overlord to whom Ingram would someday give an accounting. If such an overlord did weigh the hearts of men and kings, Bhaltair thought, surely he was displeased with MacMurrough, the king who had misled his own men. Was he also displeased with Bhaltair for abandoning his fellow and friend?

His conscience had bothered him on the entire journey across the sea, and now that they ate and drank in relative ease and comfort, Bhaltair could not enjoy himself. If Ingram still lived, did he face torture? Would he be killed in retribution for the destruction carried out by MacMurrough's men over the years of rival feuding?

Bhaltair stared at his food and wine, unable to eat or drink.

"What ails you, Bhaltair?" MacMurrough's hoarse voice cut through the hubbub at the warriors' table, and every voice stilled.

Bhaltair hesitated. It might not be wise to speak the entire truth. "I was thinking of Ingram," he said slowly.

"Aye," MacMurrough said. He lifted his cup to his lips in a silent salute, then drank deeply. When he had put his cup down and wiped his mouth on his sleeve, he spoke. "That brave and estimable warrior is now certainly dead; don't you agree, me lad?"

"Aye, that's what I was thinking."

MacMurrough nodded. "Well, I should think he died the way he wanted, eh, lad? Rode out in a blaze of glory, fighting for a cause and against strong odds—"

"We were supposed to protect his southern flank!" Bhaltair interrupted, slamming his meaty fist down upon the table. "He could have held 'em for a while. Ingram was a good warrior; he could have thought of something!"

"He knew what he was doing, Bhaltair." Eva's voice cut through his confusion like a hot knife. "He knew the situation was grim, and he didn't want to fight. But when I asked him to proceed, for me, he submitted."

Bhaltair felt his jaw drop, and his face burned with embarrassment. Princess Eva had asked Ingram to fight for *her*? Suddenly, Bhaltair understood the glances he had intercepted, the occasions he had found Eva and Ingram together in the stable.

Eva shot him a frosty glance. "Close your mouth, Bhaltair, and know this: Ingram loved me and was willing to die for me. That's all there is to it. You should not feel guilt for leaving him to do what he chose to do."

"Then why . . ." He paused, the words forming with difficulty. "Then why did we sneak away? Why didn't we tell him we were leaving?"

"Because," MacMurrough said, anger edging his voice,

"like all great warriors, Ingram wanted to pretend he had a chance of winning. You wouldn't deny him that illusion, would you, Bhaltair?"

Bhaltair shook his head slowly, and MacMurrough nodded in satisfaction. "It is good we've had this discourse," he said, slicing a piece of beef with his dagger as he raised his voice so all could hear. "Now let us forget the past and move into the future. Tomorrow we ride south, in search of Henry of England, and all that he can give us."

Eva stood in the muddy courtyard of the house the next morning and watched as her father's men prepared for departure. All ten warriors were already mounted, as were Niall, Peadar, and Bhaltair; her father was still inside with Bert and Gladys, doubtless giving more instructions. When he finally came from the building, she ran forward and caught his arm. "Wait, Father, before you go. I could not sleep last night—something troubles me."

"What is it?" His voice was rough, his mind obviously preoccupied. Eva hurried to make her feelings known.

"Why should Henry agree to our request? What have we to give him, Father? He has no need of our gold. There is no kingdom left to give, and our only asset is—" she hesitated— "me. And why would you give me, Father, to a king who has already married and had sons?"

The question caught him by surprise. "Give you to Henry?" He threw back his head and laughed. "No, my dear. Though you are beautiful enough for the wenching Henry, I would not give you to a man already married. You would be nothing more than a king's toy, and no daughter of mine will be used in such a way."

"Then why should Henry help us?"

A misty veil seemed to come down over his eyes. "Ah, my darling Eva, what I will offer is Ireland itself. Henry will hear tales of our Emerald Isle and will so covet it that he will be required to come to our aid."

"Ireland? But you, Father, want to be high king."

"You're forgetting what I've taught you, Eva," he answered, wagging his finger at her like a scolding tutor. He walked to his horse and mounted in one smooth movement. "Know your enemy," he whispered, leaning down to her. "Henry is a mighty king, with a vast empire. He will not be able to rule Ireland, Normandy, England, and all those other kingdoms alone. He must have a deputy, one to rule in his place. And who better than Dermot MacMurrough?"

He sat upright and pulled back the reins so swiftly that his horse wheeled and snorted in protest. "Forward, men!" he cried, scraping his spur across the horse's tender flank. "Henry awaits us."

TWENTY-FOUR

Donal Kavanaugh reclined by the fire in the woods with three of his fellow outlaws. The men were in high spirits, having robbed and killed a prosperous merchant and his wife that afternoon. Now, as they drank the merchant's ale, they called for their leader to join them.

But Donal Kavanaugh was in no mood for sport. The memory of his father's words set his teeth on edge . . . words of praise for the warrior named Ingram, a man his father had admired and appreciated. The fact that his father had sent Ingram to die was a small and insufficient consolation.

Frustrated, he put down his dagger and the slender branch he had been whittling. "What have you heard of a warrior called Ingram?" he called, his nasal voice stilling the revelry of his men. They paused; the only sound that remained was the sharp and brittle crack of weathered wood in the fire.

"Ingram? I do not know the name," Frang answered.

"He rode with MacMurrough's men. He led the charge against O'Connor."

Kavanaugh's other two cohorts, Cailean and Iain, looked at each other and shrugged. "We know nothing of him."

"I would know whether he is living or dead," Donal said, turning back to the fire. He picked up his branch and dagger and resumed whittling. "Find out for me."

Cailean's dark face blanched. "Now, Donal?"

"Now," Kavanaugh said, the blade of his knife reflecting

241

the flames. "Ride north to Meath or into Breifne, and find out who this man is and whether or not he lives. I will meet you later, at the hut by the River Barrow."

The three moved slowly toward their horses. Cailean paused and ran his hands through his hair. "The merchant and his woman," he said, spreading his hands. "Should we bury them?"

Kavanaugh did not look up. "Did you pull them away from the road?"

"Yes," Cailean said, his brows rising in relief. "They lie under shrubbery twenty paces from the road."

"They are nothing. Leave them for the wolves."

Donal Kavanaugh slept by the fire, his dagger at his side, dreaming fitfully of a warrior in black who shadowed his movements and stole his horse, his boots, his blade. "Who are you?" Kavanaugh called in his dreams, grasping through a dark mist for the elusive gremlin who haunted him. "Who are you?"

When he awoke, the frustrated rage within him had become a living thing, a jealousy that did not dissipate as the fog of sleep lifted. He stood from the sand, brushed leaves and dirt from his cloak, and ran his dagger over a stone to whet the blade. He had not felt like killing last night; his men had murdered the merchant couple. But today Kavanaugh's blade thirsted for the blood of one man—this mysterious Ingram who dared surface in his dreams. Donal hoped the man had not died in battle, for he could not rest until he had killed the man himself.

Kavanaugh went to his horse and tightened the leather strap that tied his bow and arrows across the saddle. It would be a day's ride to the hut by the River Barrow.

Iain, Frang, and Cailean met him at the hut two days later, breathless and upon fresh horses. "We returned straight-away," Iain explained, dismounting. "We have news."

"Tell it then," Kavanaugh said, looking up from the rabbit he was skinning. He glanced from one face to the other, even as his men looked to each other to see who would speak first.

"Ingram is alive," Frang said finally. "And not a prisoner. He sat yesterday at the kings' dinner table with Tiernán O'Rourke and Rory O'Connor."

Kavanaugh felt a curious, tingling shock. "The man who led my father's force sits with two enemy kings?" he asked, wiping his bloody hands on his tunic. "The battle at Ferns—how many died?"

"Of MacMurrough's men, nearly all. They were but farmers."

"And of O'Rourke's men?"

"Very few," Iain answered. "'Twas said that Ingram's men fought bravely to the end but were felled by the mud and a superior force. Ingram surrendered when he knew the battle was done."

"Of course." Kavanaugh slammed his dagger into the ground. "The scoundrel plotted from the beginning to surrender to his friends. He has betrayed my father!"

He stalked to Cailean and grabbed the man by the throat. "Who is this Ingram? Where does he come from? What is his family?"

"I-I cannot say," Cailean answered, his face distorted with fear. "No one knew. Some called him a knight; others said he was a farmer."

"Where did he serve before he came to Ferns?"

Kavanaugh released Cailean and turned his furious glance upon Iain. The younger man squinted. "I heard one of O'Rourke's captains say that Ingram used to train that king's warriors. Another said Ingram came from Waterford, where he had once been wounded."

"Waterford." Kavanaugh's smile overflowed with cruel confidence. "We're but a day's ride from Waterford, and I'll be wanting to talk to the good folk of that city. 'Tis a bit strange, don't you think, that no one claims this mysterious Ingram?"

"O'Rourke and O'Connor claimed him readily enough," Frang grumbled. "Don't you want to ride for Dromahair and take this man on for yourself?"

"Patience, Frang." Kavanaugh plucked his dagger from the ground and nestled it into his belt. "Though my dagger yearns to slake its appetite on his blood, me father has taught me well. If you wish to destroy an enemy, you don't come at him face-to-face. You come from the side, or from behind, and when he least expects your attack."

"But if this Ingram is as strong as the warriors say he is—," Iain began.

"Even then, we shall conquer him," Kavanaugh answered. "It will take time and persistence. But make no mistake, we shall defeat him."

The road before Donal Kavanaugh and his three companions cleared as they entered Waterford. As if they smelled the warning stench of decay, passersby sensed trouble in the men's seditious glances. Women pulled their children out of the street, and men stepped away from their doorways as the four rode into town.

"Where do we begin?" Cailean asked, peering into a house where a pretty young girl had fled. "Do we go from house to house and ask for news of this man?"

"No," Kavanaugh answered. "We visit the places most likely to be visited by a warrior—the inn, the doctor, the shipyard, the smithy. Someone in this place knows this man."

Signe heard the news first from her neighbor, Diana. "Donal Kavanaugh and his men are in the city," Diana whispered at the window, her pretty, plump face tinged with pink. "Me husband saw Donal limping about at the inn, and the tanner's wife said he spent the morning at the shipyard."

"What brings that bag of trouble to Waterford?" Signe remarked carelessly, pulling her young son's dirty hands from her skirt.

Diana's eyes went round. "They are searching, I heard, for a man called Ingram. This man supposedly was wounded here and came to see the doctor or something. . . ."

Signe's heart began to pound as Diana peered down the road. "Och, and me husband's coming, Signe. He won't take to me gossiping about anything to do with that snake Donal Kavanaugh—that's for certain."

Diana's curly head disappeared in a flash between the shutters. Signe turned automatically to lift her son into her arms as her mind blew open with memories she had long suppressed. Ingram! Had he come to Waterford without seeing her? Why would Donal Kavanaugh be interested in him?

As she turned, her eyes fell on her cot. She groaned. *Holy Father, preserve us!* It had been fifteen years since Ingram had thwarted Donal Kavanaugh and been wounded in her defense. Was it possible that Kavanaugh searched for Ingram because of that bloody day? No one else in town would know Ingram or his name unless he had visited Waterford recently, and in her heart, she knew he had not. He would have come to see her if he had.

She tightened her grip around her son, grabbed her six-year-old daughter firmly by the hand, and led them to Diana's house. "You're going to stay with Auntie Diana while Mother runs to see Grandfather," she said lightly, her steps skimming the damp pavement beneath her feet. "No crying now, and no questions. Mommy must hurry."

She thrust her children into Diana's outstretched arms and flew away before her inquisitive neighbor had a chance to ask what urgent errand compelled her to go.

The sun blazed unusually hot for September, and Donal Kavanaugh felt his temper growing short with every moment he stood in its relentless heat. The shipyards had yielded no information, neither had the inn, and the young doctor in Waterford had only been practicing medicine for five years. Aggravated, Kavanaugh sent his companions to sample the innkeeper's ale while he rode alone to the smithy.

Once he dismounted, he was glad he had come alone. The stocky smith might have looked askance at four mounted men, but he smiled pleasantly at Kavanaugh and took a moment to wipe a veil of moisture from his shining forehead before advancing to meet his guest. His helper, a younger man, stood as well, carefully regarding Kavanaugh's appearance.

"Good day, and may I help you, me friend?" the older man asked. "I am Erik Lombay, and I am pleased to serve you."

"Yes, you may help, but my business does not concern your forge," Kavanaugh answered, taking pains to be pleasant as he walked into the shade of the smithy. He shifted his weight to take pressure off his weak leg. "I have come searching for news of a friend—I know him only as Ingram, a mighty warrior, and confederate of kings."

The aged smith put his hands to his back and stretched slowly, as if taking a moment to think. He had rounded shoulders, a bent back, and a protruding potbelly—not at all the sort who would fellowship with a warrior. The younger man said nothing but wiped his hands on his leather breeches, and after a moment Kavanaugh decided that these men knew nothing.

"Excuse me, good sirs, for taking your time. But I have urgent news for me friend Ingram—"

"Don't go," the smith interrupted, his eyes twinkling. "It's been so long since I heard from the knight, I took a moment to consider your question. Are you truly a friend of his? Where did you meet him?"

"At Ferns," Kavanaugh replied slowly, hoping the man would ask nothing further. "Where did you meet him?"

"Ah, 'twas a long time ago, and I'm not really remembering."

The smith grinned pleasantly enough, but suspicion lurked in his eyes. And Kavanaugh felt himself growing impatient. "I assure you, sir, that I have only honorable intentions in mind—"

"And why would you be seeking Ingram?"

Kavanaugh scratched his beard, searching for a plausible lie.

"You hesitate, sir. A noble man would not hesitate but would speak the truth clearly and honestly."

The rushing sounds of a long tunic and a quick step interrupted Kavanaugh's reply, and he looked over his shoulder. A woman had entered, her cloak askew. She did not pause to look behind the door but walked directly to the older man.

"Father, Donal Kavanaugh and his men are in the city seeking news of Ingram."

The smith's eye flashed in warning, but Kavanaugh stepped out from behind the doorway. "You speak, gentle lady, of me."

She whirled around at his voice, and something in her wide, frightened eyes struck a chord of memory within him. Where had he seen those green eyes, fringed with fear? Not in the city, like this, but in the woods, where she ran from him with the speed and grace of a deer. . . .

He pointed at her, then pressed his fingertip to his lips. "Can it be that we have met before, my pretty colleen?"

"You will not speak so to her," the younger man at the forge bellowed, stepping forward.

"Whisht! Be quiet," Kavanaugh ordered, scowling at the man.

The girl lifted her chin in a flash of arrogance, and Kavanaugh smiled in total recognition. Of course! He had seen her in the woods, had given chase, and had met with a troublesome knight on the road to Waterford. The knight had been dispatched easily enough, but this green-eyed wench had taken up a sword and threatened him, Donal Kavanaugh!

A dim ripple ran across his mind. By all the fairies of Ireland, was it possible that the knight *lived*? And could he be the cursed Ingram he had come to find?

Kavanaugh forced himself to remain calm. "You speak of me, lady, and of one called Ingram. I would know more about him. Did he materialize from the fairy glens in the wood on the day we last met, or is he, perhaps, an old lover?"

She flushed to the roots of her hair and glanced at the younger man at the forge. Intuitively, Kavanaugh understood that these two were husband and wife. "You must tell me all you know, or I will tell your husband here what I know of you and Ingram!"

"There is nothing to tell! I will say nothing!"

"Oh no?"

In one swift movement he stood behind her, his arm around her throat. He pulled his dagger from his belt and poised it above her heart. "While our lady here remains silent, old man, you will tell me all you know of Ingram. Tell me truly, and speak quickly, or the lady dies."

The smith trembled, his jaw flapped wordlessly, and Kavanaugh was afraid the old man would drop dead before he could speak.

"Listen, now, I don't know this Ingram, but you must unhand my wife!" the younger man roared, his face purple with rage.

"You will be quiet or lose your wife," Kavanaugh replied smoothly. "Sit still, man, and be patient until the tale is told. Erik Lombay, start at the beginning and do not stop until I know all there is to know of the man called Ingram."

"Sir Ingram," Erik breathed softly.

"A knight?"

"Yes, a knight." The old man drew a ragged breath. "From England."

"Go on."

The old man spoke slowly, feeling his way through the memories. "The knight was wounded and left in the road to die. Me own Signe brought help, and we took the knight to our house and nursed him till he was fit."

"What was he doing in Waterford?"

"I don't know. He came to Ireland to search for his parents."

"His parents?"

"Aye. He told an unusual tale—a monk stole him away from a monastery in Ireland, took him to England, and left him at a castle where he was reared as a knight."

"The name of this castle!"

"South something." The smith lifted a trembling finger to his lips, and Kavanaugh twisted the point of the blade into the fabric of Signe's tunic. She gasped, and the old man continued: "Southwick, that was it! There he was much loved and reared as a knight."

"Everyone loves him," Kavanaugh repeated dully. So the knight he had left for dead in the road had risen to haunt him again. This time the man usurped Donal Kavanaugh's place not with a wench but in his father's affection.

"Of course his upbringing was obvious in those days," the smith went on, his tongue loosening as the blade remained above his daughter's heart. "He didn't speak a word of Gaelic. But when he came through here three years ago, he spoke the language like he had been born to it."

"Now it gets interesting," Kavanaugh interrupted smoothly, the knife twisting in the dim light of the fire. "Tell me, please, Erik Lombay, where had the knight been? Did he find his parents?"

"Aye." The smith frowned and scratched his head. "In Leinster somewhere. A mountainous place, he said."

"Wicklow? Glendalough? Kildare? Speak, man!"

The old man nodded vigorously. "Glendalough, that's it. He found his parents, had a son—"

"Good." Kavanaugh smiled with genuine feeling. "That is good. Erik Lombay, you and your lovely daughter have been of much help to me. Perhaps I will let you live."

He released his arm from Signe and felt her shudder as

he moved away from her. "Good day," he called pleasantly, moving toward the door.

Without warning the younger man at the forge erupted in violence, leaping over the flaming hearth. "Monster! I will kill you!" the man screamed. Kavanaugh turned in surprise.

No effort was needed; the younger man threw himself onto the dagger in Kavanaugh's hand, impaling himself neatly. Kavanaugh struggled with the weight of the dead man on his arms, then let the man slide to the floor before bending to retrieve his dagger.

"It's a good blade," he said, wiping it carefully on the folds of the dead man's tunic as the wife and smith watched in horror. "I'll not leave it behind."

Kavanaugh sheathed his dagger and moved quickly to his horse. He would fetch his men and be out of the city before any of these tightly knit Ostmen put his head on a pole.

TWENTY-FIVE

At eighteen, Lucais was the youngest of MacMurrough's warriors and the best horseman. He left his royal master at the Norman seaport of Cherbourg and engaged the swiftest horse possible for a frantic ride to the castle Gisors, where Henry II was holding court. The honor of responsibility bore heavily on his shoulders, and when he finally rode through the castle gates, lather dripped from his trembling horse.

Masons and carpenters buzzed about the inner courtyard of the castle where a new tower was under construction, and a highly decorated knight at the gate stopped Lucais. The knight cast a censuring look at the quivering stallion and murmured something in French.

"I'm sorry, I do not understand," Lucais answered in English, nodding respectfully at the knight.

"What business commands you to ride a horse till he nearly drops?" the guard demanded, his hand gripping the hilt of his sword. "Speak, boy, and quickly, before I lop off your head for doing injury to this beast!"

"I come with an urgent message for His Royal Highness," Lucais answered, taking a deep breath. "From the King of Leinster of Ireland, Dermot MacMurrough."

The guard smirked at this announcement. "From whom? I've never heard of such a king."

"You will soon!" Lucais's face blazed red in indignation. "My master is marching south even now to meet with Henry about an issue of vital concern to both kings."

"Give me the letter and be off with you," the guard replied, holding out his gloved hand.

Lucais shook his head and clutched the leather satchel containing MacMurrough's letter. "No. My orders are to place this missive in the hand of none other but the king himself. I'll gladly die if you ask me to do otherwise."

An unwilling smile flitted across the guard's face. "Have your way then, young man. I'll escort you to the chamber where His Highness is holding court, but he is so taken now with the building of his tower, you'll be lucky if he even glances your way."

The great hall into which Lucais was led was grander than anything he had seen in Ireland. The ceiling loomed high overhead; the aged, dark wood under his feet echoed with his footsteps and the movements of a score of other men. An enormous fire roared in the fireplace to ward off October's chill. At the end of the room, on a raised dais, a man in a scarlet cloak sat and regarded a series of parchments laid on the floor. Two men in simple robes gestured frantically to the scrawled drawings and murmured to the king in French.

The guard motioned for Lucais to take a seat on a bench against the far wall, where other men in various forms of dress waited for an audience or word with the king. Lucais took his place, relaxed his hold on the leather satchel, and evaluated his surroundings as the desperation of youth goaded him to formulate a plan.

There were but three knights in the room, two by the doorway and one by the fire. A daring plan might cost him his life, but he would have no life if he returned to MacMurrough without giving his message to Henry.

Lucais turned his attention to the man on the dais. Henry II was not old—indeed, could not be past his third decade. His eyes were alert, carefully regarding one architect and then the other, his manner relaxed. His auburn hair barely touched his shoulders; a brown beard covered his chin and upper lip only; his cheeks were bare. He had a durably boyish face, and Lucais felt comforted. This was not the face of a madman or tyrant.

Without further consideration, Lucais stood. "Live forever, King Henry!" he shouted, as every man in the room froze at the unexpected sound. "I bring you an urgent message from King Dermot MacMurrough of Leinster." Lucais pulled the parchment from his satchel with a great flourish and advanced toward the king. The two knights at the door sprang to intercept him with drawn swords, but Lucais simply dropped to one knee and held the letter forth. "Please, sir, with the honor one king would give another, my master begs that you consider his plea."

Henry glanced at his knights with amusement and wonder; then he smiled at Lucais, leaned forward in his chair, and spoke in French while motioning to a monk who stood at the back of the room.

The monk came forward, bowed to the king, and replied smoothly in words Lucais couldn't understand. The king spoke again, laughing, and the monk turned to Lucais. "His Royal Highness wishes me to serve as interpreter for you," he said. "The king would like to know if you are the best your king has to offer?"

Henry's voice had been soft and eminently reasonable, and Lucais found hope in his words.

"Tell him, please, that I am not the best, but the youngest. My king of Leinster has been forced to flee his kingdom in Ireland and now rides south with the hope of apprehending His Royal Highness so that they may speak face-to-face."

The message was translated; Henry pursed his lips, then leaned back in his chair and replied. The monk translated: "His Highness will excuse your rude actions here today on behalf of your master. You may tell him that the king will see him when he arrives, and until then—" Henry waved his hand in a gesture of dismissal and shrugged. "Until then," the monk went on, "may God keep him safe."

Lucais stood and bowed.

The king barked an order; the monk bowed and turned again to Lucais. "You are to go now," he said, stepping back to clear the way for the two knights who stood at Lucais's side.

The guards grasped the boy by the arms and dragged him from the chamber, but not before Lucais managed to toss the sealed parchment at Henry's feet.

"Another letter from Dermot MacMurrough, Irish king of Leinster, awaits your pleasure." The nobleman in attendance upon King Henry II spoke in flawless French and with the stiffest of expressions.

Henry dismissed the man and the letter upon his tray with a gesture of impatience. "Confound the man! Why does he hound me thus? We left Gisors and rode south to escape him in Normandy, Maine, and Anjou, and still the Irishman follows!" Henry lifted the letter, broke the seal, then frowned in impatience and thrust it away from him. "The fool writes in English, too. Does he not know I choose to speak only French?"

"He will not be dissuaded, my king. Perhaps you should grant him an audience and consider Ireland."

The notion struck Henry as so ridiculous that he laughed. "Bah! Consider Ireland? Henry I considered Ireland, and so did William called the Conqueror. Both, in their wisdom, deigned it better to leave that backward land alone."

"My son."

The words were offered as a polite introduction, and every noble head save one bowed to the elderly lady who approached the throne. Henry sat in polite indifference as his mother, Empress Matilda, made her way through the knot of men who waited before him. As much as he would like to undo the velvet cords with which she bound him, Henry could never forget that she had bargained his way onto the throne. More than that, the empress, his mother, possessed an ageless wisdom that served him well.

"Welcome, Mother," he said, giving her a barely perceptible nod. "Have you heard much of the conversation?"

"All." The empress took a seat on a padded chair near her son's side. "I know that Dermot MacMurrough of Leinster seeks your aid."

"I won't go there. The Irish are unpredictable and archaic. Their ridiculous notions—"

"—are the talk of the markets and seaports," his mother finished for him. "Surely you have heard, my son, of the wealth of Dublin? The monasteries of Ireland alone, I have heard, contain gold enough to entice Viking raiders for hundreds of years, and the countryside is green and productive. Perhaps it is time to think of Ireland."

Henry gaped at his mother. "Time, now? Years ago I mentioned the idea to you, and you dissuaded me!"

"Your hold on England alone was tenuous at that time," his mother replied, pulling a bit of embroidery from the pocket hidden in the voluminous folds of her tunic. "You were young and untried. But now, Henry, may be the time to consider Ireland."

He turned to the nobleman before him, who assiduously raised his eyes to the ceiling and pretended not to notice his king's discomfiture. Henry clenched his fists in silence. They would say his mother ruled the kingdom through her son, a mere puppet king. But still, if there were riches in Ireland . . .

"Begging Your Highness's permission." The tall counselor, Ambroise, bowed and took a step forward.

"Speak."

"If you will recall, noble sire, a dozen years ago His Holiness, Pope Adrian, issued a bull investing Your Highness with the right to rule Ireland. The emerald ring, which the pope sent as a symbol of your royal investiture, still waits in the royal strongbox."

A rush of anticipatory adrenaline struck Henry. "You speak truly, Ambroise," he said, snapping his fingers at a knight near the doorway. "Quick, knight, bring the ring. It is an emerald, set in gold, and probably still contained in the velvet pouch in which it arrived from Rome. . . ."

The knight rushed to do his king's bidding, and Henry smiled at his mother in an overflow of well-being. "Ireland, after all, is ours for the taking," he told her. "Pope Adrian was most concerned that we see to the affairs of the church in that riotous land. We have heard rumors, have we not, of terrible deeds, atrocious lapses in religion—"

"Married monks," his mother added, not looking up from her needlework. "Monasteries given as inheritances to abbots' sons."

"Undisciplined collection of tithes," added Ambroise, bowing again.

"Yes!" Henry clapped his hands in approval, then rubbed them together as he considered the new idea before him. "We shall let this Dermot MacMurrough pursue us farther into Aquitaine, as not to appear too eager—"

"Too eager we cannot be," the empress interrupted. "The pope does not smile on you now, Henry. If you march into Ireland under the flag of God, the issue of Thomas à Becket will arise to haunt you."

At the mention of the name, Henry shrank visibly into his seat. Thomas Becket, once his trusted friend and chief counselor, had turned traitor on the day Henry had begged him to take on the robes of the church and serve the throne of England as Archbishop of Canterbury. Henry had hoped to sway the rebellious English clergy with Becket's appointment, but instead Becket had turned against him, telling Henry that as archbishop he was compelled to obey God rather than the king. Becket had flung himself with passion into his new role and overnight became a staunch defender of the church.

The battle lines were drawn; Henry pursued his former friend zealously while Becket clung more and more fervently to the cause of Christ. For the past two years Becket had exiled himself in France, refusing to face or submit to Henry. During that time Henry stubbornly avoided discussion of Becket with his mother and skirted issues that dealt with the church.

Perhaps his mother was right. Entering Ireland now under the banner of religious restoration would be risky indeed, for the current pope, Alexander III, clearly would not approve of anything Henry did until the king made peace with Thomas à Becket. And Henry, still nursing wounds inflicted by an unfaithful friend, would not make peace until Becket agreed to meet the king's terms.

"Ireland waits not for us, but for Thomas à Becket," Henry said finally, glaring at his mother's profile as if she were the hated Becket himself. "When he agrees to our demands to subject the clergy to the law of the land, we shall be rid of the problem and free to enter Ireland with the blessing of the pope."

A knight approached; the emerald ring, a gift from Pope Adrian IV, shone in his hand.

Henry leaned forward and slipped the ring on his finger.

"Let this Dermot MacMurrough come, and do not forbid him when he finds us at last," he pronounced to all who listened. "We will test the man's mettle and his persistence, and God will show us what time and method we should use to enter Ireland."

In the thick of winter, 1166, Dermot MacMurrough's party found Henry in the southern region of Aquitaine. Henry had heard news of their arrival long before the group reached the house where he had lodged, and he made certain all stood in readiness when MacMurrough of Leinster finally swept through the doorway. This throneless king meant nothing to him, but he presented an opportunity through which Ireland might be won and won easily. In the persistent ambition of Dermot MacMurrough, Henry saw an occasion to let another raise the necessary fortune to wage war *and* fight its battles.

When Dermot MacMurrough and his men at last stood before Henry, the king found an unexpected advantage in the fact that they did not speak the same language. "He speaks no French at all?" Henry asked his counselor, his voice low.

"None, Your Highness. Dermot MacMurrough and his people speak English, Gaelic, and a smattering of Latin, I would presume."

Henry smiled. "Then an interpreter will be necessary. Give him my greetings."

The interpreter bowed to MacMurrough, then extended the king's best wishes in Gaelic. MacMurrough bowed in return and answered in an odd and strangely musical tongue.

"He extends his greetings, his love, and asks your permission to present his request."

"First, tell me what you have learned. What do his people say of this man?" Henry's mouth barely moved; he continued smiling at MacMurrough.

The interpreter's lips drooped in a dry smile as he answered in French. "I spoke to his sons and his men as they waited outside for your attention. They acknowledge that Dermot MacMurrough is a brave and warlike man; his hoarse voice is the result of constantly screaming orders as if in the din of battle. He prefers to be feared rather than loved. He treats his nobles harshly, his sons with cruelty, and his daughter with respect. He is vicious toward his own people and thoroughly hated by most."

Henry forgot himself; his jaw dropped. "His own people say this about him?"

"Aye, my king. Those who journey with him are like martyrs; they take great pleasure in serving such a hard father and taskmaster."

Henry turned to MacMurrough again, newfound respect and knowledge shining in his eyes. "He will be an ideal revolutionary, then," he said, placing his hand upon the chain of gold upon his chest. "Tell him that he has found favor in our sight and that we are willing to hear his request."

The interpreter nodded and repeated the message in Gaelic, and Dermot MacMurrough rose to make his offer.

Stepping forward in the confidence of triumph, MacMurrough put out his hand toward Niall, who produced a calfskin parchment. MacMurrough unrolled it and began to speak clearly, pausing after every few words so the interpreter might explain it fully to the powerful king who sat before him:

"Hear, noble King Henry, whence I was born, of what country.

Of Ireland I was born a lord, in Ireland acknowledged king; but wrongfully my own people have cast me out of my kingdom. To you I come to make complaint, good sire, in the presence of the barons of your empire. Your liege man I shall become henceforth all the days of my life; on condition that you be my helper, so that I do not lose everything, I shall acknowledge you as sire and lord, in the presence of your barons and earls."

Henry waited for a moment in silence as MacMurrough lowered the parchment and studied the young king. After murmuring to his counselor, Henry spoke again, and the interpreter bowed and returned the reply to MacMurrough: "His Royal Highness King Henry, *Rex Angliae, Dux Normaniae, et Aquitainiae, et Comes Andigaviae,* thanks you for your request and your offer of fealty. He will consider your words today and have an answer for you by nightfall. You and your men are welcome here, to eat and drink of our supply and observe our hospitality to its fullest."

Dermot MacMurrough felt his ambition deflate. Henry's response was less than enthusiastic, yet still there was hope. MacMurrough nodded stiffly to the counselor, bowed deeply to the greater king, and led his people out of the hall.

"I don't quite trust him, Empress Mother."

Henry made the bold assertion in the privacy of his bed-chamber, where his wife, mother, and three of his most trusted counselors waited in attendance upon him.

"What is not to trust?" Queen Eleanor asked, her hands fluttering over the needlework in her lap. "He has nothing, so he cannot harm you. Send him on his way, and be done with him."

"Such advice will cause you to lose a great deal," the empress spoke up, her voice querulous with age. "Dermot MacMurrough is an open door to Ireland, and the door has opened to you, Henry. If you send MacMurrough away, to whom will he go? Would you lose Ireland to Louis of France?"

The thought of Louis the Pious in Ireland brought a flush to Henry's cheek. His mother knew just which chords to strike to arouse his fury. Louis was Henry's bitterest rival. . . .

"Louis would not care for Ireland; he is too caught up in the trials of the Holy Land," Eleanor replied, wagging her head.

"Shut up!" Henry roared. "Do not remind me that you know him! Do you think I can forget that he married you first?"

Eleanor flushed to the roots of her hair, and the pretty piece of needlework fell from her hands to the floor. "You are most unkind, my lord," she said, her voice a tremulous whisper. "For you know that I did not love him—"

"Just like I don't love you now," Henry replied automatically. He turned from the sight of his weeping wife and looked to his counselors. "What shall we do, then, to aid Dermot MacMurrough?"

❖ ❖ ❖

The king's answer reached MacMurrough by nightfall, as promised. MacMurrough was disappointed that Henry did not appear personally, but he recognized the bearer of the king's letter as one of the trusted counselors who had stood at Henry's right hand. He bowed deeply as a sign of respect.

"His Highness King Henry wishes me to give you this," the counselor said in careful English, offering a sealed parchment. "It is a letter inviting all citizens of Henry's realm to come to your assistance. All men, whether from Normandy, England, Wales, or Scotland, are encouraged to rally to your cause and may fight for you with His Highness's blessing."

MacMurrough took the parchment and tapped the seal absently with his finger as he thought. He had hoped for more—an army, provisions, weapons—but a letter of approval and support was better than nothing.

"Before you depart, His Highness also wishes me to provision your men with fresh horses, new clothes, and shields painted in His Highness's colors."

"His Highness is most generous." MacMurrough forced a smile.

"Yes."

The counselor bowed and retreated, leaving MacMurrough with the parchment in his hand. After a moment of deliberation, he felt a tug on his sleeve. Niall stood there, a question on his handsome face. "Good news, Father?"

"Not the best, but it will do," MacMurrough replied coldly, turning from his son to his men. "Rest well, warriors, for tomorrow we ride from this place to secure our army. We'll soon be making our way back to reclaim what we lost under Rory O'Connor."

TWENTY-SIX

Donal Kavanaugh and his men rode through the night and slept in the woods by day. Kavanaugh felt more secure moving in darkness, for his entire life had been spent on the shadowed side of respectability, family, and inheritance. His mother, a prostitute of Wexford, had died of disease when he was ten. Kavanaugh had reared himself on the streets of the Norse city, confident of only two things: first, that despite the physical shortcoming that caused him to limp, he was capable of besting stronger and less motivated men; and second, that his father was a king.

His mother had assured him of this latter truth before she died, and when, at thirteen, Donal Kavanaugh had boldly approached Dermot MacMurrough with his assertion, the king had the good sense to recognize his own stern qualities in the boy. MacMurrough had turned everyone from the room save Kavanaugh, and in that hour the king recalled Donal's mother fondly and promised the boy that he would be provided for as long as he kept his parentage a secret and remained loyal to MacMurrough.

For his part in Donal Kavanaugh's birth, Dermot Mac-Murrough had freely given of his time but not his home, his money but not an inheritance, his regard but not his family name. He bade Donal Kavanaugh patrol the woods of Leinster—fully aware of his thievery, Donal was sure, but also quietly proud of his ability to rob and plunder at will. Kavanaugh's reputation grew among the people of the south, and while the common people did not know *why* Donal Kavanaugh escaped the fate reserved for murderers, it was clear that he did and thus was to be feared.

In one way Kavanaugh's activities supported his father's kingship, for MacMurrough was occasionally forced to organize a party of warriors to "cleanse" the woods of robbers and highwaymen. Kavanaugh and his men regularly joined these excursions, celebrated with the king's men afterward at the castle, and then returned to the woods, where their real pleasure lay.

But lately Donal Kavanaugh had found pleasure only in imagining cruel tortures for the knight known as Ingram of Southwick. He could not blame his father for embracing a traitor, for it was like MacMurrough to accept a man because he was adept with a sword, not caring where he came from. The realization that MacMurrough had actually nursed a confederate of O'Rourke's and O'Connor's fascinated Kavanaugh. The more he thought about it, the more he became convinced that Ingram had somehow arranged MacMurrough's downfall and forced his father into exile.

Now, as they neared the monastery at Glendalough, Kavanaugh bid his companions make camp in the woods and wait, for he knew the sight of four armed men riding through the gate would likely arouse suspicion in the monks. "I feel an urgent need to pray," he said, jerking his head toward the walled monastery as his men laughed. "I will join you by nightfall."

The men saluted and turned their horses into the woods while Kavanaugh rode toward the house of God and properly composed his face into lines more fitting for a man in need of spiritual succor.

"May I help you, my son?" A small, bald monk stood before him, his hands hidden in the wide sleeves of his robe. The man's dark eyes were bright with interest, and Kavanaugh assumed that strangers did not often find their way to this remote monastery.

"I am looking for a friend," Kavanaugh said, keeping his eyes on the altar as he crossed himself. "I have not seen him in over fifteen years, and God has directed my footsteps to this place."

"Bless God's name, then, my son, and ask for the help which I may be able to give. Does your friend have a name?"

"Aye." Kavanaugh rose slowly from his knees as though reluctant to depart from the presence of God. "He is, or was, called Ingram of Southwick. A knight."

The monk drew in his breath and ran his eyes quickly up and down Kavanaugh while one corner of his mouth quirked in a smile. "Are you a knight?"

"No." Kavanaugh gave the monk a look of shamefaced humility. "I am a simple man, Father. But I do not know these mountains, and I know the family *rath* of Ingram is somewhere near here. I crave directions, so that I might visit his family with some news."

"As abbot here, I visit the man's family often," the monk said, "though all is not well with that family in the eyes of God. Ingram himself married a girl with only the belated blessing of the church, then allowed his wife to leave after a year and a day." The monk clucked in disapproval.

"My soul aches to hear that the marriage failed," Kavanaugh whispered fervently. "To whom was he married? I heard he had a child—"

"Yes, a fine boy called Alden," the monk answered. He motioned for Kavanaugh to follow him. "The girl was called Brenna, from a family in Wicklow."

"Does she keep the child in Wicklow?" Kavanaugh struggled to contain his burning impatience.

"No, Alden remains with Ingram's family," the monk replied, nodding his head like a bright-eyed, eager bird. "It is a simple matter to reach the *rath;* one only needs follow the road to the top of the mountain directly west of this place."

"Thank you, Father," Kavanaugh said, tipping his cap to the abbot. His strides lengthened as he neared the door. "I thank you most sincerely."

Philip paused from his hunting and lowered his crossbow. The sound of steady hoofbeats on the narrow road echoed across the winter landscape, and Philip hoped to see Ingram, for it had been six months since his brother had last visited. Rumors of battle and unrest had reached them through the occasional visitor to their mountain, and Philip promised his *fine* that no harm would come to them if they kept to themselves and tended their own crops.

The rider came into view. Though the visitor wore a sword, it was not Ingram but another, younger man with golden brown hair and an alert, weakly handsome face. The rider carried himself proudly and rode with both hands on his reins; his sword hung unguarded by his side. Philip relaxed his grip on the crossbow and stepped forward to meet the unknown rider.

The stranger reined in his horse. "Peace be unto you and your house," he called, looking carefully at Philip. "I seek the family of one called Ingram, a warrior."

"What business have you with this family?" Philip answered, studying the man carefully. Something about him did not seem right; a veil hung behind his eyes.

"I bring sorrowful news," the man answered, turning his gaze from Philip to stare at the ground. "I am Donal of Leinster, and I am sad to tell you that Ingram lies near death. He has sent me to fetch his son so that he may look upon the boy once more before he dies."

The words were a stab in Philip's heart; he swayed on his feet before answering. "Ingram cannot be dying," he said flatly, finally finding his tongue. "He is younger and stronger than I."

"'Twas a folly," Kavanaugh answered, his cool blue eyes darting again to Philip's face. "A contest, a mere game. By an accident, Ingram's leg was pierced with a lance, and now he has a fever. He fears he will die and asks for Alden."

"Alden is too young to leave; he is only four—"

"Ingram says that Alden is to live with Brenna after his death," Kavanaugh added. "And that I am to give his love and regard to all in his family." The man paused delicately while his horse shifted under him. "Who are you?"

"Philip, his brother," Philip mumbled, feeling as though the sky had darkened above him. Strange that he should feel such pain at this news, when he had so resented Ingram's arrival into the family years before. But even though Ingram no longer dwelt here, he had left his mark and his son, and those influences had brought new life and strength to what had been a monotonous existence.

"Ah, yes, Philip," Kavanaugh said, his eyes almost disappearing into his bony cheeks as he smiled. "He has spoken often of you."

"Follow me," Philip mumbled, turning to walk up the road. "You shall dine with us, and we will prepare Alden for the journey."

"There is no time," Kavanaugh answered, the slap of his reins urging his horse forward. "Though it may appear indelicate, I must take the boy and leave immediately. Ingram is too near death for me to tarry."

"So be it then," Philip mumbled, leading the way up the mountain road. Suddenly, he felt very old and very tired.

Kavanaugh found it difficult to conceal a grin as the plain-faced mountain family passed the small boy around for one last hug and kiss before placing him squarely on Kavanaugh's saddle. How simple it had been to fool these uncomplicated people! Because he had mentioned the right names and appeared properly sorrowful, they handed him the child without complaint or question.

Even now, as the small boy whimpered on the horse and Kavanaugh mounted behind him, these people did nothing but wish him Godspeed. How ignorant they were, and how blind! For as Kavanaugh regarded the shining blond child before him, he knew the child was not of this family. The boy was as different from them as salt from pepper, as day from night. The picture of Ingram's handsome face was dim in Kavanaugh's memory, but he knew in one glance that neither the knight nor this boy belonged in this *fine*. The abbot of Glendalough may have been blinded by his own ambition, Ingram by his desire to find a family, and the family by their need for a strong man. But Kavanaugh suspected an error had been made, and he knew how to prove it.

Kavanaugh placed the child's hands on the broad pommel of the saddle, gave a final bow to Philip and the other men of the *fine,* and turned his horse to ride away. The child's whimpering became a loud, sobbing cry before Kavanaugh had reached his friends in the forest, and when he finally found his men, he impatiently plucked the screaming boy from his saddle.

"Give him something to eat, and keep him quiet," he told Cailean crossly. "Tie him to a tree, and put something in his mouth if you have to. But keep him here through the night. I'll return in the morning, and we'll be off."

"Och, you never said nothing about taking a child," Iain said, a tiny flicker of defiance in his eyes.

Kavanaugh glared at him. "I don't tell you everything. Just keep him quiet and wait here if you want to see the sun rise on the morrow. Tomorrow we ride for Ferns."

"And tonight? Where are you going?" Frang asked.

"To the monastery." A smile crawled to his lips and curved there like a snake. "I feel the need to confess my sins."

Kavanaugh left his horse in the care of a monk at the monastery gate, then proceeded directly into the hallowed halls of the cloister, pausing outside the scriptorium, where thick manuscripts hung in their leather satchels from the walls. He had advanced to one of the manuscripts when he heard a discreet cough from behind him.

"May I help you again, my son? You should not be here without permission."

"I do not need permission." Kavanaugh turned and saw the abbot. "I have come to correct a grave error. It is my sincere belief that my friend Ingram is not related to the family I have just visited on yonder mountain."

"But he is—it is all here in the records."

"Prove it."

The abbot stepped forward and pulled down a book, then opened its soft pages. "Ingram owes his life to the church, and his son's life, as well," he said, running his finger down the notations in the book.

"Why is that, Father?"

"Because he was given at birth as an oblation. It's all here in the records." The abbot's yellow finger paused on the parchment as he read: "One infant son, given to God by his parents, Donnchad and Afrecca of Glendalough, in thanksgiving to God for his goodness and faithfulness. The infant joins the twenty-eight consecrated souls at this house of God."

"Impossible," Kavanaugh countered. "Why would that poor family give a strong and able-bodied boy to the church when every hand is needed for plowing or planting? How can you know that this reference pertains to the knight Ingram?"

The abbot shrugged. "Donnchad and Afrecca accepted him without reservation. He stayed with the family for years, then ran away when he thought I was on the verge of having the pope return him to this monastery."

Kavanaugh chuckled. "How very unsporting of him."

The abbot stiffened. "I can assure you, my son, there is nothing *sporting* about a religious vocation. Indeed, it is the highest calling on a man's life—"

"I meant no offense, Father," Kavanaugh answered, his eyes skimming the pages of the parchment. A notation caught his eye, and he gestured to the monk. "Look, Father, at this next notation: In March, only two months later, another baby was given to the church, and still there were only twenty-eight consecrated souls here."

Abbot Steaphan nodded. "True. That is, in fact, confirmation of Ingram's story, that as a babe, he was stolen from the monastery."

Kavanaugh shook his head. "The knight's story is that a *monk* stole him away from the monastery. If this situation is his, Father, there should only have been twenty-seven souls present. Don't you see? The monk *and* the baby should have been missing."

The abbot stared stupidly forward and stammered. "There must be a m-mistake. . . ."

"No mistake, Father," Kavanaugh said, turning again to the parchment. "These appear to be accurate notes, but something is wrong. There are no deaths recorded between the time that babe and the next was received. Your community is missing one child, not a child and a monk. Something happened to that child of Donnchad and Afrecca—what was it?"

The abbot had no answer.

"I have called together the brethren," the abbot explained carefully an hour later. "I asked news of those who were here in that year when the baby was placed, and none have recollection of what happened to that particular child. Some speculated that the child was spirited away by a wet nurse, others that the child died and the scribe merely failed to record it."

"How many of your monks were here in 1125?" Kavanaugh asked, his temper rising. "I will speak to them myself."

"Two. And you will not speak to them, for they are under my rule."

"You had no success."

"One is a lay brother, and I am certain he knows nothing. The second is an anchorite, Father Pòl, and he lives in a hut on the outskirts of the community. Pòl has chosen a life of silence and solitude in order to devote himself to prayer."

"We can talk to him."

"We cannot. He has not come forth in over forty years."

Kavanaugh laughed. "You have a mystery monk that has not been seen in forty years? How do you know this Father Pòl still lives?"

The abbot stiffened. "We take his food tray at dinner every day. The food is eaten, the empty tray left outside the door. He is alive, I assure you."

"I will talk to him," Kavanaugh said, pulling his dagger from his belt. "And we will know the truth of this matter, Abbot, before the sun sets today."

The abbot refused to help, even with a dagger at his throat, and Kavanaugh decided it was better to search for the anchorite's hut alone than to risk eternal damnation for slitting the throat of a monk. He rode west along the outer walls of the monastery until the stone wall merged with a timber fence and then melded with the forest itself. Tall conifers grew overhead, shielding him from the setting sun.

He found the anchorite's hut easily, for a narrow trail existed, the result of the refectory monk's tireless daily jog to feed the spiritual brother who aided his community solely by prayer. A narrow stream of smoke rose from the center of the beehive-shaped hut, and Kavanaugh smiled. The monk had lit a fire to ward off the chill of evening, a sure sign of the man's humanity.

The hut stood at the crest of a hill, and Kavanaugh dismounted and tied his horse to a tree some distance away. He crept forward and crouched in the bushes, wondering how to proceed. Small and dark, the hut was not the best place to confront a man unwilling to talk and sworn to avoid his fellow men.

'Twould be better to meet him outside, Donal reasoned. And if the man had no reason to expect a visitor at sunset, he might decide to step out and stretch his legs or fetch wood for his evening fire. With encouragement, perhaps, the man would come out.

Kavanaugh crept closer and hid in a thicket of greenery. Cupping his hands around his mouth, he gave his best imitation of an owl's cry, then threw a stick toward the animal skin that covered the doorway.

The ruse, however commonplace, worked. A broad hand lifted the flap. After a moment the crown of a man's head appeared, and Kavanaugh noted with satisfaction that the hair was dark and coarse, like Philip's. When the man hesitated, Kavanaugh threw another twig farther into the brush. The man stepped out of the hut and turned his face toward the source of the sound.

Kavanaugh gasped. Before him stood a giant, fully six and a half feet tall, with shoulders as broad as an oak and hands the size of oars. He wore a simple dark robe, sandals, and a crucifix about his neck, but the man's face held Kavanaugh's attention. His dark eyes were slightly slanted, his skull broad and short. He blinked uncertainly in the gathering darkness, and from his hiding place Kavanaugh recognized a childish innocence shining from the man's eyes.

A twig snapped under his feet as Kavanaugh stood. The sound and movement caught the man's eye, and his mouth opened silently in abject terror.

"It's all right," Kavanaugh said, smiling pleasantly as he extended his hand. "I'm a friend. Are you Father Pòl?"

The big man shook his head, then put his finger in his mouth. The gesture reminded Kavanaugh of a child about to cry.

"Father Pòl is inside." The man-child stepped timidly aside and motioned toward the doorway.

Kavanaugh stepped forward carefully. The man's dark eyes widened further still when he observed Kavanaugh's pronounced limp. "It's all right, I won't hurt you," Kavanaugh said, soothing him. "I hurt my foot."

The monk nodded, comprehension slowly settling over his features, and Kavanaugh lifted the flap of animal skin and stepped inside the hut. Nothing on earth could have prepared him for what he found there.

In a rotting wooden chair reposed a corpse, a tufted skeleton dressed in a monk's robe, a shining silver crucifix around his neck. The eyeless sockets leered horribly forward; the rotten teeth grimaced in a ghastly eternal grin.

The giant stepped into the hut behind Kavanaugh and waited. "This is Father Pòl?" Kavanaugh asked gently, pointing to the skeleton.

The man nodded. He opened his mouth to speak, and Kavanaugh was shocked by the lyrical beauty of the words that came from the idiot's lips. He could not possibly understand what he was saying, and yet he recited the office for the dead perfectly. "Leave this world, Christian soul," he repeated in a beautiful and eloquent Latin, "in the name of the all-powerful Father who created you . . . in the name of the angels and archangels, in the name of the thrones and the dominions, have pity on his tremblings, have pity on his tears, refuse not to admit him to the mystery of the reconciliation."

The giant made a sweeping sign of the cross over the dead priest, then sat before the glowing embers of the small hearth in the center of the hut. "Benedicite," the monk said, closing his eyes in peace as if he welcomed a visitor every day.

"Dominus." Kavanaugh gave the customary reply without thinking, so intent was he on the situation before him. The answer was clear now. The hapless giant before him was not Father Pòl at all but a victim of *amadanachd,* or idiotism. Donnchad and Afrecca had surrendered him at birth, recognizing the signs, and one monk, Father Pòl, had pity on the child, choosing to seclude him in an anchorite's solitary existence rather than subject him to the role of a servant in the monastery.

Donnchad and Afrecca's son sat with his eyes closed as his lips murmured Latin prayers; it was the time for the saying of Vespers. Kavanaugh paused for a moment, surprised at the stir of envy in his breast, then turned and left the monk's hut as he had found it.

TWENTY-SEVEN

With every day that passed that winter, Dermot MacMurrough felt the heaviness in his chest increasing. At every village, castle, and estate they stopped and proclaimed the contents of Henry's letter, yet no one had joined their cause—neither freeman, nor knight, nor nobleman. MacMurrough began to offer further rewards, speaking of gold, silver, and the riches of Ireland, but still his invitations were refused. None were willing to leave the security of their land for an unknown country.

By the time the biting winds of February drove them home to Bristol, MacMurrough was caught in a devouring gulf of despair. "What good is a letter from the king of this dominion if no one heeds its message?" he railed to Eva in the kitchen one day when he found her directing the cooks. "I have offered riches, titles, power beyond anything these people can imagine. Yet the knights are content to serve their lords; the lords are content to serve their estates; the freemen stay at their little hovels and work their trades."

"Eva—" he turned to her, his eyes heavy-lidded with despair— "what am I to do?"

Eva sighed and settled herself at the rough worktable. "Sit down, Father, and consider what I have to say. In the months you have been gone, I have come to know something of the people here."

"Bert and Gladys?"

"No, the *English*. You have asked freemen, knights, and

274

lords of France and the south of England to enjoin your cause, but they are content. You must find men who are discontented, Father, and speak to them."

"Discontented?" MacMurrough frowned.

Eva nodded. "Not far from here, across the river called Severn, the native Welsh still battle the Normans for possession of their lands. The fabric of their society is smooth enough, for the Normans have intermarried with the Welsh, but underneath, they squabble and war with one another. No one is content."

MacMurrough said nothing, but his eyes gleamed with interest.

"The Norman-Welsh of the north," Eva went on, "are a mixed race. They have no special allegiance to England, Wales, or France. Ruthless and cunning, they are expert sailors and horsemen, men with a sure instinct for discipline and order. They are tough, intelligent, and hungry for their own land. There isn't enough land in Wales to satisfy the ancient Welsh claims and those of the Normans."

"You are a true gift from God," MacMurrough said, catching her face between his hands and kissing her lightly on the forehead. "Worth more than ten sons to me you are, Eva! We'll ride tomorrow for Wales and assemble a force to leave within a month. If these men are as able as you say . . ."

He stood and walked out of the kitchen, mumbling to himself. Eva remained at the table, put her head in her hands, and sighed.

MacMurrough kept his word, setting off the next morning. If his men were tired or discouraged, they did not dare show their reluctance in the face of his intense eagerness. MacMurrough pushed the horses in the cool of the early morning, determined to make good time. The air along the coast road knifed their lungs and tingled bare skin; 'twas perfect for keeping men awake and focused on their task.

His first stop, at the town of Cardiff, resulted in the

promise of ten Norman knights, and the next day, at
Swansea, a dozen more men signed on to his cause. Mac-
Murrough was at once thrilled and dismayed at the ease
with which the Norman-Welsh knights committed themselves to the expedition to Ireland. True, they were land
hungry, as Eva said, but Dermot thought a man ought not
to be so quick in signing his life away. Among the men he
had signed up thus far, not one seemed careful or prudent
enough to lead an army capable of taking Leinster, much
less all of Ireland.

At an inn of St. Govan's Head, MacMurrough heard the
story and situation of Richard FitzGilbert de Clare, affectionately referred to by the innkeeper as "Strongbow."
Strongbow, the innkeeper assured MacMurrough, was experienced in war, strong in will, and noble, a descendant of a
powerful Norman family. "But now," sighed the innkeeper,
"the earl finds himself without a wife, out of favor with King
Henry, and land poor as well. His intended wife died two
years ago, and with her, his hope for a larger estate."

"Tell me more," MacMurrough said, placing a silver
coin of Henry's realm upon the table between them.

The innkeeper's eyes lit up at the sight of silver, and his
tongue loosened considerably. "He's a generous, easygoing
man, the earl is. Though some would call his voice weak, 'tis
commanding enough when it has to be. He's persuasive, I'd
say—could charm cats out of trees, you know. The knights
around here like him and would do anything for him. I've
heard it said that he's brave but not stupid, reliable, and possesses the best quality of a soldier—"

"Which is?"

"Self-control," the innkeeper finished proudly, thrusting
his chin upward. "He's a rock of a man, Strongbow is. A ver-
ifiable rock."

"I see." MacMurrough took a moment to rub the whis-
kers on his chin, then turned to the innkeeper again. "Has
this earl yet remarried?"

"No, sirrah, for he's particular in that area, you see.

Can't marry just anyone—must be a lady of uncommon breeding and nobility." The innkeeper lowered his voice carefully and leaned forward. "I'd say she's got to have lands of her own, too, and plenty of 'em. The earl's estate isn't what it once was."

"Thank you, my good man." MacMurrough slid the silver coin across the table, where the wizened little man caught it with glee. "Now, if you would be good enough to tell me where I might find this Strongbow, I think I'd like to call upon his hospitality."

Richard FitzGilbert de Clare was not as imposing in person as his name first led MacMurrough to believe. The man Strongbow stood tall, though not so tall as MacMurrough, with reddish hair, gray eyes, a feminine, sharp face, and a weak voice that echoed timidly through the halls of his small manor house in direct contrast to MacMurrough's hoarse blustering. A girlish dusting of freckles lay across the earl's nose and cheeks.

Upon his first close examination of the man, MacMurrough was tempted to laugh aloud and beat a hasty retreat from the earl's home. But the hand that gripped his in greeting was large and firm, and his manner most gracious. Strongbow invited MacMurrough and his sons into his small but neatly furnished hall. When they had taken comfortable seats around the fire, Strongbow read Henry's letter with interest and handed it back to MacMurrough without a word.

"So?" MacMurrough said, hesitating to force the question. "Does my mission interest you?"

"At present, no," Strongbow replied. "Here I have a home, you see, and men of my own to serve me. The king who promises to aid your venture does not think highly of me. Why should I heed his invitation and leave my home for Ireland?"

"For many reasons." MacMurrough smiled. He had

seen the flicker of interest in Strongbow's eyes, and he knew the man was really asking what the king of Leinster planned to offer in addition to Henry's challenge.

"You have no wife, you have only a small portion of land, and the importance of your title has been greatly diminished."

The man across from him flushed slightly. "You have made investigation."

MacMurrough shrugged. "Perhaps God has sent me to you, for I have the things you lack. I have a daughter as fair as she is noble, I have a throne and title to lands great and mighty, and I plan to rule all of Ireland under the protection and favor of King Henry."

"How do you know I desire these things? I am a happy and contented man, my lord."

"What man is truly contented?" MacMurrough drew his lips into a tight smile. "Can you honestly say that you are?"

"I am."

"We shall see." MacMurrough snapped his fingers at Niall, who removed another parchment from the leather satchel that had held the king's letter. "There is one other thing I'd like you to examine, my lord. This is a miniature of my daughter, Eva—the prize I offer to the man willing to lead my expedition to Ireland. She is a princess of Leinster, and it shall be arranged that her husband will inherit my throne. If I rule all of Ireland, all I possess will one day be his."

Strongbow took the portrait into his hand as if it were a minor consideration, but the nobleman's eyes gleamed with interest as he studied it. A vein in the man's throat swelled and pulsed in time with his quickening heartbeat, and Mac-Murrough knew he had struck a sensitive nerve. So the man was a romantic, then, and desperate for love. Well, Eva could certainly provide on that score.

"I can assure you, the portrait is no exaggeration," Mac-Murrough murmured after a moment of silence. "As any of the men in yonder courtyard will tell you, this portrait is a mere shadow of my daughter's beauty."

"Truly?" His voice was detached, noncommittal. So he would be difficult until the end.

MacMurrough stood and motioned to his sons. "We are riding up the coast to St. David's, my lord, and then to Pembrokeshire. We shall be returning this way in a few days. Perhaps you will have an answer for us then."

Strongbow stood and held out the portrait, but Mac-Murrough lifted a restraining hand. "Keep it, my lord, as you ponder your decision. Envision her as your wife and love, and then, perhaps, you will consent to join us."

At Rhos in Pembrokeshire, Dermot MacMurrough obtained promises of support from Flemish fighting men in the vigorous colony that had come from Flanders sixty years earlier. The fathers had settled the land, the sons had inherited it, and now the grandsons were eager to conquer lands of their own. To all who would join him, MacMurrough promised pleasure and plunder; to the nobles who hesitated, he eagerly gave out smaller prizes such as the cities of Wexford and Waterford. All could be had, he told those who would listen, if they would but follow him into the battle and enter the land of emerald grass and silver lakes.

As he turned south again, MacMurrough paid a final call on Richard FitzGilbert de Clare and was not surprised to find the earl now willing to lead an army to Ireland. "You drive a hard bargain," MacMurrough said, after agreeing that Eva should marry Strongbow when the battle was done. "To take a daughter from her father . . ."

Strongbow preened as if he had bargained cunningly. The fool. "I need a wife," the knight said, his eyes wandering again to the portrait of Eva on the table near his fireplace. "And your daughter is most lovely, MacMurrough."

"It is settled, then. I shall return to Ireland immediately, make a passable peace with the tribal kings, and keep you informed through letters. You will train the army and advance when I call upon you."

"Do not fear," Strongbow said, standing to his feet. "For her hand, I would conquer Henry himself."

"Count yourself fortunate, then, that I wish only to conquer Ireland," MacMurrough answered dryly.

TWENTY-EIGHT

Donal Kavanaugh shifted restlessly where he was sitting, the whimpering of the child grating on his nerves. He glared at his companion who seemed impervious to the sound—then threw his cup at her. "Ouch," she yelped, sitting upright. "That hurt, Donal!"

"See to the boy," he mumbled. "Shut him up, will you?"

"Why don't you get his mother to do it?" the wench snapped. "Whose brat is he, anyway? Donal, you have had him here for a week now. If you are not going to tell me how long he'll be living here with us—"

He surged toward her, and his grasp upon her throat was sudden and vicious. "If you don't do what I tell you, *when* I tell you—"

She made a choking sound, and he relaxed his hand, smiling at her coldly. "Be a good colleen and tend to the boy."

She darted quickly away. "I'm coming, dearie," he heard her call to the boy who lay whimpering in the corner. "Would a bite of biscuit sound good to ye, me boy? Let me see what I can find for ye."

When she returned, the boy was quiet, but Beitiris moved about, preparing the meal in sullen silence. Kavanaugh glared at her. "What's troubling you?" he asked, annoyed.

"It's the boy," she said, folding her arms resolutely across her chest. "Whose boy is he, Donal? Have you fathered a son by some other woman?"

He chuckled. "No, my love, trust me. 'Tis the son of an old friend—an old enemy."

"Are you thinking to do him harm?" Her voice was as cold as her eyes.

"The boy doesn't matter," he said, smiling as he came to slip his arms about her waist. "For now he is my hostage." He drew her to him despite her frostiness.

"Oh." She relaxed somewhat; perhaps she was even flattered at the idea of holding an important hostage in her house.

"He is a noble child, then?" Her voice teased him now; her hand crooked around his neck while her fingers began to explore his hair.

"I don't know what he is," Kavanaugh answered, nuzzling her throat. "But today we shall cut a lock of the boy's hair and seal it in a letter for the boy's father. You shall stain your best robe with the blood of a chicken—"

She gasped in protest, and he placed his finger across her lips. "Oh, yes, you will, and it will be worth your while. The father will think his son dead and my vengeance complete, never dreaming that I have just begun to do my work."

"Who will keep the boy, then?" she demanded, a worried edge to her voice.

"You will, my love, for a time," he answered. "And some day, when the time is ripe, the father will be at my mercy with his son's life in me hands."

"If you only want a hostage, why tell the father the boy is dead?"

"Because," he answered, his voice growing impatient against his will, "I would have his father suffer once, and suffer again, and again. Then my father and I shall destroy him in battle. On that day, Beitiris, I'll be known as Dermot MacMurrough's son, and you shall be my wife."

She giggled and thrust her arms around him. "Sure, and don't I know you lie, Donal Kavanaugh."

"Not always, my love," he whispered, bringing his lips to her ear. "In love and war, my words are true enough."

DONAL KAVANAUGH
1167

He did evil in the eyes of the LORD,
because he walked in the ways of his father and mother.

1 KINGS 22:52

Twenty-nine

Upon MacMurrough's order, a small troop of Norman, Flemish, and Welsh warriors assembled in Bristol, then boarded a ship with the deposed king and his family. The journey to Ireland was uneventful, their landing at Wicklow routine. From reports written by Donal Kavanaugh, MacMurrough knew the Irish kings did not expect his arrival. It was amazingly simple to advance to his ruined castle at Ferns, establish a base camp, and direct the men to rebuild a temporary fortress.

The land around the blackened ruin of the castle stood deserted and desolate. The widows of men killed in MacMurrough's last attempt at rebellion had gathered their children and elderly and moved to the compounds of extended family members. MacMurrough was pleased with the silence of the region: He wanted solitude.

The news of MacMurrough's return reached Rory O'Connor within a week. The high king assembled his counselors and rode to Dromahair to meet with Tiernán O'Rourke, and the two kings sat together at dinner with their most trusted and valuable warriors. When the high king mentioned Dermot MacMurrough's reappearance on Irish soil, Ingram felt the eyes of every warrior in the room fasten on him.

Even his loyal friends, Donnan and Ailean, turned to

Ingram with curious glances at the mention of MacMurrough's name, and Ingram groaned. He had hoped to forever distance himself from that ambitious and ruthless king, but 'twas a vain hope, surely. Ingram knew, far better than most, of MacMurrough's measureless ambition. That king coveted nothing less than the title of *ard-ri*.

"Like a blood-sucking mosquito, he always comes back!" O'Rourke growled, slapping his hands together explosively. "I thought we had chased the troublesome pest away for the last time."

"You didn't kill him." Ingram's voice broke the tension in the room, and every eye slanted again in his direction. "Begging your pardons, my kings, but a pest like MacMurrough will only be still when he is dead."

"We tried to kill him," O'Connor said with a grim smile. "But you were determined to stop us—or have you forgotten, Ingram? Shall we be forgetting the day you rode to face us with MacMurrough's own men?"

Ingram felt himself reddening. "I thought we would forget that," he said pleasantly, breaking a hunk of bread from the loaf in the center of the table. "I thought we agreed I acted on an impulse of love, not war."

"The daughter," O'Rourke reminded O'Connor, looking across the table. "She is a beauty, 'tis true. Ah, sure, I don't suppose we can be blaming Ingram for his confusion."

"Still, we're lucky he didn't kill one of us," O'Connor grumbled. "But what are we to do now?"

Ailean cleared his throat. "My kings, if I may be so bold—"

O'Connor nodded, giving him permission to speak.

"Ingram is a valuable tool in our hands. Suppose we send him back to MacMurrough, to spy out Leinster's weaknesses?"

"Too risky," O'Rourke said, waving his hand dismissively. "MacMurrough will wonder where Ingram has been for the past year. He will not trust him."

"And can we be forgetting that our friend Ingram's

head was turned once before by that ebony-haired daughter?" O'Connor inserted. "Suppose he sees her again and betrays us in the name of love?"

"You can trust me," Ingram replied, frowning. "I have put that love behind me. Let me lead the force against this rebel king and prove my loyalty to Ireland."

"Loyalty, Ingram?" O'Rourke asked softly. "Is loyalty not a relative virtue, driven by the desires of a warrior? My warriors are loyal until their farms are threatened; then they rush home to protect their wives and children."

"I am no warrior," Ingram replied. He smiled with rueful acceptance. "Let me from this day be Ingram *na nRidireachd,* Ingram of the Knighthood. I am who I am; I can deny my calling no longer. I am a knight, sworn to obey God and my king, and loyalty is part of my service to you."

"Very well." O'Connor lifted his tankard; all at the table did likewise. "Let us pin our strength and hope for peace on this Ingram of the Knighthood and see how we are rewarded."

The combined forces of O'Rourke and O'Connor met Mac-Murrough's ragtag warriors on a plain outside Ferns, and Ingram was wholly taken aback when MacMurrough surrendered after virtually no fight at all. The mercenary warriors from Ferns, poorly armed and wearing clothes and colors of a foreign texture, laid down their weapons without a struggle as Dermot MacMurrough himself rode out to meet the conquering kings.

They met on a rise outside the mended castle walls, and Ingram caught the flash of surprise in MacMurrough's eyes when he saw Ingram riding beside O'Rourke and O'Connor. MacMurrough lifted his brows in Ingram's direction, but there was no time to speak, for O'Rourke and O'Connor demanded his immediate attention.

The elder king held out his sword and bowed his graying head to the two northern kings. Ingram noticed that

MacMurrough's legs seemed to have grown spindly; his arm quivered with the tremors of advancing age. Dermot Mac-Murrough was neither the warrior nor the leader he had once been. Had he come home to die in peace?

As O'Rourke and O'Connor received MacMurrough's pledge of fealty and surrender, Ingram glanced toward the castle with suspicion. Bhaltair, MacMurrough's chief warrior and champion, was nowhere to be seen, nor were Niall and Peadar. And of course, Eva was not on the field. He forced himself to settle his imagination and concentrate on the conversation between the three Irish kings.

MacMurrough stood before O'Connor and O'Rourke in humble contrition. "I have come home to the land of my fathers," he was saying. "I have come to make reparation for my wrongs and secure my heritage for my children's children."

"Why do you bring foreigners to fight for you?" O'Rourke asked, his hand hovering near the knife at his belt.

MacMurrough lifted his head with stiff, brittle dignity. "I knew my people were slaughtered. I have a daughter and sons to protect and could not be sure of a safe welcome to my own kingdom. If it were you, O'Rourke, would you be doing any different?"

"The devil himself could not have pained us more," O'Connor said, his blue eyes flashing like daggers in the sun. "You have destroyed the peace of Ireland."

"For that, I confess my wrong and will seek to right it," MacMurrough replied, his great, heavy head hanging on his chest. Deep crescents of flesh sagged beneath his eyes; he was a picture of sorrowful regret. "This bag of gold, one hundred ounces, is the honor price for a noble lady," Mac-Murrough said, pulling a pouch from his robe. "This I give to you, O'Rourke, for the harm I did in taking your wife so many years ago."

O'Rourke caught the bag in stunned silence.

"And you, most honored *ard-ri*, have reason to doubt my sincerity, I know. I give you my sacred word that I will not disturb the peace of this land, upon the worth of my soul and according to the laws of the brehon."

O'Connor and O'Rourke blinked in astonished silence. They had expected wrathful indignation, threats, a brutal ambush, but never repentance and restitution!

O'Connor recovered first and bowed his head to Mac-Murrough. "'Tis well spoken, Dermot MacMurrough," he said, a veil of tears filling his eyes. "I will take your word and receive your reign in Leinster as long as peace remains in our land."

"And I," O'Rourke said, hefting the bag of gold in his hands, "do accept this on your behalf, Dermot MacMurrough."

"So be it." MacMurrough bowed his head to each of them.

O'Connor held up his hand. "Go in peace, Dermot Mac-Murrough," he said. "Keep these foreigners you have brought in this place. Let them not destroy the peace of the country, and all will be well."

"You have my word upon it," MacMurrough replied.

Two weeks later a signal trumpet blared from the tower of O'Rourke's castle, and Ingram lifted his head from the letter he had been writing to Philip. The signal required his attention, and Ingram was relieved that he would be able to postpone his letter explaining why he had been unable to visit Glendalough during harvest season. Ingram missed seeing Alden, but since MacMurrough's arrival back in Ireland, O'Rourke had been skittish, demanding that his warriors stay fit and in top form. Extra warriors had been recruited from the farms throughout Breifne, and Ingram had been placed in charge of training the men. Unable to shed his misgivings about Dermot MacMurrough, O'Rourke wanted to be sure his warriors could defeat any mischief MacMurrough might instigate in the south.

Ingram left the garrison and walked through the courtyard as the gates swung open. Two men in blue tunics and cloaks approached; a brehon and his student. The flicker of a smile rose at the edges of Ingram's mouth. The elder brehon was Griogiar.

"Griogiar!" he shouted, stepping forward to embrace his friend. *"Céad míle fáilte."*

"A hundred thousand welcomes to you, too, Ingram."

They clasped each other firmly, then Ingram stepped back to study the youth that walked with his friend. "And who is this?"

"This is Dòmhnull," Griogiar answered, placing his tanned hand on the youth's back. "He has a quick mind and an apt tongue, Ingram. He would make a good warrior, but you cannot have him. I caught him first."

"Though I can use a good warrior, I am glad to see you no longer travel alone, my friend," Ingram said. "Come inside, both of you. O'Rourke will be pleased to see you. The land is poised for trouble, you know."

"I know." Griogiar's smile faded. "I hoped I would be the first to reach you."

"We have known of MacMurrough's return for weeks," Ingram said, waving his hand to dismiss the brehon's concern. "O'Rourke does not trust MacMurrough, but the peace is holding, and we are ready if it does not. MacMurrough actually repented, Griogiar! I would not have believed it had I not been there and heard his words."

Griogiar's blue eyes searched Ingram's face; then he sighed.

"I do not bring news of MacMurrough, Ingram. I bring private news for you, and a letter. I have carried a terrible knowledge for many days."

The brehon's eyes narrowed in pain, and Ingram shook his head in confusion. "What news is this?" he said, his voice artificially bright. "What could possibly bring such pain to a learned brehon?"

"The thought of your grief, me friend." Griogiar motioned toward Dòmhnull, who pulled a folded sheet of parchment and a bloody bit of cloth from a pack on his back. Griogiar took the parchment and handed it to Ingram. "An Irish woman living among the Ostmen in Wexford gave me both the cloth and the letter. She made me swear not to reveal her name, for she fears your wrath, and I have judged her innocent of any crime."

"What crime?" Ingram said slowly, a knot of fear growing in his stomach.

"Shall I read the letter?"

"I'll read it." Ingram took the parchment and unfolded it. Surprisingly neat and tidy, the message was written in Gaelic:

> *To the honored warrior called Ingram, who serves O'Rourke and O'Connor. Dear Sir:*
>
> *I have today buried a boy, aged four years or less, who was known as Alden of Glendalough. The boy died in me arms, his throat having been cruelly cut by one Donal Kavanaugh of Leinster, who killed the boy for some injustice you did to him years before. I know this, for Donal Kavanaugh told me so before he fled.*
>
> *Enclosed is the cloth with which I wiped his wounds and a lock of the child's hair. I sorrow with you, sir, and pray God's peace upon you.*

Ingram looked up from the parchment, and his hand began to shake. "This cannot be true—"

"Aye, it is," Griogiar answered. "I saw the grave, and here are the proofs—"

"Why would Donal Kavanaugh do this to my innocent child?" Ingram cried, flashing into sudden fury. "How did he find Alden?"

He threw the parchment onto the ground and stared at the scrap of bloody cloth and tuft of golden hair in the young brehon's hand. "No, that can't be Alden's," he whispered, knocking the youth's hand away. "By all that is in heaven, you can't make me believe it is true!"

"Ingram, the woman tells the truth," Griogiar said, stepping between his student and the knight. "After hearing her story, I went to Glendalough. Philip himself told me that a man answering to the description of Donal Kavanaugh came to the *rath* more than a month ago and took the child. He told them he was a friend of yours, that you were dying, and had asked for your son. He further told them that you had ordered that Alden live with Brenna after your death."

"Philip let Kavanaugh take Alden?" The truth sank in slowly, like painful stabs of reality.

"Philip had no choice. Donal Kavanaugh, if indeed it was he, knew everything about you—your wife, where you were, who you fought for—"

"He knows? How? I have not seen Donal Kavanaugh in over fifteen years, Griogiar! What forces him to hate me now, and with such fury?"

"I don't know." The brehon's face twisted, and he struggled to regain his usual composure. "But what I do know of this man, Ingram, is that he bears a hard grudge and bears it forever. If you have wronged him—"

"I, wronged *him*? He put an arrow between my shoulders, Griogiar, and left me in the road to die! For this he takes the life of my son?"

Griogiar put his hand into a pocket of his robe and pulled out a bundle of silk. "And there is this. Eamhair bade me return it to you. She said she could not keep it."

Ingram took the folded silk and recognized the weight and shape of the jeweled brooch Father Colum had given him. The brooch that was to lead him home . . .

Grief hit him suddenly, like a fist in the stomach, and Ingram crumpled forward, his arms crossing his body as he groaned. A monster from his past had reappeared to snatch the only living person Ingram could call his own, and for this there could be no understanding or forgiveness. Ingram bent over double, like an old woman, and Griogiar and Dòmhnull helped him to his quarters.

Two weeks later Ingram stood before O'Rourke. "My king, if I have served you wisely and well—"

"You have," O'Rourke said, nodding. "What is your request, Ingram?"

"Leave to go," Ingram answered, feeling strangely tired. "I have trained your men. All is in readiness in case an attack should arise, but I do not feel one will come. . . ."

His words trailed off; lately he had trouble collecting his thoughts. He had prayed and received no answer, wept and found no comfort. Even the simplest tasks had become difficult since the news of Alden's death; darkness seemed to press down on him even at noontime, and a cloud of gloom engulfed his head.

He did not carry his grief alone, for the news had spread quickly throughout the castle. Now servants hushed when he entered the room, the men in his charge avoided his eyes, and even O'Rourke treated him with a most unflattering kindness and deference. Ingram was sick of it all, tired of regret, and worn out from sleepless nights in which he plotted his own plans for vengeance.

O'Rourke knew him too well. "I will grant you leave to go, but on one condition," he said, motioning for his scribe. The scribe picked up a quill and poised it above a sheet of parchment: The next words, Ingram knew, would be recorded for posterity and should be considered a royal proclamation.

"You, most loyal Ingram," O'Rourke said, his stentorian voice rumbling through the chamber, "may leave this place and travel throughout my kingdom in safety and with my leave, but upon no circumstances are you to pursue one called Donal Kavanaugh."

Ingram made no answer. He had expected such a reply.

"Because you are loyal to your king and high king, and because the tranquility of this land is tenuous at best, you are not to disturb the peace by venturing into the land called Leinster, whose king is Dermot MacMurrough."

295

Tiernán O'Rourke fixed his one good eye on Ingram. "Do you understand these conditions for your leave?"

"I do," Ingram replied.

"Then you may depart with my blessing and my hope that you will soon return," O'Rourke said, standing. He extended his hand and lowered his voice. "And if we have need of you, Ingram, where shall we send for you?"

Ingram spoke without thinking. "Waterford," he said. "The house of Erik Lombay."

THIRTY

Ingram rode steadily toward Waterford, stopping only to feed and water his horse. He ate nothing, avoided speech with everyone he met, and skirted Leinster lands as O'Rourke had commanded him, traveling instead through the valleys of Meath, Connacht, and Munster. The farmers' fields lay brown in the aftermath of harvest and the chill of autumn, mirroring the pain and loneliness in his own heart.

On one bleak, rainy day when the clouds hung as low as his spirits, Ingram thought about freeing the horse and sitting down to open his veins under a tree. 'Twould be so easy to give up the struggle, to join Donnchad and Afrecca and Alden in that vast heavenly realm where the dead watched the living. But Signe's ministering hands waited in Waterford, and even if she was married to another, she and her father would know what to do and say.

The gatekeepers at Waterford were preparing to close the gates as Ingram rode through at sunset, but with one look at his gaunt face, the guard wordlessly held the gate open for him. Ingram rode without hesitation to the house of Erik Lombay and pulled his horse into the small and tidy courtyard. A light gleamed from a window, someone cracked the door open in the fading daylight, and a muffled voice called out through a gathering mist.

He felt himself slumping, then falling from the saddle. He was aware of earth under his hands, then suddenly Signe's arms were about him, her tears on his face. Ingram

allowed the world to fade to blackness and lost himself in
the warmth of Signe's embrace.

He lay in the dark sea of nothingness, a formless void
where a single light shone from some place behind him.
Whispers sounded from the darkness; voices called from
his past. Lord Galbert, a half-shadow, half-light creature,
whispered from the darkness: "If you seek to serve God as
a knight, the prize must bring you pain." Rory O'Connor,
the high king himself, rose from behind Lord Galbert and
pointed an accusing finger at Ingram. "Will you find what
you seek?" his ghostly voice called through the strangely
thickened air.

A low, throbbing sound muffled the whispers and the
darkness filled with faces—round faces, brown faces, English
faces, Irish faces, common faces, haughty faces. "What of
your ancestors?" the disembodied faces demanded. "If we
are murderers or kings or harlots or brehons or farmers or
lords . . . what does it matter?"

Ingram covered his ears with his hands and cried out.
The visions faded abruptly, dark patches of emptiness appear-
ing in the darkness, but a large, more ominous vision took
their place. Dermot MacMurrough appeared, but he seemed
all face, suspended in nothing, flesh shriveled and thickened
so that only ambition gleamed in his eyes. "If you find what
you seek," MacMurrough's ghastly mouth called, "you will
pay for it with everything you hold dear." The vision smiled
in cruel confidence, then he began to laugh. . . .

When Ingram awoke, he lay in silence for some time. He
had slept long and heavily, troubled by nightmares, but he
woke to find himself in a cot next to the fire.

He turned his head to glance around the room. Over in
the corner two wide-eyed, red-haired children perched at
the foot of their cot, their blue eyes fixed on him. The house

had not changed much since his time there, but the sight of the children confused him. Did Signe still keep house for her father?

Her quick footsteps entered the house, then stilled as she surveyed him, one hand on her hip. "Are you going to sleep the day away?" she asked, her voice more gentle than he remembered. "Or are you going to get up and tell me what's brought you here, and in such a condition. Sure, and I thought you were wounded, then drunk, but me father said you were neither."

"No," Ingram answered, moistening his dry lips. "Neither."

She knelt at the side of the cot and placed her hand on his. "What then?" she asked, coaxing him. "What brings you back to us, sir knight?"

He didn't know if it was the old endearment or the warmth of her eyes upon him, but something brought the wall between Ingram and his emotions tumbling down. Unembarrassed, he laid his head on her hand and began to cry, stopping only when his tears were spent and his heart empty of all feeling but remorse.

Signe sent her children outside to play while she listened to Ingram's tale. When he first mentioned the name of Donal Kavanaugh, she paled and her green eyes glittered with an emotion he didn't recognize, but he kept on until the story was completely told.

He shrugged when he had finished. "I came here because I had nowhere else to go," he said simply. "I cannot go back to Glendalough, for Alden is no longer there, and neither are my parents. My brother, Philip, is head of the family now, and I could never serve under him."

"Still proud," she said, but her eyes smiled.

He shook his head. "I came to your father's house, Signe. I would not intrude upon your marriage."

She lowered her eyes for a moment, then murmured,

"There is no marriage. Donal Kavanaugh killed me husband a year ago."

"What?" His hand squeezed hers in sympathy. "When?"

"Kavanaugh came to Waterford seeking word of a man called Ingram," she said, without a trace of blame or bitterness in her eyes. "Me father told him that you had gone to Glendalough, and from us Kavanaugh also learned that you were the knight who helped me on the road that day. . . ."

Ingram frowned. "If Donal Kavanaugh searched for me before he knew that I was the knight on the road, then *why* did he seek me? What harm have I done to him?"

Signe shook her head. "He is full of his own importance, Ingram, though only the devil knows what his importance could be. As proud as you are, you could have offended him in any number of ways, had you reason to meet him."

"But I never met him after that day," Ingram answered. "What possible reason could drive him to destroy me, to murder my son?"

"I don't know."

"Well, that's not the important thing." He placed her hand in his and gently stroked her fingers. "He has done both of us a wrong, Signe, and I shall find him and take his miserable life. Where does he live? Who is his family?"

She shook her head. "Better not pursue this, Ingram. Donal Kavanaugh is without a family, a *ni truaillidn*—illegitimate. It is widely known that his mother was a prostitute, and only God knows who fathered the monster. Some have said that Donal Kavanaugh is the son of Dermot MacMurrough himself. Only a king's son could escape the consequences of his horrid crimes."

Ingram snorted. "'Tis unlikely that he is MacMurrough's son. How could one who spawned the beautiful Eva also bring forth such a monster?"

At the mention of Eva's name Signe withdrew her hand, and Ingram sensed that the atmosphere changed. He softened his tone. "Surely this Kavanaugh has a house, a fortress somewhere. . . ."

"In hades, perhaps." Abruptly, she stood and moved toward the window, turning her back to him. "You said you swore that you would not seek revenge."

"Some vows are better broken."

"A vow that can be broken should not be taken." She lifted her chin in the stubborn gesture he remembered well, and for the first time in weeks, Ingram wanted to laugh.

"Oh, Signe," he said, rising from the cot. Hunger had made him weak, but he walked to her and placed his arms around her shoulders. "How I have missed you," he said, pulling her toward him. "Despite everything, I am glad to see you have not changed."

"Haven't I?" She stood stiffly in his embrace at first, but as he held her quietly, he felt her relax and lean against him. "Two children, mind you, change a woman considerably. There are gray hairs under me cap, and wrinkles by me eyes. . . ."

"I don't care," Ingram whispered fervently, closing his eyes. "You will always be beautiful to me."

Donal Kavanaugh, his men, and one small boy rode to the stone palace at Ferns and saluted the guard on the tower of charred stone and green lumber. "Donal Kavanaugh has come to answer the summons of the king of Leinster," Donal called out, loving the echo of his voice over the quiet hillside.

The guard nodded and saluted stiffly. "Enter," he said, and the massive gate swung open.

Once they had entered the king's hall, Kavanaugh received the ebullient welcome he had long waited for. The mighty Dermot MacMurrough rose from his chair and came forward to clap Kavanaugh on the shoulders, then drew him close in a warm embrace. "Ah, Donal, me son," MacMurrough said, well-defined creases in his flesh angling toward the corner of his eyes. "It is good you have come at last to join us. And who are these you bring with you?"

"My men are Cailean, an archer; Iain, a horseman; and Frang, an expert in swordplay," Kavanaugh said, introducing his men.

"And the boy?" Eva stepped forward from behind MacMurrough's chair, a flicker of interest in her eyes. She smiled warmly at the child. "Where did you get such a boy?"

"The boy is the son of Ingram, the traitor who now rides with O'Rourke and O'Connor," Kavanaugh answered, pulling the silent boy in front of him. He placed his hands on Alden's shoulders. "He is our hostage, my king, for the same treachery that drove Ingram to desert your forces might yet cause him to bring harm to this house. But if you would rather use him as a slave—"

"We can't be making such a handsome boy a slave," Eva interrupted, coming forward. She smiled and stooped to Alden's eye level. "Are you hungry, little one?" she asked.

The boy looked as if he might cry, but he nodded.

Eva stood and put out her hand. "Then come with me, son of Ingram, and I will find you something good to eat. You might like it here, and you can stay with us as long as your father does his duty."

She led the boy away, and MacMurrough threw Kavanaugh a questioning look. "Ingram knows the boy is here? That is dangerous, Donal, for he will doubtless try to regain his son. I am trying to keep peace in the land until the time is right for our advancement—"

"Have no fear, my king," Kavanaugh interrupted. "Ingram thinks the boy dead. He will be our secret until it is time for us to move, and we shall have the assurance that Ingram will not attack a castle where his own son is held captive." He raised an eyebrow. "Was this not well done?"

"Excellently done," MacMurrough replied, raising his eyes to his son in an oddly keen, swift look. "A just reward for such a traitor as Ingram. This may be the best revenge you have ever taken, and I have heard many tales of your exploits, Donal."

Kavanaugh warmed to his father's praise. "I have tried to live up to your reputation."

The old king leaned forward. "Ah, there's the rub. I doubt you can ever do it, but 'twould do you good to try. Remind me sometime to tell you of the worst thing I ever did as a young prince. Thwarted the laws of God and man, I did, and proved that a king may do as he will. If he has bravery and ambition enough, Donal, a man may do anything."

"Even take the throne of the *ard-ri?*"

"Aye." MacMurrough grinned, standing. "Even that. As we speak our army is assembling, for I send constant letters to Wales, promising plunder and riches to any and all men who would come to our aid. And every week we receive a letter from Strongbow assuring us that all will be in readiness."

"Strongbow?" Kavanaugh's brows lifted in question. "Who is he?"

MacMurrough clapped Kavanaugh on the shoulder and led him toward the banquet hall. "He is Eva's betrothed and an earl in Wales, land hungry and eager for the marriage bed. You'll like him, Donal, as a brother-in-law. He's nearly as ruthless as you are."

Kavanaugh looked over his shoulder at Niall and Peadar, who followed their father into the banquet hall. Narrowing his eyes, he gave each of them a killing look and resisted the urge to smile when they cowered visibly and fell back a step. Eva had obviously inherited all their mother's cunning, he thought, swiveling his glance back to MacMurrough. Even so, 'twould be best to have Niall and Peadar out of the way, to leave the male line of succession properly open. Unless MacMurrough had sired another son away from his marriage bed, the only remaining male heir to the throne of all Ireland would be Donal Kavanaugh.

He dutifully turned his attention once again to his

father's prattle about the coming battle to gain the high kingship.

Ingram stood above the tiny grave in the courtyard of Erik Lombay's house and whispered a prayer: "God, forgive me for not being the protector I promised to be. Keep his soul safe, and let him know that I loved him truly."

Anna, who looked more like her mother every day, came through the gate and paused at the sight of Ingram leaning on a shovel. "What are you doing there?" she asked innocently, her freckles gleaming in the sun. "Burying a cat?"

"No, a leather purse," Ingram answered. He smiled at the girl and placed his hand on the silkiness of her red hair.

"A purse?" She crinkled her nose and made a face. "Why, Ingram? Did it die?"

"No." His smile twisted a little. "It contained a brooch that I had given to my son. Since I no longer have him, I no longer want the brooch." He dropped the shovel and moved to the bench in the courtyard. "I know it sounds foolish, Anna, but the brooch was all I had left of Alden. I thought I should lay it to rest."

She hopped up onto the bench next to him and nestled under his arm. She must have sensed his grief, for she patted his arm in quiet pity, then sat up and tented her fingers. "I'll say a prayer," she said.

THIRTY-ONE

"So when are you going to marry me daughter?" Erik
Lombay demanded, slapping his hands to his knees. He and
Ingram were sitting in the courtyard of the house that had
belonged to Signe and her husband—a house that had, for
the last year, belonged solely to Ingram.

"Marry Signe?" Ingram asked in mock surprise, as though
the idea hadn't occurred to him a thousand times. "Why
should I marry the girl, Erik? She has two children, more than
a few gray hairs, and she's temperamental besides."

"You love her, and you know it. What's more, the colleen loves you, too, though I'll never understand the mind
of women. You know," Erik said, leaning forward and lowering his voice, "she never loved her husband, and that's
God's honest truth. Ailbert was a good man, a fair man, but
he never stirred her heart, not at all. She never lit into him
the way she quarrels with you."

Ingram smiled at the enthusiasm in Erik's bright little
eyes. Poor thing, he probably realized his age and wanted
nothing more than to see his daughter married and settled.
Ingram felt a wave of protective concern sweep over him,
and he threw an arm loosely around the old man's shoulders. "You shouldn't worry, Erik," he said. "Signe will be
fine, no matter what happens in the future. She's a strong
woman, and I'll always look after her. But I can't marry her
now, no more than I could years ago, when you first proposed this idea."

"And why not? You were fit for each other then; you'd be fit for each other now. 'Tis not a bad thing to be married, Ingram. Me own wife was a jewel, just like her beautiful daughter."

"I'm not afraid of marriage. You're forgetting that I was married once before. I thought things were fine, but my wife walked out after a year."

"Perhaps she didn't love you like me Signe does."

Ingram laughed. "Your daughter has a strange way of showing love. A more headstrong, stubborn, willful girl I've never met. Most men couldn't handle her."

"But you could, sir knight."

The corner of Ingram's mouth lifted in a wry smile at the compliment; then he shook his head. "I can't marry your daughter, Erik. Years ago, I couldn't marry her because I didn't know who my parents were. Now I can't marry her because I do know who they were. My parents were poor dirt farmers, and what freeman's daughter would wed beneath her? Besides, both then and now, I am a man of war, and I am bound to obey a king. I am a knight, Erik, not a husband. I cannot wed her or any other woman."

Erik fell silent and seemed to stare at the ground in front of them while Ingram leaned back against the rough daub of the wall and sighed. He had found a home here in Water-ford—not what he had imagined but a home nevertheless. In order to appease the neighbors' gossiping tongues, he had moved out of the house Signe and her children shared with her father and into the vacant house she had owned with her husband. But Ingram spent little time in his house, preferring to pass his hours either helping Erik at the smithy or playing with Signe's children at Erik's house. Life had settled into a blessed normalcy, and though he heard Alden's voice and laugh in every syllable uttered by Signe's youngsters, he had slowly learned to deal with his pain and accept his loss.

Did he love Signe? He supposed he did. Her touch did not burn him as Eva's had; unlike Eva, Signe did not exude the scent of wildflowers and exotic spices but instead smelled comfortingly of vanilla and fresh-baked bread. Eva's flesh had been pale and chill; Signe's skin was freckled and warm. The two women were as different as night and day, and Ingram knew he had burned for one while cherishing the other.

And yet he could have neither of them. Marrying Eva would be like binding himself to a flaming meteor; marrying Signe would forge a millstone around her neck. And what was the harm in continuing as they had been? Signe was his friend, confidante, and companion; Eva, the ideal beauty whose memory frustrated him on occasional lonely nights.

Why should he consider marrying at all? In his new life Ingram had found a sort of peace and sense of belonging. He had Signe's children to enjoy and remind him of Alden, work that kept him busy, and friends who laughed at his jokes and listened to his stories of adventure. The people of Waterford knew and liked him; Erik Lombay peacocked through the city streets with Ingram as a surrogate son at his side, and the earl of the city, Sitric, bragged to any who would listen about Ingram's elevated standing with the high king. Sitric often invited Ingram to dinner, where scores of Waterford's citizens were treated to tales of bravery and courage on the fields of battle. In less than a year Ingram became an icon of the town—*Ingram of the Knighthood,* the personal good luck charm of Waterford, who kept evil and outlaws far from the city streets.

He should have been happy and content. But often he awoke in darkness, drenched in sweat and engulfed in a vague uneasiness that had no name or cause. He shivered on such nights, torn between an urge to flee and the desire to hide himself from nameless, intangible terrors that shadowed his dreams.

If Signe slept next to him as his wife, would his fear and restlessness depart? Ingram didn't think so.

He withdrew his arm from about Erik's shoulders and stood up. "Come, Erik, the forge awaits us," he said, opening the creaking gate that led to the narrow street beyond. "Another day of work, then another of Signe's delicious suppers. All's well in our home and in Ireland."

"There, me boy, you are showing your ignorance," Erik said, shuffling to his feet. "Ireland's like her weather—if you don't like what you see on any given day, just wait a wee bit. Things will change. Upon my word, they will."

STRONGBOW
1169

The fathers have eaten sour grapes,
and the children's teeth are set on edge.

JEREMIAH 31:29

THIRTY-TWO

Three companies of two hundred men each ran their flat boats upon the sandy beach at Bannow Bay. Dermot Mac-Murrough, Bhaltair, Niall, Peadar, and Donal Kavanaugh watched the landing from proud stallions on a windblown dune overlooking the beach, and Donal realized he had never seen such an assortment of warriors. Unlike the Irish warriors, who depended more on their own bravery than expertise, each advancing soldier of the Norman force had a distinct role defined by his garb. In the company of warriors, there were knights in glistening coats of mail, sturdy foot soldiers in jackets of leather and thickly quilted cloth, and archers in dull green tunics with dreaded Welsh longbows in their hands.

As the ranks assembled on the beach, three men in full military garb approached on horseback. Splendidly dressed, they wore loose-flowing embroidered surcoats over their mesh coats of mail. The mail sleeves ended in fingerless gloves, and jeweled rings adorned the men's fingers. Each carried a long, kite-shaped shield decorated with colorful designs, and each wore a conical helmet of iron. The iron nasals of their helmets protected the fragile cartilage of their noses but left the men's ambitious and determined eyes unobstructed.

The tallest of the three, a bearded man with a steady eye and blond hair flowing from beneath his helmet, rode forward to MacMurrough and pulled a letter from his surcoat.

"From our Lord Strongbow," the man said, nodding with more dignity than respect. "I beg to introduce myself and my companions to you. I am Robert FitzStephen; to my left is Hervey de Montmorency; and to my right, Maurice de Prendergast."

Donal Kavanaugh squinted as he listened to the strangely flat tone of the man's accent. Where had Strongbow procured these men?

Apparently, MacMurrough did not care. "Welcome," he said, smiling with obvious delight. "This land awaits you, and like a fat hen, it is ready for plucking. These are my sons—" Kavanaugh saw the king's eyes sweep over him— "Niall, Peadar, and Donal. Donal commands the four hundred men I have with me. Esteem him, my good sirs, as you would me, for he and my captain, Bhaltair, will lead our loyal warriors to assist your cause."

"We have no need of your warriors," FitzStephen replied, one corner of his mouth drooping slightly. "We have come for one purpose and will not stop until we have fulfilled it."

"Well, naturally," MacMurrough said, turning his horse. "Then let us move forward to Wexford."

Without wasting time the invading force marched forward, and Donal followed with his father's warriors at the rear. All together, one thousand armed men glutted the narrow road, and Kavanaugh chuckled as he thought of the surprise in store for the citizens of quiet Wexford. What would the high king Rory O'Connor do when he heard that city had fallen?

Donal squirmed impatiently in his saddle. Perhaps O'Connor had spies in the area, and news was on its way to him even now. O'Connor would call for his best warriors. Perhaps he would even call for the knight Ingram. He would assemble his troops and ride from the north, but he could not stop MacMurrough's men today, even this week. It would take time to assemble an Irish army worthy of this

foreign force, and until O'Connor had managed it, Wexford, Waterford, and perhaps even Dublin would fall.

Yes, the Normans have arrived, Kavanaugh thought, looking ahead to the living sea of knights, archers, and soldiers
on the road. Those Norman eyes burned for land, riches,
and royalty. They would not be dissuaded, and Donal
doubted that O'Connor would be able to stop them.

The Norse city-state of Wexford lay twelve miles northeast of Bannow Bay. The fleet Norman scouts on horseback
who had whipped their horses into a tearing gallop would
scan the city in less than an hour; the marching army would
arrive in less than three. Undoubtedly, the lookouts on the
city walls would see the scouts or hear rumors from frightened peasants who scurried into the safety of the city before
the approaching tide of enemy soldiers, but Wexford had no
force with which to launch an offensive attack.

Donal smirked at the thought of sure and easy victory
and proffered a question to the stone-faced Bhaltair. "What
will the peasants say after beholding us?" he asked, reining
in his eager stallion. "What will they think of such an assortment of knights, archers, swords, maces, shields, and lances?
Has there ever been such a force upon Irish soil, Bhaltair?"

The giant Bhaltair turned his eyes from the road ahead
and gave Kavanaugh a withering look. "I think not, me
lord," he said, giving due respect to Kavanaugh's newly
acknowledged status as MacMurrough's son. "Though we
have oft met with invaders, Vikings, savages, and the
Fomorians of old, none have come like this."

"'Twill be a great victory," Donal prophesied. "You and
I, Bhaltair, will be great lords in Ireland. My father will be
the *ard-ri,* and we shall sit on thrones worthy of our help in
this venture."

"You, perhaps," Bhaltair answered, apparently uninter-
ested in the prospect of power. "But I wonder if the king,
your father, will find cause to regret his decision to bring in
the foreigners."

"Why should he?" Kavanaugh snapped, clenching his jaw.

"Because their boats have turned away. Didn't you notice it? These warriors have not come to plunder and leave, Donal Kavanaugh. Methinks they have come to stay."

Kavanaugh suddenly remembered the look of fierce ambition in the eyes of FitzStephen, de Montmorency, and de Prendergast. Perhaps his own personal throne would not be won so easily now that there were more contenders for positions of power. The thought so unsettled him that he spurred his horse and left Bhaltair behind.

When at last the gray-brown walls of Wexford rose into view, Dermot MacMurrough hung back and smiled in approval as the three captains of the Norman force hid their companies in the forest at points northwest, southwest, and northeast of the city walls. The northernmost point of Wexford opened to the bay, but MacMurrough knew the Normans would not worry about defending the waterfront. Let the women and children rush to boats and flee; the proud Ostmen of Wexford would stand and fight, not realizing the strength of the army that had encamped around their walls. And they would be defeated, if not today, then surely by tomorrow.

He and his four hundred Irish warriors settled back on the crest of a hill to watch and wait for victory while the Normans organized their attack in the valley. Gleaming in their armor, the mounted knights came forth from the forest in straight rows with no more than two feet of empty space between them. The stout-armed archers, with their deadly longbows and arrows that could pin a man to the ground, stood in groups on either side of the knights. The common foot soldiers marched behind the knights with swords, axes, maces, and clubs in their hands.

The army separated into this arrangement on three sides of Wexford, and a hot and heavy silence fell over the land.

There was no movement on the city walls, no creaking from the stout oak gates, no traffic on the roads leading to the city. MacMurrough squinted ahead. Perhaps the city's earl debated with his counselors. Would the gates open and bring a message of surrender? Would the battle be easier than even he had expected?

He saw a red banner rise above the knights' heads at the northwest—FitzStephen's signal. A blue banner arose from de Montmorency's contingent at the southern point, and finally, a yellow banner bloomed from the east, where de Prendergast waited with his men.

A Norman trumpet blew; the knights lowered their lances to charge an enemy yet unseen. MacMurrough held his breath and leaned over the pommel of his saddle as he heard the smooth rolling sound of a bolting beam sliding from its supports on the huge gate of the city. Would the citizens of Wexford surrender without any struggle at all?

The gate opened, and through it a horde of men streamed forth. Armed with axes, swords, and shovels, they came; old men, young men, and boys too young to shave. Screaming *Abú!,* the ancient Irish war cry, they poured out of the city to face the invaders. MacMurrough's pulse quickened with the thrill of the chase even as he smiled in admiration for the doomed Ostmen's courage.

The men of Wexford advanced two hundred yards before the Normans moved; then another trumpet blew, and a volley of arrows flew forth and struck the onrushing mob. Down they went, the courageous Ostmen. The Norman knights lowered their lances, spurred their horses, and charged the brave fools who still stood, spearing them like fish on a skewer.

The neatly arranged battle lines vanished in the melee, and MacMurrough stood in his stirrups to gain a better vantage point. The Norman foot soldiers advanced to attack the Ostmen who had survived the archers and the knights, and MacMurrough was surprised to see that so many persisted in the fight. The men of Wexford fought bravely, pulling the heavy knights from their horses, ignoring the sharp pain of arrows that pierced their own limbs, and hacking mercilessly with their Irish axes at any Norman who dared step in their way.

The air clouded with dust, and the ground ran red with blood. Swords and axes raised and slashed downward; men locked themselves together in a grisly dance as they struggled for supremacy. One mounted knight pursued a youth who had stolen a horse and slipped through the Norman line; with a quick flick of his wrist MacMurrough signaled Bhaltair, who would make certain the youth did not pass through *his* line.

Within an hour the surviving Ostmen managed to retreat behind the city walls. The gates clanged shut, and the Normans closed their ranks and regrouped in the forest.

In the deforested fields outside the city walls, men sweltered in hot gore and struggled to draw their last breaths. Wounded bodies lay strewn about and trampled from the hooves of frightened horses; knights in heavy armor staggered in exhaustion, weighed down by muck and mire and metal.

A young knight carrying the red banner of FitzStephen galloped toward MacMurrough and raised one hand in salute as he reined in his horse.

"Come you from FitzStephen?" MacMurrough said, noting the banner. "Is he going to scale the walls?"

"My lord Robert FitzStephen counsels mercy and patience," the boy answered. "He says we should camp here tonight and resume the battle in the morning."

"Camp?" MacMurrough's jaw clenched as he rejected the boy's message. "Why not continue? We could scale the walls, take the city, burn the entire place."

"My lord Robert FitzStephen wants to win an unblemished city, not a burned-out shell," the youth replied, gripping the pole of the red banner firmly. "He is adamant in this feeling, and Hervey de Montmorency and Maurice de Prendergast agree with him."

"I am not alone here," MacMurrough answered, drawing himself upright in the saddle. "I have four hundred warriors, me sons and me captain—"

"My lord Robert FitzStephen says the battle is his and will be won his way," the boy answered, a disrespectful and greedy gleam in his eye. "The battle will be won tomorrow, else my lord will take his men and leave Ireland. Further, he will report of this day to Strongbow."

MacMurrough held up his hand in acquiescence and bit his lip. This disagreement was too trivial; Wexford was but one small dot on his map. MacMurrough's warriors could take the weakened city now. But all of Ireland stood to the north, and he could do nothing without Strongbow and the mighty army yet to come.

MacMurrough pressed his lips together and closed his eyes. "We shall camp here for the night," he said, iron in his voice. "We shall take the city in the morning, at the pleasure of me lord Robert FitzStephen."

There was no further battle. Shortly after sunrise the next day, a contingent of bruised and bloodied men from Wexford opened the city gates and laid their pitiful weapons down before the enemy. The Normans accepted the Ostmen's surrender with dignity, then threw the city gates open and celebrated their success. The invaders plundered homes, stealing jewelry, robes, furs, and horses. The few women who remained were treated as spoils of war; men who dared to defend their wives and mothers were killed. Children watched the horror with wide and frightened eyes.

The Normans did nothing to guard the harbor gate until the excess of their celebration had passed. Several families who escaped the Norman atrocities of Wexford sailed to other Irish ports. In less than five days the horrific news of the invasion had spread throughout Ireland like a grass fire. The call for loyal Irishmen went out as if on the wind, and fathers and sons left their farms and families to join the high king's army.

On a hot May afternoon in 1169, Ingram stepped out of the smithy into the street as a breathless rider dismounted. "Orders from Tiernán O'Rourke," the lad said, his voice high-pitched and reedy with youth. "Foreigners have landed at Bannow Bay in Leinster and taken Wexford. O'Rourke wills that you rejoin him at once."

"Bannow Bay!" Erik's eyes bugged from his bald head. "That's only a four-hour ride from here!"

"The king and his men are preparing to advance," the youth replied. "He bids me give you this letter."

Ingram took the sealed parchment, tore it open, and read:

> *To Ingram, our greetings:*
> *This troublesome king, Dermot MacMurrough, has brought invaders from Normandy to bring trouble upon our fair kingdom. Wexford has fallen, as will other cities, unless we stop this pestilence. The invaders, it is said, wear helmets, armor, and carry weapons with which we are not familiar. If you bear any loyalty to your high king and friend, join our force immediately. By the time you receive this letter, we should be assembled in the hills north of Ferns. We march on MacMurrough's palace in the hope that we may stop this man's ruthless ambition.*

The letter was sealed with Tiernán O'Rourke's ring.

The parchment felt heavy in his hands as Ingram turned to face Erik. "I must go." Ingram untied his leather apron and dropped it at Erik's feet. "Kiss Signe and the children for me, Erik, and pray for us. The change you anticipated is upon Ireland—may God preserve us!"

Ingram motioned to the boy. "Come with me while I

prepare my horse. You can feed and water your mare at my house."

The boy nodded, then closed his eyes and slumped toward the earth in a deep faint.

He would not have gone to Signe's house, but the boy needed attention and Ingram knew Signe would be pleased to give it. She was waiting in the doorway with a bundle of food when he arrived, and she wordlessly stepped out of the way as he brought the pale boy inside and laid him on a cot.

"He's nothing but exhausted," Signe said, wetting a cloth with water from the bucket she kept near the table. She wiped a trickle of sweat from the boy's brow and smoothed his clammy cheeks with her hand. "Leave him here with me, Ingram, and go do what you must."

"You know, then," he said, feeling foolish. Of course she knew. The boy must have stopped here first and inquired where Ingram could be found.

"Yes." She did not look up from the boy's face. "I'll explain things to the children, and we'll look after the house until you come back. . . ."

Her last words hung between them, and Ingram knew she was thinking that he probably wouldn't be back. At forty-four, he was no longer a youth and no longer equipped with armor, helmet, shield. . . .

"I am still a knight," he said softly.

She looked at him then, her expression pained, as if he had struck a nerve. "You always were," she answered, rising from the boy's bedside.

The fear, desperation, and loneliness in her eyes chilled his soul. He caught her, pulled her to him, and felt her arms close hesitantly, then roughly, about his neck. He squeezed her tightly and heard the rush of air expel from her lungs in one wild gasp. Then his head lowered, and his mouth met hers.

He hadn't intended to kiss her; he never imagined he'd

want more than an affectionate embrace. But suddenly the memory of all the nights they'd spent in each other's company surrounded him in priceless warmth, and he realized he was leaving that comfort for the cold, brutal world he had known before. Like an infant about to leave the security of the womb for an uncertain and explosively painful world, he clung to her and felt her return his kiss with an urgency he'd never known she possessed.

He might have stood there forever, but a sound from the cot brought them back to reality. "Faith, it's good to see a woman send her man off with proper affection," the boy mumbled, pushing himself upright. "I'll be wanting to go with you now, Ingram, if you're ready."

Ingram lifted his head; Signe steadily pushed him away. "I'll be making you a new tunic for when you've returned," she said, her voice clotted with emotion. "So go on now, and take care of yourself."

Ingram couldn't trust his voice to reply. He picked up his bundle from the table, jerked his head toward the boy, and left the house in Waterford.

Probably, he thought, for the last time.

He and the boy rode forth immediately and followed the River Barrow north into Leinster. They found the encampment of O'Connor's men at sunset on the second day, and the shadows of early evening cloaked him and his companion as they approached a young sentry on the outer perimeter.

"Halt!" the boy yelped, a shrill note of terror in his voice. He fumbled with the spear at his side. "Who are you?"

"Sir Ingram of Southwick, to see O'Connor," Ingram answered, dismounting. He caught his horse's bridle and led the animal to a makeshift corral in the trees. "You had better wake yourself, boy," he called to the blushing sentry. "If I had been a Norman, I'd have cut your throat by now."

Ingram found O'Connor and O'Rourke surrounded by

their captains at a roaring fire. All the men wore stubbled beards and worried frowns, and their eyes lit up at the sight of him. "Ingram!" O'Rourke stood and embraced him fondly, and O'Connor extended his hand.

"We are glad you have come," O'Rourke said, clearing a space for Ingram at his side. "MacMurrough has brought the *coimheach* to do his fighting for him."

Ingram took his place by the fire. "The foreigners will do more than fight," he said, looking grim. "They will also take your lands. A lord in England will leave his land or release his knights only by a command of the king or for a holy crusade. Since this excursion is neither by the command of King Henry or committed in God's name, it is reasonable to assume that these knights and nobles seek more than adventure. They covet riches and a country of their own."

"I believe MacMurrough seeks to master the circuit of the *ard-ri*," O'Connor said suddenly, his eyes on the fire before him. "His ambition is limitless, and though me father was *ard-ri* before me—"

"MacMurrough's ally was *ard-ri* before you," O'Rourke pointed out. "And don't I know his cursed ambition has led him to bring the *coimheach*? But these foreigners are few in number—"

"How many?" Ingram asked.

O'Connor tilted his head. "Above five hundred, probably."

"A small force."

"True enough."

Ingram hesitated to ask the crucial question. "How many are we?"

O'Rourke's mouth curved in a confident smile. "A thousand, easily. We gather more men the farther we move south through Leinster, for MacMurrough's own people are well ready to be rid of him. His peace has been false, his kingship burdensome."

"And when do we move?"

O'Connor answered, "When MacMurrough returns. The foreigners have settled into Wexford; God knows they're draining the city of life. MacMurrough will come home to Ferns. We're not sure how long he'll be taking, but we'll be waiting when that vulture flies home."

"Are we certain he is not bringing the Normans with him?"

O'Rourke's single eye gleamed in the firelight. "Our scouts saw MacMurrough leave Wexford today, and he rode with only his Irish warriors. He camps tonight in the forest and should reach Ferns tomorrow."

"Then tomorrow, the day will be ours," Ingram said, standing. His blood pulsed steadily through his veins; it felt good to have a clear purpose and enemy to fight. He bowed to O'Rourke and O'Connor. "Good night, my kings. May tomorrow bring us the victory we seek."

THIRTY-THREE

Led by Ingram, O'Connor, and O'Rourke, the forces of the high king hid themselves in the forest outside MacMurrough's stone palace at Ferns and waited for the sun to rise. As the fog lifted from the quiet meadow surrounding the castle, Ingram heard the twittering of the birds and wondered idly if this day would be his last. He had not dared to voice his fears aloud last night, but he doubted if even a thousand poorly armed Irish warriors could face and defeat five hundred Norman knights and archers. Normans were born and bred to battle; Irishmen were primarily farmers, fathers, and philosophers, not fighters.

Two hours passed as they waited in silence. Ingram was wondering if the element of surprise was worth the tedium of waiting when he spied a cloud of dust arising from the south. Horses were on the move, a large number, and soon they would be within range. He gave the signal, the cry of a wood pigeon, and heard it repeated through the forest. His adrenaline level began to rise; even the air seemed to hold its breath at the threshold of battle.

Ingram tightened his grip on his sword when the first riders came into view—not Norman knights but simple Irish warriors. He allowed them to pass on the road, barely fifty feet from his hiding place, until the entire company was in view. In the midst of the company's ranks rode Dermot MacMurrough himself.

Ingram raised his sword and nodded to Donnan and

323

Ailean, who waited at his left hand. They lifted their swords as well; the signal went down the line, and as one man, the force released a battle cry and spurred their horses. From out of the forest, the concealed army of the high king burst forth into the startled ranks on the road.

'Twas not really a battle, Ingram thought later, but merely a skirmish. Within ten minutes MacMurrough's Irish army had scattered through the open fields before Ferns, and MacMurrough himself had come forward to sue for peace with his two sons, a third man, and Bhaltair. Surrounded by O'Connor's nobles, MacMurrough and his captains sat in silence and listened as O'Connor put forth the terms of MacMurrough's surrender.

MacMurrough was to rid himself of his foreign allies, O'Connor stated flatly, and recognize O'Connor as high king. In return for his surrender, O'Connor and O'Rourke would recognize MacMurrough as king of Leinster south of Dublin. Wexford could remain under MacMurrough's control.

With perspiration dripping down his sagging cheeks, MacMurrough nodded in agreement.

O'Connor paused for a moment and looked at MacMurrough with suspicion and surprise in his eyes. Ingram's hand went automatically to his sword when the third man with MacMurrough raised his head to address the high king. There was something familiar about the man's thin, nasal voice, and Ingram strained to remember where he had heard it before.

"Excuse me, most honored *ard-ri*," the man said, with the faint beginnings of a smile. "But surely you know that in battle and peace alike, it is beneficial to accept the giving of hostages. I myself now have custody of a hostage and am assured of my peace and safety as long as the hostage remains in my care. If you hesitate to accept this man's word—" he nodded toward MacMurrough— "might you accept his sons as hostages?"

Ingram saw MacMurrough send the man a quick warning glance, but the man only smiled and nodded carefully. After a moment MacMurrough smiled, too. "'Tis well spoken," he said, with an odd mingling of amusement and regret in his eyes. "Take my two sons, I beg you, high king, to insure the peace of the land."

Folding his hands in an elaborate display of resignation, MacMurrough nodded toward Bhaltair, who dismounted and bound Niall and Peadar's hands with quick efficiency. MacMurrough's sons gaped in astonishment when Bhaltair pulled the reins away and led their horses forward to Rory O'Connor. The third man, Ingram noticed, watched the proceedings with amused interest.

"For the sake of peace and our mutual respect, unloose their hands," O'Connor commanded, gesturing to Ingram. He hesitated and winced. Niall and Peadar were the sons of a treacherous father, and who knew what further mischief MacMurrough had planned? Could O'Connor be certain that these two would not fling daggers into his back as he rode through the northern kingdoms?

"No, my lord." MacMurrough himself held up a restraining hand. "Do not unbind them, lest your suspicion undermine my sincerity. Leave them bound until you reach your palace, then keep them in your care."

MacMurrough turned to his sons. "God go with you, my sons, until we meet again." Niall and Peadar did not speak but silently glared at the stranger who rode by their father.

A cloud passed before the sun, a vague premonition of disaster, and Ingram shivered. How quickly this surrender had been arranged! But it was not like MacMurrough to surrender easily, especially after his considerable victory at Wexford. The forfeiture of his sons had been no great sacrifice, for Ingram knew MacMurrough did not especially esteem Niall and Peadar, but what of the Norman army that still loitered in Wexford? How could O'Connor be sure that MacMurrough intended to rid himself of them?

Ingram opened his mouth to protest, but Rory

O'Connor held up his hand. "So be it between us this day, Dermot MacMurrough," he said. "Remember, I beg you, that the justness of the king is the peace and protection of the people, care for the weak, the joy of our daughters, mildness of the air and calmness of the sea, fertility of the soil, consolation for the poor, the heritage of the sons, the hope for future salvation, the abundance of corn, and the fruitfulness of the trees."

"I will remember," Dermot MacMurrough replied, his eyes watering in the bright sunlight.

"Then there will be peace between us," O'Connor said, his classically handsome features shining in his generosity. "Depart in peace, Dermot MacMurrough."

The two parties separated like the Red Sea; O'Connor leading his men northward, MacMurrough leading his band eastward toward the castle at Ferns. As they pulled away, the mysterious third man with MacMurrough gave Ingram a wry smile of superiority, and Ingram felt the hair on the back of his neck rise. MacMurrough had just surrendered. Why did this man smile as if he had just won a victory?

Ingram followed his king, but a vague sense of trouble continued to plague him. Tonight at supper in the king's camp, he would voice his reservations and see if an answer could be found.

Talk of MacMurrough at dinner was forbidden; the high king wished to celebrate. A cask of ale appeared, the men drank freely and long, and apparently no one else shared Ingram's inclination to doubt MacMurrough's word or his honor. "'Tis the way of Irish kings to be true to one another," O'Rourke snapped when Ingram dared to voice his concerns. "'Tis been this way since the beginning of time."

"We, the Irish," continued O'Connor, "living at the edge of the world, followers of St. Peter and St. Paul—there has never been a traitor or a heretic among us."

326

"Amen," chorused O'Rourke lustily, raising his cup to O'Connor's. Ingram watched them gambol like two dogs who had just snared a bone more than big enough for two. *We, the Irish*, O'Connor had said, pointedly excluding him. *We Irish don't break our vows. We Irish are loyal, and you wouldn't understand.*

O'Connor's implication stung Ingram's soul. Was he not as Irish as they? Was he never to be forgiven for serving Dermot MacMurrough? Disgusted, he ignored a pair of concerned looks from Donnan and Ailean and left the king's campfire, avoiding even the fires of the other men who feasted and drank on a lesser scale.

He should ride back to Waterford. 'Twould be easy enough; his job was done. In two days' time, three at the most, he would be back in the city, where Signe and her children doubtless waited for some news of him. He paused and leaned against a tree. Travel after dark was dangerous for anyone, even in times of peace. But the land seemed to breathe easier tonight, and perhaps even the brigands of Leinster had scurried away with their tails between their legs as their king had retreated to his palace.

He moved steadily through the dark toward the group of hobbled horses. An unexpected snap in the woods made his heart thump against his rib cage, and he glanced around. Only a sliver of moon hung in the sky, and he was far from the light of the campfires. Did a shadow move in the woods beyond? No, he was imagining things. He walked forward again, taking care to place his steps in the darkened hollows where rain had left sticks and twigs too sodden to snap.

Another flurry of noise rose behind him, the swift bending and rising of a green branch. "Who is there?" he demanded, impatience searing his voice. "Show yourself, immediately."

Only the wind answered, then a shadow moved from behind him. A dark, slight form advanced gracefully, a familiar feminine figure, bewitching in its beauty. Dark curls peeped from the edge of the hood, and as she drew closer, icy blue eyes radiated from a perfectly oval face.

Eva stepped forward until she was close enough to touch him.

"Ingram." She whispered his name, pressing her hands against his chest.

"What?" He stepped back and grabbed her arms. So he was glad to see her!

"I had to see you. I must speak with you."

His face darkened. "You betrayed me. You used your beauty and my love for you, and I dishonored myself on your behalf." He glared at her, and his mouth twitched in anger. "What are you doing here?"

"I came on an errand—for you." She pressed close to him again, looking up into his handsome face. But her charms did not seem to move him this time.

"And what is your errand? I suppose you have come with soft words and willing lips to atone for your past sins."

"No." Her voice hardened. "I'll be wanting to dissuade you from fighting for O'Connor and O'Rourke."

He threw back his head and laughed, and she glanced around, trying to shush him. "Do you know where you are, woman?" he said finally. "You are in an enemy camp. You take a great risk coming here and suggesting such a thing. What if I took you now before the high king and announced your treachery?"

She jerked her head upright. "You wouldn't do that," she whispered. "They would kill me, Ingram. They'd take my flesh and cut it, use me like a common *stríopach*. . . ."

"And would it be less than you deserve?" Ingram answered, gripping her arms until his fingers marked her tender skin.

She drew back and rubbed at the painful marks. "Why do you seek to hurt me, Ingram?" She fluttered her eyelashes at him. Surely with the right words, the right ges-

tures, she could have him in her power once more. "I came
here only for you, my knight. My heart is broken because
you ride with my father's dearest enemy."

Ingram laughed harshly. "You have no heart. And we
are no longer enemies; the peace was made today." He
leaned forward, and his eyes bored into hers. "Your two
brothers sit yonder as hostages. They will enjoy the hospitality of O'Connor's castle for as long as the peace holds."

"And our hostage, too, will stay in our care," she
answered. She took a deep breath. "Ingram, my brother
holds another hostage, and bids me tell you that you must
leave O'Connor and O'Rourke immediately. If you're planning to do otherwise, our hostage will die."

"Your brothers are with O'Connor."

"Och, you *amadon,* and do you know everything? I
have a third brother; me father has just acknowledged him.
Donal Kavanaugh, who rode with me father today. Donal
knows that you are skilled in the ways of the Normans, and
me father does not want you to guide the armies of his enemies."

Ingram blinked in astonished silence, and Eva congratulated herself on her success. If that information rendered
him speechless, her next news would drive him to the
ground.

"Donal Kavanaugh was the man with your father
today," Ingram finally managed.

She nodded.

"His voice! I thought it was familiar, but—" Cold fury
filled his eyes, and his hands closed about her throat. "Donal
Kavanaugh killed my son, Eva! For nothing other than spite,
he killed a helpless child!"

His fingers tightened around her neck. His eyes blazed
like a madman's, his breath came hot and quick in the darkness. Struggling for air, she made a strangled sound and
flailed at him with her arms. One slap struck his handsome
face, and miraculously, he loosened his grip, then released
her and walked away to pace in the shrubbery.

She took a deep breath and rubbed her throat. Tomorrow she would have bruises, but for now she could bear this pain and indignity. "Donal Kavanaugh did not kill your son," she finally managed to say. "The boy is a hostage at Ferns. I myself have cared for him; he is well."

Ingram stopped in mid step; his eyes froze upon her face. "Are you telling the truth?" he demanded. "But the proofs—what of the hair and the bloody tunic I received?"

"Donal is clever. He paid his mistress to stain a garment and cut the boy's hair." She laughed softly. "The wench cannot even read or write, Ingram; 'twas all a lie. The boy has been at Ferns for two years. He is very handsome, with golden hair and blue eyes like yours. . . ."

In an instant his fury seemed to fade into relief, and she was genuinely surprised when he fell to his knees and covered his face with his hands, sobbing. She had never seen a grown man cry, save for those who begged for mercy from her father.

After a moment she drew her cloak about her and knelt at his side. "Return with me to Ferns, Ingram, and rejoin my father's warriors. You are a knight, and surely you would be content living with your son. We would give much to have a skilled defender in our company."

Ingram found his voice. "Your father has hired Norman knights waiting in Wexford. He does not need another."

"He has promised to rid himself of his foreign allies," she said. She reached up a hand to stroke his hair. "Do you not value the life of your son?"

His hand caught hers roughly, and he stood, startling her with the vehemence that shone in his eyes. "I value my son's life above yours," he said, jerking her arm behind her back. She cried aloud in pain, but the sound seemed only to increase his determination. "Go to your father, Eva, temptress that you are. Tell him I have quit the camp of O'Connor. But I will not fight for the man who has opened the gates of hades upon Ireland."

"Let me go!"

"One more thing." His grip tightened on her arm. "Tell your *brother*, Donal Kavanaugh, that I will redeem my son."

"He will kill the boy if you so much as approach the castle," she spat out, clenching her teeth against the pain. "You are known, Ingram, and you are a fool. You should have taken the chance to join us."

"Donal Kavanaugh may be a devil, but he is not invincible," Ingram answered, pulling her closer until she felt the hot breath of his anger on her face. "As God is my witness, if Alden dies or suffers, Donal Kavanaugh will suffer tenfold. Swear that you'll tell him."

She said nothing but merely glared at him. He twisted her arm. "I swear!" she gasped, jerking away in pain.

Ingram released her and disappeared into the night.

He went immediately to Rory O'Connor and Tiernán O'Rourke with his news but found the two kings reluctant to break their treaty with MacMurrough. "He told us he had a hostage, as we have his," O'Rourke said, jerking his head toward Niall and Peadar, who sat under a tree with guards on either side of them. "For the sake of peace, Ingram, we cannot raid MacMurrough's castle, even for your son. 'Twould be a grievous injustice."

"There is no honor in it," O'Connor agreed, his careful blue eyes studying Ingram's reaction. "Alden is not a king's son, nor a member of the *rigdamnae*. For such a one we cannot go to war."

"Do only fathers of the royal family love their children?" Ingram protested, clenching his hands. "Give me ten men, my king, archers to take out the guards on the wall, and I will ride alone into the castle—"

"No." O'Connor shook his head with finality. His expression softened, and he looked at Ingram with compassion. "I am sorry, Ingram. But the peace of Ireland is tenuous. We cannot risk the future of these kingdoms for one small boy." He paused and gave Ingram a halfhearted smile.

"All will be well, Ingram. Because the boy is of no great parentage, 'tis not likely any great harm will come to him. This appears to be a personal vendetta, and I cannot break the peace of Ireland for one man's son."

Ingram stifled the roar that threatened to rip from his throat. O'Rourke fought MacMurrough for the sake of his kidnapped wife and wounded pride; O'Connor fought to hold the title of high king. Would no one fight for a scared little boy who had been wrongfully torn from his home?

"I am going to Waterford," Ingram said abruptly, bowing his head sharply toward the two kings. "If there is peace in Ireland, you have no need of me. But if the peace ends, know, my kings, that I will not fight with your armies again unless they ride to save my son."

Signe hung her washing out to dry and heard quiet clucks of sympathy from Diana's open window. "'Tis a lonely washing that has no man's tunic in it," Diana said, eyeing the garments on the thin rope in Signe's courtyard. "Have you heard nothing from your knight?"

"He's not my knight," Signe answered crossly. "He belongs to himself; he always has."

"Still, the women at the well wonder where he's been," Diana went on, pretending to study her hands in the morning light. "They say O'Rourke and O'Connor's men settled things rightly, and all is at peace in Leinster. Haven't you wondered where the knight has been these past days? Seems to me, if he was planning to come back a'tall, he'd be here already."

"I'm sure I haven't had a thought of him in me head," Signe answered, turning to face her neighbor. "If he comes back, well, sure, I'd be pleased to see him, but if he's decided to live with the high king himself, I don't think anything of it one way or the other."

Anna's freckled face suddenly appeared over the hedge of the courtyard. "Mama," she said, dimples deepening in both cheeks. "Ingram's here, at the forge with Grandpa. He's back!"

Knowing full well that her reaction disproved her words, Signe dropped everything and ran for the smithy.

That night, after the children were asleep, Signe stepped out into her courtyard. Her father sat on a bench under the arbor; Ingram knelt in a corner of the garden, a dirt-encrusted leather bag in his hand. She watched in silence as Ingram opened the bag and removed the jeweled brooch. Studying the bronze circle in weary dignity, he told Signe and Erik that his son lived as a hostage of Donal Kavanaugh.

"I've been wandering the woods for days, trying to think of a plan to bring Alden home," he explained, turning the brooch over and over in his hands. "But I can't think of anything. Now I realize I should have gone to Ferns to serve Dermot, but I was sure O'Rourke would aid me. How can I face Alden if he knows I had the chance to free him and chose *not* to come to him?"

"How could you face him if you sold your soul to that devil Dermot?" Erik asked. "You did the right thing, me boy. As precious as a child is, still every man is responsible to God for himself, not his parents or his children. You must trust God and know that by doing right, all will be well."

"Will it?" Ingram lifted tired eyes to Erik's, and Signe felt her heart breaking for him. Engulfed by the ashes of his dreams, Ingram had never seemed so vulnerable.

"All I ever wanted was a noble family," Ingram whispered as the cool breath of evening blew upon them. "Is that too much for a knight to ask?"

THIRTY-FOUR

The peace of Ireland lasted barely three months. O'Connor and O'Rourke returned to their castles, dismissed their men, and settled into their normal affairs. Within weeks of their arrival at their castles, frantic messengers rode from the south, bearing news that a daring Norman called Raymond Carew, *Le Gros,* had landed with a hundred men and horses at a rocky headland called Baginbun. The invaders had not pressed inland, the scouts reported, but had erected earthen ramparts and fortified the rocky stretch of beach between Bannow Bay and the Hook, a point closer to Waterford than Wexford.

All the muscles in Rory O'Connor's face tightened in rage at the news. His sergeant at arms looked gravely toward the garrison, where only a handful of men awaited battle, and O'Connor turned toward his scribe, who lifted a quill and poised to inscribe a parchment.

O'Connor nodded to the messenger. "You must ride again, my friend, and carry this message to one called Ingram, who lives in Waterford. Write that Ireland's peace is broken, for the foreign enemy has landed at Baginbun. Ask Ingram to gather an army and lead an attack from the south, and assure him that I will join him as soon as I assemble my men."

The scribe scribbled furiously and paused. "Anything else, sir?"

O'Connor bit his lip. "Only this—be certain to write

that I promise my support for an attack on Ferns after this enemy is defeated."

Ingram folded the parchment from Rory O'Connor and laid it without comment on the table. So the high king had relented. He would attack Ferns for Alden's sake, but only after this new enemy had been defeated. Ingram felt a somber satisfaction in knowing the end of his trial was near.

Signe watched him, her eyes filled with fear. When he did not speak, she broke the silence. "Another attack is coming, isn't it? Those who escaped from Wexford have been saying more Normans would soon come, and even now they may be outside our walls—"

"I have suspected it for some time, and I have already sent word to the kingdoms of Decies, Ossory, and Idrone," Ingram said, finally turning to look at her. "I did not need a word from O'Connor to proceed. I knew more Normans would come. They will take Ireland as they took Saxon England. . . ."

Reluctantly, he remembered the time he and Father Colum were attacked by resentful but conquered Saxons on the road to Bristol. By all that was holy, was this the beginning of the end for Ireland as he had come to know it? Would the Gaelic Irish be overcome and conquered as had the Saxon chieftains of England?

"Will they come and murder us in our beds?" Signe paced in agitation; Ingram had never seen her this flustered. "Me children, Ingram—what if they hurt the children? We would flee, but where are the other *coimheach* that attacked Wexford? What if they are outside the city in the forests and would attack travelers on the road?"

"You will be safe as long as you stay here," Ingram said, crossing the room. He pulled on his cloak, fastened it with the jeweled brooch, and opened the door. A light rain had begun to fall; the air was heavy and close. "Trust God, as you have always done, Signe. And trust me. I will not fail you."

She lifted her hand to stop him. "Will you swear on your son's brooch that you will come back?"

He paused, and his eyes lit with a smile. "You told me once that a vow should not be given if it might be broken."

"That's why I want your word of honor now."

He looked out the door and took a deep breath. The weight in his chest felt like a millstone. But she waited, and she deserved an answer.

"You have my word," he said, going out the door.

Three thousand Ostmen and Irishmen from several neighboring communities and kingdoms assembled in the hot summer sun the next day, and Ingram found it difficult to contain his delight. Three thousand to rout one hundred! Though the Normans had entrenched themselves on the shore at Baginbun with weapons the Irish did not possess, they would be easily driven into the sea.

Ingram looked over the assembly. The men who stood in the meadow before him were not warriors. Some wore the trousers of farmers; others, the fine woven tunics and voluminous cloaks of the aristocracy. Golden brooches gleamed in the early morning sunlight; dark, soil-stained hands gripped iron hoes and axes. As their grandfathers had defended their homes against Viking pillagers, so these men stood ready to make war against the unknown Normans who had spoiled Wexford, their sister city.

Erik Lombay, his bald head dewy with perspiration, stood in the front of the line, an iron poker in his hand. He caught Ingram's eye and nodded grimly, and Ingram felt a stab of regret pierce his heart. By summoning foreigners, men like Ingram himself, Dermot MacMurrough had forced grandfathers and boys to pick up weapons of death.

Ingram directed the crowd into companies and appointed capable-looking men as captains. Very few of the three thousand had ever killed anything other than a hog or cow, but today they might yet taste of bloodshed. Had they the stomach for it? Ingram couldn't tell. Their eyes were resolute enough, their faces grim. Still, instinct told Ingram that only those truly born and bred to battle could successfully challenge a Norman knight.

But time had run out. Since six hundred or more Normans were already encamped in the ruins of Wexford, the two Norman contingents must be prevented from joining and launching an assault on Waterford.

Ingram led the group in a prayer for God's mercy, then gave directions and motioned for the men to proceed toward Baginbun.

The battle was short and decisive. As Ingram and his force approached the earthen ramparts of the Norman fort, a wooden gate swung open, and a herd of long-horned cattle stampeded forth against the oncoming troops. The startled farmers in the front line, well acquainted with the fury of horned cattle, broke from their formations and ran like mindless rabbits. Those who did not run were trampled.

The mare Ingram was riding reared in the stampede; it took every bit of his concentration to hold the horse steady and push forward. All around him, men dropped their make-shift arms and fled into the sea or ran for the open meadows. One screaming youth ran past Ingram in abject terror, a raging bull at his heels. Ingram spurred his horse forward, cutting in front of the bull to spare the boy. The bull lowered his head and snorted, charging blindly forward. The horse screamed, her flank torn open, and fell to the ground as the bull raked her tender belly with razor-sharp horns.

Ingram pulled himself from beneath his horse's body as the bull stumbled away. Then he heard an agonized scream. As Ingram looked up, the boy flew through the air, tossed by the mighty horns of the beast, and fell beneath the hooves of a Norman knight who galloped forward in pursuit of Irish prey.

While confusion reigned, the Norman and Flemish

knights behind the ramparts rode forth, brandishing lances and swords. They corralled the confused Irish foot soldiers like animals, killed the farmers on the spot, and herded the better-dressed warriors behind the walls of the fort.

Ingram scrambled to his feet, drew his sword, and crouched beside the body of his mare. The sea of cattle had swept past him. The foremost enemy knights thundered in the distance, and his army of three thousand had been scattered like chaff in a tornado. Sweat stung his eyes as it poured down his head, and through the dust of the melee he saw Donal Kavanaugh ride forth from the fortress on a dainty-footed mare.

Ingram felt caution and sense slip away. He roared and charged with his sword extended. He would have run Kavanaugh through but for a stout Norman knight who stepped into his path. Grinning oddly, the man parried Ingram's initial blow with ease and returned it with a sideways swipe that cut through the fabric of Ingram's cloak like paper.

Startled, Ingram pressed his hand to his side and felt the warm stickiness of blood. He looked up not at his attacker but at Kavanaugh, who rode easily through the carnage without seeming to notice that he had been under attack. Frustration and anger drove Ingram to his knees, and a flying kick from the booted knight made him lose consciousness.

When Ingram opened his eyes, the bloody meadow lay in absolute silence. He groaned as the pain in his side intensified. He lifted his head: Death surrounded him. Young men in trousers, boys in short tunics, old men in their cloaks—all stared unblinking at the blazing summer sun.

But the battle had not been completely one-sided. A dead Norman knight lay not far away. Ingram groaned as he pulled himself upright and crawled to the man's body. The knight's throat had been cut, and the blood pooled thickly beneath his neck. But the man wore a helmet and hauberk. His sword lay in his hand.

Groaning with the pain of exertion, Ingram pulled the iron helmet from the dead knight and put it on his own head. Keeping an eye out for the victorious Normans who would soon return to kill the remaining wounded, Ingram rose to his knees and pulled the mesh hauberk from the dead knight, then slipped it over his own torn tunic. In the helmet and hauberk, with a Norman sword, he could disguise himself, enter the fort, and find Donal Kavanaugh.

Of the three thousand assembled at the creek of Baginbun, two thousand nine hundred ninety-nine had fought for their homes. He, Ingram of the Knighthood, had fought only for his son and his vengeance upon Donal Kavanaugh.

The stout Norman at the gate peered anxiously at the blood-stained warrior who approached from the battlefield. "Are you injured?" the man called in French.

Ingram quietly thanked God that eighteen years in Ireland had not dimmed his understanding of the Normans' language. "If I am sick, I will go to the doctor," he answered in French. He forced a smile. "I'll do what I have to do."

The man relaxed and waved Ingram forward, and Ingram halted and pressed his hand to the wound in his side after climbing the steep earthen ramp. Before him lay the most pitiful sight he had ever seen.

At least seventy Ostmen and Irishmen, aristocrats by the look of them, stood bound hand-to-hand in a single line that coiled inside the fortress like a snake. The air was heavy with the stench of cow manure, smoking fires, and blood.

At an end of the line, a balding Norman with a ponderous belly interrogated a white-haired man Ingram recognized from Waterford. "Tell me, old man, of the treasures in Waterford," the Norman demanded, his thumb sliding over the ripe skin of an apple as he spoke. "Of the church—where are their golden relics? Tell me now!"

The man would not reply, and at a nod from the interrogator, two knights laid the man upon a bench and raised heavy cudgels to the sky. Within a second the cudgels fell, breaking the man's legs, and as he screamed in agony, the cudgels raised and lowered again, breaking his arms.

With his limbs shattered, the old man was hauled to the highest point of the fortress and tossed off the cliff into the sea. The heavy, flour-faced Norman then motioned for another prisoner to be brought forward, and Ingram felt his body grow rigid when he recognized the face and form of Erik Lombay.

Had he been fifteen years younger, he would have charged blindly into the enemy guard to free Erik. But Ingram felt every one of his forty-four years, and the pain in his side reminded him that he was mortal and wounded. Worse yet, he had never felt more like the son of a farmer.

As Erik eyed his tormentor and refused to answer intimidating questions with no real purpose, Ingram silently dropped his sword to the earth and lifted his heart in an anguished prayer. Why must Erik Lombay pay the penalty for Dermot MacMurrough's vile ambition? Frustrated beyond reason, Ingram prayed that God would end Erik's pain quickly.

The cudgels rose and fell; Erik's hoarse screams chilled him to the marrow. Ingram turned and walked out of the fort, his blood roaring in his ears.

God, forgive me. . . .

The guard at the gate called something to him, but Ingram waved the man away and walked northward toward Waterford.

'Twas over. Three thousand had been routed by one hundred. The Irish had been led by a former knight and defeated by a herd of cattle. And Alden, wherever he was, would be better off not knowing his father.

Donal Kavanaugh rode into the earthen fortress later, pulling two struggling Irishmen behind his saddle. With a satisfied smile he noted the line of prisoners who stood before the executioner, then nodded to a knight who stood nearby. "Cut these two loose and put them with the rest," he said, bringing his leg over his saddle. At the knight's questioning gaze, he pulled himself upright. "Don't dawdle! The son of MacMurrough addresses you!"

The knight moved away without complaint, but his sly grin implied an insult that Donal found hard to bear. He stalked toward Raymond Carew, who sat in front of the line of prisoners and ate his dinner. His limp bothered him greatly, for he was tired, but he held his head high. Let them smirk, these landless fools from across the sea. They were but poorly paid guests in Ireland, hired hands brought in to do their work and then do as they were told. If all went according to his plan, in a year, maybe two, they'd be gone from Ireland entirely, and the Emerald Isle would be in his hands.

He paused next to Carew and pretended to be interested in the tearful "confession" of the merchant who knelt before the Norman, but his mind was far from Baginbun. If O'Connor followed Irish law, his half brothers, Niall and Peadar, would soon be dead. And Strongbow, that misfit from Wales, would never be accepted by the Irish tribes, not even with an Irish princess as his wife. Only one, Donal Kavanaugh, would remain to assume MacMurrough's expanding power, and assume it he would, whatever it took to gain control. Only one other remained to threaten him, and that one would soon be dead, too.

He waited until the merchant had been broken and carried away before clearing his throat. Raymond Carew looked up.

"Why do you ask these useless questions about gold and treasure?" Kavanaugh said, stroking his beard. "A real threat

341

lies in Waterford, and a threat is more important than a treasure."

"A threat?" Carew laughed. "In that town? We took their best today, Kavanaugh, and see how easily they fly from the cliff to the sea they love so much!"

"The threat I speak of is not an Ostman, but a Norman knight." He saw Carew's brow rise. "Yes, a man who knows more of Normandy *and* Ireland than you could hope to know. He has grown famous in these parts: Ingram *na nRidireachd.*"

"Speak so I can understand you," Carew snapped, his jowls darkening.

"Ingram of the Knighthood," Kavanaugh answered, his voice light. "He lies in wait in Waterford, of that you may be certain. Chief of O'Connor's army, champion of Tiernán O'Rourke, formerly of Southwick Castle. 'Twas he who led the opposition today, I'd stake me life on it."

Carew stared at the next prisoner in front of him. "Is this true?" he barked as the man trembled before him. "Do you know this Ingram who dares to call himself a knight?"

The man's eyes rolled back in his head; sweat poured from his brow.

"Speak!" Carew commanded, rising from his chair.

A tremendous shudder wrenched the prisoner's body. Carew paused and lowered his face until his eyes were even with the prisoner's.

"What is your name, sir?" Carew asked patiently, confidentially.

"Lorcan."

"Lorcan, do you wish to demonstrate my knowledge of Viking torture to your countrymen?"

More shudders. "No."

"Then, I ask again, Lorcan. Do you know this one called Ingram?"

"Aye," the man answered, sobbing for his life. A flood of words broke forth; he would not be silent. "I know Ingram, he is our captain, he led our army, he lives in the home of Signe Lombay of Waterford, by day he works in the smithy." The man stopped sobbing and raised tearful eyes to Raymond Carew. "What else would you know, master?"

"One thing," Donal Kavanaugh interrupted, stepping forward. "This Signe Lombay—has Ingram married her?"

The man looked puzzled for a moment, then shook his head. "No, my lord. Signe is a widow."

"But does he love her?" Kavanaugh asked, more to himself than to the prisoner, and the man shrugged helplessly.

Raymond Carew turned to Kavanaugh, and his brows lifted the question: "Anything else?"

Kavanaugh shook his head.

"Take this man, break his limbs, and throw him off the cliff with the others."

It was dark when Ingram crept back through the unguarded gates of Waterford, and all was silent within the house of Erik Lombay. Signe's children lay asleep in their bed, and a bowl of cattle dung burned slowly, casting a dim light over the room.

Ingram sat upon Erik's narrow cot and tried to focus his eyes. Had he deluded himself for an entire lifetime? A knight was honorable, dedicated, and true, a defender of the people. A knight never turned from battle, and surrendered only with honor. A knight sought God's victory and settled for nothing less.

His actions today had been most unchivalrous. He had stolen from a dead man, allowed his worst enemy to escape, stood uselessly by while his dearest friend was tortured and killed. He had resorted to deceit to save his own worthless life.

He fell onto the bed as dark despair slipped over him. The Normans would doubtless march on Waterford next, then probably Dublin or Cork. Other Normans surely waited on the sea or in Bristol or a port of Normandy, and once they knew that the Irish were helpless and hopeless, they'd come in like vultures for the kill.

Why had he ever thought that he could actually help? He was no longer a knight, not brave, not worthy of serving a king—even an Irish king. Ingram of the Knighthood— 'twas all a lie.

Sighing in defeat, he clutched the rough wool of the blanket and fell into a dreamless sleep.

Signe found him before dawn. Ingram lay on his side in her father's cot, his feet still on the floor. Blood and mud stained his leather boots; clotted blood filled the mesh of the strange armor he wore over his tunic. She struggled to pull it over his head and gasped when she yanked it free of a gaping wound in his side, but he did not wake or move as she ministered to him.

A dim memory ran across her mind as she cleaned and stitched his wound. She had tended to him before, bathed his face and feet, and tucked him properly into bed. The last time she had done these things, he had healed, regained his strength, and left her life for years. Would he do the same again, now that the enemy was upon them?

Once he was settled, she went to the window, opened the shutters, and peered down the slowly brightening street for some sign of her father. She had not dared to hope that he would come back; still, miracles could happen. But Erik had kissed her forehead, embraced his grandchildren, and bade her farewell with the wide eyes of a man who fears that each glimpse of a beloved object will be his last.

And now Ingram slept in his bed. Signe wiped a tear from her eye. She would not see her father again.

A sharp rap on her door after sunrise told Signe what she already knew—the battle was lost, and the Normans were advancing. Already there were reports that more ships had

landed at Passage East, a small village just outside Waterford, where the Suir and Barrow rivers met. "They say two
hundred knights and a thousand foot soldiers have landed,"
Diana whispered breathlessly as she clutched her thin summer cloak around her. "The Normans from Wexford and
Baginbun are on the march, too. They will be here before
midday, to be sure."

"I'll pass the message," Signe promised, bidding her
neighbor farewell. She watched Diana scuttle back to her
own small house, then threw a cloak over her own tunic and
stepped out into the sultry August morning to speed the
message to her other neighbors.

Ingram was sitting up and awake when Signe returned.
She hung her cloak on a hook by the door and crossed to
the rough-hewn table to cut bread for her hungry children.
"Signe, there is something I must tell you," he said, his
voice gruff with exhaustion. "Your father—he will not come
home today."

"Didn't you think I'd be knowing that already?" she
answered, trying to smile through her tears. She stopped
moving, though, her knife poised above the loaf of brown
bread, and steeled herself to keep moving. There was no
time for grief today, no time to dwell on memories or love
lost. The knife came down; she handed bread to the children, who were struck speechless in their bed by the sight of
Ingram in their grandfather's cot and their mother's flowing
tears.

"The *coimheach* have landed again, twelve hundred of
them, at Passage," she said, slicing bread and cheese for
Ingram. "They'll be here before midday, to be sure. I'm
sending the children to the church."

"That's good," Ingram answered, nodding slowly. "You
go, too."

"Och, and you're a fool if you think I'd be doing so."
The knife clattered to the table as she scooped up bread and
cheese and handed it to Ingram. "For all your talk of being
one of us, you don't know the Irish, sir knight. In days not

long past, the best of women had to go to battle. On her one side me grandmother would carry her bag of provisions; on the other, her babe. A thirty-foot pole she carried on her back, at one end an iron hook, which she would thrust into some woman in the opposite battalion. Her husband would walk behind her, flogging her on to battle, a fence stake in his hand—"

"Surely you don't mean what you're saying. You can't intend to fight."

She gave him a quick, startled glance. "Surely you couldn't be meaning I should do anything else." She lowered her face until her eyes were level with his. "They're coming for our homes, Ingram; they will make slaves of me children. How can we do anything but fight?"

"But you're not a knight; you don't know how to—"

"I know what's right. I know I won't lie down and be taken by the cursed *coimheach,* nor will they touch me children if there's a breath in me body."

She crossed the room, threw open a trunk, and pulled out a pair of her father's leather trousers, dark with wear and age. Without hesitation she drew them on under her skirt, tied them at her waist, and fumbled in the trunk for a short tunic to replace her long gown.

Surprised, she felt hands upon her shoulders and stood to find Ingram at her back. "Calm yourself, brave girl," he said, his eyes strangely vulnerable. "I will fight for you, Signe. I don't know that I'll win, or that the men of Waterford will keep the *coimheach* outside the gates, but with God's help I'll do my best for you."

He turned her, held her close, and whispered something she never thought she'd hear, not in a thousand years: "And if I fail, my brave one, then you can pick up my sword and fight. Fight for all you're worth, Signe, for this enemy is stronger than we thought."

THIRTY-FIVE

Two days passed without incident as the Ostmen and Irish of Waterford fortified their city walls, and the Normans solidified their force. On August 23, Richard FitzGilbert de Clare, called Strongbow, came ashore with his captains and joined the nineteen hundred Flemish and Welsh Normans who comprised his army. Together with four hundred troops assembled by Dermot MacMurrough, they poised on the outskirts of Waterford and anticipated their great victory.

The latest troops, Strongbow's personal army, covered the area of their camp, and just the sight of them terrified the peasants, who ran from the area with their lives. These knights, outfitted completely in Strongbow's royal purple, carried silver lances from which hung violet pennons appliquéd with golden crosses. Surcoats of purple silk fluttered over their armor as they practiced jousting in the fields, and their painted shields bore frightening images of fierce lions.

Nervous and eager, Dermot MacMurrough brought Eva and Bhaltair to meet Raymond Carew, mastermind of the Baginbun massacre. They met Carew with Donal Kavanaugh in a tent erected on a rocky cliff near the sea, and Eva heard her father cackle with pleasure when Donal Kavanaugh rehearsed the battle at Baginbun.

"'At the creek of Baginbun, Ireland was lost and won,'" Kavanaugh said, nodding in respect toward Raymond Carew after telling the story, complete with theatrics. "The peasants are already foretelling your victory. It is understood that Waterford will be ours when we proceed, and then all Ireland waits for us, my king."

"Splendid!" MacMurrough rubbed his weathered hands together. "And as soon as Waterford is mine—"

"Your beautiful Eva will be mine." A light voice interrupted the king's prophesy, and MacMurrough turned toward the tall figure who blocked the sun from the tent's doorway.

Eva started in surprise, forgetting to drop her eyes as a modest maiden should. The man who stood before her with his hands on his hips would have made a beautiful woman. Tall and slim, his lush red hair lay obediently in place while his gray eyes gently surveyed her. His face was narrow and well defined, his hands long and slender. His thin beard, though attractive, did a poor job of hiding the freckles sprinkled across his face. But there was something in his manner that offset his gentle appearance—a masculine force, a great presence born of certainty.

Her mouth curved gently. He looked more Irish than she did.

He noticed the smile. "I hope I please you, Princess Eva," he said, bowing gallantly before her.

"How can I know, sir?" she asked, remembering her role as a modest maiden. She lowered her eyes and her voice. "I scarce know of you and know you not at all."

She felt her father's quick glance of reprimand, and she knew she had spoken too coyly. Yet she sensed that Strongbow would be the kind of man to delight in verbal games. She ignored her father and pressed her instinct. "What would you have me know of you, sir?"

Ignoring her father's obvious discomfort, Strongbow came forward and knelt at her feet. Taking her hand in his, he looked up into her eyes, exuding the confidence of one who had already won a crown and a fortune. "You should know that I desire a wife, and love, and children. This, above all else, drives me to win the battles before me. So before I press further, lady, perhaps I should hear what you desire of me?"

She tilted her head slightly, fully aware of the effect of her blue eyes upon him. The hand that gripped hers trembled; his confidence in battle apparently did not extend to the conquest of women.

"You should know, sir, that I was born a princess. My children should be kings, like their grandfather before them. Any man who will serve me may love me, and he who serves me most shall I love most fully."

He smiled and glanced down at her hand. She had to strain to hear his next words, so quiet was his voice: "And will you give your fidelity as well as your love?"

"Completely, sir."

"Then we have an agreement. For you, beautiful Eva, I will conquer the whole of Ireland if need be. And for me, you will bear children to wear a crown. May God honor the covenant between us made."

"May it be so."

He stood, brushed his lips across her hand, then turned and exited the tent. Raymond Carew followed him, as did Donal Kavanaugh. Her father turned on her in fury: "You thankless wench! What are you thinking, speaking so smartly to the earl? Suppose he had declared you impertinent and sent you packing?"

"Never fear, Father," Eva answered, twirling a loose dark curl around her finger. "No man has sent me packing yet."

For two days Ingram worked with the city's earl and governor, Sitric, to fortify the city, but on the morning of the third day, as the Normans advanced to within yards of Waterford's walls, Signe found Ingram delirious with fever and too weak to rise from his bed. The wound in his side had festered with infection. She instructed Anna to give him cool water and rub the wound with salt and pounded garlic.

Cries of confusion and fear echoed in the city streets beyond, and she quickly tied her hair back. "Tend Ingram well," she told Anna, forcing a smile. "And watch after your brother. I'll be back, never you worry."

She lifted Ingram's heavy sword from its hiding place under his bed, blew a kiss to her children, and paused at the door to murmur a quick prayer for God's protection on all in the house.

When the assault on Waterford began, the besieged Irish and Ostmen fought bravely and long. Their battle plan consisted purely of defensive maneuvers, for most of the city's warriors had been killed or wounded in the battle at Baginbun. Women, elderly men, and beardless teenagers led the defense of the city.

Sitric followed Ingram's plan and directed Waterford's defense from the courtyard of the cathedral in the center of town. He sent women to buttress various points of weakness and young boys to guard strategic positions. The women were directed to pour hot oil on those who came near the city walls; the inexperienced boys shot arrows from tall wooden towers inside the city, then ducked and ran for buckets of water when flaming arrows were returned from the Normans. Boiling tar and "Greek fire," an explosive mixture of asphalt and crude petroleum, were projected from siphons over soldiers brave enough to attempt the climb over the city walls. Twice the heroic inhabitants of Waterford actually repelled vicious frontal assaults, and each time the Normans drew back, Signe thanked God that Ingram had been able to tutor Sitric in Norman warfare.

But as the hot day of battle wore on, it became obvious to even the most optimistic defenders that Ingram of the Knighthood's help had not been enough. The Normans had brought strange contraptions with them, machines of wood and metal that struck fear into the hearts of those who had never seen an organized military force.

At Sitric's command Signe flew to her house, thankful for the opportunity to check on her children. Ingram lay still and pale on his cot, his upper lip dotted with sweat. Anna and Brian crouched wide-eyed at Ingram's side. Brian had curled his tiny hand inside Ingram's.

"Ingram," she whispered intently, moving into the blessed shade of the house. "The earl has sent me to ask your help."

The knight's eyelids fluttered weakly, and he tried to rise but fell back in exhaustion and weakness.

"Don't sit up," she said, kneeling by his side. "Just listen. The Normans have a wooden machine on wheels, which tosses boulders over the wall." She paused to mop her face with a kerchief. "What is it? How do we stop it?"

"A *trebuchet,*" he said, feebly waving his hand. "A catapult. There is no defense. Move the women and children away from that section of the wall when the *trebuchet* approaches. Send men to reinforce the wall with green lumber that will not burn. . . ."

"There are no men available." She bit her lip; desperation made her blunt. "Sitric has also heard reports that the Normans are constructing a tall timber tower in the woods. What is that, Ingram?"

"Burn it, if you can, with a flaming arrow," Ingram mumbled, "or they will put men in it and roll it right up to the city wall. They will have us, Signe; do not doubt it."

"I do doubt it; I must doubt it!" she cried, rising from her knees. She took a moment to douse a rag with cool water, then wiped the perspiration from Ingram's forehead and lips. "We cannot lose, Ingram, else we die."

She could not take time to decipher his vague mumbling; the battle awaited. She kissed her children's heads, then ran through the door.

The city was in the hands of the Normans by sunset. A weak point in the wall was ultimately breached by Raymond Carew, and soon a stream of Norman foot soldiers scaled the walls and opened the gates for the victorious knights to take their spoils.

The knights wasted no time. Riding with fiendish glee through the city, they spared no house, no woman, no man. All homes were torched. The women were taken captive, the men of Waterford killed or enslaved. Sitric formally surrendered to Strongbow in the courtyard of the cathedral and was promptly beheaded for not surrendering sooner.

Signe's heart went into sudden shock when she saw the first gleam of Norman armor atop the city walls. Her whole body tightened; then she took a breath and ran for home, forgetting all but her children and the man who lay near death in her house. Once she reached her courtyard, she screamed for Anna and Brian.

"You must obey me and hide now, quickly, in the hedge," she said, making a desperate effort to calm her voice. "No noise at all, do you hear? Pretend you're hiding from Ingram."

The children recognized the urgency in her tone and ran to hide. Once they were safely away, she rushed to Ingram's side.

His eyes were closed; she slapped his cheek to rouse him from his delirium. "Hurry, Ingram, wake up. You must do as I say, and do not question me. Can you think?"

He blinked his eyes uncertainly but nodded.

"Good. You must don the helmet and the armor." She lifted the heavy hauberk as she spoke and draped it onto his shoulders. He struggled as he lifted his arm and winced as the cold metal mesh touched the bandage over his festering wound, but he did not resist her. She fitted the helmet on his head, then searched frantically for the sword. At last she found it outside in the courtyard, where she had dropped it when she called the children.

"Now, Ingram," she said, propping herself under his right arm. "We must walk to the courtyard, for the house will surely be burned over our heads." She glanced at his bare feet and grimaced. "Shoes. You must wear shoes."

She slipped from beneath his arm, then found a pair of Erik's leather *pampooties* near the doorway. They were old and three inches too short, but she propped them over Ingram's feet and nestled under his arm again. "They're coming, do you hear?" she said, lifting him from the bed. Sheer terror gave her strength. "You must pretend to be one of them, the way you did before; do you remember telling me about that? Good. Now come, Ingram, we must walk to the courtyard."

He was heavy on her shoulders, but she managed to get him out of the house. The sun had disappeared, and the city was alight with burning homes and shops. Screams and cries of frightened women and children rent the air, and Signe prayed with all her soul that her ruse would work.

She found a spot in the courtyard near the gate, far from the thatched roof. She turned Ingram to face her and told him firmly that he must stand upright.

"Now, Ingram," she said, propping his weighty arms upon her shoulders, "your life and me honor depend upon your strength. They will take the women." Her voice shook as she tried to make him understand. "You must stand over me, Ingram, and pretend that you are a Norman. I will scream and protest, and you must—"

He shook his head in confusion and pulled away, but she held tightly to his arms and would not let him go. The steady rumble of hooves approached, a woman screamed outside the tall hedge that surrounded the courtyard, and Signe grasped the mesh of his armor in desperation. "Kiss me or kill me, Ingram, but do something!" she cried, and he lowered the iron helmet onto her shoulder just as a mounted rider burst through the gate with a blazing torch in his hand. She screamed in honest fear, struggling under Ingram's heavy arms, while the Norman knight looked down from his saddle and grinned.

"Que regardez-vous?" Ingram growled, lifting his head and turning to the knight. His voice was heavy and slurred.

"Je suis désolé," the knight replied, still grinning. "Sorry, I'll find another wench."

The knight spurred his horse forward long enough to touch the torch to the thatched roof of the house, then rode out again in search of more interesting prey.

Back in the courtyard, Signe hung onto Ingram and sobbed in mingled relief and humiliation.

As the innocents wept and the city burned, Dermot Mac-Murrough and Donal Kavanaugh rode to the cathedral. Shortly after their arrival, Richard FitzGilbert de Clare, commonly called Strongbow, took Eva, princess of Leinster, as his wife in the eyes of God and man.

Two days later, when news of Waterford's conquest reached the palace of Rory O'Connor, the high king of all Ireland gave the command that Niall and Peadar, the hostage sons of Dermot MacMurrough, should be beheaded. Donnan and Ailean, two of O'Rourke's most faithful warriors, volunteered to carry out the king's command.

"You know," Tiernán O'Rourke said, tugging on the sleeve of his royal ally as the brothers left to perform their distasteful task, "things are come to a sad state when the king of Leinster allows his sons to be killed and his daughter to marry a foreigner. If it were not impossible, 'twould almost seem that another of the *rigdamnae* sought Leinster's throne by eliminating all rivals, would it not?"

"Is it impossible?" O'Connor asked, little lightning bolts of worry darting into his eyes. "Who would that person be?"

Signe
1169

God sets the lonely in families,
he leads forth the prisoners with singing.

PSALM 68:6

THIRTY-SIX

The once proud and free city-state of Waterford had
become an occupied garrison. The warriors who had freely
prowled and plundered the city on the day of their victory
were now contained in the former earl's house in the center
of town. Signe heard frightened whispers that Strongbow
and MacMurrough were headquartered there, too, with
Donal Kavanaugh and other Norman knights fiercer than
the Fomorians of ancient legend.

But she gave little thought to the conquerors of the
ruined city as she struggled to find food and shelter for her
family. While Ingram convalesced under the shelter Signe
had constructed from branches and blankets, Anna was kept
busy shooing flies from Ingram and fetching cool water to
wet his parched lips. Signe put little Brian to work gathering
the chickens who had taken flight, and she herself tried to
rebuild enough of a home to ensure their survival.

Only the charred walls of her house remained. She had
managed to salvage only her table, which was badly burned
but still serviceable. Besides the few chickens, all that had
survived the fire were a few vegetables in the garden and the
clothes on their backs. Theirs had once been a prosperous
household, Signe thought, wiping her forehead with the
hem of her tunic. Now, if they were to survive the winter,
they would have to beg food and provisions from the invaders.

She looked over the blackened remains of her hedge and

surveyed her neighborhood. The street now ran past a row of burned-out shells, the occupants long vanished into the night or dispatched to heaven by Norman swords. If not for Ingram, she might have fled into the forest or to the sea, but she and the children would not have survived long. The sea teemed with pirates; the forest crawled with looters and people more desperate than she. *Perhaps,* she thought, looking down at the wounded knight, *since I saved his life, his inability to travel may have spared us as well.*

Her patient groaned, and Anna's frightened glance brought Signe back to reality. "Mama, he is not well," Anna called, running to bury her head in her mother's skirt as if she could no longer bear to look at the pale man who lay in the dust. "Is he dying?"

"I don't know," Signe answered, patting her daughter's shoulder. "If he dies . . ." She waved her hands helplessly. It was hard to believe they would not all die within the week.

Donal Kavanaugh let his dirty boots fall to the floor and glared at the Normans in the garrison, who gorged themselves on the best meat Waterford had to offer. "I say we search until we find him," he snarled, his face tightening into a mask of rage. "Ingram *na nRidireachd* is here in Waterford; he could not have escaped us."

"If he is here, he is dead," Raymond Carew said, waving a chicken leg carelessly. He paused to take another bite and spoke as he chewed. "No brave knight came riding out to meet us here, Kavanaugh, and I think none exists. If this Ingram is the knight you think he is, he would have died bravely in the fight."

"I have searched among the dead, and he is not there," Kavanaugh answered, his patience straining against MacMurrough's order to treat the Normans with respect. If Donal had his way, he'd order all of them, including Strongbow, back across the Irish Sea.

A light voice from the doorway cut through the tension

in the room. "Perhaps our brave knight fears to fight because of the hostage you hold, my dear brother," Eva said, moving into the chamber.

Every man present, including the besotted and useless Strongbow, stopped eating to stare at Eva. She smiled gently, but within the depths of her eyes, Kavanaugh saw the dark fire of her fierce intelligence, the same flame that burned in his soul.

"What of my hostage?" Kavanaugh asked, his brows lifting the question. "The boy is not here and is in no danger. Why won't the knight come forward to face me?"

"Because one word from you, one fleet horse, one letter, could end his son's life," Eva answered, gracefully sinking onto a bench at her husband's side. Her hand fell on Strongbow's head, and the Norman seemed to melt under her touch. Kavanaugh forced himself to look away.

"Perhaps Ingram works to encourage a revolt against you; perhaps he even hides in the forest outside the city," Eva went on, her voice lazy in the stillness of the afternoon. "But he will not attack openly, for you hold his dear son." She paused and smiled serenely at her new husband. "Ingram is a man of virtue, of compassion and honor. He would die himself before bringing harm to the boy."

"If he is a threat, he should be found," Strongbow said, his eyes darkening as he looked at his wife. Whether his action sprang from jealousy or the desire to please Eva, Kavanaugh could not tell, but Strongbow made a quick gesture with his freckled arm. "Carew, gather men and search house to house. FitzStephen and de Prendergast will comb the forest outside the city. Every man found alive is to be brought here for an accounting."

"Every man, my lord?" Carew asked, his fingers curled around a pastry.

"You heard me; make it so," Strongbow answered. His eyes shone with a possessive gleam as he looked at his new bride.

Eva threw a triumphant half-smile in Donal Kavanaugh's

359

direction, and he grinned in acknowledgment of her shrewdness. He had condemned and railed against Ingram for half an hour, and Strongbow had not moved. But one word of praise for the knight from Eva had set the Norman armies into motion.

His smile faded, however, when he considered Eva's motivation. He had known her long enough to learn that she never did anything without a reason. Why had she encouraged Strongbow to find Ingram?

Kavanaugh waited until she left the room, then followed her out into the hall. "Eva, a word with you," he called, lengthening his stride even though a quick pace accented his limp. When he reached her, he took her hand and watched her eyes carefully. She stepped back as if to ward off his touch.

"You set the armies upon the knight," he said flatly, avoiding all pleasantries. "What interest do you have in his capture?"

Her eyes searched his for a moment, then her mouth curved in a predatory smile. "Why does it matter, Donal?" she asked, pulling her cold hand from his. "Perhaps I seek to aid your quest."

"I find that hard to believe."

She shrugged lightly, then gathered her skirts to move away. "Then accept the truth: If the knight is dead, the boy will be mine. I've grown quite fond of him." She took two steps, then tossed a casual question over her shoulder. "Have you never loved anyone, Donal?"

Kavanaugh felt an unexpected tug at his heart as the memory of his mother floated through his mind—a thin, once-pretty woman who had cried pitifully during long nights and finally died, leaving him alone.

"No," he said, his mouth curving in a mirthless smile. "No one."

"Then you wouldn't understand," Eva answered as she left him in the empty hallway.

Signe had just gathered a group of wilted vegetables from the garden patch when she heard Anna and Brian scream. She dropped her scanty load and ran to the courtyard gate as three mounted Normans pushed their way in, their horses' hooves trampling the meager possessions she had managed to salvage.

One of the Normans, a heavy man with a pale, pitiless face, reined in his mount when he saw her. His eyebrows rose in obvious admiration, and Signe remembered too late that she had belted her tunic and raised her skirt so her legs could escape the stifling heat.

She unclasped the belt at her waist, and the hem of her tunic fell to the ground. She lifted her chin. "What have you to do with us?" she demanded in English. She felt herself trembling, and she recognized the heat in her chest and belly as pure rage. "Your men have already burned the house and taken everything of value."

"We are not come to plunder today, my beauty," the man said, his eyes narrowing as he studied her. "We search for a man. Have you seen or heard of one called Ingram? He is often called Ingram of the Knighthood."

She felt herself flinch at Ingram's name. If the idiot before her had any sense, he'd realize he had hit a sore spot.

But his eyes had dropped as if he sought the outline of her legs through her tunic. "No," she said evenly. "I know no Ingram and no knight."

"Perhaps, then, you know of a woman called Signe Lombay? We know the knight has lived with her family." He gave her a lopsided grin. "Quite unchivalrous of him, actually, to live with an Irish wench."

She flushed to the roots of her hair but took a deep breath and forced herself to remain calm. When she paused, the knight offered another comment: "We have prisoners, you see, who can draw us a map to this wom-

361

an's house, but I am asking you freely, my lady. Do you know this Signe Lombay?"

She ran her hands through her unruly hair as if searching absently for a name, and a shout interrupted their conversation. "Sir Carew!" one of the other knights called. "A man! Nearly dead, but a man in armor lies here!"

Carew kept his eyes steadily upon her. "Know you that a knight lies in your yard?" he asked, leaning forward confidentially. "Could it be that you are a sympathizer? Did you give aid to one of my men?"

"Sir," she answered, tipping her head back to look better at him. "I believe God would have us give aid and succor to all beings in need."

He smiled then, glanced to the side yard, and called to his men. "Bring the man across your saddle. We'll not trouble this woman any longer."

Dutifully, he raised his hand to his gleaming helmet and saluted. "*Au revoir*, my lady," he called, turning his horse. "Perhaps I will visit you again sometime."

❖ ❖ ❖

Donal Kavanaugh, Eva, and MacMurrough, a fierce trio of conquerors, searched the motley crowd of assembled men for a sign of the knight called Ingram. Eva scanned the faces of wounded, sick, and infirm men without pity, but the face of a frightened child held her attention for a moment. "Have these Normans no sense?" she complained, forcing herself to turn from the boy. "Ingram will not be among these. He is likely halfway to O'Connor's camp by now."

"I beg to disagree," Kavanaugh answered, roughly grasping the gray head of a man who bore only a bloody stump where his right arm should have been. He studied the wounded warrior as casually as if a head of lettuce lay in his hand. "Ingram will stay nearby and rouse the populace. He delights in his legendary status; the man has sought nothing so much as glory and fame."

"You are mistaken, Donal," Eva said, moving on to glance at the face of the next prisoner. "The knight has done nothing more than search for his family." She cocked her head and looked at her half brother quizzically. "You asked why I sought the knight, and I told you. Why do *you* pursue him so zealously?"

"Because my son hates a traitor," MacMurrough interrupted, throwing a stout arm around Kavanaugh's shoulders. The grooves around his mouth deepened as he fondly regarded his illegitimate son. "This, Eva, is the son who should have been lawfully mine. His is the mettle of the MacMurroughs, the ancient line of the MacMurchada. This Ingram has dishonored our family and throne, leaving our camp to fight for the O'Connor—"

"Only after you abandoned him to certain death," Eva interjected, forcing a polite smile.

MacMurrough grunted and said nothing as Kavanaugh moved ahead and scanned the last of the prisoners. "Not here!" he stammered, stamping his good foot before Raymond Carew. "Did you not inquire at the house of Signe Lombay?"

"Excuse me, my lord Kavanaugh," Carew answered dryly, scratching his pale beard. "But the city is destroyed, and the survivors are not eager to answer my questions. You see before you every man we found within the city and in the forest. We found but one other, a Norman, who is ill with a festered wound and fever—"

"You fool," Eva hissed, glaring at Carew. "Ingram is Norman." She lifted her eyes from Carew's heavy face and saw two foot soldiers carrying a blond, bearded knight on a stretcher. She gasped in recognition, and Kavanaugh flew from Carew's side, limping beside the stretcher in the dust as the men hurried to find the doctor.

"Oh yes," Eva heard her brother call as he kept pace with the stretcher bearers. "Run, my good men, run for the doctor, for this man is my prisoner and no Norman. Whatever it takes, he must be kept alive."

363

Through a careful regime of herbs, baths, and regular bleedings, Ingram's fever broke. Within a week he was discharged from the Norman doctor's care and consigned to a prison in Waterford. When he asked his crime, his gaoler merely smiled and walked away.

Exhausted, still weak, Ingram leaned against the wall in despair.

Yet again, Lord, you have spared me. But why?

Softly, gently, the answer came: *I have loved you with an unending love.*

Closing his eyes in confusion, he sank to the floor.

Through the heat of August and the cold of January, Ingram waited in prison. As his body healed, his soul struggled to make sense of his trials. Had God brought him to Ireland only to mock him? Was his faith in knightly ideals worthless? Only one fact was undeniable: He, the so-called Ingram of the Knighthood, had failed miserably. Hundreds, perhaps thousands of his countrymen had paid for his failure in battle with their lives. How many more would die before the inexorable Norman onslaught?

How could he have thought himself a knight? He was nothing but the son of a farmer, a simple peasant. He should never have left Glendalough.

Silently, bitterly, he railed against the monk who had stolen him away for knighthood and cursed Donnchad and Afrecca for surrendering him to the monastery. He was not fit for God or glory but for the earth. Well, in time, the earth would claim him. His execution could not be far off.

On a freezing day in late February the guard unlocked the door to the pit that served as Ingram's prison. Ingram stood, alarmed at the sight of well-shod feet on the stairs, and his blood rose in a jet when he recognized the nasal voice of Donal Kavanaugh. The man descended the stairs and smiled at Ingram as if greeting a long-lost friend.

"Kavanaugh." Ingram spat the name as if it were a foul curse.

Kavanaugh merely smiled and nodded to the Norman gaoler who had led him in. "You may go, good man, for I trust the chains that hold this man to the wall. My words are for his ears alone."

The gaoler muttered something in reply and slammed the creaking door—hurrying, no doubt, back to the warmth of his fire. Ingram could not speak but gave Kavanaugh a killing look. The man had been nothing but a torment since Ingram's arrival in Ireland.

Kavanaugh clapped his hands and rubbed them briskly together, his breath misting in the cold. "Brr! Amazing, isn't it, how frigid these dungeons can be?"

"By all rights, you should know," Ingram replied evenly. "You above all men deserve to spend your life in a prison."

Donal Kavanaugh smiled and wagged his index finger at Ingram like a scolding tutor. "Come, come, me friend, or should I say, me brother? For we served together once, you and I. You rode as a leader of Dermot MacMurrough's warriors, while I rode in the forest and aided the king's cause in more subtle ways. Still, we both sought MacMurrough's favor, didn't we?"

"That king's favor means nothing to me."

"Ah, but it should." Kavanaugh drew his fur-lined cloak about him and enfolded his hands in the warmth of the garment's heaviness. "I am glad to see you have regained much of your health and strength, Sir Ingram. I would have come to see you sooner, but I have been busy leading MacMurrough's armies. There is also a boy who needs me, a little lad whose face is stamped with your handsome features."

Ingram leaped toward Donal Kavanaugh, but the chains held him fast and cut into his raw flesh. Kavanaugh raised an eyebrow. "Did I say something wrong?"

Ingram swallowed his urge to roar in anger and hatred.

Still straining against his chains, he muttered, "Surely you know that I will kill you if my son is hurt."

"Don't threaten me, Ingram. The boy is alive and well. I wished to keep him as a slave, but our own dear Eva dotes on him as she would a pet. He serves her even now at Mac-Murrough's palace. When she tires of him, well—" he shrugged— "then he'll become me slave. Time enough for that later."

Ingram's fists rose involuntarily, but he was again caught short by his shackles. Kavanaugh noted the violent movement and drew his lips in a tight smile. "You know, we are much alike, you and I. Both of us have searched throughout our lives for our parents' blessing, though of course, I knew I was an illegitimate castoff. But though the villagers called me *ni truaillidn,* me mother called me her son. After a long while, I learned not to let vile names bother me." He paused and squinted at Ingram. "A good lesson to learn."

"We are nothing alike," Ingram spat.

"That's where you're wrong, me friend. We are much alike: both fighters, both determined, both prouder than we ought to be." Kavanaugh paced slowly through the narrow cell, taking care to keep out of Ingram's reach. "Have you never thought, Sir Ingram, that a man is the sum of his ancestors? He is like the lower end of a suspended chain— he may be swayed to the left or the right, but remove your hand and he falls into line with the other links, his predecessors."

Kavanaugh stopped pacing and stood inches outside Ingram's reach. "We *are* alike, you and I; we are forged of the same chain. Both of us knew our father; and for a time neither of us were acknowledged by him."

Ingram frowned. "You speak as though we share a father," he said, curling his lip in distaste. "Donnchad was poor, but he was a faithful man and not likely to beget a devil like you."

Kavanaugh raised an eyebrow in disbelief. "Faith, and surely you don't believe those peasants from Glendalough

are your true *màthair* and *athair*? 'Tis folly to believe such a
lie, for I swear to you that the true son of the farmer
Donnchad lives even now as a hermit in the monastery of
Abbot Steaphan. I have seen the man, a pious simpleton.
Donnchad's blood flows as evidently in his face as your
father's does in yours."

Ingram's denial caught in his throat as reality shattered
his misconceptions. Suddenly everything became clear.
From the beginning Donnchad had doubted Ingram's claim
to their family, and Ingram knew now he had been accepted
as a son because Afrecca desperately needed to reclaim the
child she had surrendered. Philip and the others had
accepted him reluctantly not because he was a poor farmer
but because he was alien. He didn't belong in the mountains of Glendalough, and he never had.

In a breathless instant of release, he was freed. He would
miss Philip and the others, but he would no longer feel like
a traitor to the clan or a misfit. Pure and simple relief
flooded his soul.

Then a mocking inner voice reminded him of Kavanaugh's words: *"Both of us knew our father. . . ."*

Ingram glanced up, slanting the hideous unspoken question to his tormentor, and Kavanaugh gave him a mirthless
smile. "Aye, there is more, sir knight," he said, folding his
hands outside his robe. "Would you like to hear it?"

Ingram inhaled slowly, like a man about to plunge into
freezing water. Kavanaugh paid no attention. "I would tell
you even if you had no wish to hear the story. For this is a
tale of pain and violence and betrayal. The story was
recorded by a monk, the parchment discovered years ago
by an illiterate peasant woman in an abandoned stone hut
outside the monastery at Clonmacnoise. The circumstances
were most strange. For with the parchment, you see, lay the
dead body of a young girl, a crucifix around her neck and
her belly slit open. For the price of a bag of gold, the
woman sold the parchment to me and showed me the
young girl's grave."

"What has this to do with me?" Ingram asked.

"Patience, my good knight. I read the parchment, and it has a great deal to do with you." Kavanaugh backed away and took a seat on a stone step. "You should know, my brother warrior, that the princes of Ireland have voracious appetites. Over forty years ago, a youthful prince went hunting in the Kingdom of Meath and paused to pray in the chapel for a successful hunt. There he spied a most beautiful young nun. Disregarding all that was proper and holy in the eyes of God and man, the prince took the nun to feed his own desires."

Ingram lowered his eyes in shame and heard Kavanaugh chuckle contentedly. "Yes, me brother, 'twas a terrible thing to do. A monk, however, heard the girl's pitiful cries and frightened the prince away. This monk cared for the girl until the child that sprang from the youth's loins was born. To help the nun's child in birth, the monk cut her belly open, and the blade of the dagger sliced the child's left leg. If you bear such a scar, Ingram of the proud and mighty Knighthood, then you are the nun's child, and there is no doubt."

Ingram did not have to look down to know that Donal Kavanaugh told the truth. Kavanaugh paused a moment, glancing at Ingram's filthy leg, then leaned against the wall to continue his tale. "Before the girl died, she begged the monk to give the child to God, but the monk, filled with bitterness toward the God he served, stole the baby away and left nothing but a parchment record of all that had transpired. The nun would be pleased, don't you think, to know that her child serves God with a sword instead of a monk's prayers?"

Donal Kavanaugh folded his arms and smiled in smug satisfaction as Ingram sank back against the cold wall of the prison. "This prince," he finally asked, pausing to moisten his dry lips. "Who was he?"

Kavanaugh's cold eyes glowed with the black fire of vengeance as he smiled at Ingram. "The author of the parchment could not name the girl's attacker. But I would never have found the parchment or the peasant woman if an aging prince of Ireland had not confessed in a moment of confidence that his worst offense was committed on a day when his youthful lusts led him to ravish a bride of Christ at Clonmacnoise."

Kavanaugh's smile flattened. "That prince is now king of Leinster, Dermot MacMurrough. Ingram of the Knighthood, you are truly me own brother."

THIRTY-SEVEN

Despite the foul warmth of the soiled hay under him on the prison floor, Ingram could not stop shivering. After his startling declaration, Donal Kavanaugh had announced that for the crimes of treason, insurrection, and attempted patricide, Ingram would be executed within a week. A priest would hear Ingram's final confession. Then Kavanaugh turned and fled up the stone steps as if he could not bear to remain in Ingram's presence one minute more.

Ingram's mind still reeled from Kavanaugh's news. The relief he had felt upon hearing that he was not the child of peasants had blossomed into brief joy when he thought himself the son of a prince. But oh, the horror of learning *which* prince! Dermot MacMurrough had risen to power by murder, bloodshed, and cruelty; he had no noble lineage to recommend him. If Ingram truly was of the MacMurroughs, his prayers for a noble family had been answered in the cruelest way he could imagine.

In the merciless light of reality, Ingram realized that he was as loathsome and illegitimate as Donal Kavanaugh and descended from the same heartless monster.

The appointed day of his execution dawned clear and bright, and a guard rattled keys at the top of the stairs before Ingram had fully awakened. "A visitor," the gaoler called, pushing the heavy oak door open. A small pair of leather boots stepped into view, and Ingram sat up and blinked the sleep from his eyes. "Be quick, lady," the gaoler warned. "The priest awaits. This man dies today."

The door slammed shut; the boots came farther into the cell. A woman in a plain brown tunic moved toward him and allowed the hood to fall from her head. Signe!

Ingram rose to his feet. She clung tightly to him for a moment, then pulled away. "There is little time for talk," she said, keeping her voice low as she pulled a square of cloth from her sleeve and wiped at her wet eyes. "But never fear, Ingram, you have friends. During the six months you've been locked away from us, your friends have slipped into the city."

"I don't deserve to live, Signe." He lowered his hands from her shoulders. "I know things you do not. Perhaps my death will be a good thing."

She pulled away, horror filling her eyes. "Do not say such things! You are Ingram *na nRidireachd*, the one who will lead us forward!"

He laid a pale, cold finger across her warm lips. "No. I am the son of Dermot MacMurrough, as much a shame as Donal Kavanaugh himself. My pride is fueled with MacMurrough's own cold ambition—'tis his cruelty that has made my hands swift with a sword."

"No, no!" She threw her arms around him, as if to comfort a child. "Ingram, if there be truth in these false imaginings of yours, remember that if you look forward you need not look back. God is with you, sir knight. For today, me love, friends stand outside to help you. You will not die today."

"I will. When the executioner comes, I will not resist."

"Think of your son!" Her eyes blazed up at him; her face was gently lined with creases that had not existed when he had last seen her. He brushed her fiery hair with his hand and pulled her close.

"I have spent six months thinking," he said, pressing his lips to her ear. "A man is all that he can call his, Signe. He has a body and soul, clothes, perhaps a house, a wife and children, ancestors and friends, reputation and honor, lands and horses." He pulled back and looked deep into her emerald eyes. "I have nothing but an aging body and a weary soul. No wife, no honor, no house, no family, and only the vilest of ancestors. My son will not know or remember me. If I do not claim him, he may never know that my tainted blood flows in his veins."

"You underestimate yourself." Her voice was like a warm embrace in the chill air, and he smiled at her earnest attempts to dissuade him. "You have so much, Ingram! You are a true follower of God, and he has graced you with his strength and goodness. Even now the Irish speak of Ingram the *ridirich*. Your friends have come from Dromahair; me home is your home, and Anna, Brian, and I will be your family!"

"I would not bring the wickedness of MacMurrough upon you. You have suffered too much already."

Tenderly he drew her to him, kissed her forehead, then ignored her tears as he held her at arm's length and called for the gaoler to bring the priest.

After confessing to a litany of sins, Ingram held his hands forth to be bound with stout rope and obediently walked between his executioners to the top of the tower outpost that overlooked the inlet of the sea. The wild wind howled around him, slapping the guards' cloaks against their faces as they cursed the foul winds and the lingering clouds that threatened to drown them in freezing rain.

"Ingram of the Knighthood," a guard recited, hastily glancing at the parchment in his hand. "By order of Strongbow, ruler of Waterford, and Dermot MacMurrough, king of Leinster, Wexford, and Waterford, I sentence you to be thrown from this tower into the sea. May God have mercy upon your soul."

Ingram did not resist when he was led to the edge of the

precipice, nor did he balk when the guards motioned for him to climb upon the stout stone wall. He pulled himself up, creeping steadily along the crumbling stone, and he placed the edge of his worn boots into the expanse of sky that surrounded him. The wind shrilled as he looked over the broad expanse of the deep. The guard cursed and jabbed Ingram's cloak with the point of a sword, and Ingram stepped casually off the wall and into the gray firmament.

For a moment he flew. Then the churning ocean pulled him down until his chest hit the wall of water. He felt the blow and the sting of pain. Above him the heads of the guards on the tower disappeared as they retreated from the bawling weather, and the world went black.

"Now," Signe urged, her teeth chattering as she hid behind the rocks on the beach. "Hurry, Ailean, lest he drown!"

Ailean and Donnan moved swiftly toward the water, diving with the practiced ease of fishermen. They seemed to search forever in the angry gray waters; then Signe saw a hand waving from the water's surface. Three heads appeared. The brothers struggled out of the surf, carrying a pale, thin body between them. Though Ingram was blue with cold when they reached Signe, Donnan assured her that the knight lived.

She had a small fire glowing behind the rocks, and while Signe piled more wood on the fire, the brothers stripped Ingram of his wet clothing and wrapped him in a fur-lined mantle. Once they had propped him near the roaring fire, Ailean slapped Ingram's face steadily, almost rhythmically, until the knight's hand finally flew up in defense.

Ailean's ruddy face spread in a wide smile. "He lives," he said simply.

"God be praised," Signe echoed fervently. She pulled a bag forward. "In there you'll find boots, a tunic, a dagger. Dress him quickly, and speed him to O'Rourke, will you? They'll have someone searching for the body soon, and it won't do if he's found near here."

"Don't worry, mistress," Donnan answered, furiously rubbing Ingram's blue feet. "We'll have him warmed up and out of here in an hour. O'Rourke waits for us at Enniskerry."

"God bless you, and God bless Tiernán O'Rourke for sending you," Signe said, planting a quick kiss on the brothers' heads. She paused and laid her hand gently on Ingram's cold cheek for a moment before turning and scampering up the rocky cliffs.

He thought he saw a billowy figure clambering among the rocks, but the insistent and clumsy hands who dressed and warmed him diverted his attention. Ingram frowned. He had hoped to awaken in heaven; what was this?

A man near him laughed. "Look, brother, he awakens," he said, gathering a tunic in his strong hands. He slipped the rough material over Ingram's head and struggled to pull Ingram's leaden arm through the sleeves. "Do you not recognize us, old friend?"

Ingram blinked. The voices were familiar, the bodies stout and strong—

"Ailean and Donnan!" he mumbled, consciousness resurfacing. "What are you doing here?"

"O'Rourke sent us to find you; Signe Lombay told us of your execution," Ailean explained, tying a leather belt around Ingram's waist. "She visited the prison every day, but they would not allow her to see you until this morning. Didn't she tell you of our plan?"

"I wanted to die," Ingram said simply, a painful warmth spreading along his toes and fingers.

"Och, you can't be meaning that," Donnan answered, slipping new leather boots over Ingram's cold feet. "What good would you do us in the underworld?"

"In heaven," Ingram insisted, scowling at his friend. "I confessed to everything. My soul is clean."

"Is it now?" Ailean asked, fastening a heavy winter cloak around Ingram's neck with an iron brooch. He stood back and examined their handiwork. "Sure, and a finer looking corpse I've never seen; have you, brother?"

"Nay."

"Then let's be off. Can you walk, Ingram?"

"Of course," Ingram grumbled. But when he stood, his legs turned to jelly, and he collapsed in a pile on the sand.

The brothers laughed and propped his arms around their brawny necks. "'Tis good enough," Ailean said as they dragged Ingram from the beach. "As long as you can sit on a horse, we'll have you to O'Rourke's camp before 'tis too late."

THIRTY-EIGHT

Donal Kavanaugh smirked as the Normans behind him grumbled, their complaints surrounding him as always. They wanted to take the roads. Their horses weren't used to this thick forest; they were strong destriers, stallions more suited for running on broad fields of conquest. But as his nimble mare picked her way over the damp and thawing ground, Kavanaugh held up his hand for silence and lifted his chin in stubborn pride. His father had placed the troops in his command, elevated him above even Raymond Carew and Robert FitzStephen.

He led the army because he knew the land better than any Norman. Strongbow had listened to his suggestions intently, then surprised Kavanaugh by supporting his idea. "Donal's plan makes sense," Strongbow had said, turning carefully to his father-in-law. "If O'Rourke and O'Connor guard the only road to Dublin—"

"The geography of the land leaves only two defiles through which an army could proceed," Donal had pointed out, gesturing at the rough map on the table. "There are sure to be warriors at Enniskerry and Clondalkin."

"And you propose to lead my men *where?*" MacMurrough had asked, peering at his son in proud amazement.

"Through the forest, over the mountains," Kavanaugh replied, lifting his head. "I have spent considerable time there. I can lead the knights through, find a place for training, and arrive at the gates of Dublin without O'Connor ever suspecting that we are anywhere near."

MacMurrough seemed to ponder Donal's proposal, and Donal clenched his teeth when the aging king's eyes went again to Strongbow for confirmation. This Welsh earl was unworthy of the honors MacMurrough had bestowed—why did MacMurrough seek Strongbow's opinion instead of trusting his own *son*?

Donal forced himself to remain calm. He would have to be patient. 'Twas only a matter of time before Strongbow met his demise.

"I suggest we let Kavanaugh lead the men according to his plan," Strongbow said graciously, his hand claiming Eva's. She sat by his side, one hand on her rapidly expanding belly, the other tousling Alden's hair.

Another usurper. The child had made a home in MacMurrough's castle and looked every inch a prince. Kavanaugh felt his soul burn with resentment as he stared at the boy.

MacMurrough must have noticed his gaze. "The lad you brought us is handsome, Donal," he said, shifting slightly in his chair, "but I fear Eva will tire of him when the new MacMurrough prince is born. What a wonderful day that will be—the best of Ireland and the best of Wales combined into me first grandson, a strong new prince."

Eva protested that she would never grow tired of Alden, but something in the king's proud tone stirred jealousy in Kavanaugh's breast. He felt himself coil and prepare to strike. How easy it would be to tell the old man that he had a grandson already—Eva's pet! But MacMurrough did not deserve that pleasure.

"When the new prince is born, give Alden to me," Kavanaugh said, making an effort to keep his voice light. "I have often wished for a lad to help with me target practice."

Eva's cold blue eyes met his, and his mouth curved into a bitter smile. "To fetch the arrows, of course, me dear sister."

The wind rushed out from the Wicklow Mountains with snow in its breath, and Ingram braced himself against its frigid embrace and urged his horse onward. Tiernán O'Rourke had not wanted Ingram to leave camp after only a week of rest, but since the enemy was nowhere in sight, Ingram had been granted leave to gather additional warriors. Ingram justified his detour by telling himself that he *would* return with additional men, but not before he accomplished another, far more difficult task.

The road to the family *rath* of Donnchad and Afrecca lay naked in the barrenness of winter, and Ingram's horse snorted in protest at the steep climb. The brittle ground was hard under the animal's hooves, and Ingram stopped often to rest the mare, who doubtless preferred the warmth of the crowded corral back at Enniskerry.

During one of these restful pauses, Ingram saw a falcon rise from her nest and circle overhead, screeching angrily at a disturbance in the forest. He withdrew from the road, slipped from the saddle, and hid the horse behind the fullness of an evergreen.

Horses were approaching through the woods, a great many, and the unusual aspect of such a force lifted the hair on the back of Ingram's neck. No travelers, no family, no man would travel these steep, mountainous paths in winter, unless—

A thin, nasal voice echoed through the stillness, and Ingram stiffened when he recognized the voice and the face of the man who came into view. "Yes, my friend Carew," Donal Kavanaugh was saying, "just beyond this ridge lies a monastery. The monks will gladly feed us a warm supper in exchange for a purse of gold."

Ingram slipped behind a bare tree and closed his eyes. What was Donal Kavanaugh doing in the Wicklow Mountains with an army? O'Rourke and O'Connor expected the Normans to come by way of the Wicklow coast or the road to Clondalkin. No one dreamed that Kavanaugh would choose a treacherous, time-consuming overland route.

Ingram smiled ruefully and shook his head. He had to give Kavanaugh credit; the move was bold and ingenious. "So, little brother," he whispered, not daring to move from behind the tree. "Now begins the race to the finish."

The children at the *rath* were thinner than he remembered, but Philip's broad grin was warm and genuine as Ingram dismounted beyond the gate. Ingram stared at the man who had briefly been his brother and marveled that he could have ever believed himself of the same blood and bone of this man. Philip was now bald, save for two patches of dark hair above his ears; the telltale widow's peak of the clan had been erased from his wide forehead.

"Ingram." Philip's wife, Eamhair, held out her hands to him, and he took her hands in his and chafed them gently.

"Welcome home."

Ingram turned at Philip's greeting and extended his hand. "I have news to tell you, Philip, that must be told quickly. Can we go into your hut and speak freely? And can you spare men for a battle? Even now the enemy rides below us across the mountains."

Philip's eyes darkened, but he nodded and led the way to Donnchad's beehive hut of stone, lifting the flap of leather so Ingram could enter first.

When the entire tale had been told, Philip blinked unsteadily, and Ingram was startled to see tears in the man's eyes. "I never thought much of ye, truth to tell," Philip said. His hands trembled on his knees, but whether from cold or emotion, Ingram could not tell. "But when you left us, I watched you go with pride. You were not a farmer, of little use save as a hunter—"

"I owe you a great deal," Ingram said, reaching out to

rest his hand on Philip's arm. "You and Eamhair took care of Alden; you taught me all I know of farming, and you allowed me into the family. But today I must renounce my place in it; I have no inheritance here. My portion must be divided with the others when the time comes."

Philip nodded stiffly. "It will be as you say. Though you were not one of us, Ingram, still, I must admit—" he looked to his wife for assurance, and a smile brushed across Eamhair's face— "we were proud when the brehons told us stories of Ingram *na nRidireachd.*"

Ingram acknowledged the compliment with a nod. "Now, Philip, I must ask a more crucial question: Donal Kavanaugh leads the invaders to Dublin, and if the port is lost, all of Ireland will fall to the Normans. The high king needs men, and I am here to beg your help in his name. But before you consider the king's plea, will you consider mine?"

Philip raised his chin and regarded Ingram carefully. "What do you need?"

"Alden." Ingram spoke quickly, without premeditation. "If Donal Kavanaugh rides with an army in these woods, Ferns is likely to be unguarded, or nearly so. Alden is there, Philip, and I must free him or die trying. Though he is not of your blood, still, he nursed at your wife's breast."

Eamhair stirred at the mention of Alden's name, and now she leaned forward, a wisp of gray hair falling into her eyes. "Alden can be saved?" she asked, her eyes strangely haunted. She turned toward her husband. "Philip, since the day he was taken from us, I have not slept without dreaming of him."

Philip reached for the hunting spear propped against the wall. "We may have taught you farming, Ingram," Philip answered, "but you have taught us much about courage and honor." He paused and smiled. "All the men of this *deirb-fhine* stand ready to go with ye. Lead us where you will, Ingram *na nRidireachd,* and we will follow."

Tears rose in Ingram's eyes at the sight of Philip's devotion. "Let us go, then," he said, nodding in satisfaction. He stood and smiled at Eamhair. "If God smiles on us, there will be few guards at Ferns. I will return your men safely."

The journey to Ferns was slow and arduous. The ten men from Glendalough traveled on foot, and though they were as surefooted as any mountain packhorse, they were unused to marching in a procession or with any military discipline. Ingram gave up trying to keep order in their line as they progressed through the mountains. He especially tried not to think about their choice of weapons—axes, hoes, and spears. They were not equipped to deal with any Norman troops MacMurrough might have left behind to guard his castle.

They crossed the mountains, heading westward, until they reached the River Slaney, then followed the river southward until they reached Ferns. Ingram motioned for his men to hide in the forest while he rode out alone to survey the rebuilt stone fortress.

Dressed in the simple tunic and cloak Donnan and Ailean had given him, he rode slowly. Nothing in his appearance should have alarmed any guard on the tower. He squinted toward the castle. One guard stood on the rampart, his hand at his sword, and another leaned inside a window of the stone tower. But no trumpet sounded; no one seemed the least bit troubled by his easygoing ride across the open pasture.

Presently the gate opened, and a hulking man on horseback rode forth to greet him. Ingram's blood froze in his veins when the two were close enough to recognize each other. Ingram's hand automatically went for the dagger hidden at his waist; Bhaltair's hand hovered above his sword. But both weapons remained sheathed as the men circled each other on horseback, each unwilling to make a definite move.

"Greetings, Bhaltair," Ingram called, speaking slowly, feeling his way. "I come in peace, only to take my son."

"Greetings, Ingram," Bhaltair answered, keeping a

steady hand on the sword at his side. "If your words are true, I would like to let you come in peace."

"They are." Ingram could find no malice in either Bhaltair's words or his manner, and he reined in his horse and rested his hands on his saddle as if to emphasize that he was unarmed and harmless. "Why are you not riding with your master, Bhaltair?"

The captain of MacMurrough's guard spat on the ground. "I am not needed. My master has brought knights from Wales, Flemish captains who command men in strange tongues I can't grasp. They fight with tools I've never seen, for reasons I don't understand."

Ingram leaned forward on his horse. "Why don't you come with us, Bhaltair? O'Connor needs men like you, men who understand the Irish. These foreigners, these Normans, are of no use to us! MacMurrough did wrong to bring them in."

"He did wrong to leave you, too," Bhaltair said, holding up a scarred and stubby finger. "Do you remember, Ingram? I was to fight with the archers on your southern flank, but MacMurrough commanded me to follow him to England."

"I remember."

"I wouldn't have you thinking I am a coward."

"I've never thought that, Bhaltair. You are a champion, truly. And I could use your help."

The old warrior looked down at his hands as if weighing the choice; then he nodded to Ingram. "You were always clever," he said, admiration clearly in his face. "Like Donal Kavanaugh—he's clever, too."

"We're all too clever for our own good," Ingram answered, his smile tight. Confusion flickered across Bhaltair's face, and Ingram laughed to ease the giant's tension. "Never fear, my friend, just follow my plan. We are here to take my son Alden, make no mistake, and not to hurt anyone else. If you like, we'll take you with us to O'Connor, where you'll be a mighty warrior, probably a captain over a company of Irish."

Bhaltair beamed like a child, then moved closer to hear Ingram's plan.

The plan, as Ingram explained it to his men in the woods, seemed insultingly simple to the farmers who had hoped for a taste of adventure. Bhaltair confirmed that MacMurrough had taken nearly all the Normans with him, leaving only a handful at his already conquered territories. Hence, only a few Normans guarded Waterford and Wexford, and only a score of weak and wounded foot soldiers remained in the garrison at Ferns.

The boy, Alden, Ingram explained, could be sleeping anywhere, so all rooms were to be checked. Bhaltair knew only that the boy did not sleep in the garrison. They would advance into the castle at night. No one was to be awakened. They would get the boy and get out.

When darkness finally covered the pasture and castle, Ingram gave the signal and led his men toward the stone walls. The solitary guard on the wall, yawning at his post, was silently knocked unconscious by a well-thrown axe handle. Within a moment of the man's falling to the ground, Bhaltair opened the gate from the inside. He directed Ingram's men to the kitchens and the servants' quarters. Slipping through the shadows, they searched each area, clutching their rustic weapons before them like good luck charms.

Ingram watched each man return to the courtyard and shake his head. When all had returned, Ingram sighed and motioned to Bhaltair. They would have to search each room and chamber of the palace itself until the boy was found. Bhaltair nodded and walked confidently to the youthful guard who slept on a bench outside the huge oak door.

"Wake up, lad!" Bhaltair barked, and Ingram had to stifle a laugh when the boy jerked to wakefulness and dropped his dagger on the ground. "You're relieved of duty, you worthless fool! To the garrison, straightaway, and you'd best not let me see your sorry face until morning!"

The boy scurried away like a rat, and Ingram and his men slipped behind Bhaltair into the palace. The men of Glendalough slowed their pace once they stepped inside, and Ingram realized they had never seen such riches, probably had never even imagined them.

"Quickly, brothers," he whispered, pointing down two halls, one to the left and one to the right. He darted upstairs to the family's chambers and hoped for a brief second that Donal Kavanaugh had come home to roost. Just once, he'd like to face Kavanaugh without chains on his ankles and wrists or archers hidden in the bushes.

The front chamber, MacMurrough's, was empty. A thin stream of golden light shone under the second door, however, and Ingram threw his weight against the door, breaking the thin latch. Someone gasped as he drew his dagger; the silhouette of a figure rose from behind the bed-curtains. On a small cot at the foot of the bed, a small boy stirred and rubbed his eyes.

Ingram stared in wonder, momentarily forgetting who and where he was. But a screech from behind the bed-curtains rattled his nerves, and he sprang forward and thrust his knife into the filmy fabric, ripping downward until the curtains hung in two pieces, slashed from top to bottom.

Eva lay curled in the bed, a fur covering clutched to her chest. Anger shone in her eyes until she recognized him; then her face paled, and her blue eyes gleamed in genuine fear. "You are dead!" she whispered, scrambling awkwardly to the head of the bed. She drew the fur over her mouth. "In the name of God, leave us!"

"I'm not dead. And that's no way to greet your brother," Ingram answered, leaving her bedside. He turned to the foot of the bed, where the boy whimpered in fear. Alden was so big! His wide eyes were as blue as the lakes of Connacht, his hair like golden fields of wheat, his form slender and well favored. How Signe would adore him!

He replaced his dagger in his belt, and apparently that flesh-and-blood action convinced Eva that he was no ghost. "You are such a fool, Ingram," she said, flinging furs toward him as she crawled over the bed. "Leave the boy alone! Donal gave him to me."

Ingram knelt at Alden's side and put his hands on the boy's shoulders. The lad stiffened; his chin quivered as if he would cry.

"He doesn't know you," Eva cried, pulling herself out of the bed. She stumbled toward the boy and pushed Ingram's hands from the child's shoulders.

Ingram looked at her in surprise. She wore a shapeless cotton gown, and the unmistakable bulge of an unborn baby hung at her waist. So, Eva was going to be a mother. She ought to understand what he felt for his son.

"I am Alden's father. Kavanaugh stole him from me, and I will have him back."

"You haven't seen him in four years. He is mine." As if to reinforce her words, Alden whimpered and turned, wrapping his arms about her thickened waist. "You see how it is, Ingram?" she said, holding the boy's head to her side. "When I knew I could not have you, I chose to keep your son. Donal carelessly delivered him to me, and I now hold the boy's heart."

"You never wanted me," Ingram answered, the urge to flee straining his patience. "You only wanted power over me. That's all you want of any man, Eva. I gave you that power, and you used it against me. You shall not use it against my son."

"You forget that I am Strongbow's wife. I have more power than you could dream of, Ingram of the Knighthood." She spat the words at him and gripped Alden more tightly. "The boy is mine."

"The boy is your nephew, that much I'll grant," Ingram answered, looking steadily into her eyes. "But he is my son, and I'm taking him from this place tonight. No son of mine will grow up in the shadow of a king who would destroy his own country to slake his vile ambition!"

"What are you jabbering about?" Eva insisted as Alden squirmed in her arms. "My nephew? How can your son be—"

"Because I am another son of Dermot MacMurrough," Ingram said, standing to his feet. She gasped in genuine surprise, and he paused as he looked down at her. His fingers closed more tightly around the dagger at his belt. "Eva, I don't want to hurt you, but I will if you don't give my son to me. Even now my men are scattered throughout this place—"

"You're lying," she said, closing her eyes in fury. "Now get out of here before I—"

She tried to move away, but pregnancy had slowed her catlike grace. Ingram caught Alden easily and wrested him from her desperate grasp. Despite the boy's screams, he heaved the child onto his hip and stalked out of the room.

Eva paused only for a moment, then ran after him like a crazed animal. She caught hold of Alden's foot, clutching at him even as she tried to brace her feet against the slippery wooden floor. Ingram was tempted to slap her off, but he could not bring himself to do it. She was pregnant, after all, and his sister.

Blocking the child's cries from his mind, he dragged the boy, with Eva in tow, to the landing of the staircase. Lifting Alden in his arms, he forcefully yanked the child from her grasp and began to make his way down the stairs.

Caught off balance, Eva swayed on the threshold of the first step, then teetered forward, tumbling head over heels down the steps. Ingram reached out to catch her and grasped nothing but empty air. Calling hoarsely for Bhaltair, he shielded Alden's eyes from the sight of Eva lying still at the bottom of the stairs.

❖ ❖ ❖

Philip and Bhaltair were quick to answer his cries. Ingram gave the boy to Philip with instructions to take horses and ride for Glendalough. Ingram sent Bhaltair for a midwife, for Eva lay on the floor in a puddle of watery fluid, and Ingram knew enough about childbirth to know that the arrival of Eva's child was imminent.

Eva thrashed on the ground, blood on her forehead. Delirious in her pain, she rolled her head over the hard floor and tore at her tunic. Ingram pulled a tapestry from the wall and placed it under her head, and for a moment her eyes widened as if she recognized him. But then Bhaltair returned with the midwife and urged Ingram to flee.

"You cannot stay here," Bhaltair said, pulling roughly on Ingram's cloak. "'Twas not your fault. We must run, before someone rings the alarm bell. Though there aren't many in the garrison, 'twould only take two swords to kill us."

Ingram looked at his old friend, and a twinge of guilt struck him. Bhaltair would die, too, if Ingram were found, for the captain's guilt would be obvious. But to leave Eva like this—

She groaned, and the midwife chuckled in pleasure and held up a slimy, red creature that opened its mouth and let out a pitiful wail.

"See? The child and mother both live," Bhaltair said, forcefully pulling Ingram away. "We must ride."

The old midwife did not understand all that had transpired in the castle of MacMurrough. But she had attended births in all sorts of situations, and this was not the most bizarre. In fact, the unusual circumstances made her task easier. The mother still groaned on the floor, semiconscious from the blow to her head, and the tiny baby, born too soon, squirmed restlessly in her hands.

The midwife absently shushed the infant and placed it again between the mother's legs. Donal Kavanaugh had paid her ten pieces of silver for the deed she was about to commit and had promised an additional five if the child proved to be a boy.

"'Twouldn't do to have a son born to Strongbow," Kavanaugh had said, placing the silver coins in the midwife's hand. "Can you imagine the son of a foreigner ruling Leinster? Can't you see, good woman, what grief that would bring us?"

She had agreed, for MacMurrough himself had brought her family more than enough grief, and so she accepted the silver easily. Now came the part that gave her conscience pause, but it wasn't so hard, really. She wrapped the baby's umbilical cord around its tiny neck and quietly mumbled reasons for the child's death until the babe stopped breathing. *'Twas born too soon. The lady had an accident. 'Twas a cursed night. 'Twas the seed of the cruel Dermot MacMurrough.*

She unwrapped the umbilical cord and gently prodded the baby's chest with her finger. No response. She had earned her fifteen pieces of silver. To a grandson of the bloodthirsty MacMurrough, she would have done it for nothing.

THIRTY-NINE

Ingram and Bhaltair rode hard for the forest, then gave their horses their heads as the animals picked their way through the woods that would lead them to the River Slaney. Soon they would meet Philip, Alden, and the other men; from that point the journey would be slow and steady.

Ingram knew he should have been happy, even thrilled. But a strange ambivalence filled his mind. On one hand, as Bhaltair did not cease to remind him, he had foiled his enemy and righted a serious wrong by rescuing his son. On the other hand, he had been forced to wait four long years to bring Alden home, and the boy had spent over half his life in the company of either Donal Kavanaugh or Eva . . . Ingram's brother and sister.

The irony of the situation made him laugh, and Bhaltair cast a worried look in his direction. "What's wrong, sir knight?" Bhaltair asked, and Ingram grimaced. The title sounded strange coming from Bhaltair's lips.

"What would you do, Bhaltair, if you were a lad of seven years and were forcibly snatched in the dead of night from the woman you knew as mother? if a man calling himself your father practically brandished a dagger in your face? if you saw the mother you loved plunge down the stairs and lie broken below?"

Bhaltair frowned in thought. "If I knew me father was Ingram *na nRidireachd*, I'd be glad he didn't wait until I was eight," he finally answered.

Ingram sighed. 'Twas a loyal answer, but it did little to assuage his guilt.

A celebration had begun when they arrived back at the family *rath*. The children played music, the women danced, and fresh April flowers adorned the tables, where a feast had been spread. Dressed in her brightest tunic, Eamhair approached the arriving group and threw her arms about her husband while the other women and children welcomed the company home.

"We've been cooking for two days," Eamhair said, casting a fond look at her husband as he dismounted. "Philip said ye'd be back in ten or twelve days. I pray the venture went well."

"It did," Philip answered, slipping his arm about her waist. "No one was hurt."

"And Alden is returned," Ingram said, casting a tentative look at his saddle, where his small son waited in silence. The boy had spoken little on the entire trip. But his eyes were no longer troubled, and he had actually smiled at Bhaltair once or twice.

"Come and eat; I'm sure you're all starving," Eamhair said, pulling her husband toward the table laden with food.

Ingram turned and extended a hand to his son, who took it and slowly hoisted his right leg over the saddle. With trust shining from his eyes, he slipped from the horse's back into his father's arms.

After dinner father and son took a walk through the forest outside the walls of the *rath*. Ingram walked slowly, breathing in the sights and smells of early spring, and Alden walked silently by his side. Ingram had hoped to see more childish enthusiasm from his son, and it suddenly occurred to him that he did not know the boy.

"Do you remember this place?" he asked finally, taking a

seat on a large rock. He patted the spot next to him. Alden
dutifully sat down, then shook his head.

"You were born here," Ingram said, waving his hand
at the majesty of the tall conifers that surrounded them.
"In the family *rath*. I helped pull you from your mother's
womb, and you fell into my hands."

"Eva?" Alden asked slowly.

"No." Ingram shook his head and gentled his voice.
"She is not your mother, but your aunt, and I am sure she
cared for you very much. Your mother's name was Brenna.
She was my wife, and she lived in a clan from Wicklow
before coming here. Remember this, my son. You'll want
to understand these things one day."

The boy squinted up at him. "Where is my mother
now?"

Ingram shook his head. "I don't know. She left here
after a year and a day, as the law allows. I didn't want her to
go, and I know you needed her. But Eamhair took care of
you for three years when I went to battle. I am a knight
sworn to obey God and defend his people, and my life is
often spent in fighting those who would disturb the peace."

The boy digested this news in silence. "I have made enemies," Ingram went on, feeling his way carefully, "and someone who hated me came here, told Philip and Eamhair a
falsehood, and took you away. That is how you came to be
with Eva. I have tried to find you, but the evil man who
took you from this place made it difficult for me. Only when
he thought me dead was I able to risk bringing you back."

A rabbit ran through the bushes, and the boy's head
turned to follow the animal. Ingram did not know if his
words were making any impression at all.

"But I've always loved you, Alden. I had great plans
for your happiness, and I hope that one day, with God's
gracious help, you will fulfill them."

The boy slipped from the rock and turned away. "Can
we go back now?"

Ingram sighed. "Yes," he said, standing. But as he led the way, he was surprised to feel Alden's hand creep into his.

Ingram decided it would not be right to presume upon the hospitality of Philip's family any longer than necessary. So the next morning he and Bhaltair saddled their horses, collected Alden, and said a bittersweet farewell to the men and women of the clan at Glendalough. Philip promised to join O'Connor's men if and when war broke out, and Ingram nodded solemnly in respect for the man's courage and commitment to his family. Eamhair placed her hands on Alden's head and murmured a prayer for their safety as he waited in the saddle, then swiftly embraced Ingram and Bhaltair before they mounted.

Halfway down the mountain, Ingram watched as the curling smoke from the family's fires rose and blended with the gray clouds. He knew he would never see Glendalough again.

Three days later, as the sun settled beneath the horizon, he and Bhaltair drew their hoods over their heads, slumped in their saddles, and allowed their horses to walk slowly past the Norman guards at the rebuilt gates of Waterford. The men on duty were clearly bored, having seen only merchants and peasants all day, and Ingram knew there was nothing in his or Bhaltair's appearance to cause alarm. Spies from O'Connor would not travel unarmed and with a child. Besides, every fighting man in Ireland knew the real battle was being staged around the hills outside Dublin.

No light shone through the shutters at Signe's window, and Ingram feared for a moment that she had fled the town in search of prosperity elsewhere. But the faint aroma of burning wood scented the darkness of her courtyard, and he knocked on the door, hoping that it was her hearth that burned.

The door cracked open an inch, a green eye peered forth, then the door flung back, and she pulled him inside with both hands. "Ingram! You're here! I thought you had gone to O'Rourke!"

"I had other business to attend to." He drew back from her warm embrace and jerked his head toward the courtyard. "Come and meet Bhaltair. Even MacMurrough's own captain now rides with me in the service of the high king."

"MacMurrough's captain?"

"And someone else even more important. Signe, I want you to meet my son."

Signe smoothed her hair, then stepped into the darkness and smiled at Bhaltair. Her eyes lingered on Alden, though, and her smile softened. "Wouldn't you like to come inside with Anna and Brian?" she asked, her voice warm with maternal tenderness. "There's extra porridge by the hearth, poor though it may be, and bread."

"Your bread could never be equaled," Ingram declared, motioning for Bhaltair to dismount. "If you have any to spare, we'd be in your debt."

"You're already hopelessly in my debt, Ingram," she replied smoothly as she led the way into her house.

"And so I must go to O'Rourke, and I cannot take Alden," Ingram explained, even though he really didn't have to say anything. She had known from the instant he arrived why he had come, and she knew just as certainly that he would ride out again, leaving his son at her side. Another mouth to feed, and in wartime, when food was scarce and she strived from daybreak till dusk just to keep herself and her little ones alive! But she would work for Ingram's son as if he were her own. And Ingram had known this, of course.

When the children were asleep in their cots, Signe took a seat next to Ingram and watched the small fire dance in the darkness.

"Must you go?" she asked. A foolish question, but she

persisted. "The war is far away, and Donal Kavanaugh and his men think you dead. Let them believe so; stay here with me, and help us here in Waterford. There are not so many men here, and we can do little, but we dream of casting off the few Normans who control the city."

"I must go; I am a knight, called by God."

"You mean you are Ingram *na nRidireachd.*" She bit her lip. She hadn't meant to be so sharp.

His pained expression confirmed that she had hurt him. "It's not merely a title to me, Signe, it's who I am. *My father* stirs this country to war, and I must do something!"

"You are not responsible for Dermot MacMurrough's actions. Don't you know God holds us responsible for our own? If you go and fight, you are following in MacMurrough's footsteps, molding yourself in his image."

His face was unreadable in the fire-tinted darkness. "I am a link in a chain forged years ago. Now I can only seek to undo the damage done by the MacMurroughs. Dermot fills the land with invaders. Donal Kavanaugh has raped and pillaged and plundered; even Eva seduces men and children to her advantage."

His voice changed subtly at the mention of Eva's name, and Signe's intuition signaled that something was amiss. Taking a deep breath, she dared to ask the question that lay foremost in her mind: "Has this Eva seduced you?"

She had hit a nerve, for he flinched. "She tried," Ingram admitted, lowering his eyes. "But on the night I took Alden from her at Ferns, she was delivered of a child. There will be others to fulfill MacMurrough's legacy of war if O'Connor cannot stop the Normans."

"And so it all depends on you, Ingram of the Knighthood," she whispered softly. He stared at the smoldering embers in her fireplace without speaking, and she put her hand on his arm. "I will keep your son and pray for your safety, Ingram, but there is one thing you must do for me before you go."

"Speak your price."

She hesitated, thinking of the gossip in town. People had talked about her and Ingram for years, and if it was known that she kept Ingram's child, no one would believe that the knight visited her out of a purely platonic love. But was it right to snare his heart with such an excuse? She cast aside her doubts and lifted her eyes to his: "If I am to act as your son's mother, you must marry me."

"That—" he held up a warning finger and pulled away from her— "I cannot do."

"Why not?" Sudden warmth flooded her cheeks.

"I once thought myself too good for you, Signe. Now I know I am not good enough. *My father* raped a nun! *My family* provides safe haven for murderers and infidels!" He shook his head, a horrified expression of disapproval marring his handsome face. "Never could I marry you or any woman. I was wrong to marry Brenna. I'm sorry, but I shall not marry again."

Still shaking his head, he left her side and walked to the courtyard, where Bhaltair had already spread a blanket and lay snoring on the ground.

FORTY

Ingram and Bhaltair left the next day and rode immediately to Clondalkin, where Rory O'Connor had camped to wait for the massing of Norman troops. Ingram requested an immediate audience with the high king and was surprised when it was granted.

"Ingram *na nRidireachd*," O'Connor said, extending his hand in easy informality as Ingram entered his tent. "We wondered if we would see you again. Such rumors have reached our ears!"

"Captivity, execution, my own rescue by Ailean and Donnan, and the rescue of my son," Ingram summed up his exploits in a few words. "All are true, my king. And so are the rumors that Donal Kavanaugh is leading the Normans through the Wicklow Mountains."

"This is harder to believe than your fantastic tales," O'Connor answered, tenting his hands before him. "We heard the story some months ago and have sent scouts into the mountains. There is no trace of the Normans."

"They were in the mountains," Ingram insisted. "And they are not at Waterford or Ferns; Bhaltair and I can verify that. So if they are not at Baginbun or Wexford, MacMurrough has hidden them."

O'Connor considered this, then roared in a loud guffaw. "It is not important. When they come, they will come by the road at Enniskerry or through the narrow passages along the coast. We will be waiting, no matter where they come. We are ready."

"I hope you are," Ingram answered. He saluted, then left the tent.

Ingram remained with the high king's camp at Clondalkin throughout the summer of 1170, waiting each day for some sign or sound of the approaching Normans. Often he volunteered to ride with the scouts who compassed the forest and the base of the Wicklow Mountains, but never did they find any sign of Normans or Donal Kavanaugh.

O'Connor seemed to think his show of strength had forced the Normans into hiding or retreat, but the threat of the enemy haunted Ingram at every turn. On guard duty at night he kept his back to his tent and his face toward the mountains, straining to hear and identify every snap and buzz in the darkness. Even in the common calm of daylight, he stiffened at the approach of an unknown warrior and constantly scanned the woods for the bright reflection of a Norman sword in the sunlight. But he saw nothing. Through June, July, August, and early September, nothing.

On a windy day in mid September, Ingram looked out across the fields and noticed two figures in long, blue tunics on the road. Brehons, certainly. As they came closer, he recognized the handsome and distinguished features of Griogiar, and he hurried forward to meet his friend.

Griogiar placed his hands on Ingram's arms in greeting. "'Tis good to see you, me friend, but we have urgent news for the high king."

Ingram jerked his head toward the brightly colored tent behind him. "I'll lead you. What news?"

Griogiar hesitated for a moment, then spoke in a low voice. "My apprentice and I have been held hostage these past twenty days at a monastery."

"A monastery!"

The brehon nodded soberly. "What I have seen and

heard goes against all the traditional laws and the laws of God. Donal Kavanaugh has sequestered an army in the monastery near Glendalough. They have marched forth from that place, and only now have released us. We are fortunate that we are fleet of foot—the Normans are fat and slow from months of eating and sleeping."

"Abbot Steaphan—"

"He is dead," Griogiar said, his dark eyes snapping. "Kavanaugh killed him and any monk who dared to question him." The brehon paused and put his arm on Ingram's shoulder. "And again, it saddens me to bring you news of sorrow, me friend. But the Normans went in search of food, and they raided the *ratha* of families in the area. . . ."

Ingram felt his mouth go dry. "Philip?"

Griogiar nodded. "Everyone in the *rath*—every man, woman, and child. The Normans left none alive."

Ingram stared past the brehon into his own thoughts and heard Griogiar as if from a distance: "Kavanaugh will surely burn in hell for this action."

The words sprang to Ingram's lips automatically: "Donal Kavanaugh cares not for his soul, nor anyone else's." He turned toward the high king's tent and motioned for Griogiar to follow, his anger rising up like a living thing within him.

❖ ❖ ❖

As Ingram listened in numb silence, Griogiar repeated his story before Rory O'Connor; Dòmhnull confirmed every word. O'Connor paused, looking toward his captains for advice, but they had none to give. "All right," he said finally, his posture militantly erect. "We mount up and ride to Dublin. If we surround the city walls, we are sure to beat Donal Kavanaugh to the prize."

The trumpets blew, and men scrambled to their horses. Messengers were sent to Enniskerry to warn O'Rourke, but before they had been gone an hour, other breathless messengers met O'Connor and his men on the road.

"Most honored *ard-ri,*" one of them shouted, reining in

his horse in a cloud of dust. "The enemy has marched forward from Rathfarnham and surrounded the city."

"MacMurrough is at Dublin already?" O'Connor asked, blinking in astonishment.

"Aye, sir, with Strongbow, Donal Kavanaugh, and a host of men. The Archbishop of Dublin is already suing for peace."

"Laurence O'Toole," O'Connor muttered, looking to his captains for confirmation. "What a peace that will be! O'Toole is MacMurrough's brother-in-law!"

"He might as well hand Dublin to the Normans on a platter," another captain groused. "Why are we riding forward, my king? The men of Dublin are determined to give themselves to MacMurrough."

"'Twould seem that way," O'Connor agreed.

"My king," Ingram interrupted, urging his horse forward until he sat within easy speaking distance. He made an effort to remain calm and reasonable. If O'Connor saw the gleam of anger in his eye, he would discount his advice. "To stop now will ensure MacMurrough's victory. Perhaps if the men of Dublin know that we wait to aid them, they will be less likely to surrender themselves. And how do we know that O'Toole is sympathetic to MacMurrough? I heard from the brehons that MacMurrough once held this O'Toole hostage."

"'Twas a long time ago." O'Connor dismissed Ingram's concerns with a wave of his hand.

"Thousands will die if we proceed," another captain prophesied. "Let the Ostmen in Dublin take care of their own. Askulv, their king, has done nothing for us."

"There are Irish in Dublin, too," Ingram insisted. "God-fearing men, women, and children—"

Rory O'Connor held up a hand for silence, then regarded the weary messenger with a steely gaze. "Ride to O'Rourke at once, and tell him that we are returning to our homes. The Ostmen of Dublin have not asked for our help, and we need not give it to those who bargain with our enemies. I have spoken."

Ingram opened his mouth to protest, but O'Connor's face had darkened in sober resolve. The men around him turned their horses to return and break camp.

The news arrived the next day, carried in part by refugees and in part by a messenger from Askulv, the king of Dublin. The captains of O'Connor assembled in the heat of the day to hear the messenger's tale.

"We had just sent our king's envoy forth to Strongbow," the messenger said, sweat dripping down his forehead despite the balmy September breeze. "Negotiations were proceeding, and the archbishop had promised that peace lay within our reach—"

"O'Toole," O'Connor interrupted, frowning. "Giving the city to his brother-in-law."

The messenger paused out of respect for the king, then continued his tale. "The king's representative, Strongbow, and Donal Kavanaugh conversed at the city gates. In the midst of the negotiations, at another point of the city's wall, two Norman knights crept into the city, cut down the guards, and led their companies to take the city before our king even knew what had happened. There was no time to protest and little time to escape. One called Raymond Carew threw open the city gates from the inside; then Kavanaugh pulled forth his dagger and killed the king's negotiator."

"What of Askulv?" O'Connor asked, his eyes glittering with interest.

"He managed to sail away, probably to the Hebrides," the messenger replied. "But not before vowing vengeance. 'Twas most dishonorable, what Strongbow did."

Ingram snorted in derision and felt every eye in the circle come to rest on him. "Why are we surprised that these men have no honor?" he asked, searching the eyes of Rory O'Connor. "They never do what we expect; they do not follow the rules of war. I refuse to call them knights; to do so is a shame upon God's holy ordination of knighthood."

O'Connor closed his eyes to Ingram's words and turned back to the messenger. "Where are the Normans now?"

The messenger shrugged. "I fled with my life, me king. They could be dancin' with the devil, but I care not."

"They are inside the city, you may be sure," Ingram said, feeling the pressure of the captains' eyes again. "Pillaging, plundering, and polluting innocent women and children. The men who remained inside will be killed. And MacMurrough reigns over three port cities and the entire coast of Leinster."

He might well have said, *And MacMurrough truly rules as high king of Ireland.* O'Connor read the rebuke in Ingram's eyes, acknowledged it with a grim stare, and bowed his head.

"We will return to our homes and pray that God will show us what to do," O'Connor said finally, his voice broken in humility. "The circuit of the *ard-ri,* the unity of Ireland, must be preserved if we are to know peace and prosperity."

The high king raised his hand and lowered it again, giving his men permission to depart. Ingram went to his tent, gathered his few belongings, and said good-bye to Bhaltair. He would ride south to Waterford and remain with the little family that waited for him there. The day would come, most certainly, when his son needed a knight's protection as Philip and Eamhair had. It was only a matter of time before the Normans vanquished Ireland as thoroughly as they had annihilated the small family *rath* on the mountains outside Glendalough.

Griogiar caught Ingram before he left camp and pulled him aside for a private word. "I am worried for you, me friend," he said, his dark eyes narrowing with concern as he studied Ingram's face. "Once hope made its home in your heart, but something else resides there now."

Ingram sank onto a small stool and drew the back of his hand across his brow. "Even a knight grows old and tired, Griogiar," said, trying to muster a smile for his old friend. "Are you never weary?"

"I am settled in meself and content," Griogiar answered, folding his arms. "You, Ingram, have never been settled. You are like a leaf twisting in the wind, blown one way and then another. Will you never reach out for the tree that gives you life?"

Ingram snorted. "Will you never speak plainly? You have Cathal's gift for speaking in riddles. He visits me in nightmares, you know, and offers me the Holy Grail of Airt Mac Con. Now you're offering me a tree. And I don't need anything from either of you, for I'm as settled as a knight can be in the winds of war."

Griogiar shook his head. "I heard your words to O'Connor. You said that the Norman knights were not worthy to be called knights."

"So?"

"They behave as knights, Ingram. 'Tis you who are different. They live by the earthly laws of knighthood. They have given their allegiance to men; your knightly service has been dedicated to the spirit and righteousness of God. You have striven for him, fought for him, and sacrificed for him. You have done all for him, me friend, and yet you've never accepted the things God would do for you."

Ingram stared at the brehon in a paralysis of astonishment. "What would God possibly want to do for me?" he asked in a hoarse whisper. "He provides me with food, shelter, and strength—"

Griogiar smiled slowly. "He would give you peace, Ingram *na nRidireachd.*"

❖ ❖ ❖

With Signe's help Ingram found an empty house, repaired it, and made two beds—one for him and one for Alden. They slept there each night, but during the day Ingram found himself irresistibly drawn to Signe and her children. Together their small family group labored and played, hunting, preparing food, tending the horse and chickens. The experience was nearly all Ingram imagined a family to be, and he found a simple satisfaction in the humble chores that had been beneath his dignity as a knight.

The festivity of Christmas in Signe's house that year reminded him of the earlier time when Erik had confidently proposed a Christmas toast to Ingram and Signe's marriage. Now, as then, bits of evergreen and ivy from the forest adorned the table and the window, and a strong fire roared at the hearth. Ingram was amazed at the Christmas feast Signe managed to prepare: two loaves of white bread, a dish of pork, a venison pie, and a bountiful supply of apples and nuts. After they had eaten their fill, Signe sang while the children danced and clapped. Then Ingram drew Signe into his arms for a dance while the children sang a sprightly carol.

Alden's countenance glowed in the happiness Signe had created for them, and Ingram found himself falling helplessly into her green eyes. She had to be nearing forty, Ingram realized, but her eyes still sparkled with mischief, and her step was as light as it had been on the day he met her running through the woods. She smelled wonderfully of soap and baking bread, and as he held her, he found himself wishing that the dance might go on forever, that he could wrap her in an embrace and never let her go.

But eventually he must let go. War was coming. As long as Rory O'Connor claimed the high kingship, Dermot Mac-Murrough would not be satisfied. He would send the Normans yet again to finish their work. Despite what Griogiar said, there would be no peace for Ireland . . . nor for Ingram.

Signe must have felt his arms instinctively tighten around her, for she pulled away, and surprise shone in her eyes. "Why, Ingram, you're getting sentimental," she chided, pulling out of his arms. She walked away and began clearing dishes from her table.

"Imagine that," he said, his voice husky with his unspoken thoughts.

Life fell into a predictable routine, and the city of Waterford bloomed again in the spring of 1171. No longer conquerors, the few Normans who remained in the city settled into the role of grudgingly tolerated governors, and the city gradually returned to the business of life. New immigrants arrived from the Norse islands of the Hebrides and the Isle of Man; the scorched houses and gardens of the townspeople were repaired or replaced. The Normans, too, brought in a steady stream of immigrants and clerics, and the flavor of the city became even more exotic. The accents of the Irish and Norse mingled freely with the French and Welsh of the newcomers.

Signe reveled in the town's new life and laughed when Ingram urged her to be cautious. "Surely you can't be thinking that the Normans will come again," she chided him, brushing a lock of graying hair from his eyes. "And even if they do, what army will want you, Sir Ingram—a forty-six-year-old knight? Let things rest as they are, me friend, and rejoice that God has blessed you."

Alden, too, seemed content and happy in Waterford, although he often awoke screaming in the night. On these nights Ingram crawled into his son's bed and held the boy until the tears and fears had passed. Ingram always enjoyed the sweet solace he felt acting as his son's protector. But the feeling evaporated, as it always did, when Alden stopped crying and whispered one request: "I want Signe."

'Twas difficult to explain why Signe was not with them and why she could not be. It would be almost worth forgetting his own principles and asking her to marry him, Ingram thought as he tucked Alden into bed one night, for the sake of the children. But he had humiliated her twice before by rejecting her hand, and she would never agree to marry him now. He abruptly ceased his imaginings and returned to his own straw mattress.

In early April 1171, two men dismounted at Signe's gate. Ingram felt Signe's tug on his sleeve, and he quietly turned from his gardening to survey the strangers that stood outside her gate. They were cloaked, both of them, with hooded faces and dark eyes that gleamed through the light rain that had soaked the city for more than an hour. The first man was slight and hunched; the second, a giant.

He left his hoe and went to the gate. "Peace be unto you and all in this house," the first man said, his voice heavy with weariness.

"Peace to all who enter here," Ingram said, moving to open the gate. "Have you come far?"

"From Connacht," the first man replied. He pushed the hood from his head, and Ingram stared. The high king, Rory O'Connor, stood before him.

The second man dropped his hood and grinned a toothy smile. "Bhaltair!" Ingram eagerly accepted each man's outstretched hand, and Signe curtsied politely before them.

"My king, meet Signe Lombay," Ingram said as Signe flushed deeply. He turned to her and lifted an eyebrow. "Have we anything to feed these good men?"

"Aye," she said, scurrying inside. "Bring them in."

Resting by Signe's hearth, the king explained the reason for their sudden appearance. "Bhaltair was sent to scout around Ferns at Christmas," O'Connor explained, buttering a slice of Signe's brown bread. "MacMurrough had retired there for the holiday."

"Is all well?" Ingram asked. "Who holds Dublin?"

"Strongbow," O'Connor replied. "But he does not hold it well. Askulv is building a force in the Hebrides and preparing to attack when the time is right. That time is approaching, Ingram, for MacMurrough is an old man. They say he lies in his chamber at Ferns and waits to die."

Ingram shrugged. "Do not trust their word, my king. 'Twould be like him to lure us by his death and then rise from hell to ambush us later."

O'Connor gave him a grudging smile. "This is no ruse. Eva is with him, as is Donal Kavanaugh—who, by the way," the king added, his eyes twinkling, "roared like a bull when he discovered that you were not dead, after all. But Strongbow silenced his threats and bade him swear that he would not retaliate against you. Strongbow knows that the people have not accepted him, and when MacMurrough dies, he will have trouble on his hands. I daresay he hopes that you will convince the people that he is a better choice for king than Kavanaugh."

"Could he possibly believe that the throne of Leinster will be his?" Ingram asked. "He is not a blood member of the king's *deirbfhine* and not eligible to be elected king."

"You are right," the king said, wiping his mouth on the sleeve of his tunic. "But though he is not an eligible member of the *rigdamnae,* apparently MacMurrough designated Strongbow the heir apparent when he married Eva. Eva's children are supposed to inherit their grandfather's throne."

"Her son—"

"There is no son." O'Connor watched Ingram's face carefully. "The child she bore did not survive. Eva swears that you killed her child."

Ingram gasped. "Before God, I did not! Bhaltair is my witness; when we left, the midwife held a breathing child in her arms—"

O'Connor lifted his hand. "So Bhaltair has told me. But Eva is set on your destruction, Ingram, no less than is Donal Kavanaugh. 'Tis only Strongbow, we hear, who keeps them from sending assassins to kill you." The king laughed. "Strongbow wants you alive, it seems, for the people love Ingram *na nRidireachd*. And if you, a Norman knight, can find acceptance in Ireland, why can't an earl of Wales?"

Ingram chuckled. "Donal Kavanaugh cannot be happy about Strongbow's power."

"Nor am I." The king took a bite of the bread, and Ingram waited in silence until he was ready to speak. "But I have learned startling information that pleases me better. I know, for instance, that you are a blood member of the MacMurrough *deirbfhine.*"

Ingram choked on the ale he was attempting to swallow. When he had lowered his cup, he managed a weak smile. "Do the brehons know *every* genealogy of Ireland?" he asked.

O'Connor nodded. "Apparently they do now. And, me friend knight, you are as fit to be king of Leinster as Donal Kavanaugh—more fit, in fact. I want you to ride with me to Connacht, where I am assembling a troop to rally against Strongbow on the day Dermot MacMurrough dies. Askulv has sent word to me; he will attack Dublin west from the sea; we will counter from the north, east, and south. We cannot lose, Ingram. And we will install you as king of Leinster and restore the peace of Ireland."

Ingram froze in stunned silence. For years he had felt himself alone, without a blood relative in the world. From that obscurity he had come to be a peasant, then the illegitimate son of a ruthless king. He had sought the Grail and found it, but the price was far too high. Now he was being offered a position more powerful than the one presently held by Rory O'Connor.

"I will remain high king, of course," O'Connor said, correctly guessing Ingram's thoughts. "And Askulv wants to regain control of Dublin. But Waterford's earl is dead, as is Wexford's, and there is no reason you could not rule those two cities as well as Leinster."

"I cannot." Ingram shook his head, unable to do anything but deny the incredible opportunity. He looked up at Signe. She had heard all and had backed away from the hearth into a corner of the room. Her eyes blazed like emeralds in the center of her pale face, and her hands covered her mouth as if she had just heard news too terrible to contemplate.

O'Connor, however, smiled with the confidence of a king. "If your words of longing for peace have been true, Ingram, you must join with us. 'Tis your duty."

"I am not a king. I am a knight, a defender. I know nothing else. I am Ingram—"

"Ingram of the Knighthood, I know that well," O'Connor said, leaning forward intently. "Just as Strongbow was the earl of meaningless Strigoil and now rules Ireland. *Is ferr fer a chiniud,* Ingram—a man is better than his birth. 'Tis the law of the Irish."

From the corner of his eye, he could see Signe weeping into her apron. But though as a man he could not answer, as a knight his duty was to serve his king.

"I will leave with you in the morning," he said, rising stiffly to his feet. "Tonight you will sleep with my son and me in our house. It is not far from here."

The king nodded in satisfaction. He and Bhaltair followed Ingram and Alden out into the night.

❖ ❖ ❖

Ingram slept little that night, thinking of Signe's haunted face, and he arose early the next morning to take Alden to her house. On the way he told Alden that the high king of all Ireland needed him, and he might be gone for a long, long time. "But Signe loves you," he said, stopping in the dusty street outside Signe's house. He knelt at his son's eye level. "She will never let you be lonely, Alden. And you must always know that your father loves you very much."

The boy threw his arms around Ingram's neck in response, and the gate to Signe's courtyard creaked open. She stood there, dressed in a simple green tunic, her eyes swollen and red-rimmed. "I see that you are going," she said, her hands crossed defensively. She gave Alden a brief smile and patted his shoulder as he walked past her on his way into the house.

Ingram planted his feet apart as he stood before her and

assumed an air of confidence he did not feel. "You heard the king, Signe. What am I supposed to do?"

"Be true to yourself, Ingram. What do you want to do?"

"What do I want? I am a knight; I do what my king tells me to do. I want nothing!"

"That's a lie." Her words were quiet and spoken without anger, but they cut him to the heart. He had never lied to her. He had always been honest about his responsibilities and feelings, even about Eva—

Her angry words cut off his thoughts. "Though you do not know it, Ingram, you want two things, and they are at odds with one another. You want nobility, and your blood races even now at the thought of gaining MacMurrough's throne. And you want a family, but on your own terms. Here you have a home, children, yes, even a wife, if you'd have me. But we're not good enough, not noble enough for you."

He gritted his teeth. "I cannot walk away from my king."

"But you walk away from your son, from Brian, from Anna. They all love you dearly; you are the only father they have ever known—"

"Say what you mean, Signe. You're only upset because I won't marry you!"

"Yes!" She stamped her foot and clenched her hands, a flush of anger flooding her face. "You will walk away from me today as you did all those years ago when you knew I loved you! You have all the happiness a man could want waiting in this house, and yet you have left it repeatedly to search for what you felt is your noble destiny. You will leave us now because you want to be a king. If you leave now, Ingram, don't come back!"

"My duty calls—"

"I don't care about your duty! Don't you think I know you are a knight? Fight if you must—someone has to—but that is not what pulls you away from us! You don't care about your duty! You care only about your pride, O Ingram of the Knighthood! You moan and fret and say you do not

409

want this plan of O'Connor's, yet the thought of winning a king's throne leaves you speechless!"

Her eyes flickered over his face, searching for something he did not know how to give. After a moment she lowered her eyes and pressed her palm to her forehead. Tears streamed down her face, and he approached cautiously and wrapped his arms around her. *Let the neighbors see,* he thought, glancing over the courtyard hedge for spying eyes. *Let them know that I love this woman.*

An ugly sound escaped her, a sob of both laughter and sorrow, and she pulled away and wiped her eyes on her apron. "Come inside for a moment; I have something for you," she mumbled, her nose red.

"The king and Bhaltair will be here soon," he said, hesitating.

"This will take only a moment," she said, stepping into the house.

He lingered in the courtyard and was relieved when he heard the *clip-clop* of approaching hooves. O'Connor and Bhaltair appeared, leading Ingram's horse, and he signaled to them that he would be ready to leave in a moment. O'Connor nodded, looking down from his vantage place in the saddle, and sighed impatiently.

Signe came out of the house, an object in her hand. "You haven't worn this since Baginbun," she said, making an effort to smile up at him. "Do you remember? I took it off when I nursed you, and when Alden came home, I hesitated to bring it out; . . . I thought it might bring you pain."

She opened her palm, and Ingram was surprised to see the jeweled brooch in her hand. "The brooch! I thought it was lost in the battle or destroyed when the house burned." He looked at it a moment, then waved it away. "It is valuable, Signe. You should sell it. Since you will have the expense of caring for Alden until I can send for him—"

"No." She shook her head and pulled the simple iron brooch from his cloak. "If you are indeed riding to claim the throne of a king, you must look the part. Wear this, sir knight, and wear it well."

The gate creaked again. O'Connor stalked into the courtyard and stared at the brooch Signe was fastening onto Ingram's cloak. "Where did you get that?" he asked Signe, breathless. "Who gave it to you?"

"It's mine," Ingram answered, perplexed. "She has kept it for me. She didn't steal it—"

Without a comment or explanation, O'Connor reached out. He flipped the pin from the brooch and caught the round circlet in his hand. Ingram's cloak sagged and fell to the ground, and as he bent to pick it up, he heard O'Connor exclaim, *"An bráist of ua Conchobair."*

"What?" Ingram asked, tossing his cloak over his arm.

O'Connor held the brooch beneath Ingram's nose and whispered intently. "Have you lived in Ireland so long without knowing what you've possessed? Let's go inside, my friends, for I feel the need of some ale and a strong seat. There's a tale here, Ingram, and I don't think we can go farther unless 'tis told."

FORTY-ONE

"I was the oldest of three children," Rory O'Connor said, sitting by the cold fireplace with the brooch in his hand. "Me father was *ard-ri,* a truly great high king. His second child, me brother, died of a fever at age ten, and his third child, me sister, was most pious and holy. She entered the old and esteemed convent at Clonmacnoise when she was thirteen."

He paused, and Signe did not dare breathe. The children played behind the house, and the sounds of their play seemed a world away, so deep was her concentration upon the circlet of bronze in the king's hand.

"After me brother's death, me father the high king commissioned three brooches, identical in every respect, and wonders of metalwork. One he wore always in memory of me brother; on his death he wore it to his grave. This I saw with me own eyes. Another brooch was given to me; I'm wearing it now."

Signe glanced up. Indeed, another brooch, seemingly identical to the one in O'Connor's hand, lay nearly hidden in the folds of his hooded cloak.

"The last brooch was given to me sister. She took it with her to the convent, and a special dispensation from the archbishop allowed her to keep it. The brooch was her only tie to our family, her only worldly possession, and she kept it with her always."

The king's eyes overflowed with tears. "We did not visit

412

her often, as she gave much of her time to prayer. But one day the archbishop brought word that me sister had died. A peasant woman had found her body in a stone hut like those in which the hermits dwell. The peasant woman, the archbishop told us, was perverse, and suggested that me sister had given birth to a child, but we knew that could not be true. The archbishop told the woman she lied, and the woman left in anger and would not reveal where me sister had been buried. We had no confirmation of the woman's story and never found me sister's grave, her brooch, or her child. Until now."

Signe glanced at Ingram's face. His eyes, too, were riveted on the brooch, his mouth agape at the story the king told.

O'Connor placed the brooch in Ingram's hand. "If this is yours, sir knight, I would hear more of how you came to have it."

Ingram did not speak for a moment. "A wandering and rebellious monk, Father Colum, gave it to me," he finally said, his voice heavy with awe. "He told me it would lead me to my home. And since that day I have learned that I am the son of Dermot MacMurrough, who forced himself on a young nun. The girl died in childbirth and was buried by a peasant woman who kept a parchment upon which the monk had transcribed the story."

O'Connor did not lift his eyes from the brooch, and Ingram went on. "In rebellion, the monk spirited the babe away from God, to whom the child had been promised, but he had a change of heart years later as God revealed himself. The monk visited me in my twenty-sixth year, to bring the babe home at last."

"And now you are home," O'Connor echoed, folding his hands. "Welcome home, Ingram of *ua Conchobair*. As God lives, you are my *mac peathar na bràther*—my nephew."

Signe felt the room swirl around her as she studied Ingram through a veil of tears. As heir to two thrones, Ingram would certainly leave her forever.

Bhaltair slipped out of the house, seemingly embarrassed by Ingram's weeping and the king's tears. After a while O'Connor left, too, struggling to regain his composure. Ingram sat alone by the dark fireplace, unable to stop his weeping. Signe faced him, watching from a bench at the table, but she did not approach him. Idly, some still functioning part of his mind wondered why.

A conversation from his past rippled through his mind. *"Do you have faith, me son?"* Father Colum's voice echoed through the corridors of Ingram's memory.

"Aye, in some things. But not in all men."

"In God?"

"I believe in God, yes. And as a knight, I am sworn to serve him."

"You speak with reluctance, I think."

"I speak as one who has never seen God's hand. Have I known parents? Have I known love?"

Ingram paused as a word suddenly resounded in his mind: *Yes.* He had known parents and love. Lady Wynne had mothered him; Donnchad and Afrecca had opened their home and family; Donnan and Ailean, Cathal and Griogiar, Signe and Erik had given freely of all they had possessed. Through every trial, every disappointment, someone had been by Ingram's side, nudged by the hand of God.

For what purpose? He was no saint.

You are mine. The voice came again, unbidden, inaudible, and Ingram felt it lift the hairs on his arm. *You are not a saint, nor were your parents. You are not a child of kings or murderers or a nun or a harlot; you are mine.*

Ingram listened and believed. In that moment, a circle closed, a wound healed. One grandfather had been a murderous MacMurrough, but the other had been Turloch O'Connor, the greatest high king Ireland had ever known. But it did not matter that treachery, goodness, cruelty, and piety resided in his heritage, for, like each of his ancestors,

Ingram had struggled within himself against ambition, pride, and dishonor. And through God's grace alone, because of God's love and mercy, he had found the strength and ability to choose according to the will of the heavenly father. 'Twas all that mattered. Knowing that.

After a long while, he stood, pinned the brooch to his cloak, and walked outside, where O'Connor sat on a bench and studied the darkening sky.

"What was my mother's name?" Ingram asked quietly.

"Sorcha," O'Connor replied, never taking his eyes from the gathering rain clouds.

"Sorcha." Ingram tried the word on his tongue. How easy it would be to remember that name, how difficult to forget the name of his father. But he remembered the voice: *You are mine.*

"You probably have more right to rule Ireland than I," O'Connor said, a thread of laughter in his voice. "Descended from the lines of two kings, you are, Ingram *na nRidireachd.* I suppose you'll be demanding me throne next."

Ingram wanted to joke that O'Connor would simply have to take the risk, but something stirred in the aging king's eyes and silenced him. "No, my king," he said finally. "It is enough to have a name and a heritage. I do not wish to have a throne. God has called me, by his grace, to be his servant as a knight."

"Let us ride, then, sir knight. MacMurrough draws his last breaths even now."

"If you could wait, my king, my *uncle*—" He tried the word out on his tongue, and both men smiled when it seemed to fit. "If you could wait, I must settle something with a lady," Ingram finished, smiling as a flicker of amusement passed over the king's face. "It will take an hour, perhaps."

O'Connor waved his hand as if the matter were nothing. "We will wait," he said simply.

❖ ❖ ❖

Signe had not moved since he left her. She still sat at her table, a look of complete and utter astonishment on her delicate face. He put his hands under her elbows and lifted her from the bench.

"Come, my love, we must talk," he said, lifting her chin so her eyes met his. "You were right, Signe. I have been unfair to you."

Her eyes widened in continued surprise, and her fingers flew up to touch his lips. "Speak no more," she whispered. "I'm dreaming."

He laughed at the telltale flash of mischief in her eyes. "No, don't joke with me now, Signe. You were right. My mistake was not marrying you on the day your father offered me your hand all those years ago."

"What has changed?" she whispered, her eyes searching his. "You would not marry me then because you were a knight and I a humble village girl. I'm still a humble village girl, and now you are the son of kings—"

"No, I am only a man who owes his life and service to God. I've realized too late that one of God's commands is humility." He cleared his throat awkwardly. "I would not be alive today if God hadn't sent me to you."

He took her hands and knelt on the floor at her feet. "Signe, you were right. All I've wanted, all my life, is a family to be proud of." He caught himself and shook his head. "Nay, forget pride. All I've wanted is a family to love me. I couldn't see that God had provided a home for me here. I couldn't admit that I needed you, Signe, that I needed to find my place at your side."

Her small hands were cool in his, and he found himself looking at them; her eyes were too piercing for comfort. "So God sent me to Glendalough. God allowed me to fail in everything that mattered. But with the mercy of a loving father, he brought me back to you."

He brought her hands together and surrounded them

with his, the old gesture with which he had long ago
pledged service and fealty to Lord Galbert of Southwick.
"Signe, will you let me love you with my life? Will you
marry me today? O'Connor is ready to leave, but he has
given me an hour to take you to the church steps. Say you'll
marry me, Signe, and then my family will be complete."

"'Tis always what *you* want," she whispered, pulling one
hand free. "And will you be thinking of me at all?"

Ingram shook his head. Was there no end to his mis-
takes? "Noble, beautiful Signe, could you possibly want
me?" he asked, hoping she would believe the humility and
sincerity in his eyes. "I've always loved you. I've hurt you,
I know—"

"Aye. 'Tis true." She nodded primly.

"Can you forgive me, then?"

She tore her eyes from his and seemed to search the
thatched roof above them for her answers. "Och, you
amadon," she said finally, her voice breaking. "How often
I've wanted to be your family, haven't I said so? But you
would not let me, you know. You kept me at arm's length,
welcoming the children, me father, the townspeople—
everyone but me. 'Tis a bit strange, don't you think, that I,
who longed most to love you, found meself shut out?"

"I'm sorry."

"Sorry? Are you thinking one simple word can heal the
hurt of twenty years?"

He could not answer. He knew he could not command
words eloquent enough to win her heart. But she loved
him, he knew she did. She kept her hand free of his grasp,
but her eyes glittered with hope and love. And he felt his
heart turn over. The impulse to reach out and hold her overwhelmed him, and he wrapped his arms around her waist
and looked up into her eyes. He could feel the heat in his
face; she trembled at his touch.

"Signe, I love you now and forever," he said, words leap-
frogging in his mind as he knelt before her. "Be my family,
my wife, my life, and mother to my child as I am a father to

yours. Whether we have an hour or an eternity, whether we live here or in the forest, in a house or in a castle, be my family, be my love."

A tear hung on the fringe of her lashes, but her hands fell on his shoulders in mute acceptance. He struggled upward to stand beside her and drew her into his arms. She laughed gently through her tears and laced her fingers in his hair, and he kissed her as a man who has just discovered that one woman who holds the key to joy and fulfillment. Her kisses were sweet on his lips, her breath warm in his ear.

"I suppose I had better marry you," she whispered finally, locking her hands around his neck. "Faith, imagine what the children would say if they were to walk in and find us thus!"

He laughed and kept his arm about her waist as they walked through the house and reached the door. Flinging the door open with his free hand, he grinned at his uncle and Bhaltair. "We'll meet you at the church," he said, winking at Bhaltair, who watched with his mouth open. "Bring the children, will you, my friend?"

They were quietly and properly married by a priest on the church steps. No sooner had the priest said "amen" to the nuptial benediction than the heavy rain clouds burst overhead, soaking all in the wedding party to the skin. Ingram kissed Signe's wet face as her tears mingled with raindrops; then she gathered the children around her skirts, and her husband mounted the empty horse between Rory O'Connor and Bhaltair.

A moment ago she had been relaxed and invincible in happiness. Now that she saw Ingram poised to ride away, she felt the sickening sensation of loneliness and vulnerability.

He gestured for her to come closer, and she did. Bending low from the saddle, he kissed her forehead and took a moment to brush her wet hair back from her face. "I love your hair when it's wet," he remarked absently, the warmth of his hand on her head causing her to shiver. "Mark this, my love—on this day, Ingram *na nRidireachd* has discovered God's purpose for his life. He lives to follow and serve his lord. He lives for his children. For his wife."

"I love you," she whispered, closing her eyes. "Go with God."

"I will be back," he answered, kissing her again and again. "As I am God's knight, beloved, I will return to you."

"Always a knight." She opened her eyes and forced a smile as the horses snorted and moved away; she felt the children pull on her skirt as the sound of hooves diminished. Looking toward the horizon, she saw three men in the distance. One of them, the knight in the center, turned and saluted her, placing his hand across his heart. She did not move until the trio had disappeared from sight; then she gathered the children and walked to her house.

He would come back. Despite the Normans who waited inside Waterford, Wexford, and Dublin, Ingram would come back. The strong and invincible enemy had changed the course of her country on the invitation of one man, but as one ambitious man could move a country toward destruction, surely another righteous man could bring it back from despair.

Her husband was such a man: Ingram *na nRidireachd*. Ingram of the Knighthood. Ingram of the Irish.

GLOSSARY

abú—ancient Irish war cry

aes dana—nobility

aire tuise—chiefs

amadon—idiot

amadanachd—idiotism

An bráist of ua Conchobair—The brooch of Conchobair

ard-ri—Gaelic high king

athair—father

boaire—freeman

Céad míle fáilte—One hundred thousand welcomes

cenn fine—senior member of geilfhine

coimheach—foreigner

deirbfhine—extended family

destrier—battle horse

Diarmaid na nGall—McMurrough of the Foreigners

eraic—blood money

Formorians—warriors who came against the Irish in ancient
    legend

geilfhine—family clan

gibht—gift

Ingram na nRidireachd—Ingram of the Knighthood

íochtar—youngest child

Is ferr fer a chiniud—"A man is better than his birth."

mac peathar na bràther—nephew

máthair—mother

mortair—murderer

ni truaillidn—illegitimate

pampooties—leather boots

rath—farming community

ridirich—knight

rigdamnae—royalty
saer cheili—freemen
siùrach, strìopach—harlot, loose woman
trebuchet—catapult
tuath(a)—kingdom(s)

If you enjoyed this book, be sure to read the rest of the Theyn Chronicles!

THE THEYN CHRONICLES

Additional titles by Angela Elwell Hunt

CALICO BEAR   0-8423-0302-2
A warm bedtime story that reassures children of God's love for them in a changing world.

CASSIE PERKINS SERIES   Volumes 1–9
This bright, ambitious heroine teaches junior high readers about finding God in the challenges of growing up.

LOVING SOMEONE ELSE'S CHILD   0-8423-3863-2
A supportive, practical book for adults who are taking the responsibility to care for children not their own.